The Wanderer

Also from Tor Books by Cherry Wilder

Signs of Life

Also from Tor Books by Katya Reimann

THE TIELMARAN CHRONICLES

Wind from a Foreign Sky

A Tremor in the Bitter Earth

Prince of Fire and Ashes

SF

CHERRY WILDER AND KATYA REIMANN

The Wanderer

A TOM DOHERTY ASSOCIATES BOOK

NEW YORK

THE WANDERER

This book is printed on acid-free paper.

Edited by David G. Hartwell

Map by John M. Ford and Katya Reimann

A Tor Book
Published by Tom Doherty Associates, LLC
175 Fifth Avenue
New York, NY 10010

www.tor.com

Tor® is a registered trademark of Tom Doherty Associates, LLC.

Library of Congress Cataloging-in-Publication Data

Wilder, Cherry.
The wanderer / Cherry Wilder & Katya Reimann.—1st ed.
p. cm.
"A Tom Doherty Associates book."
ISBN 0-312-87405-7 (alk. paper)
EAN 978-0312-87405-6
1. Woman soldiers—Fiction. 2. Fairies—Fiction. I. Reimann, Katya. II. Title

PS3573.I4227W36 2004
813'.54—dc22

2003071138

First Edition: May 2004

Printed in the United States of America

0 9 8 7 6 5 4 3 2 1

To Cathie and Louisa

In memory of a mother whose writing
stirred and spurred
so many imaginations—including my own.
—KR

CONTENTS

BOOK III

BOOK IV

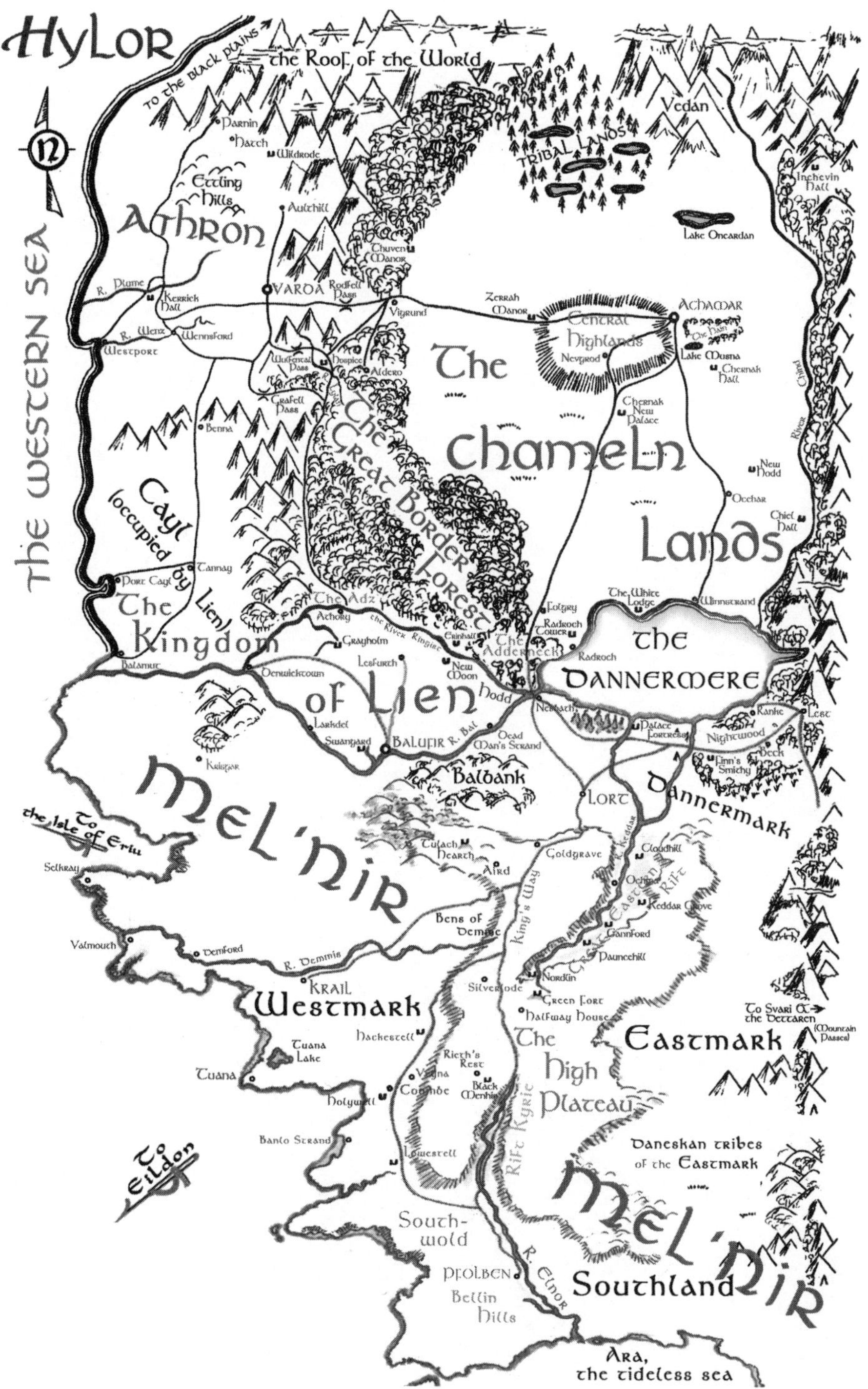
Hylor
The Western Sea
To the Black Plains
the Roof of the World
Parnin
Hatch
Wildrode
Ettling Hills
Athron
Aulthill
Tribal Lands
Vedan
Inchevin Hall
Lake Oneardan
Chuven Manor
R. Plume
Kerrick Hall
Varda
Rodfell Pass
Vigrund
Zerrah Manor
Central Highlands
Achamar
The Horn
Lake Musna
Chernak Hall
R. Wenz
Wennsford
Westport
Wulfental Pass
Hospice
Aldero
The
Nevgrod
Crafell Pass
Chernak New Palace
Benna
The Great Border Forest
The Chameln Lands
New Hodd
Otchar
Chief Hall
River Chind
Cayl (occupied by Lien)
Tannay
Port Cayl
The Adz
Folgry
The White Lodge
Winnstrand
The Kingdom of Lien
Athorg
the River Ringise
Erinhall
Radroch Tower
Grayholm
Lesfurth
The Adderneck
Radroch
The Dannermere
Balamut
Denwicktown
New Moon
Hodd
Nesbath
Lesfurth
Rankie
Lest
Larkdel
Swangard
Balufir
R. Bal
Dead Man's Strand
Palace Fortress
Nightwood
Beck
Finn's Smithy
Kristar
Balbank
Lort
Dannermark
Mel'nir
To the Isle of Eriu
Selkray
Tulach Hearth
Aird
Goldgrave
R. Keddar
Cloudhill
Eastern Rift
Keddar Grove
Bens of Demise
King's Way
Gannford
Valmouth
Demford
R. Deminis
Pauncehill
Nordlin
Krail
Silverlode
Green Fort
Westmark
Halfway House
To Svari & the Dettaren
(Mountain Passes)
Hackestell
The High Plateau
Eastmark
Tuana Lake
Tuana
Rieth's Rest
Black Menhir
Holywell
Banlo Strand
Lowestell
Rift Kyrie
Daneskan tribes of the Eastmark
To Eildon
South-wold
Mel'nir
R. Elnor
Pelbben
Bellin Hills
Southland
Ara, the tideless sea

PROLOGUE

Of all the lands of Hylor, Mel'Nir has the shortest history and the longest chronicles. The scribes, working away in relays, at cross purposes, and in different colored inks, try to set down everything there is to be known. Kings, warlords, heroes, these are grist to their mill; a single battle gives them employment for years; a war, in their pages, never ends.

These busy chroniclers are always hungry for legends, for marvelous tales, for tall stories to enliven the endless feats of arms, the mustering and deployment of a race of giant warriors. Where can they find such tales? On the Chyrian coast, perhaps, within sound of the Western Sea. On the High Plateau, where the last of the Shee, the fairy folk, linger in the mist. In the Southland? Yes, for the air is warmer there, strange fruits hang on the trees, and over Ara, the tideless sea, lie the Burnt Lands.

What tales of intrigue and love and human folly might come out of the new Kingdom of Lien, with its young god and ancient heritage of poetry, art, and music? What secrets have been brought over the Western Sea from Eildon, which calls itself the most ancient of all lands? Who dwells in the distant north in lost Ystamar, the vale of the oak trees? What is stirring among the Chameln, in the Land of the Two Queens, Old Aidris the Witch-Queen and beautiful Tanit Am Zor, the virgin maid, whose heart is cold? Who can tell what strange songs are sung in peaceful Athron? Who has ventured beyond its northern mountains, into the Black Plains?

In all these places the scribes stumble gleefully over a strange figure: the Wanderer, who comes out of the mists of time. (But what of the sighting last year or in the winter of the great snow?) Sometimes the Wanderer comes mounted on a black horse, alone or with shadowy companions. Sometimes there are a whole troop of wanderers, an army of the lost, thin and brown, crossing the endless sands. Reliable witnesses saw them come home to Pfolben in the Southland, heard their names and the name of their leader.

There is magic involved, magical objects . . . a ring, a sword (a nervous scribe might change to green ink, which wards off evil influences and at the same time expresses doubt). A kedran captain, a battlemaid, has been pitched headlong into the chronicles among the kings, princes, generals. For the Wanderer is a woman. Tall, red-haired—one scribe writes "beautiful," because beauty is in the eye of the beholder. Tall, red-haired, steadfast, a trained soldier: a heroine for Mel'Nir.

BOOK I

CHAPTER I

GAEL MADDOC

Gael Maddoc grew up on a hill farm in the Chyrian lands of Mel'Nir. Holywell Croft was the land of the Maddoc family by deed and by custom. It was all they had: a wretched croft that hardly nourished the farmer, his wife, and their two surviving children. There was little else in their lives except the backbreaking struggle with the stony pasture. It seemed they had always been poor: Rab Maddoc could hardly look back to a happier time, and Shivorn, his wife, had grown very quiet.

Gael, their third child, was strong from birth. She survived and was not brought behind the hill to the graveyard where so many Maddocs lay under the tumbled stones.

Then again there were two bad years, and at last Shivorn bore her third son, her sixth child, the second survivor. The boy, Bress, was a year old, then two years, crowned with his father's dark curling hair, and he was all their joy.

One spring night when Gael was seven years old and her brother three, it was certain Bress would die. Their mother had not slept for two nights, but still the fever would not shift. Gael crouched by the fire, for they had forgotten to send her to bed. She heard her mother say:

"I will go!"

And Maddoc made some reply, half angry, full of dread.

"Go, then!"

Her mother snatched up the child, wrapped him in her second shawl, and ran out of the stone hut. The yard was muddy, crusted in the shadows with ice. It was Crocusmoon. The breath of winter yet lay upon the ground around them, not quite ceded to the gentle winds of spring. Gael followed Shivorn through the yard, past the well; her mother had never run so fast. She ran and ran, little Gael stumbling after her, round the corner of the hill. She ran to the sacred Holywell that gave the farm its name. The moon looked through clouds as Shivorn Maddoc parted the bushes and the dead grass of the last season and opened the dark mouth of the grotto and its flowing spring, in the sacred precinct of the Goddess. Clutching her son against her breast, Shivorn bowed her head and entered.

In a moment, Gael had gathered her courage and followed her mother. With one hand against the coolness of the limestone wall, she entered the darkness of the passage, keeping always to the right, away from the waters of the spring. She stumbled on the age-polished tiers of the flowstone floor, for the light was poor and her memory dulled by the passage of many days since the Holywell's last ceremony. Ahead, already within the grotto, she saw her mother dip the boy in the sacred font, heard her utter a prayer before the altar. Then the cave was filled with the radiance of the moon, shining through an opening in the roof, and it was a sign the prayer was answered. So the boy lived, and he was a beautiful child who repaid all their love and attention.

Gael grew up taller than Maddoc, her father; her skin was lighter. The blood of the incomers, the giant, tawny warriors of Mel'Nir, was mixed in the veins of the dark Chyrian folk. Her mother had old Chyrian tales she told by the fireside to Gael as they did the baking. In winter she had family stories for Bress and his sister. Shivorn's father, Euan Macord, had been an incomer, in Chyrian the word was *Fallan,* one who came from beyond the campfire, a traveler, perhaps, or a wanderer. He was a Chyrian, certainly, but pale-faced and with hair dark red. He was a hunter and something of a harp player and had taken service at Ardven House, by the Cresset Burn, where he wed Gael Rhodd, one of the spinning girls—the grandmother for whom young Gael was named.

Now the great house by the river was a ruin. When Sir Oweyn Murrin had passed on, his eldest son, the Heir of Ardven, was well set up on family lands in Balbank, and the elder girl, Avaurn, had married in Rift Kyrie, to the southeast. The younger daughter, Emeris, had gone for a kedran battlemaid and led a wandering life in all the lands of Hylor and beyond. Now there was no one living in the ruined house but this half-cripple kedran captain, Old Murrin.

In summer Gael took her brother down by the Cresset Burn, and Old Murrin let them fish within the grounds of the manor. They were shy children, unused to strangers, unused to the simplest comings and goings of village life. Besides the occasional desperate ceremony, such as that which had preserved Bress's health and life, there were festivals and ceremonies held about twice or three times a year at the Holywell. The reeve of Coombe village came along, with the Druda Kilian Strawn and the old woman Fion Allrada, one of the half-Shee, to conduct the ceremony.

On these occasions, the Maddocs cleaned the grotto and set greenery about and readied the ancient urns for flowers, brought by the village wives. There was a small dark place, a cave, hidden within the passage to the grotto—across the spring, and too far a step for those unfamiliar with the water's course. Gael took Bress there to hide and watch all that went on. They knew it was dangerous—Maddoc was not a harsh man but he might have given them the flat of his hand if he had found them there.

When Bress was a big lad of eight, ten, he stood with the rest of the people, but Gael, growing tall, awkward, and shy, still kept watch from her hiding place. She told her mother that she must stand guard to see that no one stole the sacred stone cups or the ancient urns but in fact it was because she liked to be there. The place was full of magic. One winter at the beginning of the feast days, after she had seen the small gathering of worshippers leave the grotto, she heard a sound close by. A piece of stone fell down beside her feet where she sat curled up. Investigating further, she discovered a sort of shelf, natural but bearing signs of ancient chisel work, from where the stone had fallen. The stone left a square hole in the wall and inside there was a metal casket, a small thing, no bigger than a thick slice of bread. She snatched it up, tucked it inside the slack of her tunic—for she would not wear a gown and shawl—and took it home to the storeroom where she was allowed to sleep in winter.

There, in the first pale light of dawn, Gael opened the grey metal casket and found an ancient parchment, folded small, and covered with writing and strange drawings. There was nothing else but a small leather pouch at the bottom of the casket—inside was a joined loop of fine silvery chain. She slipped it over her head but took it off again, returning it to the pouch. The casket and its contents she hid far away under the sacks of winter vegetables. She tried to think no more of the casket—she had hoped for some gold to give her father.

On the night of the Winter Feast, when even the Maddocs made shift to celebrate a little by the fireside, she brought out the chain and gave it to her mother, saying she had found it under a stone before the grotto, which was very nearly the truth. This was the year that Maddoc had made Bress a bow and arrows and there were sweet honeycakes after the rabbit stew.

One person had a care for such poor folk as they, and it was the village priest, Druda Kilian Strawn. He knew they were as needy as the wandering tinkers and the mad old men who lived in the woods. Winter and summer he came to them, reminding them that a feast day was coming so they would accept his gifts. He brought bacon, rabbits, woven stuff, and bundles of tailings from the fleece so that Mother Maddoc could spin them up.

The Druda was a tall bony fellow with a lank braid of black hair streaked with grey. He was middle-aged, a few years older than Maddoc. He came and went in all the cottages round about. Men admired him because he had been a soldier and served with the men of Mel'Nir during the Great King's War, in the sad days of civil strife when opposing war-leaders' men had torn apart the country. Women talked freely to him because he had been married. He was widowed of a fair young wife from Banlo Strand down by the sea, a woman whom he had wed after the war, and the touch of that coastal life had held close on him, in his faraway gaze. "Druda" was a title jealously reserved, but Kilian Strawn was not a distant celibate, like those of the priestly colleges in far-off Eildon. He was a Guardian, so-called, from the Holy Grove by Tuana, the old Chyrian capital, and deeptrained in Chyrian ways.

In sacred Tuana, now overgrown and faded—Mel'Nir's overlords distrusted magic and did what they could to discourage the old folkways—there had been always three priestesses, holy virgins, the Lady of the Grove and her two Maidens, who ruled the hearth and saw to the care of women. Then there were the warrior priests, the Guardians. In old times they had lived among the people and advised the chieftains in their councils. Kilian Strawn was of this old strain, perhaps among the last so trained.

Gael Maddoc trusted Druda Strawn so much that at last she brought out the ancient parchment she had kept hidden and told him she had found it by the Holywell. He unfolded it at night by the fire in their small cot and laughed with delight.

"See here!" he cried. "It is a map of Coombe!"

They looked, and when it was laid on a settle the right way round they all could see it—there was the road through the village, there was the Holywell marked with a sacred kell. There also were the crossroads. North and south were the twin fortresses: Hackestell, which still belonged to their liege lord, Knaar of Val'Nur, and Lowestell, which remained in the hands of Lord Pfolben, ruler of the Southland. There were words written in the ancient Chyrian tongue, and when the Druda, half teasing, helped Gael to sound them out, a strange thing happened: there came a glowing upon the parchment, and just for one moment, the outline of a great cup, with double handles.

Gael laughed, she was so frightened. "Is it Taran's Kelch?" she asked, for that cup was a great Chyrian treasure and occupied a place of pride in many of the old stories Shivorn had told her.

The Druda looked at her, and his gaze was uncomfortably sharp. "Who is to say it is not?" he said softly, and then Gael was embarrassed, for the cup was a thing of legend, and she thought he must be teasing her. "By your leave, I will take this paper away with me, and study it."

Then Druda Strawn did a strange thing. He brought out a box of polished wood, his writing case, and he taught Gael Maddoc straightaway to write her name, first on the parchment of the map itself and then on a sheet of thinner stuff, writing paper, from his case. "One day you will need to know this," he told her, and again she was frightened. For all she knew, there had never been a Maddoc before her who had needed to know how to write.

When spring was upon them in the new year Druda Strawn came by on his old mare. Gael Maddoc was on the hill above the croft, breaking stone. The Druda came over the crest of their hill as Maddoc and his daughter ploughed the hillside.

"Your daughter wields that hand plough well enough!" he said.

Maddoc agreed, mopping his brow, and they watched her urging the simple furrow maker up toward them.

"What age is your daughter?" asked the Druda.

"The boy, our Bress, is thirteen," said Maddoc, "so she will be seventeen."

"I have a plan," said Druda Strawn, "that will be pleasing to the Goddess."

He explained it to the family at their hearthside. Gael Maddoc blushed to feel herself the center of attention, then her heart beat faster as the priest told of his plan. She, Gael, would go into training with the Summer Riders, and become a kedran after one year, when she was of age. This would not just be preparation for the Westmark's required military training: she would train to be a true battlemaid, perhaps even be selected to join the muster for Coombe's liege lord's house. The family's back taxes would be written off; the boy, Bress, could be spared from military service until he was turned sixteen, ready for *his* summer training.

Gael did not look at her parents but spoke up, mastering her shyness. Yes, she would do it, she said eagerly. Her mother looked out into the yard where Bress was drawing water from the well and echoed her daughter's words. If the Druda believed Gael could be made into a kedran . . .

Rab Maddoc was more hesitant. The Maddocs had ever performed their training for the Westmark, but never in living memory had they gone for soldiers. Their croft held the Holywell, perhaps few came there now, but the Maddocs were yet its guardians . . . Shivorn gave her husband a sharp look, a look that had a little of stomach hunger in its sharpness. "The girl is willing," she told him. "Besides, Bress will stay with us still—think on that!" Rab Maddoc shook his head and sighed, but after that he kept quiet and did not give further voice to his protest.

At the Plantation in Krail, the golden city of the Westmark, their liege lord, Knaar of Val'Nur, kept and maintained the Westlings, three hundred warriors recruited from the Chyrian lands. Lord Knaar, though aging, was a restless man, and these three hundred were his pride. Knaar's father before him had held fast against the outrages of Mel'Nir's tyrant, Ghanor the so-called Great King, but now, in the peace of Ghanor's son, Good King Gol, Knaar was treaty-bound to maintain his house's army at this diminished strength. But those three hundred! A family with even one kern or kedran in the Lord of the Westmark's service was lifted out of poverty.

Gone for a kedran in Knaar's service—it was a golden dream. More practically speaking, the Melniros were a martial race, and if a kedran was not accepted into Knaar's army . . . well, there were many lordly households throughout Val'Nur and beyond where a battlemaid could find good service.

A chance at training for one such as Gael was something to seize upon and not let go.

II

Now began the happiest time at Coombe that Gael Maddoc could ever remember. Before the Elmmoon came, and the fullness of summer, Maddoc taught his daughter to handle a bow and the Druda taught her to ride his tall old mare. On the croft they had not even a donkey, but as a child she had once or twice been "given a ride" on a horse. Now riding and horses were to be her life. She was fond of Friya, the priest's patient old mare, but she dreamed of other horses, more spirited. There would be a special horse, maybe, to understand and love.

The training of potential Westling recruits was a great matter for all the towns and villages in the Chyrian lands of Mel'Nir. Recruits were drawn from Tuana, faded now but still almost a city, and from the thriving port at Banlo Strand and the villages around Coombe, on the edge of the High

Ground. It was not always possible to raise "a full muster" of five hundred for Knaar to chose from—this was peacetime, the weather and the harvests were always uncertain. Coombe, one of the oldest villages on the coast, was very poor, but it kept up its proud tradition, remembering the Westmark's great hero, General Yorath, who, while camped in Coombe, had summoned the first muster of the Westlings for Valko Firehammer, Lord Knaar's famous father.

The war had been a terrible thing for Mel'Nir: Ghanor, the so-called Great King, had been a power-mad monster, a warring king who thrust the borders of Mel'Nir outward until the sad day when his excesses collapsed the country inward on itself. Men like the Westmark's war-leader, Valko Firehammer of Val'Nur, held loyal at first, then turned against their king when it became clear Ghanor was mad: he conspired against the families of his war-leaders; for fear of prophecy, he had his own grandchildren set to the sword. Infamously, at the field of Silverlode, he arranged for the treacherous murder of all those his heated mind had come to believe were set against him. The land had need of great heroes to turn the tide against such a tyrant—and Yorath, who had called the muster at Coombe, had been first among the men to stand against him.

Mel'Nir was quiet now, but Val'Nur's honor was still remembered in the little villages. Coombe always sent its full share of the muster, or near to it.

Young men and women, ready to serve as kerns or kedran, came from round about to do their early training under Druda Strawn or under Sergeant Helm Rhodd, younger brother of Rhodd the Innkeeper. On a certain day at the beginning of summer Bress cried out from the yard and Gael, dressed already as a kedran in a brown tunic and green trunkhose, was ready for the great adventure.

Fast approaching from the village was a tall dark girl on a beautiful roan horse. She led another saddled horse, a brown mare with one white foot. This was Jehane Vey, daughter of a wealthy farmer, down toward the forest hamlet of Veyna. She was granddaughter of the old wise-woman, Fion Allrada. Gael had spoken to her at the house of Druda Strawn and was glad there was another kedran in training. And yes, a training horse would come from Veyna—and some other mounts, mainly ponies, would be found for the young men.

In fact it seemed to Gael that Druda Strawn had some notion of propriety—perhaps he had known Jehane would stand forth and had had an eye out for another kedran wench to bear her company. There were ten young men in this Green Muster, as it was called, and another ten seniors who had already ridden out on a forest ride to Lowestell, under the leadership of Sergeant Rhodd.

"So here is Ivy!" cried Jehane, as the Maddoc family shyly gaped.

Gael ran out and took the bridle, spoke to the brown mare, tightened the girth and stowed her gear in the saddlebags. Then she mounted up and laughed aloud with pleasure.

"Oh, Comrade Jehane," she said happily. "This is the morning of the world!"

Jehane smiled her agreement, and Gael knew they would be friends despite the great gulf (for so it seemed then to Gael) in their estates.

Mother Maddoc sent out Bress with two stirrup cups of apple wine and pieces of hot oatcake. Jehane laughed with young Bress and called out her thanks. The two new battlemaids raised their two ash staves—their training weapons—and rode off down to the crossroads.

To their right, across rough grazing land, with trees lining the roadside, the road ran due south to the fortress of Lowestell, on the border of the Southland. To the left the road wound down through the best land near Coombe, with market gardens and smaller roads leading off to Veyna and other forest hamlets. But the high road went on toward the twin fortress of Hackestell, still in the hands of Val'Nur since it was seized by Yorath Duaring and that first great muster of Chyrian folk. Ahead of the two riders the road went straight and climbed the High Ground, the great plateau, where the Eilif lords of the Shee, the fairy race, were said to linger in the mist.

"Well, by the Goddess," said Jehane, "here come two young Eilif lords . . ."

Gael laughed as two men on shaggy ponies came down from the edge of the High Ground. She did not recognize them, but Jehane named them as the Naylor twins, from a farm on the way to the southern fortress. They came up and exchanged names, Barun and Leem Naylor; they were much alike, but Leem had a scar that crossed his left cheek.

"You're a long way from home!" said Jehane.

"We took a ride up to the high ground," said Leem, "to test the ponies!"

"By Star," said Barun boldly, "proud kedran wenches are always getting the best mounts!"

"We need them the most!" put in Gael. "You'll be on foot, Kern Barun, when we join the Westlings!"

He cringed away from her on his shaggy grey pony, pretending to be afraid.

"Look alive!" said Jehane. "Here comes the main force!"

A large muster were riding down from Coombe, already at the boundary wall opposite Holywell Croft. Druda Strawn led the way and they all met together there at the crossroads. There were a few shouted greetings from the young men to the two kedran and Gael was surprised at how many of them she knew. There was Prys Oghal, the reeve's son, whom she had always liked, and that was surely Bretlow, third son of Vigo the Smith. He was a "giant warrior," a Melniro in the classic form, topping seven feet and broad besides. He rode a war horse with plumed hooves. His two brothers were already officers at the Plantation, in Krail city, the great barracks where the Westlings made their home. Then there was a tall, pale boy whom she knew but could not place—she had a chance to ask Jehane, who identified him as Nate Gemman, whose father had a kind of permanent market stall—a shop, he called it—behind the reeve's house.

"Fancy that long lump, kedran?" whispered Jehane.

"He deals with our croft, is all," Gael said, grinning. "We sell him oatcake and he has my mother make up green pickles and straw dolls for his Da's 'shop.' "

Tall Nate knew her too, it seemed—he was waving and smiling; his legs were so long they almost reached the ground on either side of his piebald pony.

"By heaven, where *did* the Druda get these ponies!" said Gael.

"Have a care," grinned Jehane. "My father sent up the whole herd of them, with no charge!"

Druda Strawn raised his voice and called the Green Muster to order; he got down from his mare and spoke in a strong voice that carried far. He called for good sense, good manners, for spirit to learn, for strength and good heart and the ability to follow orders.

"Today is a special day, a special summer day—who knows its name? Yes, Kern Oghal? Tell us all!"

Then the reeve's son rode forth on his grey pony and spoke up:

"Sir, it is Foundation Day for Hackestell Fortress. It was built or at least put in its present shape by Duro the Fox, Lord of the Westmark, father of the great Valko Firehammer and grandfather of Lord Knaar, our present liege!"

"Excellent!" cried Druda Strawn. He looked up to the sky where the summer sun was not yet overhead. "There is a ceremony today at Hackestell—the Lord Knaar will be there in person. We will ride down to the fortress to pay our respects. Lead off, Kedran Vey, Kedran Maddoc!"

They rode off down the highroad in fair order—a pony kicked up its heels and unseated one of the lads. The girls—kedran now—took it slowly, nervous at first to find themselves at the head of this great green troop, then they began to trot, and it worked well enough. Jehane complimented Gael for a natural-born rider. On they went, through the bright summer green of the roadside, with farmed plots all around and stalls with fruit under the trees. A tall dark fellow called Egon Baran, mounted on another heavy charger from the Smithy, rode up beside Jehane and spoke companionably, but Druda Strawn shouted an order to hold their ranks and he went back again.

They reached the fortress before the sun was right overhead. Already a crowd was gathering to greet their liege lord. A village had grown up before the outer wards of Hackestell to serve the men of the garrison, and it seemed everyone had come out to make the greeting. The fortress officers and their men had turned out in fine dress uniforms, brown and gold with short tunics and tan boots. They held back the crowd at wicker barriers, twined with leaves and flowers. A broad path, held open by these battening boards, led way through the village from its outskirts to the fortress's very gate. The opposite way, in a field below the village (and well clear of the highroad), the kedran could glimpse something that might have been a great cotton tent, a pavilion. Above it waved a pennant for the house of Val'Nur, showing a brown hill with a fork of lightning, one of their emblems.

The Druda rode up and spoke with an officer to get his recruits a good place. Bretlow Smith and Egon Baran, looking so fine on their massive chargers, were led over the ceremonial pathway to a prominent position in the west by the fortress gates. The remainder of the trainees from Coombe, with their scruffy ponies, were only allowed up to the barrier near the road they had taken. All of the lads got down and tethered their mounts to a hitching rail near a trough. From there they could edge into the growing crowd where the barrier came near the outer wards of Hackestell. The kedran, at a glance from the Druda, kept in their saddles and held their places at the corner where the wide ceremonial pathway turned toward the fortress.

They had not waited long when a trumpet sounded by the white pavilion. As the procession moved outward toward Hackestell's gates, the crowd began to cheer. First to come into view were men in black tabards marked with a bird's head; they carried pikes. These were Krail's Palace Guard, the Eagles, successors to a fierce Free Company. After them came the lord himself, Knaar of Val'Nur, walking with his sons Thilon and Duro and the nobles of his court.

Gael had seen a very few noblemen and -women before, and then only at ceremonies by the sacred spring or riding out from Coombe to hunt or to make a progress to the Southland. She saw now that Lord Knaar was an old man and not very tall, by no means one of Mel'Nir's giant warriors. Yet he was very strong and fit, he shone with power; his shoulder-length hair was brownish grey, like his beard. He was magnificently dressed in a knee-length robe of cloth of gold, over a white tunic. He wore no dress sword but carried his plumed hat by the brim, working it up and down as he walked, as if it helped him along.

The sons of Knaar were fair, handsome men; Thilon, the heir of Val'Nur and the Westmark, was not so tall as his brother. After this princely party came a group of men and women, finely dressed, from Krail as well as locals. Jehane knew the ordering of the procession and said these would be some of the wives and parents of the garrison and other such dignitaries. Then they spied those who made up the end of the procession and could hardly keep from smiling. Ten tall kedran upon splendid horses, white, grey, dapple-grey: on their dark grey tabards was blazoned the device of a lily in white and gold. These were the far-famed Sword Lilies, the elite troop of the Plantation, the barracks of Val'Nur.

The procession came to a halt before the gates of Hackestell. A trumpet from within answered the trumpet sounding from without, and the gates were flung open. The first of the Eagles marched in; behind them Lord Knaar strolled along more leisurely with his sons, looking keenly about him and acknowledging the cheers. He stopped to speak to a group of women, merchants' wives and their children, who held up posies. The lord smiled and took the flowers, passing them behind him to the hands of a guard and an older counselor.

A dark flash, like lightning, struck at Gael, deep behind her eyes, forcing her to turn. She took in at once a movement, a glint of metal in the crowd; she uttered a cry and gripped Jehane's arm. Thrusting forward on Ivy, the brown mare, she pushed aside the wicker barrier and shouted to the guard: "*'Ware! Danger!*"

Hardly thinking of the risks, she rushed headlong into the crowd, just behind the group of women and children. Village folk, their faces dark with fear, pushed out of her path as she urged her horse forward, shouting to clear the way. Jehane came behind her, and then suddenly they were hard up against the two men, the two assassins, as they bore down upon the Lord of the Westmark.

They were big men, one older than the other. The older man's green cowl had fallen back, showing his strong features, his thick dark brows. The younger man wore a curious close-fitting hood, brown-black, a *knitted* hood. Both attackers pressed on desperately, though it was clear that the two kedran were coming for them. The older man held a long spear with a broad gleaming blade, and the other had a short sword.

Gael struck the older man in the throat with her ash staff, drew back and beat him across the head. By now the crowd had seen what was going on and two men seized the spear wielder and wrestled him to the ground.

The danger was not over—the young man went lunging through the shrieking women and almost came to Knaar, who was dragged aside, at last, by his Eagle guards and his sons. Jehane had held on with the pursuit, and the younger assassin suddenly relinquished his attempt. He lifted his sword to heaven and came back; he uttered words in a strange tongue and went among those holding his companion. Incredibly, he was able to drag him away, and they both fled into a narrow street. The villagers gave chase, and Gael would have gone too, when her bridle was seized and two lances were crossed before her . . .

"Halt, girl!" ordered an ensign of the Sword Lilies. "Declare yourself!"

"Maddoc, of Coombe!" Gael gasped out. "They went down that alley—the assassins . . ."

"There!" cried the second Sword Lily, as big and hard faced and angry as her comrade. "Says assassin, dares to say assassin, does she! You're a prisoner, now, let fall that staff . . ."

The villagers added to the confusion—an old woman with a big voice cried out that she had been pushed aside by the horses.

"Rode us down!" she shrieked.

A tall older man said: "No, good Mother, they were after the two armed men! The two men who went to attack the Lord Knaar!"

"Quiet!" roared the ensign. "Get back, all of you!"

"Ensign," begged Jehane, drawing in closer. "I pray you, send one of your troops after those two bandits! I swear they tried to attack the lord . . ."

At last the ensign summoned two more Lilies from the bunch, and they pushed through the thickening crowd and sent their white horses hurtling down the alleyway.

"I still don't know you gals," she said angrily. "Where d'ye ride?"

"We are new recruits from Coombe," said Gael. "We are training with Druda Strawn."

"So that's it," said the ensign, still frowning. "Names?"

They gave their names and were ordered to turn their horses and get out of the way. The other kedran pointed with her lance and drew her dapple-grey skillfully aside. So Maddoc and Vey rode back to their old position. The barrier had been set upright, Lord Knaar and his closest followers had gone; the Eagles patrolled before the gates of Hackestell with lances at the ready. A young man on foot, wearing a striped yellow-and-grey tunic, came through the soldiers, together with a high-ranking guard officer. Gael noted the officer's crown and star—an obrist of the guard.

"There!" said the young man in the stripes. It was Knaar's younger son. "The two kedran wenches, the red and the black. They saw it all—went after those rogues!"

"Well, kedran!" said the obrist, staring up at them. "You heard Hem Duro—what shall we call you?"

They gave their names smartly, and the prince of Val'Nur smiled at them.

"Training with the Chyrian priest, I'll be bound," said the obrist, knowingly. "Aha, they're all brave hearts in Coombe!"

"Kedran Maddoc, Kedran Vey," said Duro of Val'Nur, "Obrist Wellach will have you brought into Hackestell. The duty officers will see to your horses and bring you to the private hearth beside the commander's quarters. I will be there soon to question certain witnesses about this attempt on my father's life."

They saluted and went round the barrier. The obrist called to another guardsman to lead them in and handed up to Jehane a duty pledge, a strap of leather with a silver badge on it, showing his own seal and marks of rank. So they rode through the wide gates into the outer wards and the guardsman pointed the way ahead across the inner bailey.

"Good Ensign," said Gael, to the guardsman by the door, "we have been given this duty call—pray you bring word to Druda Strawn, the leader of the Coombe training muster, to say where his kedran have gone!"

"I'll do that, sweetheart!" said the guard with a grin. "Just cut across to the lodge there, find the duty officer . . ."

They went slowly on their way, through hurrying crowds of soldiers and others—servants, market women, scullions, and cooks with their heads covered. Above them on all sides now were the towering walls of Hackestell central keep, built all of pinkish stone from the quarries northwest of Krail, with darker bands of greystone from the south by Rift Kyrie.

"Great Goddess!" breathed Jehane. She, as well as Gael, had heard tale of the fortress's prison cells. "How have we come to this, Gael Maddoc?"

"A pity," echoed Gael, speaking just as low, "a pity if we have such an adventure because some rogues attack the lord!"

They got down, trying not to be overawed, showed their token to a stableboy who led away their horses and pointed the way to the lodge. Inside there were more than a dozen members of the garrison; they kept up a little murmur of teasing talk until the duty officer saw the token. He waved it and gave them both a smart salute, said his name, Captain Treem, and summoned yet another ensign for their guide. There was silence as they went out and the young ensign led them into the keep under the great iron wargate.

"Godfire!" he said, on the stairs. "This is a terrible business—did you see the bastards?"

"We chased them!" admitted Gael. "Others went after them through the town—were they caught?"

"Not yet—we've heard all sorts of tales." He chattered on, said his name was Stivven, and asked their names. They kept on up the wide winding stair with its old wooden banisters, rising up on the left side of the keep within the thickness of its outer wall. Outside, through a narrow window, they saw the afternoon sunlight shining on the high ground and a wind moving the tops of the trees.

So they came to the private hearth, where witnesses were to be heard. Stivven left them at the door with a salute. It was surely not so for Jehane, but for Gael this was the finest room she had ever been in. There were rich hangings on the walls and a bank of fresh green leaves filling the hearth and the settles were padded with bright red leather. The room was empty—Jehane touched Gael's arm and led her behind an arrangement of painted screens near the door. There was a place to wash, with mirrors and a privy, thickly curtained. They each took turns keeping watch while the other removed her tunic and made a soldier's ablutions. Towels and vials of lavender water made Gael feel giddy with luxury. She combed up her hair, in its new short kedran cut. She a little regretted the loss of her thick red braids, but a quick look in one of the fine silver mirrors told her she was no plainer than before. Jehane would have to look fair for them both . . . They heard movement in the chamber and came out from behind the screens, carrying their riding caps.

Five orderlies were bringing in food and arranging it on a long trestle that had been set up along the western wall. There was an older man, one of the lord's servants, and again the young ensign, Stivven. He said their names as witnesses, and the older man looked at them keenly and pointed to a settle, with a table before it.

"Fetch yourselves food and ale," he said gently. "Sit there."

They went to the food table and were served with hot meat, buttered bread, salad greens, and a cloth each to wipe their hands. Did they each have knives? Yes. The boy would bring them their ale. So they took their places and ate as daintily as they might. Presently two civilians were shown in, and Gael recognized the tall old man who had spoken up for them outside the fortress. He stood about with the men and drank a goblet of wine. After a moment he caught sight of them and exclaimed:

"Yes, by heaven! There they are! The two young kedran—they saw it all!"

He came across to their table and bowed and bade them not to get up.

"Mentle," he said, "I am Huw Mentle, Reeve of Hackestell Village. I'm glad they brought you here to bear witness!"

"Good Sir," asked Gael, "were the men captured after they went down that alley?"

"No, they were not!" he said. "Not even the Sword Lilies could find them! And there was something strange in that . . ."

The doors were opened, and Obrist Wellach led in Duro of Val'Nur, along with a pale, striking fellow in a black scholar's gown. They were followed by two Sword Lilies. Jehane nudged Gael, recognizing the pair who had halted them. Then there came a notably handsome young man, finely dressed in blue—Gael took him for one of the courtiers who had walked with Lord Knaar and his sons. There were some others, servants of Val'Nur and soldiers of the garrison.

There was movement at once as the room was rearranged for the hearing. The obrist spoke up, saying what would be done.

"Master de Reece, head scribe of the house of Val'Nur, will be the questioner. This is not a court-martial, but all witnesses are asked to speak up plainly. There will be no penalties, no name taking, and no rewards.

"The good Master is a lay justice in Krail. We are fortunate indeed to have one so close at hand who knows how to conduct such a hearing."

Behind, while Obrist Wellach spoke, Hem Duro was instructing two kerns where to place his chair, before the food table, facing the room. Despite his words outside the fort, it seemed, at least for now, that he was there to listen rather than to speak.

Two lesser scribes, one a young woman, settled at a special table to write down the proceedings. Then the obrist held up his hand for silence. Master de Reece stepped forward and spoke in clear ringing tones.

"We will not have the witnesses sworn just at first," he said easily. "I will begin with the person who was closest to Lord Knaar—first gentleman of the bedchamber, Valent Harrad."

The handsome young fellow in blue stood up and answered to his name. Yes, it was just as the procession turned to make the approach to the fortress. He was behind Lord Knaar, who turned aside to receive flowers from some country wives and their children. No, he had seen nothing amiss until two kedran came riding from the barriers and pushed into the crowd just beyond the women. And then? Yes, indeed, said young Harrad, tossing his long scented locks. He saw the attackers, two men in dark clothes, perhaps hunting dress. He saw that one had a great spear and came at the Lord Knaar, although the kedran would have prevented it.

"So the red-haired one struck him down!" he finished.

"Do you see this kedran?" inquired Master de Reece.

The young man's gaze flicked over those present in the wide sunny room, and he pointed eagerly, smiled and nodded.

"There she is, Master de Reece, and her companion too . . ."

Gael held up her head and prayed for strength.

"Kedran?"

Master de Reece made a gesture; she stood up, saluted, and gave her name.

"Gael Maddoc, kedran recruit from Coombe village!"

She was echoed by Jehane springing up at her side:

"Jehane Vey, kedran recruit from Veyna!"

De Reece nodded to Huw Mentle, including him in the group of witnesses.

"Yes, Master Scribe," said the old man, "I first saw the danger when these two brave kedran came through and held the two brigands. Some of our citizens from the garrison village came to their aid and took hold of one of the men. The younger of the two, in a close-fitting hood, held up his sword to heaven and made some incantation. Then the pair of them made off, and two of the lord's escort, two Sword Lilies, came amongst us and ordered the kedran to declare themselves!"

Only one of the Sword Lilies, a fierce old captain called Lockie, told the tale from their side.

"Yes, Master de Reece," she said in her hoarse voice, "we had not seen anything of an attack or an attacker. We did not recognize these two recruits."

She gave Gael and Jehane a curt nod—it was recognition at last, and they acknowledged it thankfully.

"Now, was there a pursuit of these two men?" asked de Reece.

"There was," said Captain Lockie. "Two of our troop went after them and some citizens before. They had taken to a narrow alley called Oldwall that leads to the fields. The men were not found."

"They had hidden themselves? Reached the fields?"

The captain was already embarrassed by the questions. Reeve Mentle signed to de Reece and spoke up seriously, looking at Hem Duro.

"I know that our noble Lord Knaar is no friend of such talk, but it must be said. That short street, Oldwall, is bare of any doorway or possible hiding place. The younger fugitive was heard speaking strange words. Hem Duro—your father's attackers escaped with the help of magic!"

Duro gave a short laugh and shook his head.

"Yes," he said. To everyone's relief, he had taken no offense at the reeve's uncomfortable disclosure. "My father does not encourage magicians. But magic is used all throughout the lands of Hylor. Two enemies of Val'Nur might be just the fellows to fight against us with such tricks!"

As he spoke, the trumpet call sounded below, and bells were rung. The obrist whispered something to the prince.

"What? Changing of the guard? Yes, of course, any with duty may leave. If Captain Lockie or her ensign could stay back a moment—I think we are come to the most important part of this whole affair: who were these men, to set themselves against my father?"

Amidst a general movement, the room greatly emptied. Jehane and Gael remained by their settle as Master de Reece announced a break in the proceedings. There was time for the retiring room, and drinks of ale were passed around. When they all came together again, it was like a roundtable gathering; all the witnesses were seated, as well as de Reece and the scribes.

The ensign of the Sword Lilies was questioned first. She had seen two men running off. Yes, she had seen their faces. The men were tall, but she could not swear they were men of Mel'Nir. She thought one was older than the other. They wore trews or trunkhose and perhaps their cloaks were green. One had a close hood.

Reeve Mentle sat beside de Reece and gave his testimony directly and quietly to the scribes and it was taken down.

"Just so," said Master de Reece. "So now it is the turn of the two recruits from Coombe."

A glance passed between him and Hem Duro.

"Kedran Maddoc," said Duro, his pleasant voice sharpening just a little, "what made you pursue these men? How did they first come to your notice?"

It was a question she had put to herself ever since the attack, and there was no answer that would serve but the truth.

"Highness," she said, "I had some kind of foreshadowing. I suddenly knew that there was danger, there to my right among the crowd."

"Have you ever practiced magic?" he pursued. "Do you know anyone, man or woman, who could be described as a magician?"

"No, Highness!" said Gael Maddoc firmly. "But we are Chyrian folk in the village of Coombe."

"What do you mean by that?"

"We have our own natural magic, from the Goddess."

Hem Duro shook his head, as if to say "worse and worse."

Jehane Vey spoke up:

"Highness, I am Jehane Vey, of the Forest Hall, in Veyna hamlet, and my granddam is Fion Allrada, a lady of the half-Shee. She is known for her wisdom and it might be called natural magic."

Hem Duro turned to de Reece with a questioning look and the Head Scribe said evenly:

"This lady is known as a local wise woman, Highness . . ."

Duro, seeming satisfied, turned again to Gael Maddoc.

"And your family, Kedran?"

Gael had no hall to claim, and she found her cheeks burning at the form of the prince's question. "My family have always lived at Holywell Croft, by deed and by custom, as our own Reeve Oghal would bear witness. We have the care of the holy well, in its sacred grotto."

"The Well of Coombe," de Reece interjected softly. "Yes, then this witch-sight you carry cannot be surprising. Your family bears an ancient troth." He glanced at Hem Duro. "Older than Coombe itself, if truth be told."

While Gael had heard some such tale told enough times in Coombe village, it came as some surprise to know that a scribe from so mighty—and distant—a city as Krail might share any knowledge of her family's humble crofting.

"Do you know anything about the Westlings, Kedran Maddoc?" inquired Hem Duro.

"Yes, surely, Highness," she replied eagerly, "I have been told this tale. Our great hero of Coombe village, General Yorath, raised the first muster of Chyrian folk to serve Val'Nur, during the Great King's War. The siege of this same fortress, Hackestell, was broken by the Chyrian horde . . ."

"Who told you this tale?" he demanded.

"I did, Highness!" said a voice. "Pray you have mercy on my good recruits!"

Druda Strawn had come in silently. Now he walked forward and bowed to the prince. His sharp dark gaze took in the whole table round of witnesses and questioners. Gael Maddoc knew that she saw a man absolutely unafraid in this company.

"Of course," said Hem Duro, dryly. "Druda Strawn, pray take your place here at my side. We are come to a most interesting part of this strange affair. Your two recruits must describe the two men who tried to attack my father."

Jehane went first and although they had hardly spoken together of these things Gael found her description agreed almost perfectly with Gael's own picture of the two assassins. Then it was her own turn. She might have wished herself in the midst of battle rather than speaking so long before this company. Yet she spoke up as clearly and truthfully as she could, for the honor of poor Coombe and for Druda Strawn, who had chosen her for a kedran.

"A hood . . .?" queried de Reece. "The younger man wore this closely woven woolen hood?"

Gael screwed up her eyes in an effort to retrieve the scene.

"No Sir," she said. "Not woven—it seemed to me that the hood was *knitted*. And I particularly noticed the color of the thick-spun thread. It must have come from a black sheep."

There was a moment of complete silence around the table, then de Reece, Hem Duro, and young Valent all cried out at once, with oaths ranging from "By the Warriors!" to "Blood and Fire!" Druda Strawn gave a bark of laughter.

"Well said, Gael Maddoc!" he exclaimed. "And I charge all you gathered here to see that this is a tale I have not told. She uttered the words quite innocently."

He gave Gael a smile and went on: "The Black Sheep are a band of rebellious souls who farm tracts of land and do their own magic. It is said they are refugees from the island of Eriu, formerly a feof of ancient Eildon, now held firm in the iron hand of the Kingdom of Lien."

"Eildon? They have their magic of Eildon?" Gael spoke aloud in her surprise, impressed by the Druda's erudition. Eildon-across-the-sea was old and its ways were strange. She had heard magic was much used there, but all spoke that it was magic of a glamor kind, a pretty—or treacherous—illusion played by the Priest-King's court, deep opposed to the country-bound Chyrian style of magic. Even so, if these *black sheep* used magic, it was not surprising that they should find themselves Lienish castaways. From what little she knew, Lien, Mel'Nir's neighbor to the north, was a kingdom where magic was held in even greater public distrust than in Knaar of Val'Nur's domains.

"But in truth," the Druda said softly, as he looked again toward the prince, "it seems to me that this use of magic, together with Gael Maddoc's sighting of the knitted hood, is a blessed gift, for it tells us that the question here today is whether or no Knaar of Westmark has dealt fairly with some refugees living rough upon his own land, and does not, Goddess be thanked, touch anything greater. Wronged farmers are a safer enemy than a land whose gaze has slowly turned outward to its neighbors' fields."

Hem Duro's eyes glittered dangerously, and he did not answer. For a moment Gael could not believe that the Druda had really aired a fear that *Lien* itself might have been responsible for today's attack on Lord Knaar, but the prince's next words left her with no doubt that she had properly understood the Druda's meaning. "It is not fit that we should speak ungently of our northern neighbor," Duro snapped. "Lien may have taken Mel'Nir's fair Balbank into its own realm, but there its outward push has ended. Neither my father nor any of his kin will stand for such words to be spoken."

Yet, whatever the diplomatic content of Duro's words, a look of unhappy understanding flashed between the Druda and the prince. Gael could see a concern shared between them. De Reece shuffled his papers, interrupting with some small question. The moment of unease was past and gone.

And that was all the sense the kedran were able to get out of their long ordeal. No more questions were put to them, and this matter of Eriu, or perhaps of Lien, was not aired to them any further. Hem Duro and Master de Reece spoke together in quiet, and after a little time, they admitted Reeve Mentle and Druda Strawn to their council.

Valent Harrad was excused to return to Lord Knaar's service.

Gael and Jehane sat together, whispering a little. Presently Captain Lockie of the Sword Lilies and Obrist Wellach returned from their duties and joined the conference. A few moments after, the captain haled the two recruits off to quarters. They were to sleep in Hackestell this night and return to their training in the morning.

They gathered up their saddlebags and their ash staves and followed the old kedran out of the private hearth. As they went toward the stairs, she looked about for a moment as if to be sure no one was watching and drew them aside, along the gallery.

"Hem Duro is a generous man," she said. "Keep quiet about this."

She drew out from a deep pocket in her tunic two bright twists of yellow cloth and handed them to Gael and Jehane.

"Silver!" said Captain Lockie. "Five silver shields each, fresh from the Royal Mint at Goldgrave!"

She held up a hand as they both whispered their thanks. "You both drew a strange duty this day," she said. "Maybe with a bit of training you'll be seen among the Westlings."

The captain did not say "among the Sword Lilies." They were a special troop, the lord's escort. Gael could see how Lockie smiled at Jehane's retort to this cautious approval—the tall girl was nettled, her pride was touched. In her own town of Veyna, great things were expected for Jehane—and Gael, knowing how easy Jehane Vey rode, her already easy manner as she spoke with their rough green troop, would not have gainsaid those happy expectations.

But this was for the future. For now, Jehane held her peace, and the captain led them through winding passages to the kitchens. A female cook had charge of them there. She took two thick, lighted candles and brought them into a stone room with stone shelves for beds. These were covered with sacks of thick straw and each had a thick plaid blanket. There was a place to wash and presently a girl in an apron brought them broth, bread, a bottle of ale, and a basket of apples.

This was a good supper. As they enjoyed it, Gael counted her bright silver coins with the shield of the royal arms of Mel'Nir and tied them up again in their cloth. She wondered aloud where the Sword Lilies would sleep. Jehane guessed that a few would remain in the fortress to guard Lord Knaar in his guest chamber, wherever that was. The rest, they decided, would have gone back to the Val'Nur pavilion.

There was a trumpet call and another peal of bells; they heard marching feet overhead. Through a high window they could see the stars and the fields. There was a heavy bar on the inside of their door, and they slid it into place before they went to bed. Gael's nerves were still taut as a bowstring, but after a time she relaxed in the strange room and quickly fell asleep. She dreamed of men in outlandish long brown robes, herding black sheep before them.

CHAPTER II

SUMMER RIDERS

Druda Strawn led the way but he let the young men go ahead on their ponies; they rode up a firm, winding way called Larch Road and came over the edge of the plateau. Jehane and Gael brought up the rear, through a stand of noble, shaggy larch trees, and saw the lads go hallooing over tussock and green reeds. Game birds rose up into the summer sky; larks were already singing. Far away to the south there was a head of cloud rising over Rift Kyrie, but here in the center of the plateau, the air was very clear. They could see the Great Eastern Rift, a little to the northeast. Then they were all on the High Ground, and training had truly begun.

Gael was full of relief and joy—this was how things were meant to be. The episode with the attack and the questioning was like a summer storm or a flash of dark magic. That night for the first time they made camp, pitched their tents, learned about horse pickets. At the campfire they sang a marching song and a chant for good fortune.

Now they rode out every day from their camping places, drilled with Druda Strawn, cared for their horses, practiced archery. Gael did well with the short Chyrian bow and the crossbow. One of the Naylor twins, Leem, had a natural gift, hardly wasted an arrow or a bolt. Jehane rode very well and, together with Bretlow Smith on his charger, showed them all simple exercises in dressage—walk, trot, canter, counting steps, and turning closely. Once, in the stableyard of the great inn called the Halfway House, Gael felled one of the lads to the ground for beating his pony—after that all the kern recruits respected the strength of her arm.

It was fifteen years since the end of the Great King's War; Ghanor, the so-called Great King, had died in his bed at his Palace Fortress on the inland sea, the Dannermere, in the year 334 of the Farfaring, as time was reckoned in Mel'Nir. As they followed the roads built on the plateau since the war, Druda Strawn tried to teach his uncouth band about the lands of Hylor, and, closer to home, of the internal strains that lay upon Mel'Nir. They knew well enough that peace reigned between their own liege, Knaar of Val'Nur, Lord of the Westmark, and Good King Gol, son of Ghanor; but the Southland, under the Lords of Pfolben, was almost an independent state. What of the Eastmark? Huarik, the Boar of Barkdon, last of the Eastmark's Lords, had died during the Great War, in single combat with a hero of Mel'Nir—no less than Coombe's own champion, Yorath Duaring—and no other lord had arisen in his place. King Gol still held many of the Eastmark lands. Recently much clamoring had arisen among the houses of the East that these, and a Lord for the Eastmark, should be restored.

Gael was shamed to discover how little was her own learning of the lands beyond Mel'Nir's (or even Val'Nur's) borders—even the Naylor twins were better taught. The Druda smiled—assuredly Gael was not the only member of his troop whose knowledge was lacking—and he spoke to them in vivid pictures, deep into the night, as the campfire blazed before them.

First came the wide Chameln lands across the inland sea, those lands which always had two rulers, the Daindru, and, nine years past, King Sharn Am Zor had been done to death by savage tribesmen. Now the Chameln were ruled by two queens: Aidris Am Firn, the old Witch-Queen, and the beautiful young Tanit Am Zor. Mel'Nir had held these lands for a time, in the years before Gael was born; as the tale was told, the old Witch-Queen Aidris had spent those years in hidden exile, training for a kedran, awaiting the moment to strike.

Aidris in those distant days had been an enemy to Mel'Nir, but in the stories as the Druda now told them, the Queen of the Firn was a figure to admire, particularly for an impressionable kedran just taking up her training.

True also, Aidris Am Firn had been an enemy with a sense of honor. In the slaughter of Great King's Red Hundreds at Adderneck Pass, she had humiliated Old King Ghanor, but once she had retaken her land and her throne, once the border of the Chameln had been reaffirmed, Aidris had kept within her boundaries. The part of the story those around the fire found most impossible to believe—the Witch-Queen was a dwarf, a creature of the Firn, a tiny, slender-figured race. Even mounted on a Chameln steed, she stood no taller than the shortest of the Melniros. How could such a woman ever have gone for a soldier?

Then there was far-off Eildon, the magic land, with its knightly orders and reclusive Priest-King. There was quiet Cayl, where once there had been no lords—until Lien had swallowed them up, reinstated the old aristocratic lines, and—so it was claimed—brought back to light Cayl's lost honor and glory. There was gentle Athron, land of the magic Carach tree, its prince and highest lady claimed for the most beauteous in all Hylor, the most fair and comely in all their deeds and doings.

On other nights, the Druda told darker tales. North of the River Bal lay the Kingdom of Lien, ruled by King Kelen and Queen Fideth. Here the Druda's telling lost its playful tone, and Gael was brought back to the sharp looks he and Hem Duro had exchanged after the examination at Hackestell Fortress. Mel'Nir and its rough warriors yet held Lien to be a small, tame land—but there was also a history of magic, intrigue, and violence. Who had not heard of the Grand Vizier, the archmage Rosmer of Lien, who, not yet ten years past, had gathered in many lands—Mel'Nir's own Balbank included—to transform Lien into a kingdom?

The Mark of Lien had been the home of poets, actors, painters, scribes, and makers of books, a land of palaces and pleasure boats. Rosmer's unbounded ambition had remade more than its borders. For now the *Kingdom* of Lien lay under the ban of a new religion: pastime and merriment were at an end.

Rosmer had taken the life of Kelen's truelove, Zaramund of Grays—his lovely but barren wife. He had taken Zaramund's father, her brothers, all the core of the family who would have avenged her. In her place he set a young girl—foolish and hot-blooded—a woman who could give Kelen the heir his vizier so dearly wanted.

But the gods take as easily as they bequeath, and the archmage had died the triumphant day Kelen rose to wear his kingly crown. As the Druda told the story, Rosmer's life served as the final pledge that raised his liege to a king's throne—and Kelen of Lien's spirit was not strong enough to bear up beneath the burden of this last gruesome token.

Life in Lien after the coronation soon turned bitter and hard. Rudderless after Rosmer's death, the new-made king was turned by his then-young, but also penitent and implacable queen to follow the bright torches of Inokoi, the Lame God, also called the Lord of Light, and Matten his prophet. Now, instead of an archmage, the state was served by the Brotherhood of the Lame God, a fellowship who scourged the queen for her past sins—for all the world knew she had lain with Kelen and got herself with child while the king was still married to Zaramund—and preached that all the world must renounce the pleasures of earthly life and of the flesh. Queen Fideth, remorseful now, had even gone so far as to dedicate her son, Lien's heir, to the brotherhood's ranks, and there were rumblings that the day Matten—the boy had been named for the great Prophet himself—inherited the Kingdom, he would take a Brown Priest's robes, and become himself one of the Brown Order.

This was about as much stuff from the scrolls as the band of recruits could bear—a prince, the heir to all his nation's riches, voluntarily wearing sackcloth and spurning carnal pleasures! They could not—would not—believe it.

They sidetracked Druda Strawn into talk of battles. Everywhere upon the plateau, he could point out memorials of his greatest hero, Yorath Duaring. The Druda had tears in his eyes when he spoke of the cruel ambush far to the west, in the very last days of the war. In the month of chaos while Ghanor of Mel'Nir lingered on his deathbed, the great Yorath was set upon and killed by rogue warriors of the Great King's army, driven over the cliffs into the western sea, as if only the ocean could subdue his proud spirit. A sad mark of fate indeed to open Good King Gol's reign, for Yorath Duaring had been—though every recruit knew this story, they gasped to hear it told again—Yorath Duaring had been King Gol's only trueborn son, stolen from the cradle and brought to manhood in secret from his murderous grandsire, that unnatural grandfather who would have seen the child strangled at birth for a prophecy that touched at his own death.

The aftermath at least was happy: Gol lost his son, but he made peace with the Lords of the Westmark, where his son had seen all his service. Knaar, after all was said, had been the noble Yorath's bosom friend, and Valko Firehammer, Knaar's sire, had been the father to Yorath that Gol's own sire had denied him.

The young recruits always eagerly clamored for stories of the lost heir of the Duaring Kings.

Near the broad road, the "King's Way" which traversed the plateau, was the strange ghost town of Silverlode—long deserted since its veins of silver were mined out, and since the bloody day when Huarik the Boar had lost his head to Yorath Duaring inside its tall Roundhouse, following the betrayal that triggered the bloodiest phase of the Great King's War. Now Silverlode, in the gentleness of summer, was a place of pilgrimage. Druda Strawn led his troop there on a sunny day in Oakmoon, the Midsummer Month, and there they met other riders. A working party had arrived all the way from the Eastern Rift to clear away the weeds that rose up between the stones and to wash down the queer small buildings of brick and stone that stood about the Roundhouse. Gael thrilled to the tales of Silverlode, but in itself it was a cold, bereft place, and nothing could bring life or warmth to it.

Inside the tall Roundhouse daylight shone down from open shutters in the roof; there was a long table with a fine red cloth and many wreaths of flowers. A group of women from the rift had arranged the greenery; now an older man, a tutor from the great house of Pauncehill, came forward and recited for them the tale of *The Bloody Banquet of Silverlode*. He told of Huarik of Barkdon, called the Boar, both for his house's crest and for his savagery. This lord had plundered and raged up and down the eastern border of the High Plateau.

The Boar made a secret pact with the mad old King Ghanor, who used his authority to summon all the lords from the Great Eastern Rift to the neutral ground of the High Plateau, calling them as if to a peace table and a field of martial games. The Rift Lords had little reason to trust Ghanor, who had not sent his soldiers to aid them in the campaign to hold Huarik from their fields, but Ghanor sent his daughter, Princess Fadola, and her husband, Mel'Nir's vizier, as an earnest of his goodwill, so the followers of the Rift Lords put aside their wariness. In this very Roundhouse the lords and their ladies sat down to feast. As they ate and spoke and laughed, readying themselves for the tourney, their troops, housed in the compound, were treacherously brought to sleep by drugged wine. And underground, hidden within the old mine, waited fresh troops of Huarik, a secret double muster.

Then, at the appointed hour, Huarik the Boar showed his true face. The Rift Lords were set upon as they sat at table; the Boar himself slit their throats, and they lay weltering in their own blood at the festive board. Their wives were herded away from the table; servants who intervened were struck down. Even the princess and Sholt the Vizier were appalled, stricken with fear and loathing, for they had not been privy to this awful deed. Young Knaar of Val'Nur, come up from the Rift, where he had trained with Strett of Andine at Cloudhill, was seized for ransom.

Ah, but a warning had been given. The men of Cloudhill did not drink, and they warned others. A rescue party came in underground and climbed up, up—to the gallery yonder, where the musicians had played. They gazed down upon the frightful carnage in this great hall, and Yorath Nilson, a gangling untried warrior, a loyal man who had served in Strett of Cloudhill's houseguard, took charge. While some stole away and opened the outer doors, crying for their life and freedom, this Nilson strode instead to the gallery railing, and there he took his stand. He cried out in a loud voice—a champion had arisen! Calling Huarik a foul and treacherous murderer, he challenged the Eastmark's lord. Then over the rail he went, and he was so tall, such a mighty man, that it was but a little step down into the hall. There he stood, and all who beheld him in this hour believed this was truly a Godson, come to avenge the Rift Lords and their families.

So Yorath Duaring—for that was this Nilson's true name—matched broadswords with Huarik the Boar, and they were both mighty warriors: Huarik more experienced and crafty, Yorath with a greater reach, fresh and unafraid. So it was that they fought and marked each other with small wounds and at the last Huarik slipped in the spilt blood of his victims. He came to one knee, *there, right on that spot;* Yorath did what must be done. He swung a perfect blow; he struck off the head of Huarik the Boar, denying Old Ghanor the success of his treachery even as the Rift Lords' families cried out and called arms against their king, and a new battle, a new round of Mel'Nir's saddest and greatest war, had opened.

Hearing this tale, none of the listening recruits could remain unmoved. Gael caught her breath; she felt the power of that moment, she looked up to the tall broken railing over which Yorath had leapt, now so many years past. Jehane, beside her on the settle, pressed her arm, sharing the excitement. As they listened to the end, Gael was in a dream between past and present . . . she thought of course of her own liege . . . and Knaar of Val'Nur was instantly set free to clasp the hand of his brother in arms. Gael thought wistfully of this lord as he was now, as she had seen him walking before the fortress at Hackestell two weeks past, and wondered if that unbent old man yet yearned for the fiery honor days of his young manhood.

The followers of the Boar? Some were killed, taken hostage—they had lost all. Huarik's secret muster, hidden underground, were veterans of the Chameln war, Ghanor's men, returned from defeat in the Adderneck, already half in disgrace. Now, in a last stirring scene, they turned their allegiance to Yorath. He accepted their pledges, formed in that instant a Free Company to serve Val'Nur and protect the Rift from the troops of the Eastmark. He became Yorath the Wolf, the greatest ally of Westmark's lord. The rest—the rest was a history Gael and the others had already heard many times over.

As the Green Muster straggled out into the afternoon sunshine, the young men were fierce, with mock fights, flourishing their staves and practice swords. Gael Maddoc saw her chance and approached Druda

Strawn as he sat alone on a stone bench in the center of the deserted town. She sat down without asking leave and began to question him about what had taken place in Hackestell.

"Druda," she asked, "how could it come to such a pass—the Lord Knaar attacked in this way? If we had not been at that very part of the way . . ."

"You have put your finger on it, Gael Maddoc," replied the priest. "It was a grave error, a failure in the planning of the parade. Oh, of course—it was a peaceful occasion, close to a strongly garrisoned fortress of Val'Nur—but the Eagles were too far ahead and the Sword Lilies out of sight at the bend. Guards and escort kedran are there to do just that—guard the lord and his family!"

"We heard no more," she said. "We were hustled away to the maidservants' quarters. Druda, what is known of these rebellious folk, the Black Sheep . . . ?"

Druda Strawn sighed deeply.

"I know little of them," he said, "but I will try to learn more. It is almost certain that the two men came to attack the lord because farms they had, far away west of Krail, were flooded to make a dam."

"Oh," said Gael. "What then was the talk of Lien, that Hem Duro spoke of so soft and quiet?"

"Yes," said the Druda, "that is indeed talk for quiet tones. Though in Coombe we are so far to the south, it can be hoped that little will come of it. Do you remember the matter I spoke of the other night?"

"About Prince Matten, and his mother's intention that he should join the Brown Men's order?" The young men had found it a matter of laughter, a prince so cowed by his mother's sins that he might swear himself to the celibate life.

The Druda nodded. "It is a darker thing than you young folk can comprehend, if Prince Matten will cede to it. I have heard on the wind that Kelen of Lien has fallen ill, and Matten . . ." He paused. "The Prince is little older than your brother Bress. What say you, Gael? Is such a boy, even a prince, ready to make such choices in his own life?"

Gael thought seriously, wondering at the Druda's question. She thought of her own promise to train as a kedran, short months past, of the attack at Hackestell and all the things of the life to which she was now committed. "I am not sure if even one so old as myself would be ready," she said. "But where the choice is so much bigger than oneself, there is no choice but to rise to the occasion."

"That is a good answer, Gael Maddoc," said the Druda. "An answer such as I am coming ever more to expect from you." She did not know what he could mean, but with those words he smiled, and dismissed her to join her companions.

II

The work went on with the drills. Jehane and Gael trained with the bows, with the long, double-edged "kedran" swords, and, finally mounted, with the lance. Now the entire muster had settled into the Halfway House, the great inn for travelers, no more than twenty miles from the Great Eastern Rift. The folk who ran the inn were half-Shee, a populous family named Cluny. Druda Strawn received special treatment and a special rate for the recruits.

The High Ground was the domain of the Eilif lords of the Shee, and mortal men continued to respect their tenure. Armies had marched over the plateau, and the precious metals and jewels had been mined out, but there were few permanent settlements and no garrisons south of the Halfway House. Before they rode out in the early morning Druda Strawn offered greeting and prayers to the Shee. Gael believed she sensed their presence. She asked Jehane how it was to have the blood of the Shee, from her grandmother, but the dark beauty said she had no special powers. In fact it might make it harder for her to make a good match—or so her father teased her mother.

In the evenings Jehane worked with Gael at her reading. Only Jehane and Prys Oghal and a weaver's son they called Little Low could read. The Druda had a store of primer books on parchment and vellum, as well as slates and cakes of chalk, for the reading lessons. Gael worked hard, but her written script lagged behind the reading. Jehane praised her for knowing two languages already—Chyrian as well as the common speech, and swore that it would one day come in handy.

The day soon came when they all set out from the Halfway House and rode down into the Eastern Rift, that long, fertile valley, and saw the manors of the Rift Lords and the thriving Rift villages. They rode as far as the eastern end of the valley to Cloudhill, the famous horse farm where Yorath Duaring and Knaar of Val'Nur had trained with Strett of Andine. Strett had been a man legendary in his own day for his honor, his generosity, his noblesse; overcoming the bastardy of his birth, he had built his holdings upon principle and virtue. His death at Silverlode had been a great tragedy for Mel'Nir and was still spoken of with sorrow in the Rift villages they passed through.

In the village of Ochma, they met an old soldier, Captain Gorrie, who had served with the Red Hundreds of Ghanor the Great King and had survived both the eerie disaster of the Adderneck Pass and the betrayal at Silverlode before he had turned away from the King's service. He recounted how he had pledged himself to the Free Company of Yorath Duaring, and his eyes shone when he spoke of this leader, so fresh were his memories. He shook his head and said, smiling, there was no one like him. No warrior so tall and bold, yes, but he had a noble heart as well and cared for his people.

In this chance meeting Gael began to understand that the old days were not so long ago as she had believed them, that the ceaseless turn of seasons as she had understood them by the croft at Holywell was but a small drop in time, and that perhaps these men—the Druda, Gorrie, and even Knaar—were not so old, their youth not so far away. For a poor crofter's girl in her seventeenth year, these thoughts were new, and she felt herself jealous for the first time of Jehane, who'd had a tutor for more than a hand of years now, besides having her father welcome Druda Strawn to dinner in their fine forest hall many a fair night. The Maddocs' home—only on a feast day might their fare stretch so far as to include company.

This resentment might have stayed but for Jehane's kindness and light spirit, and also it was swept away by the larger ideas of Hylor's varied and much-changing lands that were slowly coming to fill Gael's waking thoughts.

As the young troop rode back from Ochma through the rift along the eastern bank of the River Keddar, they passed the splendid old houses of the Rift Lords. There was Cannford Old House, where Strett of Cloudhill's daughters had lived with their grandmother; there were Keddar Grove and Pauncehill. The Eastmark families were loyal to King Gol; the lands of Barkdon had been redistributed, but these, as Druda Strawn now pointed out, were the very families who were clamoring for a new Lord of the Eastmark to be set over them.

The balance of the Marches was out of kilter; there was no Lord of the Eastmark to stand in council where the Marchers met. The Rift Lords desired to see the Eastmark's honor restored by Gol's appointing one lord its master. Indeed, one lord had begun to rise above others, and that was Degan of Keddar, a Rift Lord with many holdings. He had survived the Silverlode massacre, aged twelve years, the page of Strett of Cloudhill. Keddar had married one of Strett's daughters, Perrine—the elder daughter, Annhad, was wed to the Lord of Pfolben, ruler of the Southland. Old Strett's memory was so highly regarded, Keddar's marriage had already in some way set him on a level with Pfolben. "But we shall see," said the Druda. "We shall see. Our king is aged and tired, and Mel'Nir yet remains sadly full of tension. We can hope for a new Lord of the Eastmark before the kingly throne changes hands, but perhaps Gol will want to leave that for his heir."

By the Druda's expression Gael could tell that he hoped the king would act.

The young men went off to explore a village with a summer fair but Jehane and Gael rode up and stood before Cannford Old House. It was fine to see, with old trees and a white road winding through an avenue. One sister, Pearl of Andine, the youngest and some said the most beautiful of Strett's daughters, yet remained. She had never married, and the great house was, of all things, a school for young women of noble birth.

"You will go in?" asked Gael, as Jehane rode boldly to the gatehouse.

"Duty call!" smiled Jehane. "My granddam knows the Lady Pearl—we'll get a look at the house!"

There was a sturdy old woman in the gatehouse who let them in, spoke reverently of Fion Allrada, Jehane's grandmother, and inquired about their training on the High Ground. They rode on up the avenue through the quiet afternoon and came to the front of Cannford Old House, facing eastward. The house was of wood and grey stone with some newly glazed windows among the narrower orioles of a former time. It was a house of women: two young girls took their horses. As they mounted the steps, the paneled wooden doors swung inward without a sound and they went into a cool, high-roofed hall.

A woman received them there and then turned toward the staircase, where a lady was descending. She was above the middle height and beautiful, with fine, even features, a radiant fairness, her thick blonde hair glowing in its silver snood. This quality, of giving off her own light, from her body, from the folds of her blue-grey gown, told Gael of magic.

"Jehane!" said Pearl of Andine, "Welcome to Cannford! I hope your grandmother is well?"

"Very well, my lady," replied Jehane.

She stepped up and exchanged a formal kiss on the cheek with the chatelaine of Cannford and then presented her companion. Gael gave a salute, and she saw that Lady Pearl had hazel eyes, very keen and sharp.

The woman who had greeted them in the hall held open a door and the lady led them into a pleasant bower, not so striking and grand as the private hearth in Hackestell Fortress, but more comfortable. They sat on a padded settle and Lady Pearl heard of their training on the High Ground and of their pilgrimage to Silverlode, where her noble father had met his death. She turned to a tall press, with a display of miniature portraits in silver frames, upon a wooden stand. There was Thilka of Andine and Jared Strett of Cloudhill; there were their three daughters, Annhad, Perrine, and Pearl. Gael found these portraits marvelous things, so fine it was difficult to think of an artist who could do such work. The painter, she was told, was Emyas Bill, a great artist from Lien who now lived in Achamar, the capital city, if so it could be called, of the wild Chameln.

Then the old woman brought lemon cordial to drink and fresh applecake. Presently the Lady Pearl reached for certain objects that stood beside a vase of roses on the table before them.

"You are blessed," she said crisply, with an unexpected change of manner. "I will give you each a reading!"

She swung back the domed lid of a black wooden box and revealed a smooth shining ball of glass, giving off rays of colored light, its own rainbows. Then she had in her hand, from a small woven basket, flat numbered sticks that Gael knew as runesticks. She did not know how to behave during fortune-telling but Jehane and the lady showed her kindly. Both girls scattered the sticks, and this showed who would go first—while Jehane had her reading, Gael was sent out onto the garden terrace and sat looking out into the orchard.

She saw a band of young girls, some of them children, picking fruit, romping and hiding among the trees. She saw and wondered at the southern wall of the rift, hundreds of feet high and striated with colored layers of earth, some where plants grew, some of bare rock. Presently it was her turn to go in and hear her own reading while Jehane wandered away into the interior of the great house.

The Lady Pearl stared at her with a keen interest and reached across the table to take Gael's hands in her own. She peered into them, made a sharp intake of breath and bit her lip. Then she gazed into the crystal ball, smiling a thin nervous smile.

"From the Holywell outside little Coombe . . ." she murmured, "and you chose the kedran life of your own free will?"

"Yes indeed!" said Gael, surprised. "I—I believe I have a calling . . ."

"More than that, child," said the lady. "Perhaps you are surprised that I have heard of your family's little well, even across this side of the High Plateau—but that Well is an ancient place, and the Goddess has long blessed it."

Gael thought of the rocky fields where her father bent his back in labor, and she withheld her own thin smile, but the lady was speaking in all seriousness, overriding her doubts. “You are people of the Cup,” she said. “Yet you, Gael Maddoc, have chosen the way of the Lance. This is a greater departure than you yet have realized.”

Gael could only stare, remembering the parchment she had deciphered with the Druda’s help, her father’s reluctance to allow her to follow the Druda’s plan that she should go for a kedran. “There is no cup at the croft now,” she said shyly. “We are humble people. Folk do not come so often to the Well—”

Pearl of Andine interrupted, her gaze fixed within the glass ball. “Gael Maddoc,” she said, “a great destiny lies before you. You will travel in many lands and know men and women of every degree. Mark well these words: I see a frightened boy, splashed by water from your own hands; you are beside him. When he looks at you, you both smile. I see a tall man, reading in a book, his pen held in readiness. O the Lance! The Krac’Duar! I see the Lance! And yes, I see a woman, an old woman sitting before a mirror—Goddess—I know her! Yet I must not speak her name.” She broke free of the glass then and turned to Gael, a little distracted, throwing a velvet cloth to cover the glass ball.

Again she took Gael’s hands. “Do not tell anyone of my reading here today. What are your plans after this training with Druda Strawn?”

“The Plantation . . .” Gael said. “To serve with the Westlings!”

Pearl of Andine shook her head.

“No,” she said. “Your training will be completed elsewhere. You will not go on to serve Knaar of Val’Nur.”

Gael could not help herself—she touched the lady’s skirts—could Lady Pearl tell her nothing more? The lady sighed, briefly covering Gael’s fingers with her own. “You may go so far as to ask the Druda this: make him tell you the history of the *Krac’Duar*. I cannot tell you further, and you must not press me.”

The reading was complete. Lady Pearl put away her aids; at the last, she reached into a drawer, under the tablecloth. She brought out a pendant on a silver chain; it was shaped like a lily flower, in white and green, with a tiny pearl in the flower’s center.

“Wear this!” she said. “It will protect you, Gael Maddoc. Till we meet again!”

As they rode away from Cannford Old House, Jehane gave a mysterious smile.

“Well,” she said, “did you get a fine fortune?”

“More than I expected,” said Gael, wondering what Jehane had been told. “But we must not breathe a word—even to each other!”

"All fortunes end that way . . ." laughed Jehane. "Look, there are those wretched boys coming back from the village!"

The summer exercises were nearly done. The Druda rode out as far as Goldgrave, a thriving town on the plateau, growing into a city. He took the two kedran recruits, along with Prys Oghal and the Naylor twins. It was a reward for good work, and certainly Gael's head was full of words and sounds. She could read at last.

Goldgrave was a fine place, where they stayed at an inn; there were market stalls on the town square, and she spent three of Hem Duro's silver shields to buy presents for the Winter Feast. It was the first money she had ever had to spend in her life.

She found a fine set of battle figures for her father and a shawl for her mother and a pair of leather gloves for Bress and sweetmeats for all the family and a little book bound in purple leather for Druda Strawn—a book of Chyrian Tales written on vellum in the common speech. She saw a whole stall full of "Emyan Ware," cheap but still attractive pictures in the style of the miniatures done by the great Lienish artist. She bought a picture of a tree, decorated for the Winter Feast, with two children dancing—perhaps they were Gael and her brother Bress.

On the third day they rode out beyond Goldgrave to the northwest. In a bleak landscape, amidst a few ancient ruins of stone, the Druda made a summoning, and there before them stood a mighty gate, with pillars, in the wilderness, slowly fading from their sight. Gael wanted then to ask him of the *Krac'Duar*, but there was no chance, no privacy. In respect to the Lady Pearl's wishes, she held her tongue and waited. They rode back through mist and rain to rejoin the others at the Halfway House: summer was at an end.

Gael Maddoc was sad to see the last of the training ride, and for reasons she would hardly admit to herself. Yes, indeed, she would miss the companionship of Jehane and the others. But not in the same way that Jehane would miss her meetings with the handsome Egon Baran—she wondered if there had been talk of this romance in her friend's fortune. What cast down Gael was the fact that she must give up her horse, the good mare Ivy of whom she had grown very fond. Where would she find another mount, even for practice? Was she truly destined to serve elsewhere—not in Krail, not with the Westlings?

Yet the season carried her along, back at the Holywell croft, getting in the firewood and the winter feed for the goats. There was the Harvest Festival in the sacred grotto, and she saw Jehane again and her granddam.

She was bidden to ride down to the Forest House before the winter came, and she knew this must be the time to bring Ivy home again. The storms of autumn held off a little in that year, so she was able to give Bress a few rides on the mare.

Gael rode round the hill and down to Ardven House, the ruined mansion by the Cresset Burn, to see Old Murrin. She sat with the old woman, who was sturdy despite her old battle wounds, and white-haired; in the lower floor of her house, they sat and talked of the kedran life. Emeris Murrin heard every detail of the strange episode with the two assassins who attacked Knaar of Val'Nur and of the enquiry that followed. Gael even went so far as to tell this veteran one part of her fortune—that it had been said she might not serve in Val'Nur. Besides all this, Old Murrin told Gael many things she had not before known of Balbank—now called King's Bank, taken as it had been under Lien's rule, though many of the Melniros had stayed on there. The old kedran's older brother, who owned Ardven still, had his home there, along with the greater part of the Murrins' land holdings. Perhaps it was such ties as these that had Knaar of Val'Nur and his sons so wary of Lien's influence—though Gael did not see that Old Murrin held any deep fondness for her brother or his loyalties to his new liege master, Lien's King Kelen.

Gael did not hint anything of this to Druda Strawn—he paid his duty call early that year because he was bound on a winter pilgrimage to ancient Tuana, the true capital of the Chyrian folk of the western coast. He brought his presents for the feast and the gifts of food, along with the wool for spinning that he carried to all the poorest crofters.

This time he brought reading exercises and a parchment sheaf with a tale of battles and magic for Gael to work at through the winter. Yes, indeed, she could make a start with Bress—it was never too soon to learn the letters and the runes. Here was a whole pot of good black ink and a bunch of wooden pens so that she might work on her practice scroll.

Before he left, she managed to take him aside and ask him of the *Krac'Duar*. He went still at her question; for a time she was afraid he would not answer.

"It is the Lance of Mel'Nir's Kings," he said at last. "It was lost in the days of Ankar Duaring, the Wizard-King—old Ghanor's sire. When Ghanor took the throne, he forbid the naming of the Lance throughout all Mel'Nir's holdings—this was years even before one so old as *I* was born, my child. It is a sacred object. Some would hold that its loss drove old Ghanor to madness, that Gol cannot chose a true heir to Mel'Nir from among his kin without its blessing—which is perhaps why all have been forbidden to speak of these matters. How did you come to hear this name, this sacred word?"

"I cannot tell you," she whispered, almost sinking down, for she had never before stood against Druda Strawn in anything, let alone a matter of such weight.

She did not know whether to feel disappointed or relieved when the Druda accepted this answer.

In the very last days of autumn Gael saddled Ivy for the last time, rode down into the forest manor of Veyna, and came to the tall Forest House.

She was made welcome by Jehane and all her family—they had the common touch, she could see that. But the difference in the fortunes of the two kedran weighed upon Gael secretly. She hoped she managed not to show it. After three days, with the weather still holding, she set out again with many promises for next spring. She walked up to Coombe village carrying her saddlebag and using her ash staff to help her along the way.

There was a cold winter in her heart even before the winter came. She recalled other winter seasons when she had had so much less—less of a life, less to remember, less to give her mother and her father and Bress at the Winter Feast. What would come to pass? She began to nourish a small flame of hope for her destiny—she thought of Lady Pearl, the wise woman's small, ill-suppressed gestures of excited surprise as she had read her crystal for Gael's fate. Yet summer and that humid day at Cannford Old House seemed so far away. How could a crofter's child aspire to any such thing as a "high destiny"?

There were the usual winter ceremonies in the Holywell Grotto before the ice closed its gate for the season. The village wives brought greenery to decorate the altar. Shivorn Maddoc was not happy at this time of the year because she was ashamed of the Maddocs' impoverishment, though this year was a little better because Gael gave her mother her last two shields, the coins she had received from the house of Val'Nur as a reward. Then Nate Gemman from the Summer Riders turned up with a good order for oatcakes and winter wreaths and straw dolls. He asked Gael to bring the orders to the family shop and step in for mulled wine.

"By the Goddess," rumbled Maddoc when the young man had gone, "I think he fancies our Gael, eh, Mother?"

Gael blushed and gave Bress a cuff for his laughter. But it was true—Nate Gemman had been friendly during their riding days and had kissed her once in the stable of the Halfway House. And she had let him, more or less. She began to understand how it might be with a man she "fancied."

Now it was the time of the first snow and there were heavy falls, a pleasure for the children who brought out their sleds and had snowball fights. The chores went on, hauling supplies on the sleds—Gael and Bress brought food and firewood round the hill to Old Murrin in Ardven House. She invited them in, as she did every year, for winter treats, and they sat in the lower floor of the old house, at the fireside with Oona the grey cat. They sang songs for the season: "The Wintering of Culain" and "Raise Up the Tree" and "Lady, Bless House and Byre." Gael and Bress could both sing in harmony and Bress could play a pipe he had made from a hollow reed. Then they went back round the hill through the snowy night, with Gael drawing Bress part of the way on the sled, and a blazing torch to guide them home.

She went along, warily, to Master Gemman's shop, in a courtyard near the reeve's house, and Nate welcomed her in and introduced her proudly to his parents.

The evening turned out to be happy and noisy—others came in to play games with counters, dice, and cards with pictures. There was music from a bagpiper and a fiddler and Nate brought her home on a sled drawn by a sleek brown pony. She did not begrudge him several kisses for the Winter Feast. She told the family about the games and her father went on a little about good old days when the harvests were better and the soil sweeter and the Maddoc family had given great evenings.

"Those days will come again, Da," said Gael firmly. "Great good fortune will come to us, and to Coombe village! I swear it by the Goddess!"

"I'll ride out with the Summer Riders!" cried Bress. "I'll come to the Westlings, where you are a kedran, sister!" She cast a look at her little brother then, not knowing what to think, and saw her whisper of worry echoed in her father's expression. If Bress too was a "person of the Cup," as Lady Pearl of Andine had called her, would it be right for him too to take up a sword?

Then at last there came the feast days, and things were as warm and merry in the old croft as they had ever been. Her presents from Goldgrave suited well. In return she had a paper Lienbook from the Druda, which he had left for her mother to give her, and a smart riding cap, as the kedran wore, with a place for a badge and a feather. The Emyan card with the tree and the two children was set on the shelf in the chimney wall.

There were heavy falls of snow and the Maddocs, even Gael's mother, dug out the approaches to the Holywell—the path from the croft under the trees, some leafless, and the lower entrance from the roadway. Some older folk in the village were taken, and there was talk of a bad round of winter croup in the villages to the south and southwest. Mostly the folk moved between house and byre, keeping themselves and their animals as warm and well fed as they could. At the Holywell Croft there were only the four goats to care for, and they did well enough.

Then, just as the weather eased a little, there was a sound at the door one night, and there, of all things, was a thin brown cat, mewing to come in. Gael saw how much better things had become for the Maddocs—they let Bress bring it inside by the fire and gave it a bowl of milk. Maddoc said that the beast could earn its keep hunting rats and mice in the storeroom and the lean-to. Her mother remembered other housecats—this was a Mouser, a gelded tomcat, who would stay and grow fat, and not go wandering. Gael thought for a day or two and then asked Bress if the cat might be called Kenit, for the old Chyrian hero who had rid a king's palace of mice and rats. So, Kenit. The winter stray sat by the fire in early spring and grew fat on mice, and they all loved him.

Gael went on with her reading, and the days grew warmer. Nothing changed in the daily round until the Willowmoon, in her eighteenth year.

CHAPTER III

THE PRINCE OF THE SOUTHLAND

It was the seventh day of the Willowmoon, the month of planting, a mild evening in early spring. Gael was out late, hunting a strayed goat, and she came round by the sacred grotto. Riders went by below her in the dusk, on the south road from Lowestell fortress. There was a shout followed by the clash of metal; the horsemen began casting about. Gael crouched in the gorse and did not move when one man urged his charger up the bank. She heard his loud cry:

"My lord? Hem Blayn?"

Then he cursed and said:

"Where is the young devil?"

As the big horse went crashing down to the roadway Gael heard another horse whinny softly in the bushes behind her. She went quickly through to the thorn trees, white and red, that guarded the entrance to the cave.

A bay horse, caparisoned in blue and gold, stood shivering by the whitethorn. In the light of the rising moon, she found its rider, fallen onto the path. He was lightly built by the standards of Mel'Nir and all arrayed in painted strip mail; his shield showed the device of a white horse and a golden star. Gael knelt down, uttered a prayer to the Goddess, and managed to remove the warrior's helm. He was very pale and his hair was pure gold.

Gael thought of the Shee, the fairy race, who still walked upon the High Plateau. This young lord was more beautiful than any mortal. He was so pale she feared for his life. She found a nasty gash on his leg just above his boot top and bound it with her own kerchief, none too clean.

She could find no other hurt but a swelling bruise on the side of his head, where he had fallen from his horse.

Then from below came a sound of hoofbeats, returning, and the lord opened his eyes. He saw Gael kneeling over him.

"Kedran," he whispered. "Kedran, I have no sword. They must not find me!"

She said nothing but gripped the lord under his arms and drew him into the passage that led to the grotto. Then she went out again, spoke sweetly to his horse and led it in. So they waited, with no light but a little sparkle of moonbeams through the fretted roof and no sound except the plashing of spring water. Gael went to stand at the mouth of the passage and heard the riders pass by, returning to the south.

She went about near the cave gathering bracken for the lord's bed. Their eyes became accustomed to the darkness of the grotto. Gael watered the horse from the sacred spring, pouring water from the old leather dipper into a hollow of the rock. Then she rinsed her kerchief in the clear water and dressed the lord's wound again and gave him drink. The lord spoke his name:

"I am Blayn of Pfolben."

Even Gael Maddoc knew this name. Pfolben was the great lord of the Southland and this was his son.

"My sword," he said. "My sword was taken from me, but it will come again."

She thought his wits were scrambled from the blow on the head. He smiled at her.

"It is a magic blade from the Burnt Lands," he said. "It is bound to my service."

Gael stared at him and felt her own head swim. She said no word but knew that she, too, was bound to his service from that hour. They spoke further, and then Hem Blayn allowed her to fetch her mother. Shivorn Maddoc brought food and blankets; the young lord hardly needed their whispers of safety and secrecy.

The story was one of mutiny. A rebellious band of officers and men from the southern border fortress of Lowestell had rejected their commander and ridden away, taking Blayn with them as a hostage. They were quickly rounded up and disciplined; two officers, the sons of other southern lords, were imprisoned as traitors. Before it came to a search, Blayn of Pfolben emerged from hiding and rode home.

He rewarded the family of Maddoc, who had hidden him in the Holywell. On the third night, Gael, after she had seen to his horse, brought the lord up the dark path to their cottage. Blayn of Pfolben, who had the common touch, sat easily at their fireside while Shivorn dressed the cut on his leg, which was healing well. He spoke to Rab Maddoc, man to man, and insisted that he take two gold pieces—they had not seen very many; the yellow glitter held them a little in awe. Blayn clapped young Bress on the shoulder and promised him a place at Lowestell when he was grown. He patted Kenit the cat and returned to the sacred grotto once more. Next morning he rode out to the south, and Gael went with the lord to be his kedran.

They set out with Blayn mounted on Daystar, his fine bay horse, and Gael running behind. Ahead loomed the fortress of Lowestell, war booty of Blayn's grandfather, for it had been seized from Val'Nur in the Great King's War and never returned. Blayn's banner had been read by the sentinels, and a captain came riding out with a small escort.

The captain, a huge man on a huge grey horse, had the look of one who did not like his duty.

"Hem Blayn," he said, "you must declare yourself."

"Captain Ulth," said Blayn, "I am safe. I made my escape from the rebels."

"The young lords Cahl and Keythril . . ."

"False friends," said Blayn, "for they carried me off as hostage to their enterprise!"

"Some would say they are true friends," said the Captain, "for they will say no word of your part in the mutiny!"

"Godfire!" cried Blayn. "I had no part in it. I was held captive! My sword was taken from me! I escaped, wounded and unarmed, and I was cared for by this good kedran wench, Maddoc, and her family."

So the whole company looked at Gael Maddoc, and it was as if she saw herself for the first time in their eyes. She was a great strapping creature with a shock of red hair and a Chyrian face that no one could call more than good humored. She had been scrubbed clean, of course, and wore her uniform from the summer training and her father's best boots.

She blushed, her heart thumped, but she stood tall and remembered the questioning she had gone through once before, at Hackestell. She could speak up in a clear voice, choosing her words carefully in the common speech. "Courage!" she told herself. "It is my destiny, as the Lady Pearl of Andine foretold. This ordeal will end, and I will be secure in the service of my lord."

"And the Lord Blayn was unarmed?" asked Captain Ulth for the second time.

"Aye, Captain!" she answered.

Then the captain sighed and nodded to one of the mounted soldiers, a kedran sergeant.

"Sergeant Witt has your sword, Hem Blayn," he said. "It was found about a half mile from this spot, in heavy brush near the roadside."

The sergeant was a sturdy woman on a spirited brown mare. She rode forward now and handed her lord a scabbard of chased leather, oddly shaped. Blayn, smiling, drew out at once the sword Ishkar.

It had a broad, curved blade, the tempered metal tinged with gold and ornamented with scrollwork. The hilt was plain save for one large gemstone, pale green with a dark star at its center that winked like a single eye. The sword shone with its own light, which came and went, pulsing, as if it were a live thing.

"Who owns thee, Sword Ishkar?" cried the young lord.

Then letters shone out plainly on the blade and they spelled out his name: Blayn of Pfolben. Gael Maddoc was proud she was able to read the letters. Now her lord flourished his magic sword and gave her one of his smiles.

"Did I not say my sword would come again?"

Then he said to the sergeant:

"Maddoc will train with your company, Sergeant Witt, and be sworn a kedran in the service of the house of Pfolben."

He rode off toward Lowestell with the captain and the rest of the escort. Sergeant Witt hung back, looking down at her new recruit.

"You can ride?" she asked.

"Aye, Sergeant!"

The Sergeant dismounted and looked Gael up and down.

"Child," she said, "you are suffering from a common complaint in these parts. You think the sun rises and sets with that young lord."

"I have sworn to serve him," said Gael Maddoc.

"What did ye do in that sacred cavern?" demanded the Sergeant. "Did he lie with you?"

Gael was shocked. She went from red to white and said angrily:

"He is a great lord! Who would think of such a thing?"

"Who indeed," said Sergeant Witt, amused. "Come, we'll make a kedran of you, then. But mark my words—the Lord Blayn will not favor you. You have seen the last of him. Now mount up on my horse and see if you can ride to the fortress yonder without falling off."

Gael Maddoc's faith was strong; she managed this first task easily and every other one besides. She had taken to soldiering from the first and wondered at the way some other wenches grumbled. Did she not have three meals a day, her own horse, clothes and stout boots, a bed in a warm barracks? She sent home a portion of her soldier's pay and planned to return to the croft on her long leave.

Sergeant Witt's company was part of the second household regiment of the Lord of Pfolben, the Kestrels. After only a few days in the kedran wing at Lowestell, their duty changed, and Gael went with the Kestrels to the city barracks at Pfolben, capital of the Southland.

Only a part of what the sergeant predicted came true: Gael was made into a kedran, fully trained, but Hem Blayn continued to favor her. He saw to it that she rode escort more than once, and he sent her on his errands. To Gael this was the work of the Goddess, nothing less, the crowning good fortune that had changed her life. To others it must have been clear that the lord in some wise recognized the quality of her devotion.

II

The Southland was warm and exotic after the Chyrian coast. Strange fruit hung from the trees, the nights were mild with a golden moon hanging over the Bellin Hills, above the city. Gael had never lived in a city; she enjoyed its closeness. There were new things to be seen and learned in every turn of the streets.

The barracks were in the north, under the hills, behind the palaces and public buildings. Gael had a fine black gelding called Ebony, and she rode with another Chyrian, Mev Arun, and with Amarah, a golden-skinned girl from the Danasken folk of the Eastmark, whose ancestors had come from the Burnt Lands.

In the south there were the wharves and warehouses: the city of Pfolben lay on the River Elnor, which went winding through the Southland to the tideless waters, the Sea of Ara. Maurik, the Lord of Pfolben, ruler of the Southland, was very rich. He had increased his great inheritance by trading with the people of the Burnt Lands and with the Zebbecks, a race of mariners who sailed in the Sea of Ara.

Yet some said that his greatest treasure was his good wife, Lady Annhad of Andine, eldest daughter of the ill-fated Strett of Cloudhill. As a young man, Maurik had ridden out with his father, the old lord, during the Great King's War, his elder brother having died in that ill-fated adventure of the Great King at the Adderneck Pass. Maurik brought home his bride from the Eastern Rift, plundered by the army of the Southland in the months following the great betrayal of Silverlode.

Lady Annhad, who had come to love her lord, had borne him three children. Her two daughters were fine girls, well married now to southern lords. Blayn, the only son, her youngest child, had been a sickly infant, not expected to live. He was cosseted as a boy because he was frail, high strung, a changeling among the big-boned sons of the southern lords. This was all the explanation his mother could find for the way he had turned out. Now, at two-and-twenty, Blayn was adroit, charming, well beloved, and it mattered little that he was a head shorter than his companions.

Lord Maurik favored a rich simplicity in dress and in the food that overflowed his palace's kitchens. All must be open handed and aboveboard in his domain. Intrigue, magic . . . these things belonged to the Burnt Lands.

Pfolben palace itself seemed almost to mock this attitude. Its older courts and colonnades had been built ages past, before the coming of the men of Mel'Nir, by princes from the Burnt Lands, from Ferss and Aghiras and Reshem-al-Djain. They had long been driven back over the Sea of Ara, but their ghosts remained. Who had not heard a whisper of silken robes on summer evenings, a sound of women murmuring in the walled garden? On the night of the full moon there was an inexplicable stench of blood in the stableyard.

Lady Annhad could only fret at her good lord's blindness in certain things. He saw no ghosts. He was genial and trusting in his dealings with all men. At the same time he flaunted his own honesty like a banner and had no patience with human frailty. He swore that his son, Blayn, was like himself, honest as the day and a true man of Mel'Nir.

So Lady Annhad was not displeased when she saw her son had acquired a big honest kedran as his henchwoman. Indeed, she would have preferred him to go about with Gael and others like her as a permanent bodyguard. The Lord Blayn had need of protection: a towering shadow fell upon him one night as he walked along Orange Flower Street to some tryst. There was a flash of metal, a cry, a splash; folk came running with torches.

Ensign Maddoc had tumbled the assassin into the river and it was the young Lord Keythril, released from prison. He was dragged from the water, half drowned. Blayn smiled and pressed no charges. The next year there was another incident of this kind involving two Danasken blades, hired by an older lord, the husband of a beautiful young wife.

Blayn, warned by his sword, Ishkar, and stoutly supported by Gael Maddoc, made short work of these men. This night was lit by the full moon: afterward the stench of death filled the little fountain court where the attack had taken place, beyond what the blood of two men could have brought there. The young lord, half-gagging, insisted that the dead be left where they had fallen. He washed at the fountain and hurried on, shadowed by his faithful kedran, to the shelter of the palace, where his brother officers were waiting to dine.

Wind of this affair came to the ears of Lady Annhad, and she sent a messenger to Ensign Maddoc. Gael was leading her horse, Ebony, down a narrow lane under the palace wall when the capricious animal went backward, tugging on his bridle. She saw that a man stood in the path. He was middle-aged, dark skinned, rather tubbily built, with a bright cummerbund under his grey silk robe and a turban of the same yellow silk. He hailed her softly by name and bowed low.

"Elim," he said, "house servant of the Lady of Pfolben. I have been entrusted to seek a token from you, Ensign Maddoc, that I may replace it with a true-handed gift and a message."

He brought from his sleeve a little ivory coffer. Gael was experienced enough now to know it must have jewels inside, but she could not think what the man might mean either by a token or by a true-handed gift, a message. Elim saw her confusion, and he smiled.

"You have been almost three years long in your lord's service," he told her. "In that time, one sister has whispered words that reached another's ear, *O child of the Holywell.*"

Gael's hand went unwillingly to her throat, where for almost four years now she had worn Pearl of Andine's lily pendant. Reluctantly, she brought it out of her clothes and held it in her hand, admiring—for perhaps the last time—the pendant's beauty, the tiny pearl's subtle spark. She did not know if this little bauble had ever given her the protection Lady Pearl had sworn of it, but it had served for these years as a hidden token to her bright destiny—she hoped. Now she found herself loath to hand it over, and that not even directly to Lady Annhad's hand.

Elim smiled again, and she wondered if he found enjoyment in the confusion that must be playing across her features. Schooling her expression more firmly, she handed the little metal flower over. "This was a great gift from a gracious lady," Gael Maddoc said, her tongue thick in her throat. "Please tell your own lady that I hold her sister in the highest regard, and ask only that she keep this token safe."

Elim gave a half-bow, acknowledging her, and handed her in his turn the ivory box. When Gael flipped back the lid, wondering, she found a silver-colored ring with a pale green stone. In its depths there was a spark of darker green that winked at her like a single eye. She thought at once of the sword Ishkar.

"My thanks to the Lady," she brought out awkwardly. "This is a fine gift, Master Elim. What have I done to deserve it?"

"Do you need to ask that?" purred the messenger.

"This ring comes from the Burnt Lands," said Gael boldly, "and so do you."

"The ring comes from the Swordmaker of Aghiras," said Elim. "It has many useful properties. Will you put it on?"

She could feel the magic of the ring already, but she would not let him see that she was afraid. In any case she trusted her lord's mother. She slipped the ring on to the middle finger of her right hand and it fitted perfectly.

"Here is the message," said Elim. "Knowing who you are, your sacred heritage, the Lady of Pfolben begs you to stay by the Lord Blayn and protect him, giving this ring as her pledge to you. In the spring he will be invited to hunt in the Burnt Lands by the Dhey of Aghiras and you will go with him, as a member of the special escort."

"I will do my duty," said Gael, not knowing how else to answer him.

She heard some echo of her own voice replying and saw the messenger's smile. She drew off the ring and said:

"Give me the message again, in exactly the same words!"

Elim bowed and rolled off the words in a foreign tongue that she guessed was the language of Aghiras. Yet before she had understood every word and been able to reply in the same language.

"As I said," continued Elim in the common speech, "the ring has many useful properties. You have found out one of them."

"Does it work for all tongues?" asked Gael Maddoc.

"No," said Elim, "only for the language of the Swordmaker. And you must be discreet in its use when acting as an interpreter. Let your own replies be imperfect as if you had learned a little of the speech from a companion in arms."

So Gael slipped on the ring again, more fearfully than before. Would she become invisible? Would it call up demons? The green stone winked up at her, comfortably, like a cat's eye, as if to say: "No such thing! Would I harm you?"

When Elim had gone, Gael touched for reassurance at the empty place against her throat where the lily pendant had hung so long, mimicking its light pressure. This was her second crossing with Strett of Cloudhill's daughters, and again a gift far beyond her stature had been brought to her. In her service to her beloved lord, she had learned much and seen a little broader view of the world. With this gift . . . alone in her plain barracks room, it was easy for the young kedran to hope she saw again the touch of destiny—even as the slight insights she'd gleaned as the Heir of Pfolben's loyal protector called a laugh, and warned her to make nothing of a lady's trifles.

Soon afterward, Blayn of Pfolben received envoys from the Dhey of Aghiras, who humbly begged him to take part in the Royal Hunt of the Lakes of Dawn, together with other princes of the Burnt Lands and of Eildon over the Western Sea. The envoys assured the young lord that this chance would come only once in the lifetime of any prince.

The Lakes of Dawn, on the very outskirts of the wide lands of Aghiras, beyond the sown land and the desert, came into being after a season of heavy rain. The tussock plain grew into a marsh, then into a string of crystal lakes. Tall reeds sprang up, the plain was green overnight; the water and the lake shores teemed with wild life. For a moon, no more, the place was a hunter's paradise, then the fierce sun dried up the lakes like so many drops of dew. Nothing was left but saltflats, to be harvested by the desert tribes. The bright caravans of the Dhey and his guests would depart with a last winding of their silver hunting horns . . .

Blayn of Pfolben received the envoys graciously and set about choosing his escort for the journey.

CHAPTER IV

A JOURNEY TO THE BURNT LANDS

The city of Aghiras was all white and gold, the domes and spires floating out of the sea mist as the galleys of the Southland drew near. The men and women of the special escort had been underway for ten days, with the long river journey from Pfolben to the Sea of Ara, but no one felt weary. They plunged into the teeming life of the wharves and the bazaars. Camels, by the Goddess, bobbing and sneering everywhere, and strange faces under turban and tarboosh. There was a desert warrior, white robed, and there three women, jet black, with huge baskets on their proud heads. There strode the much-vaunted palace guards of the Dhey, the Gaura, in bronze helmets.

Florus, Captain-General of Blayn's escort, drew his men together and consulted with Captain Verreker of the kedran. Where were the marvelous horses, the steeds bred to outrun the winds of the desert, the coursers of the sun? He began to parley with the detail of the Gaura sent to meet them. Gael Maddoc, at his side, was able to tell him that the horses were waiting behind the palace, beyond the pleasure gardens. So they marched off, sixty strong, and Gael, with the rank of acting captain, after only just short of four years' service, went in a silken litter to be near her lord.

Blayn was as happy and as well behaved as she had ever known him. He did not set much store by the glamor of the Burnt Lands, their magic and mystery, but he loved to hunt. The opportunity to test himself against the other princes: Lalmed, son of the Dhey; Meed-al-Mool, called the Red Prince, from Ferss; Kirris Paldo of Eildon, his distant cousin; not to mention Noulith, the warrior queen of the Valfutta . . . this was the sort of competition that truly excited him.

As Blayn leaned back on the silken cushions, Gael Maddoc watched the sights of the bazaar through a gap in the curtains. In the curve of a doorway outlined in raw turquoise, she saw a man watching them: he was very tall, hawk faced, in a straight black robe embroidered in gold. On his neat white turban he wore a single emerald that flamed suddenly as if the sun had caught it.

Her ring sent out a little dart of fire onto the curtain of the litter and the sword. *Ishkar* moved in its sheath under Blayn's hand.

"What the devil . . . ?" he said.

"See, my lord!" said Gael. "The tall man yonder, could it be . . . ?"

"Yes," he said, rising and peering through the curtains, "it might be Zallibar, the Swordmaker. I glimpsed him once in the Dhey's train when they came to Pfolben four years past. When I received my sword."

"He is surely a great magician as well as a craftsman," she said. "He watches us."

"Have no fear, Maddoc," laughed Blayn. "He serves the Dhey, and old Lalmed the Fat still has hopes that I will wed his daughter Farzia."

Gael gave him a questioning look, although she had heard the tale before. Blayn shook his head.

"One day you must come to it," she said, smiling.

"Maddoc, stop talking like my mother!"

Gael Maddoc glanced again into the streets of Aghiras and caught sight of a poor woman carrying a waterskin and a slender, curly-headed lad who ran after her on dusty feet. She thought of her own childhood; she seemed to see her brother Bress following as her mother did the chores and drew water from the well. She held fast to the moment and the memories it conjured. Through all the ceremonies in the palace of the Dhey, she remembered who she was, Gael Maddoc, from Holywell Croft on the Chyrian coast of Mel'Nir.

Later she saw the Dhey himself, overflowing his jeweled throne; she saw the silken luxury of the palace, where even the kedran were housed in perfumed splendor. Beyond the pleasure gardens with their fountains and groves of tamarisk, she went with the other men and women of the escort to choose a horse, one of the coursers of the sun, from the Dhey's stable.

It was here that she first met Jazeel. She examined a black mare in its box and knew that two of the Gaura and a woman house servant stood behind her in the shadow of a palm tree. One voice said in the language of Aghiras:

"That is the one . . . tall as an afreet with fox-red hair."

"Walks like a man. You know what they say about women warriors."

"Find out!" ordered the old woman. "Find out her secret heart. . . ."

Then he was before her, bowing gravely as he said his name.

"Madame Captain," he said in the common speech. "Let me show you the horse I would choose . . ."

"My thanks, good Jazeel."

Gael Maddoc laughed to herself and thought of the night back at home in Pfolben when she would be telling the tale to her friends Amarah and the light-laughing Mev Arun. The man sent to gain her favor was tall and strong; he had a rugged face and a ready smile. She knew why he was sent to her and could guess who had sent him. The Princess Farzia, a languorous, dark beauty, still cherished hopes of a match with Blayn of Pfolben. She wished to know his heart.

It had all happened before: she had been offered presents of one kind or another, she had been courted. So far she had proved incorruptible. She asked no favors of her lord Hem Blayn, and she told none of his secrets. There were times when she wished she *had* put in a word to her master. Sergeant Witt had said that the kedran escort for the Royal Hunt were showy and lightweight; they needed a leaven of experienced soldiers. The desert held uncalculated dangers, and everyone had heard of hunting accidents.

Now, far from her friends in Kestrel Company, Gael Maddoc did not put off Jazeel.

If Hem Blayn kept the poor princess dangling, why shouldn't she do the same with this guardsman? The voluptuous air of Aghiras worked its magic upon all the visitors . . . a month spent by the Lakes of Dawn was bound to be a month of pleasure. She allowed Jazeel to lead her to an inner stall where there was a fine-boned brown mare with a burnishing of black along her spine and on her delicate muzzle, mane, legs, and tail. He waved away a groom who said the visitors must all choose from the loose boxes. The mare was called Azarel, which was a name of the Goddess in the hunting field.

The caravan moved southeast from the city to the sound of flutes; the outriders, two hundred strong, were bowmen of Sarcassir, who ringed the caravan by day and by night. The palace guard rode next, then a long train of snow-white oxen with gilded hooves, who pulled the wheeled carriage of Dhey Lalmed. Under the wide canopy of cloth of gold, the Dhey rode with a few chosen men and women of his court.

Next came racing camels, led by Young Lalmed and his friend, the

Red Prince, Meed-al-Mool. Then, behind his escort, all finely dressed and well mounted, came Blayn of Pfolben, fretting because the Red Prince was placed before him. Kirris of Eildon came up to ride with his cousin and grumble about roughing it in foreign lands. The baggage train of the expedition, with silken bails of provender, with furled tents and carpet rolls, with coffers of precious herbs and donkey loads of kitchenware, trailed behind like the tail of a kite.

By day and by night, as Gael rode in her place near Hem Blayn, Jazeel came by with a basket of figs, a jar of honey, a coral amulet. They talked most companionably together and strolled about in the twilight after the camp had been set down. The low tents were spread out, first among the fields, then upon the sand. The cold air from the desert was full of music and voices. Gael kept watch for the Swordmaker and thought she saw him more than once. He descended from the Dhey's carriage; he lurked, in a different guise, among the horse pickets. He stood in a field, drawing water from an old well, as the caravan went by.

So they came at dawn to the Lakes of Dawn; in the light of the rising sun, the sheets of water seemed to hover like a vast mirage, just above the horizon. There, in the tender green of the reed forests, rose the pavilions of Noulith, the warrior queen, and the hunting platforms of the Dhey. The unearthly beauty of the place troubled Gael Maddoc; the lakes would vanish away, she knew that, but she would remember them always—they would remain in her dreams. The hunt began and she was more than ever troubled, though the killing of wildfowl and antelope had always been the sport of princes.

"Nay, come," said her friend Jazeel, "I know you do not like to see the trophies spread out, the feather carpet, but these birds must be culled. They are an overgrowth like the lakes themselves. Come the season's end, they will flock to the sown land and spoil the planting."

They sat in the reeds, and round about there were other men and women, drinking a little wine, strumming upon a lute, then growing quieter in their own green bowers. Gael Maddoc let her head rest upon Jazeel's shoulder and thought of nothing but the shimmer of the lovely lakes, so soon to pass away. So they made love, but before dawn she always slipped away and returned to the door of the tent where Blayn of Pfolben had his bed. The young noblemen had their own diversions; every night there was a feast, with music and dancing.

Blayn was having a marvelous hunt. He outran with the number of his trophies all but Meed-al-Mool, the Red Prince. There were one or two of those unfortunate incidents that seemed to pursue the young Lord of the

Southland. A beater of the Valfutta was shot with one of Blayn's arrows; there was a disagreement over the count of blue antelope: Young Lalmed swore he had been robbed.

Every morning when she saw Blayn ride out or step into his boat Gael Maddoc felt the same wonder and pride . . . she served this noble lord, she was his kedran. In the evening when they trailed back from the hunt she was relieved if things had gone well. Slowly, slowly the weather grew hotter, the reeds withered and turned brown, the lakes became more shallow. At last, before the season was quite ended, the caravan packed up and took to the desert road to return to Aghiras.

Gael Maddoc had passed the time of the hunt in a dream, and now, one day from the lakes, the dream became a nightmare. She was riding with Jazeel behind Blayn and Captain-General Florus; the trumpeters of the Dhey had just sounded the call to make camp for the night. Then a brace of camels came racing, stiff legged, through the ranks, horses reared and shrieked. Gael saw a camel boy she knew, his face a mask of fear. He cried out:

"Afreet! Afreet!"

Jazeel uttered a curse and pointed off to the west. Something moved like a cloud of oily smoke, blue and black against the pale sand. Lightning crackled at the edges of this strange cloud as it came rolling swiftly into the midst of the caravan. For a moment, holding her brown mare steady, Gael saw the cloud take shape. It reared high above the mounted columns: a blue cloud giant with a fearsome grinning face, blazing red eyes, and mighty arms, outstretched to grasp its prey.

Then she was struck to the ground, together with her mount; she saw nothing but flailing hooves. She dragged herself free of the poor struggling mare and was surrounded by howling blue darkness. The shapes of weapons, harness, pieces of cloth whirled upward and she heard a terrible voice, the voice of the Afreet, speaking in a strange tongue.

She lunged forward to the place where she knew Blayn had been riding, fell across his splendid white horse and found her lord unhurt. She dragged him upright and together they raised the horse and pressed away to the east, bent low. She heard Florus shouting and saw him still mounted beyond the cloud, with a few of the Southland escort gathering about him. She came to him with Blayn, and they all ran together, hardly looking back, and came round the shoulder of a dune.

No one could speak; they stood in darkness. The desert night had come down, and pandemonium still raged beyond the dune. It lasted only a short time, then there was an uneasy silence broken by a series of thunderclaps. A voice whispered at Gael's elbow:

"That is the Afreet moving away!"

She peered and saw it was Ali, the camel boy. Her eyes became accustomed to the darkness; she saw Blayn, unharmed, and his white horse, clearly visible in the night. She saw a crowd of fugitives, most of them men and women of the Southland. They began asking questions and Ali answered them as best he could in the common speech. The Afreet was an evil spirit that attacked caravans. An Afreet could buffet human beings in this way, could lift things up, like the whirlwind. An Afreet could be called up by a magician, and it could be put down if one knew the right words.

One of the guardsmen had torches, which were lit with a tinderbox.

Captain-General Florus said uneasily:

"Hem Blayn, I must go back and see what damage has been done."

"Go along," said Blayn. "You, boy, will the demon come back?"

"Afreet sometimes come back," said Ali. "Stay here, lord. Make camp here. Go back in daylight. The caravan will halt."

Florus and two other guardsmen still had their horses; he numbered off five more to follow him. Gael thought of Jazeel, parted from her between one word and the next. A pair of Eildon kedran, an archer of the Sarcassir, an old servant woman, all followed the guardsmen to return to the caravan. The rest made camp where they were, sharing their cloaks and eating cold lamb and oranges.

Gael remained standing by the white horse and a second horse that had come by riderless. She thought guiltily of her good mare Azarel that she had left in order to find her lord. It had been her duty to bring him to safety. Perhaps for this sad loss, the Goddess had come to her aid. At last she moved up the dune a little and settled down to sleep.

On the western slope where they had made camp, the rising sun blinded them when they woke. None of the guards Blayn had sent out during the night were returned. Gael, almost the first to wake, took a head count: seventeen Southlanders, including Blayn and herself. Three were guardsmen, one of them an older sergeant; there were twelve young kedran from the first household regiment, Kingfisher Company. Then the camel boy, Ali. Two horses. The sergeant was waking the kedran round about him. Blayn stood at the top of the eastern dune, looking back toward the road.

"Maddoc!" he called. "Come up! Bring the boy!"

She struggled up through the loose sand calling for Ali to follow her. Between the place where they had slept and the dim shapes that must be the caravan, there were tall, twisting funnels of sand, filling earth and sky. Ali turned to run, and she caught his arm.

"Run!" he said. "Go . . . we must go!"

"Is it the demon come again?" cried the sergeant.

"Sandstorm!"

The boy twisted from her grasp and fled down the dune. He paused only to point down a long shallow slope to a distant stunted palm and a short crumbled wall of masonry.

"We must go there, we must run! It will take us!"

The sand had begun to lift in a stinging curtain. Everyone ran. Blayn dragged his horse. Gael took the riderless roan. They ran through loose sand, came to a firmer footing and kept running. The air became thick. The risen sun was red; by the time they came to the tree and the edge of the ruined wall, the sun's orb was almost blotted out. The party of Southlanders clambered over the wall and took shelter, urging the frightened horses farther down into a deeper curve of the wall.

The sandstorm held them fast in the lee of the ruined wall for two days and two nights. They crouched under their cloaks, and sand crept, burning, into their boots, into their mouths, into the crevices of their bodies. Sandy morsels of food changed hands in the darkness, and their water bottles were contaminated with sand.

Gael Maddoc smoothed her magic ring and prayed for help. She crept close to Blayn and spoke into his ear, urging him to use the sword *Ishkar* to summon the Swordmaker. He shied away from her as if he hated to be touched and ate the last orange.

She returned to her place under the wall and tried to sleep. Her magic ring winked an eye, and she pried up a loose brick. In the small space underneath she found a leather pouch with six gold coins hung on a thong . . . the hoard of some priest of old time, she reckoned. Ali, the camel boy, had said this was an ancient temple. She fell into a dream of the Burnt Lands: she wandered with Jazeel by the Lakes of Dawn or reclined in a palace garden with fountains playing. Then, more puzzling, she dreamed she was flying high above all wide Hylor's lands; more elevated even than the strongest flying bird, she saw the mountains, the lakes, the great inland sea, the Dannermere, and beyond it, the curving coast of the Western Sea, the dark forests, the yellow inland plains. Sparkling at the edge of her vision, beyond the western waters, was a green line she knew must be Eildon. At last, just before dawn, Ali woke her gently. The storm was over.

"Mistress," he said, "we must go to Negib's Well."

"We must find the caravan again!"

"Mistress," he said, "behold!"

Gael stood up, as the other kedran were doing, and in the grey light of morning she saw that the desert had changed completely. New dunes reared above them; there was no trace of the desert road or the first small dunes that had given them shelter.

"The caravan is long gone," said Ali. "The new road they are following could be two or three days further west."

Blayn of Pfolben was beside them now, in fine fettle.

"What does he say, Maddoc?" he asked. "Will the rescuers soon find their way?"

The kedran were muttering; a word came out of the sandy company, gathered in the light of dawn. *Lost . . . lost . . . lost in the desert . . .*

Sergeant Freer cried out in a choked voice:

"Check all water bottles! Whose duty with the horses?"

Gael Maddoc walked along the line and came to the sergeant. He was sick, the breath rattled in his chest. He said:

"It goes ill with me, Maddoc. What does the boy say?"

"We must go south to an oasis," said Gael. "It is a day, two days . . ."

"The road?" he asked hoarsely.

"Old road is gone," said Ali. "The storm has found a new road."

He pointed and they saw the stone of an ancient causeway in the desert, leading south. Gael Maddoc sprang up on the wall and addressed the company.

"We are the lord's escort!" she said. "We must bring him to Negib's Well on this new road!"

Blayn came to her side and said:

"I see you are all in good heart, kedran. Who has a drink for me?"

She saw their faces, streaked with sand, brighten at his words and at his smile. Half a dozen water bottles were held up.

Blayn mounted his white stallion. Gael set the Sergeant upon the roan horse and the two young kerns, Dirck and Hadrik, to bring up the rear. She walked beside the horses with the two ensigns, no older than herself.

"Captain," said the dark girl fearfully, "will we come to Aghiras?"

"Better than that!" said Gael. "We will come to the Southland."

The way was hard, but everyone was in good heart. At night they sang songs of home around the campfire, and there was one kedran with a sweet voice who sang the old riding song "Pfolben Fields":

Through Pfolben fields we rode in summer,
Rich golden fields, beside the river shore,

Ride on, my soul . . .
Ride on the wide world over!
Bring me at last to Pfolben fields once more!

When her singing echoed over the cold wastes, the kedran wept; Ali bade them save their tears. Gael sat a little apart from the rest and watched her lord. She did not trust his mood. She was glad when he took a liking to the best-looking girl—though the Kingfishers were all chosen for good looks—and let her ride a short way on his horse. Blayn fretted at the water rationing; his boots gave trouble; he was badly sunburnt, as they all were, but he would not veil his face. The morale of the troop went steadily downhill; there were tussles over the last of the food.

In three days they came to a smudge of green that was not another mirage: Negib's Well. It was a disappointment to her; there was nothing but the well, two or three palm trees, some scrubby bushes, and a weathered palmwood framework, which Ali showed them how to cover with their cloaks, to make a tent. They drank deep, ate a few dates, and slept heavily.

Toward morning, Gael was suddenly awake. Her ring winked urgently in the darkness of the tent. She knew the Swordmaker had come and that Blayn had gone out to meet him. She hastened out into the night and saw lights by the well.

Zallibar the Swordmaker sat in shadow, dressed in the same black and gold robe in which she had first seen him in the bazaar. Blayn stood in the light of four torches, thrust into the sand. The Swordmaker seemed to be quite alone, without any retinue: no horses, no camels, only a small bale of woven stuff lying at his feet. She heard Blayn say:

". . . and it will bear me to Aghiras?"

"I swear it, Lord Blayn!" answered Zallibar.

Gael strode up into the light.

"Ah, Maddoc!" said Blayn. "The Swordmaker has come to take me back!"

"How will he do that, my lord?" she asked warily.

Then Zallibar gave her a darting glance from his deep-set eyes and extended a hand toward the bundle at his feet. It unrolled and she saw that it was a carpet, a good-sized, oblong carpet, with a design of leaves and flowers. In its center was a peacock spreading its tail: the colors, jewel bright, shimmered in the torches' light.

The Swordmaker gestured again, and the carpet rose up, floated upon the air a handsbreadth above the sand, then higher still, waist high, high as the torches. It circled about and Blayn, laughing, struck at it as it passed before his face. It came back slowly to its place and settled on the sand again.

"The carpet will bear Lord Blayn safely to the palace of the Dhey at Aghiras," said Zallibar, soft as velvet. "He can take ship to the coast of southern Mel'Nir."

"And the escort?" asked Gael Maddoc, looking at Blayn.

"I must come out of this!" he said. "We've been in the desert for five days."

She stared at Blayn of Pfolben and saw him plainly at last. She was the one who had changed in this instant; he had always been the same, and she had been blind.

"Gael Maddoc," said Blayn, "there is not much time. The carpet must take me before sunrise. Of course it will take us both. Zallibar has said as much."

She looked at the Swordmaker and saw how he smiled at her.

"Life is uncertain," the Swordmaker said. "Many were lost in the sandstorm and the attack of the Afreet. In Aghiras there is a guard officer, Jazeel, who waits for you."

"I am glad he is safe," she said. "Master Zallibar, is it possible to march from this place, Negib's Well, to Aghiras or to the sea?"

"Of course," he replied, "but it is a harsh journey."

"My lord, do not leave your escort in this way!" said Gael Maddoc. She met his eyes; she was not begging.

Blayn said nothing in reply; his face worked angrily. The Swordmaker spoke to him in a low voice, he stepped onto the magic carpet and steadied himself as it rose. When it hovered about four feet above the ground, he settled comfortably, cross-legged, with his sword *Ishkar* resting at his side. Gael ran forward and laid her hands on the carpet's edge.

"Hem Blayn," she said, "for your honor, do not do this thing. Do not abandon these poor souls here in the desert. In the name of the Goddess . . ."

"Don't be a fool, Maddoc!" Blayn said tersely. "I must be saved. I am the Heir of Pfolben."

She could only shake her head and step back. There was a cry from the tent; Ali came out, and a few of the kedran came stumbling after him. The carpet rose higher, and they cried out and rushed up toward the torches. Blayn was whirled about the oasis and carried away to the northwest, far above their heads. Gael saw that it took a certain sort of courage to ride on a magic carpet. Now it was no more than a black dot in the dark blue sky of morning.

"This is your doing!" she cried to the Swordmaker. "You would have him dishonored!"

"You are very bold, Gael Maddoc," said Zallibar, smiling. "The Lord Blayn has chosen his destiny, just as you have chosen yours."

Then he was gone. He made no movement, he simply vanished away and the torches were extinguished, leaving four smoking brands. The whole troop was awake now, crying out and questioning. The sergeant dragged himself from the tent, supported by the kern Hadrik.

"Quiet!" shouted Gael Maddoc.

She looked at them, rubbing sleep from their eyes. She looked to the north, and it was very dark. The endless waste spread out about them on all sides, and overhead the sky was just getting light.

"Hem Blayn has left us!" she said. "He will be brought home by the magic of the Swordmaker of Aghiras."

They grumbled and a few wept. *Lost, left alone . . . the lord taken by magic.* One voice rose, angry and harsh: *"The little bastard has left us all to die."*

"I am still here!" said Gael Maddoc. "I am your captain. I am here to lead you on a harsh journey. I am here to bring us all home to the Southland. I swear by the Goddess that it can be done, and we will do it! Now, get more sleep. We will rest here for at least a day. Dismiss!"

She turned and sat by the well, where the Swordmaker had been. The sergeant had himself brought to her side, and she beckoned Ali, the camel boy.

"Brave words!" said Sergeant Freer.

Gael Maddoc bent her head; she was close to weeping.

"Mistress," said Ali, "a caravan will come . . ."

Far to the east, there was a tiny smudge of dust.

"Is that good or bad?" she asked.

"You will barter horses," said Ali, "for camels and for food. Then we go . . ."

"To Aghiras?"

"To Seph-al-Ara," he replied, "the town of the Zebbecks."

He flattened a place with the palm of his hand and began to draw a map.

"First to the Fhadi Bakim, then to Four Palms, then to the Lion Rock, then by the Gulch of Souls, then to Rakhir . . ."

There is a legend, one of the marvelous tales told in the courts of the Dhey of Aghiras, set down by the scribes from the story tellers of the market. It is the tale of Ali and the Blue Cohort. A camel boy fell in with a lost troop of warriors and guided them through the desert to Seph-al-Ara. These were tall women . . . pale skinned, as the story goes by Fhadi Bakim, though others at Rakhir will have it that the marchers were brown and well weathered. The leader was tall as an afreet, with flame-colored hair, and her name was Galmarduc. For many days they appeared, over the brow of a dune or in an oasis about sundown, all in blue tunics, outlandish cloaks, palm-leaf hats, and red boots. They had camels . . . or perhaps they had not . . . and at night they sang, weird songs echoing through the Gulch of Souls.

It is certain in all versions of the tale that there was a whiff of magic about them and their journey. They found much treasure with the aid of a magic bracelet or a ring that housed a powerful genie. The desert took their image into itself: they may still be seen, and it is a sign of good fortune to glimpse them, coming wearily into Four Palms or threading the dry gulches east of Bakim. Sometimes the merchant caravans or a solitary traveler will find a scrap of blue cloth, a silver spur, or some other token of the Blue Cohort's passing. By the Lion Rock there is a lonely grave with a strange inscription, where travelers leave offerings.

A passing scholar once insisted it was the grave of a man, thus increasing the mystery, for these were female warriors, daughters of Ara, the Great Mother.

At Four Palms, after roll-call (*Brack, Chidderick, Dale, Dirck, she had the names by heart now . . .*) Gael Maddoc went prospecting with the magic ring, to cheer them up. Sure enough, it gave a sign by a certain bush. The dark ensign, Dale, scraped away the sand and found a coffer full of precious nutmeg and cinnamon. They waited. A caravan happened along, and they were able to purchase a third camel and more food.

Long before the Lion Rock, it went very ill with Sergeant Freer (*Dirck, Freer, Fildorn, Gruach*), and they made a litter to carry him. His brave heart gave out halfway up the rock. He died in Gael Maddoc's arms, having sent greetings to his wife and his comrades in Pfolben.

"Go on, lass!" he whispered. "You are a true kedran. You will bring them home."

Dirck and Hadrik made his grave on the very top of the rock in an old carved hollow, perhaps the empty grave of some desert chief. They all set to work and brought great pieces of shaped stone to cover the grave, then carved the inscription with a broken knife: his name and rank, then Pfolben, Mel'Nir, and the year of the Farfaring, 354.

On the long climb down the northern face of the rock, they came upon old dwellings set in the cliff and Ali would not enter them, for fear of ghosts. Gael Maddoc's ring winked at a doorway and she went in with the Kerry sisters (*Gruach, Hadrik, Kerry-Black, Kerry-Red*). They dug down under the floor and found the greatest treasure.

It was in an unpromising clay urn, and at first they thought it might contain bones . . . they did not wish to be grave robbers. Then a shard came loose at the base of the urn and they saw the glint of jewels.

"Nothing ventured, Captain!" said Kerry-Black.

She tapped the urn with the hilt of her sword and a mass of precious things spilled out upon the surface of the Lion Rock. Rings, bracelets, necklaces and chains . . . rubies, dim pearls that had lain so long in darkness, sapphires, jade, beryl, moonstones, a single diamond, larger than a pigeon's egg. The troop came to gaze at the hoard.

"We are all rich," said Gael Maddoc, sadly. "We will carry the Sergeant's share home to his widow and children. Let us go down and see how it goes with the camels."

Below them in the pass, they could see those on camel detail struggling with the contrary beasts. Camels were nothing like horses; it was almost impossible to love them. Even Ali was not very close to these animals that spat and balked and looked down their noses at the world. There was a Danasken trooper, Leshnar of the Eastmark, (*Kerry-Red, Leshnar, Maddoc, Rawl*), who had a way with these wretched creatures. She was the only one who rode them well besides Ali, but they all took turns riding.

The Gulch of Souls was a dreadful place, cold as the grave by night and so hot by day they could hardly breathe. At the end of the winding pass, the ring found a vein of gold in the rock, and it was named Ali's Goldmine, for only the camel boy would come this way again. At Rakhir, when they thought the way would never end, the desert tribes made a feast for them with music and dancing. Gael Maddoc looked at herself in a mirror of polished brass and she saw a woman of the desert, pale eyes staring from a thin, brown face.

So they plodded on behind the swaying camels and the youngest kedran, Rawl, ran on ahead to a patch of thorn on the crest of a dune. She began to call and dance about, but a stiff breeze took away her voice. They rushed up to her, knee-deep in the hot sand, and some stayed kneeling to thank the Goddess. From the crest of the dune, they beheld the sea.

II

Gael Maddoc walked upon the walls of Seph-al-Ara and looked back the way they had come. She tried to feel a moment of triumph: she would lead them home, every last one: *Rawl, Rivo, Trulach, Zarr*. Ali, the richest camel boy in town since he received his share of the spoils, saw her sorrowful look.

"Mistress," he said, "you must accept your fate."

"What fate is that?"

She swung her wrist to hear the chink of the six golden coins on their new thong, purchased in the Seph-al-Ara marketplace. She had kept this piece of treasure for herself. Once, she had intended to pass it on to her master, Blayn, but that chance was gone now, the treasure must be hers. There was magic in the coins, she was sure of it, and it did not come from the Swordmaker of Aghiras.

"You are a *Wanderer*," said Ali. "Your life lord has left you. He broke the chain, but you survived. Now you are alone to make your own judgments. Mistress, your journeying has just begun." Ali was young, but Gael Maddoc could not help but feel that his words had hold of a certain truth. The innocence of her loyalty was gone.

Next day they took ship with a trader and were brought swiftly over the tideless sea and up the river Elnor to Pfolben, in the Southland of Mel'Nir. It was summer, the golden grain was being harvested; they had come home to Pfolben fields. There were kedran whose families lived south of the capital, but they remained aboard ship, unwilling to break the bonds of comradeship. They spoke of all the trials they had passed; they missed the desert; it had stolen a part of their souls.

As they drew near the city, they saw that the wharves on either side of the lazy stream were decorated with flowers and banners. They saw a chain of dancers on Orange Flower Street; they exclaimed at the sight of kerns and kedran in their dress livery, the Kingfisher Company in their blues. They looked down at their own clean but faded uniforms, bleached by the sun, and the Zebbeck boots they wore. Music came to them on the wind; Trooper Hadrik said:

"Could the word have got out?"

"Gruach," said Gael Maddoc, "what day is it?"

Gruach had notched the days on the lid of a little cedarwood box, a souvenir from the bazaar of Aghiras.

"Captain, by our reckoning it is the ninth day of the eighth month, the Maplemoon."

"We have lost three days to the sands," said Gael. "It is the twelfth day of the Maplemoon, Lord Maurik's birthday."

They had been absent from the Southland for one hundred and twelve days; they had spent sixty days crossing the desert.

"Captain," said Rawl timidly, "will they be giving the lord his gifts in Moon Crescent?"

They came off the trader and were caught up in the press of folk coming from the wharves, all making for the Crescent. None of the townspeople recognized them. The golden trumpets of the Lord of Pfolben called the hour of the gift giving when they were a short distance away.

The Crescent was a beautiful curved courtyard from the time of the Princes of the Burnt Lands, all tiled in blue, at the eastern door of the palace. A colored barrier had been set up and there were the lord's subjects with his gifts: a fine bay horse, a giant pumpkin on a cart, a hogshead of wine from the vintners, a silken tapestry from the women of a village. These good folk had been chosen to stand at the barrier with their presents, and a kedran troop patrolled to keep the crowd back.

Already Lord Maurik and his lady had begun receiving the offerings at one end of the yard, and a herald went along to cry out the gifts. So they waited, muffled up in their cloaks, although the day was warm, and before the last gift was called, they pressed forward. Gael Maddoc reached up and tugged the bridle of a brown horse. The kedran officer looked down angrily.

"Get back!"

It was Captain Witt. She stared as Gael lowered her cloak, for she saw a ghost.

"Maddoc?"

"Bid the herald call another offering, Captain," said Gael.

The kedran on duty almost lost control of their horses. The crowd drew back, wondering, and the herald roared out the words he had been given:

"A gift from the Burnt Lands!"

So they marched proudly up to the very center of the barrier, and the Lord of the Southland turned from thanking the women for their tapestry to survey his final gift. There they stood, weather-beaten and weary, thirteen kedran and two men of the palace guard.

Lord Maurik came and stood before them with his lady, fair Annhad, as fine boned and slender as he was massive.

"But these . . ." he blustered. "Godfire! These are my Kingfishers! My guardsmen! . . . and the captain . . ."

Annhad of Pfolben prompted him quietly:

"Maddoc," she said. "That is Captain Maddoc of the Kestrels."

The good lord spread his arms wide as if he would embrace them all and called upon the Goddess and the Gods of the Farfaring, giving thanks for this great gift.

"Blayn!" he cried. "Blayn . . . see who has come home!"

The Lord Blayn came down the steps of the palace: a lightly built young man with hair of pure gold and a face perfectly handsome. Gael Maddoc still thought when she saw him of the Shee, the fairy race. She thought of the great devotion she had had for this lord, how she had sworn to serve him. Her whole life had been ordered by this bond. She had received benefits from the house of Pfolben and she had repaid what she had been given, but now she knew her service was done.

Hem Blayn came strutting to his father's side, trailed, of course, by a tall kedran, his latest bodyguard.

"Godfire!" he said boldly, "have they come again? That wily magician of the Dhey lied to me! He swore that these poor souls would never return to Aghiras . . . after the sandstorm."

"No more we did, lord," said Gael Maddoc, meeting his eye. "We came to Seph-al-Ara, the town of the Zebbecks."

The Lady Annhad understood at once. Who knew how much of the truth she had been told by her servant, Elim? She took Gael Maddoc by the hand and said softly:

"You were many days in the desert. I must rejoice that Blayn was *not* with you. How would it have been if he had taken this harsh journey?"

"Lady, I do not know," said Gael Maddoc, just as low. "Perhaps it would have made a man of him."

Lady Annhad flushed deeply at these words, but she reached and put her hand on Gael Maddoc's own, covering the ring that had been her gift to her son's protector. Her white fingers looked very slender over Gael's great weathered paw. Gael felt the lady's disappointment; there was nothing she could do. "This was destiny," Lady Annhad mouthed, so quiet only Gael could hear her. "I had such hopes, my son's path lay so open . . ."

Blayn saw the two women looking at him. He cried angrily:

"Mother, do not believe that kedran wench!"

But his words were drowned by the chorus of the thanksgiving song. Lady Annhad released the captain's hand, Lord Maurik led the homecomers into the Crescent and there they were greeted by all the kerns and kedran of the household. It was a near riot. They were embraced and made much of and carried shoulder high all the way to the barracks. It was not every day that fifteen companions in arms returned from the dead.

Late at night, while the city still celebrated the lord's birthday, Gael

Maddoc sat on a balcony with her true companions, Amarah and Mev Arun. They had heard all that she had to tell, from the first to the last.

"Ah, this Jazeel," said Amarah, with a hint of jealousy, "was he so dear to you?"

"He was a nice fellow," said Gael. "I am glad he came safe home."

"There were rumors," said Mev Arun. "Hem Blayn was no longer an honored guest of the Dhey. There was no more question of his being a suitor for the Princess Farzia."

"Life is uncertain in the Burnt Lands," said Gael, "but the bond between a ruler and his lifeguards is sacred."

"This Swordmaker rid the princess of an unworthy suitor," said Mev Arun.

"Gael, if you end your duty here, where will you go?" asked Amarah.

"Wherever my quest will lead me," said Gael Maddoc.

"Will we meet again?" asked Amarah.

"Surely!"

"Questing?" said Mev Arun. "Is that anything for a kedran?"

"Do you suppose I can buy out my good horse, Ebony?" asked Gael. "Who rides him now?"

Her two friends laughed.

"No one," said Mev Arun, "if they can help it!"

"He pines for you," said Amarah. "No one else can manage him."

"Then I will ride back to Coombe," said Gael Maddoc, "and so on into the world!"

BOOK II

CHAPTER V

COOMBE

She came home toward evening. The road was unfamiliar almost until she reached the croft's boundary wall and looked up at the stony hillside. From there she urged Ebony a little further and then stood behind an apple tree, watching the cottage. The tree was very old, almost dead; it bore a few hard, deformed fruit.

Gael Maddoc saw that the cottage was larger. A third and a fourth room had been built on, in the fashion of the district. The Maddocs had "come to a house," as the saying went. There was a fine stone chimney where the old wood box had been. From a new lean-to, there came the unmistakable honk of a donkey. In four long years, the Maddocs had done very well, had grown richer.

Beside the doorstep, in a patch of sunlight, slept a plump brown cat. The door of the cottage opened as she watched and out came a short, dark, bustling woman with an apron over her skirt, wool stockings, pattens against the muck of the yard, and a plaid against the autumn chill. It was her mother, dressed up like the reeve's wife of a Freeday. As she watched her mother draw water from the well, Gael wondered how much of the change was brought about by the soldier's pay she had sent home. It could hardly be accounted for by seven silver coins every third month.

She rode along the wall and came to the gateway. Her mother set down the new water bucket and stared. With a dreadful feeling of strangeness, Gael Maddoc got down to open the gate.

"Maddoc . . ." said her mother softly, then on a rising note, "Maddoc! Come out here! See this!"

So Maddoc came out of his house, moving as if his joints ached, and the pair of them, two short, dark Chyrian folk, stared at the tall kedran captain and her fine horse. They had had no word of her for a long time. If she had not come home from the Burnt Lands when she did, there would have been a message sent from Lowestell Fortress, brought by the same quartermaster sergeant who came by with her pay contributions. She would have been posted as missing, then later as dead. As it was, she felt very much like a ghost or a visitor from a far distant country.

"Eh, Goddess!" exclaimed Maddoc heartily. "Will that beauty fit into our lean-to?"

Gael stepped up, laughing and crying, and embraced her father and mother. Even Kenit the cat purred round her legs and seemed to remember her.

"Oh heaven and earth," said her mother, "this will surely please the boy. He is over to Coombe working on Rhodd's land. How often have I promised that you would come home and bring . . . good fortune!"

They went about in the yard and settled Ebony comfortably enough into the lean-to beside the little donkey mare. Soon Gael was sitting beside the fire with her laden saddlebags in a heap at her feet. Her mother brewed herb tea and laced their mugs with applejack from Maddoc's leather bottle. They talked first of all about Coombe, who had married, who had died—Fion Allrada was frail but hanging on, though she came to fewer rituals at the Holywell. Old Murrin was doing well: they saw to her needs, and she asked often after Gael and her kedran service.

Yes, all the young men and Jehane were at the Plantation now, full-fledged members of the Westlings. Bretlow Smith was an ensign and yes, by the Goddess, there was a whisper that he and his company had taken part in some skirmish in the west.

Jehane was in training to ride as a Sword Lily. Yes, Druda Strawn had come home after a long retreat in old Tuana and they had told him how Gael had gone to the Southland with the prince of Pfolben.

"So you have come to a house, Da," said Gael.

Maddoc nodded proudly. They had been granted three good harvests, thank the Goddess. They had all gone kelp cutting, then digging stone as day laborers. The boy worked part of each week in Coombe. Her mother had six sheep now, and not one of the Coombe wives could spin and weave better than she did.

Gael was relieved to hear all this. If her contributions had played such a small part in the family fortune, they would not be missed. She felt better about breaking the news to them, one day—not today—that she would not return to Pfolben. She felt better about her own gold that remained after buying out her horse.

She opened her saddlebag and began to give out presents. She recalled the good Winter Feast when she was last by the fireside and wondered if the things she brought were too simple now that the Maddocs had become so comfortable. Her mother felt her bolt of green cloth with pleasure. Maddoc said, "What's this?" to his new boots.

"I wore your boots when I went to the Southland," she said, and grinned.

"So! These are a replacement!"

He was pleased; he tried the boots and they fitted well. Both her parents were pleased with the bag of oranges: yes, surely, they had tasted them on feast days in Coombe. She brought out the knife in its sheath for Bress, his baldric and belt, his gloves, his ivory flute. She had remembered he liked to play on whistles. These presents for her brother pleased her parents best of all. Her father asked if the flute were made of bone.

"A kind of bone called ivory," she said. "It is from the Burnt Lands."

"From the Burnt Lands?" echoed Maddoc. "Over the Southern sea?"

"I have been there," she said. "On service."

They stared at her with an expression that was to become familiar: a kind of unbelief. Her mother turned from the fire, where she was putting more bacon and more barley into the hotpot.

"It is a very strange country," Gael continued. "All sand in places, with white cities and palms growing beside the wells. The traders use camels, strange beasts that can go for days without water. They have humped backs and great padded feet for walking on the desert sand."

Her mother laughed.

"Hush!" she said. "You are beginning to sound like Old Murrin."

Emeris Murrin had gone about in the world when she was young.

"Goddess," chuckled Maddoc, "Murrin's tall tales. The great grey beast with a castle on its back and a long nose . . ."

Gael laughed herself, looking queasily at the ivory flute.

"But there are such beasts . . ."

They did not hear her words. The door was flung open, and Bress came in. He had grown into a man, not so tall as Gael but broadly built. Their bright-faced lad had gone forever and Gael was sorry for it.

"Well, d'ye know who this is?" cried her mother.

"I know," he said.

They stared at each other, and Gael smiled to cover her first thought.

"If she is home to stay," said Bress, "then I can go for a soldier at last!"

"Hush!" said Shivorn, taking his boots and giving him her place by the fire. "See what your sister has brought you!"

Gael watched him with his knife, his belt, his gloves. For a time he would not meet her eye; he was sullen. Then at table he became more cheerful. His friend, Shim Rhodd, the innkeeper's son, would join the Westlings, and the two young men talked a lot about army life. How such and such a lad did well, came home with a golden shoulder knot, having made ensign.

"Will you try for an officer, Gael?" he asked. "Ensign Maddoc! Hear that!"

"Do you read this star, brother?" she said. "It is Captain Maddoc, since half a year."

There was a silence at table; they all stared at her. Bress, well muscled, curly haired, a picture of the village colt that maidens loved and elders feared, swore an oath under his breath.

"You have no need to lie, sister," he said. "You are under our own roof."

"I have no need to lie, brother!" she said, feeling the timbre of her voice change. Her mother said:

"Hush, let her be a captain then! Who can tell in Coombe village how things are ordered in the Southland?"

Then Shivorn Maddoc began the tale of a certain Widow Raillie, from beyond Coombe, who had one son. He had found a magic stone on their poor croft near Tuana and now they had riches to spare and had taken the Long Burn Farm. Gael could not find much point in the tale. She saw that her family accepted magic but could hardly stretch their belief to include an elephant.

When Gael went out to take a last look at Ebony in his new stabling, Bress followed her and sat with Kenit, the brown mouser, on the cope of the well.

"Take care, sister," he said, "the Voimar will get you!"

They had scared each other as children in the dark yard, talking of the Voimar. When she laughed, Bress said:

"Don't laugh! Shim Rhodd says the Voimar have come again. They were seen on the moor and on the high ground."

The Voimar were demons, half man, half beast. She thought of the Afreet, a monstrous blue shape, towering above the caravan.

"I have seen some sights," she answered. "The Voimar might not frighten me so much."

They all went to bed when the oil lamp burned low. Bress slept by the banked fire; the father and mother had one of the new rooms. Gael had a bed made up in the little old room where the winter fodder and vegetables had once been stored and now her mother's wool. It was her favorite room in the cottage; as a child she had often pretended it was hers alone. The door was left ajar so that Kenit could go on mouse patrol; there was a sound in the darkness and it was Bress picking out a tune on his ivory flute. She fell asleep at once and dreamed of the desert.

Next morning Gael woke as at a bugle call. It was still dark, but the men had gone; Shivorn sat by the fire drinking her bowl of goat's milk and eating her piece of bread. She made room for her daughter on the long settle and they broke their fast comfortably together.

"I will ride to Coombe when the sun is well up," said Gael, "and visit Druda Strawn."

Her mother urged her to go a little further on an errand. She should take a gift of oranges to the Widow Raillie at the Long Burn Farm, the same whose son had found the magic stone.

"We're beholden to them," she said. "We broke stone in their field and were well paid in kind."

"What, in grain?" asked Gael.

"We came to a house," said her mother. "They gave us cut stone and joists, and the son, Culain, sent a pair of their men to lend a hand."

Shivorn Maddoc was silent for a moment, then she said:

"The widow woman is my friend. We've often spoken together at our spinning."

II

Coombe, on an autumn morning, was quiet as the hills and the heather. The road led down from the croft then gently up again, and the village was on the crest of the rise. It had only three buildings of any size: the reeve's house, the smithy, and the Fowlers' Yard.

There was no guild of fowlers and trappers any longer, the woods were not so full of game. The solid building of wood and stone, with its cobbled yard, now served as a meeting hall, an alehouse, and a market. Rhodd, who owned the yard, had moved with the times. The Fowlers' Yard had become an inn. A newly painted sign showed a red-haired warrior, a giant, with tiny figures clustered about his knees. In one hand he held a club, in the other a spear. The inn was called the *General Yorath*.

Gael turned out of the broad road, smiling, for she knew Druda Strawn had a hand in this. She thought of his tales of Yorath Duaring during the summer training, of the words of the bard they had heard in Silverlode.

Not many persons had brought lasting help to this neglected region of the great land of Mel'Nir. General Yorath belonged with the White Lady of Nair's Hill, who drove out the wolves, and Pigger Pingally, who first used his swine to hunt for truffles.

She took her way down the lane past the smithy and saw that it was burning low, with no horses being shod, only the prentice lads working metal. She came to the holy tree and the priest's house: the two-roomed cottage nestled under the mighty oak. Druda Strawn had no need to come to a house; he lived out of doors even more than the crofters.

In the depths of winter he could be seen riding the drifts on upturned basket shoes of his own invention. In spring he was the first to ride out on his old nag, and in summer he slept in the woods or on the heather. Now, in autumn, he sat on his doorstep among the falling oak leaves and carved at his bowls and platters. He culled the woods and accepted a portion of any tree felled round about. He gave the wooden vessels that he carved to those who had need of them: the crofters who lived on the edge of things, those who were too poor to take much part in village life. The Maddocs had received their share.

He laid his work aside and sprang up from the doorstep. His old horse whinnied from its stall. He stared long and hard at horse and rider; Gael knew he saw what there was to be seen. She had gone for a kedran and done him credit.

Before they talked together, the Druda gave his blessing and uttered a prayer. Then she took her place on the thick oaken block that was the visitor's seat. All manner of men and women came and sat before the house and told their troubles to this Guardian Priest. The Druda was always a reserved man, though he inspired trust. He barely smiled when Gael gave him his first present, a knife, but he smiled indeed when she brought out the second, a book, its leather binding prettily embossed with red scrollwork.

"Child," he said, "I have a book already!"

It was a joke; they both laughed, and Gael's laughter rang a little sadly. This was exactly what Bress had said when she showed her family the priest's gift, four winters past, following that golden summer as a Green Rider.

"This is a fine book," said Druda Strawn, unwrapping the cloth package. "A printed book!"

"It is a paper Lienbook," she said, "like the one called *Tales of the Sea and Land* that you sent me for the Winter Feast."

The book had been made in Pfolben and it was called *Readings from the*

Scrolls of Mel'Nir. It was a collection of tales and legends from the chronicles, simply written. Each tale was marked for its origin: "re-told from the Dathsa," "taken from the Scroll of Vil," or "a version from the Book of the Farfarers."

"Oh very fine!" said Druda Strawn. "Have you read these tales?"

"About half of the stories," she admitted, "but if I am still here in summer and you are at home . . ."

Druda Strawn laid aside the book and stared at her very keenly.

"You will alter your service?" he asked.

"I no longer serve the Lord of Pfolben or his son," she said.

"To have come so far . . . you are a captain . . ."

"My rank counts everywhere," she said, "if I take another posting."

"Speak!" ordered the priest. "What ails you, Gael Maddoc?"

So she told him of her years of service and her journey to the Burnt Lands. At last she drew out the six heavy gold coins threaded on a thong that she had found in the desert, in the ruined temple.

"I believe I have a calling," she said. "By rights, these would have gone to Hem Blayn. As his kedran, all my loyalty was to him, all that I found of value should have passed at once into his hands. Instead . . . he deserted us. These tokens fell to *my* trust. I have learned I must go on a quest of some kind. There is . . . magic in these coins . . . perhaps they have to do with my questing."

The Druda frowned and took the coins into his deep palm. As the soft metal touched his flesh, his expression changed. He looked at each one and murmured and pressed his lips in a gesture of reverence. Then, loosening the knot on the thong, he set the gold pieces one by one on an oaken platter, between them on the leafy ground.

"Behold the Cup," he said, his voice an incantation, speaking a holy litany. "Behold the Stone, the Lamp, the Crown, the Lance, and last the blessed Fleece."

Not all the objects upon the coins were easily recognized. Cup and Crown were clear enough and the Lamp, once it was named, but the Stone and the Fleece were vague solid shapes and the Lance a mere cross-stroke on the gold surface.

"You have no idea what they are?" asked the Druda.

Gael shook her head.

"Have you heard of Taran's Kelch?"

"Of course," she said, "Taran is a Nymph of the Goddess, and her Kelch is a bowl of plenty for all the Chyrian lands. It is shown in the stars. Is it the Cup? Druda, what are these things?"

The Druda sighed.

"It is a mystery. What we have here upon the gold coins are the Hallows of Hylor. Sometimes they are called the Lost Hallows, though not all are lost . . ."

"Where are they?" she asked.

"The Stone is in the south wall of Achamar in the Chameln Lands," reeled off Druda Strawn, "and the Lamp, formerly of Cayl, is whispered to be in the Sanctuary at Larkdel, in Lien. The Crown is in Eildon in the Priest King's holy retreat, and some say the Cup, Taran's Kelch, is in Eildon too, stolen from the Chyrian Lands. The Lance—" He looked at her seriously. "I know I have spoken to you of the Lance. Well, it is lost and it belonged to Mel'Nir. As for the Fleece . . ." He shook his head, as if deeply thinking.

"Perhaps I am called to find these lost things," Gael prompted him, half hopeful.

"That would be a difficult task," said Druda Strawn.

He sat back on his step with deep creases between his thick eyebrows.

"Let me think on these things for a short while," he said. "You have another errand today?"

"Yes. I must bring the rest of the oranges to the Widow Raillie at the Long Burn Farm."

He smiled a little.

"Let this also be a quest for you, Gael Maddoc," he said, "you with your magic ring and all."

"What shall I do?"

"Look well at these folk who have come to the Long Burn Farm. Tell me how you find them."

She was not too pleased with her task, but she knew he would ask nothing in jest.

"Druda," she said, remembering the rumor, "what was this skirmish in the west where Bretlow Smith saw some action?"

Druda Strawn shook his head.

"Ask at the smithy—there is some mystery about the tale!"

On the way to the newcomers she crossed over the Long Burn twice, once when it flowed under a bridge in the road and once at the entrance to the farm. The countryside was not so fair as the Southland, but the low rough hills, red-brown for autumn, pleased her eye. On a small piece of flatland, downriver from the first bridge, there was a ring of standing stones called the Maidens. Upriver there was the mill, behind leafless trees. The Maddocs had never used the mill; they had ground their own miserable harvest of grain in their own yard.

There was a new wooden bridge before the Long Burn Farm. It was a goodly way through carefully cleared and leveled fields to the substantial house. She saw the tall figure of a man, still as a stone beside a grey boundary wall on the western skyline. It was midday, cold for the time of year, and the sun just struggling through a layer of cloud. No workers were in the fields. As she came up to the yard, hounds bayed; there was a man in a blue cloak raking by the barn. A young lad ran to take her bridle and cried out:

"What d'ye seek, kedran?"

"I will see Mistress Raillie," she said. "I have a gift from Maddoc's croft, by the Holywell."

It was as if a shadow had lifted. Perhaps she had given them a scare, riding in on her tall black horse. The lad grinned, the man laid aside his rake and quieted the dogs. Out of the kitchen came a maidservant and a quick smiling woman in dark green. Gael Maddoc's first thought was that the Widow Raillie looked like her mother. They were of an age, she guessed, and of the same height, thin and olive skinned, with dark hair drawn back. There the likeness ended. The Widow Raillie had clear, unlined skin, sparkling eyes, good teeth, an upright, youthful carriage. Her mother was still quick, but she was lined, her hair was streaked with grey . . . she was a crofter's wife.

"Ah, my dear!" cried the widow heartily. "Please to step down! Welcome to our house! See, it is the Maddocs' daughter! How your mother must have wept to see her child come home!"

Gael was impressed. Her family had earned respect, fine friends. She made the gift of oranges and the widow thanked her warmly. Ebony became skittish at first, but Gael helped the lad bring him to a stall, then followed the widow into the house.

They passed through a warm kitchen that was roughly the size of the Maddocs' old cottage. There was a reek of food, a second maid stirred at the fireplace, shadowy flitches of bacon and strings of vegetables crowded the rafters. The widow swept on into a second room with a brazier, sheepskin rugs on the wooden floor and on the settles. By the standards of Coombe, the Raillies were rich. This could have been a room in the reeve's house, where Gael Maddoc had gone with her father once, to ask permission to work off their tax.

The widow made her visitor comfortable, sent the maid, Bethne, for mulled wine and applecake. She laid a small soft hand on Gael's cold cheek and sat beside her with a rustle of silken petticoats. Somehow, despite the warmth of the greeting, this sound was like a whisper of unease.

Gael saw that the widow wore two gold rings, that there was a costly glass mirror upon the wall.

"Culain!" cried the widow. "See who is here! Maddoc's daughter from the Holywell!"

Culain Raillie had come in quietly. He was older than Gael and tall as a man of Mel'Nir. Yet his black hair and blue eyes marked him out as a type of long-boned Chyrian: Gael thought of Egon Baran of the Summer Riders. Culain, like Jehane's sweetheart, had the same fine straight features, but there was a weathering of suffering, perhaps, or guarded concern, in his countenance. When he gave his hand to the visitor and smiled, his long face did not light up.

"Well grown," he said in the common speech. "Tall enough for a Sword Lily . . ."

"I served in the Southland," said Gael.

"Why not in Krail?" asked Culain. "The Lord Knaar is always seeking tall kedran for his famed troop, the Sword Lilies."

"Come lad," said the widow. "You talk like a recruiting officer. We should be pleased that Gael Maddoc has come home!"

"I owe you thanks," said Gael, "for you have helped my family come to a house."

"We must share our good fortune," said Culain, raising his blue eyes to her own.

"I hear you have been blessed by the Goddess," said Gael, not sure why he spoke so, as if to challenge her, but also not ready to stand down before him. "You have a magic stone."

Culain continued to stare at her with a sharp, appraising look.

"Come," he said abruptly. "I am sure you will want to see our treasure."

He led the way into a smaller room with hangings of woven stuff and several chests and coffers. An altar to the Goddess had been set up, with a silver candlestick and a wreath of evergreen. In the midst of the altar was an oval polished stone, set upright like a miniature menhir. It was about a foot high, darkest green in color, and veined in red.

"A beautiful stone," she said. "May I touch it?"

"Most people do," said Culain. "They ask a blessing."

She laid her hands upon the smooth stone for a moment, then stepped back.

"You have a handsome ring," said Culain, again abruptly. "Is it a lover's gift?"

Gael Maddoc laughed.

"It is a ring from the Burnt Lands," she said. "I traveled there in the service of the house of Pfolben."

She walked to a small glazed window and looked out over the bare fields and the brown heath. Pale sunlight came in and lit up the green jewel of Lady Annhad's ring.

"You would need to protect a magic stone," she said, "against thieves and sorcerers."

"Say rather the stone protects our house and our goods!" Culain Raillie answered, coming to her side.

He patted the lid of the tall iron strongbox under the window, where her hands had come to rest. He had come uncomfortably close to her.

"Your mother and mine sit at their spinning together," he said. "They make plans like two chattering magpies . . ."

She understood suddenly that he was nervous with her, and for the first time Gael Maddoc had an inkling of what object those motherly plans might have come to. She stepped away from the window and looked Culain Raillie in the eye.

"Master Raillie," she said, "I have seen a little of the world and do not think I can bide long in Coombe village."

He made her a small bow. His smile was polite but mirthless.

"We will speak further," he said. "My greetings to your family."

He strode out of the room and out of the house without even a word to his mother. Gael came back to the widow, who was as bright and talkative as ever.

"What has brought you and your son to Coombe, Mistress Raillie?" asked Gael.

"A farm such as the Long Burn is harder to come by than you think," chattered the widow, so precisely fitting her son's image that Gael, despite her reservations about these people, found herself cracking a private grin. "Most folks hold their land by ancient deed and heritage, as your father holds Holywell Croft. There were no heirs to the Long Burn, and the deed was sold us by Reeve Oghal, who had it in his keeping."

Presently Gael took her leave and galloped back to Coombe ahead of a shower of rain; the stormy winds of autumn had already begun to strip the leaves from the trees. She took a back lane to come to the Druda's house again and sat with him indoors without a fire.

"The Raillies are strange folk indeed," she said.

"Go on . . ." nodded the priest.

"They are not farmers," said Gael, "and the son has never gone for a soldier though he is well grown. His hands are soft as his mother's. I would guess he has been a trader of some kind. They are rich, richer even than they seem to be. There is a hint of magic about the pair of them."

"Were you shown the magic stone?" asked Druda Strawn.

"The pretty stone on the household altar is no more than a polished ornament. But in a chest by the window there is some powerful magical source and much treasure. Druda, what do these folk want, coming here to Coombe?"

"Child," said the priest, "I do not know. We live too quiet in this part of the world; perhaps we are too distrustful of newcomers."

He drew out her gold coins again and fastened them upon her wrist.

"Gael Maddoc," he said, "I do not doubt that you have a calling. You must take these medals of the lost hallows up to the High Plateau and beg the Shee for guidance."

She drew her cloak about. A threshold had been crossed. Only the Druda himself ever consulted with the Shee.

"Will they speak with me?" she whispered.

"Who knows? Many a time they do not speak with me, and I am well-known to them."

He turned away, pacing a well-worn track in the dirt floor of the hut.

"There is unrest among the Eilif lords," he said at length. "The light folk have been seen more often in the past year or so. They warn travelers from their sacred grounds with bolts of fire or with singing."

"I have heard that the Voimar are about on the moor and on the high ground," said Gael, "but I hardly believed such a tale."

The Druda, who was as brave as any man she knew, put his hands to his lips again, warding off evil.

"It is some working of the Shee," he said. "Nothing passes on the High Plateau without their knowledge. The earth moved up there two years past . . . a strong quake near the ruins of Silverlode. I do not know if it was their doing."

He sighed heavily.

"I have it in my mind that the Shee will depart. It is time for them to take leave of this dark and mortal world and set sail in their glass boats for the Islands of the Sunset."

"But they are not mortal!" said Gael Maddoc, shocked. "They are the light folk! They cannot die!"

"Their nature is not like ours," said the priest. "But I fear even the Shee do not live forever."

"What must I do to speak to them?" she asked.

So at last Druda Strawn told her of the summoning of the Shee and the places on the high ground where it was best to call them.

"We have new moon," he said, "and a great storm brewing, coming in up the coast. You must not ride out until the moon is full."

Gael remembered that this was how things were in Coombe. Life was slow as a desert journey. She had been too eager to set out on her quest. She thought of the great storms they had sat out in the small house when she was a child and of the preparations that must be made—for this was a part of village life, too.

She was riding slowly past the smithy, where the fire still burnt very low, when she was hailed by Vigo the Smith himself. He was a barrel-chested man and a great gossip; now he cried heartily:

"By the Huntress! It is Maddoc's daughter from the Holywell Farm! And a captain already! D'ye need anything for your black beauty there?"

Then he looked about and came close to her stirrup.

"Captain Maddoc—I must ask a boon in the name of my son, Bretlow! Pray you come to the forge tomorrow morning. We'll groom your horse—what's he called, Ebony?—and check his hooves. We must talk, and secretly!"

"Of course, Master Smith!" said Gael. "I'll be there before noon."

"And keep your own counsel, lass!" said Vigo, anxiously.

At home she gave an account of her visit to the Druda and then her meeting with the Widow Raillie and her son Culain. Her mother seemed pleased and said no more about any plans or any debt they owed the newcomers. Gael was glad when they all settled to rest: even Coombe was full of secrets.

The next morning she rose up and presented herself back at the smithy, where the forge was going full blast, and, after yesterday's quiet, unexpectedly noisy. Vigo himself came to hold her bridle, with a young prentice. Ebony allowed this groom to lead him in. The big horse was taking all the arrangements at Coombe better than she had expected. Then Vigo led her into a small room some way from the forge, and a maid from the house brought applewine. Vigo was tense and serious, not at all his jovial self. He came at once to his son's adventure. Yes, Bretlow had taken to the life like his father who had been a farrier in the service of Val'Nur, and his brothers who were officers now in the Westlings. All the smith's sons had ridden in the "heavy cavalry" mounted on the great war horses of Mel'Nir. It was the Third Span of the Westlings, fifty riders in five companies, and now Bretlow was in Elmtree company: he was second ensign, second-in-command. Yes, they were all well-grown Chyrians, and there was another trooper from the Summer Riders, it was young Egon Baran. "It was at Midsummer," Vigo went on. "There was this call came in from the headman of a village by the Western Sea, a place too small even to have a reeve. Name of Little Bay, a nest of deep sea fishers. Their boats had been stolen—not by pirates on the seas but by marauders from the land. It was a garbled report, and the officers at the Plantation thought it was a dispute between some fightable fishermen. They sent off two companies to see to the matter, one lot of regulars, the second a city company of heavy cavalry, called 'Valko's Own,' and with them, drawn by lot, Elmtree Company of the Westlings. Our lads were glad to have the duty, I can tell you that!"

A voice said: "Let me tell it, Da!"

Gael turned her head, startled. The room was half in daylight, half in shadow, with leaping firelight from the forge. There stood Bretlow himself, like a ghost, with a cotton bandage round his head and his right arm in a sling.

"Dear Goddess!" Gael said. "Bretlow, old comrade, you're wounded! Here now—"

She and Vigo helped him to a chair. There was indeed some mystery here, not just a skirmish—a wounded ensign at home, months afterward. Had he even been treated by the army healers at the Plantation?

Bretlow started in with his tale—no, he said, he had had a blow on the head, but it had healed, and he had no brain shaking. The ten new Westlings of Elmtree company, with Bretlow as their second officer, had done very well in their drill at the Plantation; they were pleased to go on this mission to the Western beaches. With good roads lacking, it was more than ten days' ride from the Plantation back of Krail, so they went part of the way by barge on the great river Demmis which flowed to the sea further north, at Valmouth. They came ashore at a haven called Demford and rode on for four days, making camp at night in the quiet countryside, until they reached the inn at Fiveways, only a mile or so from Little Bay.

"The headman, called Old Scaith, met us there and told a strange tale indeed," said Bretlow, smiling at the memory. "At Midsummer the fishing fleet usually went out in daylight, except for some late runs of blinny, along the shore. First sign of trouble was that a small boat, newly mended and just down from its blocks, was stolen away by night. A guard was set by another vessel—a small sea-going ketch. It was the kind of boat which the fishers hoped to sell to the gentry inland for cruising to Banlo Strand, or for the crossing to Eildon. At dawn the guards were found lying as if dead and this larger ship had gone—'spirited away,' said Master Scaith."

"No one saw the thieves?" asked Gael.

"Luckily someone did," grinned Bretlow. "There was this guard whose wife brought them all some breakfast, before first light—fishermen keep the same cruel hours as soldiers! This woman—I spoke to her later—saw this ketch moving down the slipway to the sea. She had the wit to hide herself by an old stone hut on the strand. She was in great fear that her man and the other guards were knocked down, even dead. She described the marauders very well—four men, all in dark seamen's cloaks—three were big built and tall. The thing was that they could take out the ketch with a skeleton crew—their leader, a tall old man, simply threw up his arms, gesturing with his staff."

"You mean he used magic!" said Gael.

"Indeed he did," said Bretlow sadly. "And that is how I sit here disgraced and hidden away from the wrath of our liege lord, Knaar of Val'Nur."

Vigo shook his head.

"Coombe has served Val'Nur faithfully," he said, "and we have these special privileges—dating from General Yorath and the Westlings. A pity if all this is disturbed because of Lord Knaar's hatred of magic!"

"At any rate," said Bretlow, getting on with his tale, "the woman, Mallee, wife of Tamm, found her husband and his four companions struck down and sleeping. She ran to call warning, and Old Scaith, the headman, sent off runners to Demford, where his messages were taken down and sent in haste to Krail, up the river. We came as fast as we could—there had been ten days or more between the stealing of each ship. So we made plans with Headman Scaith and came as secretly as we could to Little Bay and took over the guard of a fine galley now waiting on its slipway—another ship for rich folk and by far the largest to be launched from Little Bay."

"Do you think these Land Pirates had good informers?" asked Gael.

"They might have done," said Bretlow, "but we were very careful. When we took over the guard for the first time—the second night the galley, *Brighthawk,* had been shown on the slipway, ready for launching—I swear we were well hidden, in a crude stone cobble hut, under rowboats turned up to drain. Darrah, our leader, First Ensign Darrah, stood forth as one of the guards in plain sight—four fellows in the same positions as before. I was half buried by a tangle of nets, along with Egon and a man from Tuana.

"Most of us were in position before the sun went down, with some warm provisions, but no ale or spirits. And, oh—we did not scorn to use a little humble magic ourselves, being Chyrian. Through Old Scaith, the headman, we were offered medals of protection, made by the village Helwyf or Healer. I took one—here I have it still . . ."

Vigo the Smith helped his son draw out the charm from the pocket of his tunic. It was a well-made round of bronze, decorated with mother-of-pearl. There were runes cut into the metal and it was threaded on a thong—instinctively Gael raised a hand to her own collar, missing still the long-departed lily, the amulet given to her by the wise lady of Cannford Old House. She remembered all the dangers she had passed in the Southland and in the Burnt Lands.

"The waiting was the worst part," said Bretlow. "We heard Darrah and the others moving about a little—talking softly, sometimes giving a word to those hidden, to keep up their spirits. There was some tilt-yard joking, I can tell you—about nature calls and so on. Then at last we got the signal—it was a knocking on a certain boat's hull which gave off a hollow sound. This meant the Alert—and then the call to arms, a blast on a conch shell.

"We came out of hiding but not all of us at once. I came with my lads from the tangle of nets and saw that there were no more than six of the devils come to take this great galley. We took them by surprise, I believe—they had only seen Darrah and the forward guard. I marked my man—charged him from behind and flung him down. I might have stabbed him to death there and then, but this was not our plan. We needed one of them alive. I pulled off his hood and beat him behind the ear with the hilt of my dagger, knocked him senseless. As I bound his hands and took his own weapons, there were frightful cries and shouts all around . . . I saw—I saw Darrah standing transfixed in a blaze of blue light, I saw two of our men wrestling with another pirate, who suddenly flung them off as if they were chaff. I roared out—I remember all of Elmtree Company were roaring. One pirate already stood at the helm of the boat—it was the old man, the leader, and he called to his followers in a kind of Chyrian, which we half understood. Might have been telling them to get done with us. I came to another smaller man and this time I did use my dagger, drove it into his right arm; then I felt a blow to the head and half fell down among the overturned dories. I saw that Egon had been stricken with their accursed blue fire, and he stood swaying until another of his comrades caught him and laid him down on the sand. I shouted 'Keep down! Keep down!' More pirates had boarded the galley. Then the old man raised his staff and the galley *Brighthawk* moved steadily down the slipway. Just before it reached the water, one of the other pirates uttered a cry, raised a staff of his own and directed it at me. I was standing outlined for a moment against the night sky—the air burned blue all round me. I felt a tingling through all my limbs, then I seemed to feel myself float away, and all was darkness."

Bretlow took a sup of applewine and sat there, shaking a little. Vigo went on with the tale. Yes, there had been casualties on both sides. One of the land pirates was badly hurt by Bretlow's blow to the head and one of the Westlings, another big fellow from the Tuana region, had his leg broken when he was hurled down. Three or four were in a deep sleep, Bretlow and three others, including Darrah, the leader. Then, lo and behold, the proud dogs of the senior company, Valko's Own, turned up at last and laid blame upon the men of Elmtree. The entire company was sent off, wounded and all alike, on the long way back to the Plantation Barracks. Valko's Own hung about at Little Bay and there was no further activity. Old Scaith and his fishers sailed out and searched for the stolen galley and had word that it had gone south down the coast. There was a spell of bad weather, which can surely happen in any summer, and the search was hindered.

"Bretlow," said Gael, "I can hazard a guess at these rogues. What happened to Elmtree back at the Plantation?"

"We were doctored and healed," he said. "I slept longer and heavier than all the rest. When I woke, at last, from this magical sleep, my right arm still slept, as it does to this day. I was a living example of the power of magic, or so the Healers and the Officers would have it, though there was one healer, Captain Merrick, out of Lien, who believed it might be a brainsickness which took away the power of a healthy limb. Whatever the case, I continue stricken. I was sent home all the way up river to the port nearest Hackestell, then freighted here from the garrison in a covered cart. I am on *Extended Leave,* as they call it—a kind of leave used for those who prove unequal to the soldier's life. Madmen, those who develop flat feet—there was a lad from the infantry who could not keep his food down. Kedran who get pregnant are scolded, of course, but treated well enough, at a lying-in house in the city of Krail . . ."

Gael understood his bitterness, but she thought of the other accommodations of the soldier's life, particularly in Krail: although there were houses of assignation, many respectable women married soldiers and came to live in the great city. She thought again of Bretlow among the Summer Riders and recalled that his name had been coupled with that of Ronna Oghal, the reeve's daughter. How could he court her now?

Meanwhile, Bretlow was shaking his head from side to side; Vigo put a hand on his son's shoulder and gave Gael an anguished look.

"Be of good cheer, Bretlow!" said Gael. "We must try to get your name back again!"

"How will that be?" he whispered.

"I know these rogues, these Land Pirates," she said, "and I think you do, too. You had a scrap of proof once—in your tale—do you have it still?"

"There!" cried Vigo in his booming voice. "I knew Gael Maddoc would remember!"

He reached across and felt in the pocket of Bretlow's tunic and flung the "scrap of proof" onto the table. It was crumpled and stained; Gael snatched it up and smoothed it out: a torn hood, a hood knitted from thick wool of a curious brown-black color, the wool of a black sheep.

"Was the name of this wild band of Erians, the refugees of the Brown Brotherhood in Lien, never spoken?" asked Gael. "At Krail or on the coast?"

"No, not once!" said Bretlow. "Not a word of these Black Sheep. They are scarcely known, even in Krail and at Barracks on the Plantation. It is bad luck to speak of the attempt on the life of Lord Knaar, for magic was involved. Egon had hopes of coming to that City Magistrate who took you and Jehane Vey to be questioned or even to Hem Duro. But there was no chance, and I lay there still entranced . . ."

"Well, it can be done now," said Gael. "Pray put your trust in our good Druda Strawn, for he must help me write a letter to Hem Duro, telling the tale. As for your arm, we will try one method which even Lord Knaar could not forbid us. You must come down and bathe your arm in the Holy Well—the sacred spring in the precinct of the Goddess."

"This can't do any harm, lad," said Vigo, seemingly encouraged. "We can ride down in the nighttime."

"Coombe is not Krail," said Gael Maddoc, "and our ways are different. Silence and shame have no part in your brave fight, Bretlow! Whether you try magic or the simple healing of the old wives or that of some learned healer from Lien—make no secret of your adventure!"

Bretlow lifted his great head, and the lights from the forge caught his dark brown hair.

"Well, perhaps I will speak out!" he said.

"By the Minstrels of Old Tuana!" cried Vigo Smith. "We can do better than that, by the fireside. There should be a Ballad!"

"Excellent!" said Gael Maddoc. "Come to the Holy Well at twilight tomorrow, Ensign Bretlow . . . We must not forget there is a great storm brewing up the coast. If we do not act quickly, the weather will force us to a longer wait."

CHAPTER VI

THE GREAT STORM

The simple plan for reinstating Bretlow Smith went ahead with amazing alacrity in the few days before the storm came down. In the twilight Vigo Smith drove his wife and son down to the Holywell in a covered cart drawn by matched white ponies. Gael and her mother met them at the sacred cavern; torches were already lit and there was warm water to be used after the healing water of the spring. There was a familiar procedure for aches and pains that the goodwives of Coombe often performed. Shivorn Maddoc had helped many folk in this way and was regarded as something of a healer. It was only the second time Gael had been in the sacred cavern since her return: there was the spring bubbling softly in its stone basin and a hint of starlight through the fretted roof. She thought of Blayn of Pfolben lying upon his bracken bed.

After the rites of healing, Bretlow's great arm remained pale and limp, hanging by his side when it was not supported by the sling, yet when his Mam flexed it, he swore he felt tingling near the shoulder joint and in his fingers. So this pleased them all, and the arm was bound up again. The whole party drove up in style to the Maddocs' cottage, where they sat before the fire and spoke of soldiering. Vigo brought out a bottle of brandywine for the men, and the wives brewed herb tea. Bress sat admiring Bretlow Smith and getting from him the first public version of his skirmish at Little Bay.

"Why, it sounds for all the world like the old song of Aidan, 'The Warlock of Ryall.' It will make a Ballad!" declared Bress.

"What, will you put words to that old air?" asked Rab Maddoc, with a wink at Vigo.

"Well, if you do not think *I* can do it, Da," grinned Bress, "I'll have Shim Rhodd to help me!"

The men chuckled approvingly, for they knew the innkeeper's son to be a bright spark.

Now the preparations for the storm were in full swing; everything was made fast, the livestock were brought into shelter. Bress was working on Rhodd the innkeeper's land, so Gael turned to with her father to secure the roof and hew firewood. She helped to bring the six sheep down from the top of the hill to the pen behind the house that they shared with the milch goats.

She rode out one day on Bretlow's behalf. After packing the priest's cupboard with the food that she and her mother had been baking, she told Druda Strawn the full story.

"I think you must write this letter you have spoken of to Hem Duro of Val'Nur," said Druda Strawn. "Not that he will be so very happy to be hearing from us! But we cannot have poor Bretlow set aside like this. These pirates must indeed be the same Black Sheep who threatened Lord Knaar's life when one of their brethren's farms was taken by a dam."

"Well, I have set down a few beginnings," Gael said shyly, for her writing would never please her. She drew out her sheet of paper. The priest accepted several of her sentences and together they worked them into a letter, not too long, that the Druda promised to write out fair on a parchment. Then, storm or no storm, it could be brought to Hackestell under his name and sent on from there to the lord's son, in the palace at Krail.

"Once again," the Druda told Gael seriously, "we must consider ourselves lucky that these folk have resorted to magic in their own defense." His gaze was fixed far in the distance. Gael knew he was thinking of more than Bretlow's future. "Lienish refugees—we may speak out against those, but not against Lienish men. Indeed, open talk against those of Lien is no more welcome these days than it was four summers past when you rode out with me as a Green Rider. Our Lord Knaar desires to keep the peace—and maintaining our relations with Lien outward friendly and smooth is a part of that."

Gael had heard a whisper of this since her return to Coombe. There was unrest in Lien—it was rumored that Lien's queen had taken on a coterie of evangelical counselors, men who desired to push the worship of Inokoi the Lame God and the preaching of his prophet across Lien's borders.

Still, Lien seemed little closer today than it had before her journey into the Southland. The Melniros were a vigorous, active people, a people who worked hard to wrest a living from their broad open land. Inokoi's Prophet, Matten Seyl of Hodd, had been a nobleman, and it had been a noble's dissipations he had renounced. It seemed unlikely to Gael that the severe preachings of the Brown Brotherhood—men who ranted against the "pleasures" of the world, by which they seemed to mean everything from the love between a man and a woman through to heedless spending, could ever take hold here.

Nevertheless she went home from the Druda in a thoughtful mood, glad that she had been able to aid Bretlow, but unsettled once again in the particulars of her own return.

The first night of the storm uprooted trees and hurled the well bucket a hundred yards out onto the road. Gael and her brother ran around the hillside at dawn and found that the big whitethorn tree outside the sacred cavern had fallen. They dragged it aside and set about clearing leaves and twigs that had been driven into the grotto's passage, even into the sacred chamber. Gael was sweeping the uneven stone of the floor clear of the last of the torn silver-green leaves when Bress came in, filling the doorway, and went to take a drink of spring water.

"I will ride to Banlo Strand," he said. "Let me take that black demon of yours."

"No," she replied, her hands full of broken whitethorn shards, tree of magic and of sacrifice. Her mother had cut rods from this tree every spring for the font's altar; Shivorn would certainly mourn its passing. "Ebony will hurl you down. What's at Banlo?"

"Pickings," he said. "Bits of wreckage. Maybe a haul of kelp."

"Run to Banlo!" she said. "You are the best runner in ten crofts, I am told."

"Maybe I will," he said, brightening. "Sister . . ."

"What?"

"Is it true you will not have Culain Raillie?"

"By the Goddess, now I know I am in Coombe!" she said. "He has not spoken for me and I have said no more than two words to the man, but even in this the gossips have found their food."

"It was mother's plan for you to wed Culain," said Bress. "She has kept a part of your own silver for the dowry."

"I know it," said Gael ruefully. "And the widow is her friend and we're in their debt. But the gossips are right . . . I will not have him."

"The Raillies are incomers. They're rich." He stared around at the worn ceremonial cups, the broken edge of the ancient altar. "What can they want with poor folk like us?"

He flung out of the cavern and turned back to say:

"Shim Rhodd says that they are witches!"

The storm came down again in the afternoon and by midnight the yard was a sea. Shivorn Maddoc could stand it no longer; she and Maddoc brought the six sheep one by one into the house, and also the two goats. The chimney was half blocked by a board so that the torrents of rain would not put out the fire. Gael made a hot mash and took it to Ebony and Grey Lass, the donkey mare, in the lean-to.

The family were all in good spirits; Gael remembered the excitement of stormy nights as a child. She and her mother cooked a second supper of griddlecakes, then they snatched a few more hours of sleep in the woolly, smoky darkness of the small house. Another yellow morning showed that the road was flooded, almost to the boundary wall. Their croft was like a hilly island. Maddoc said to Gael:

"Can you ride round the hill? I fear the Cresset Burn has come up by Ardven ruin."

Mother Maddoc loaded up the saddlebags with hot oatcakes, a crock of porridge with honey, a bottle of applejack. Bress helped his sister mount up in the flooded yard.

"I'll be running to Banlo Strand," he said. "I'll look for a piece of sailcloth for a new horse cover."

Gael rode behind the house and urged Ebony onto a dryish track that spiraled round the hillside. She came to a spot where she could look down on the Cresset Burn and the ruined manor on its banks. Ardven had been a fine house, taller than the Long Burn farmhouse, and it had stood a good distance from the stream. Now part of it was unroofed, with grass and nettles growing through the floor, and the stream had changed its course. She knew that the few rooms still in use were farthest from the bank of the river, but there was water ankle deep inside the streamside rooms.

Overhead, one mighty stone chimney that climbed the house's western wall had a thread of smoke arising from one of its fine brown chimney pots. There was a fire alight somewhere on the upper floor—Old Murrin must have taken shelter there.

She saw a way to ride through to the ruin. She came carefully downhill, skirting the water; Ebony found his way, snorting, over a flooded causeway. At last she called:

"Ahoy, Ardven House! Are you there, Captain Murrin?"

She called again, and a white head came up at one of the staring dark windows of the upper floor. The old woman answered the call in a strong cracked voice and directed her through the ruins. There were some bedraggled fowls, one goat and a scatter of smaller wild creatures, rats, voles, conies, all taking shelter from the flood in the ruined house. Gael let Ebony stand in a good dry place and climbed up a ladder.

"Now then," said Old Murrin. "Kedran Maddoc is it? Ensign?"

"Captain . . ." she grinned.

"Blessed Huntress!"

Old Murrin showed a few strong yellow teeth in her wrinkled leathery countenance. She was short, straight backed. She was two-and-seventy years old; she lived alone.

"Sit ye down," she said. "Bless your mother for this warm food. Water's as high as ever I've seen it."

There was a small fire on the hearth and an iron trivet for heating food. An alcove was filled with cut wood, pinecones, and kindling—Gael remembered hearing that Bress and Shim Rhodd had hauled fuel for Ardven in the summer. The room was not warm: Gael kept her cloak, and the old woman was wrapped in a blanket. The large neat room contained piles of Murrin's goods. She had carried up food baskets, garden tools, pot and pans. A grey cat lay curled on the narrow bed. On the wall behind the bed hung Murrin's riches: a magnificent banner in colored silks, green and blue, enriched with silver thread and writing in a strange language. There was a bronze shield, two banners with Chyrian words, one from Eriu, and a newer pennant from the Westlings, with a brown hill surmounted by a bolt of lightning for the house of Val'Nur.

Murrin questioned Gael about her service in the Southland, workaday stuff that only a kedran would know about or care. Was it a soft duty at Lowestell and in Pfolben city? How were the horses and the stabling?

"Whence comes your beautiful silken banner?" asked Gael.

"It is from the far-off land of Palmur," said Murrin softly. "It was made by craftsmen from the lands of Kusch."

"That is much farther than I have been," said Gael. "I have been only to the Burnt Lands."

"I am the only one left of our company of adventurers," said Murrin. "It is fifty years past. Tell me about the Burnt Lands. Were you in Aghiras?"

So they sat in the dark, ruined house in the flood and told marvelous tales. Long after Gael Maddoc had told all about her journey to the Burnt Lands, Emeris Murrin went on. She had been as far as any traveler; she had served with the fighting women of Palmur, she had seen the mountains that pierced the clouds. She had sailed southward to the Lands Below the

World and fought battles in Eildon and in the Western Isles. She took a gulp of applejack, laughed and said:

"What will you do, girl?"

"Ride out again," said Gael. "My mother would have me stay."

"Stay and marry, I'll be bound," said Murrin. "I was wed in Athron, five years long. He was a handsome man, a drummer from Varda. I had a child, a sweet girl child, but she was taken."

"So you went back to soldiering?"

"I rode off. It was a cruel thing, I'm not proud of it. My old love returned, the tall Eildon girl I told of, the companion of all my wild journeys. I left the poor man and his cottage and the grave of our little maid and went with my kedran lover. We were together then for nearly twenty years.

"We sailed for Eildon and served in a long campaign against the last Kings of Eriu. I was wounded again, and we took more peaceful duties in Athron and in the Chameln lands. Ylla died far north of Achamar, fording a river, in peacetime. It was before the Great King, old Ghanor, made his bid for the Chameln. I left the service and came home, all the way home here to Coombe, and settled in the ruins of this house, home to the Murrins of Ardven."

Gael hardly liked to ask: "How fared your brother—your sister, in Rift Kyrie? You must have nieces and nephews . . ."

"I have had a few words with all my kin, over the years," said Murrin dryly. "They did well. Avaurn, in Rift Kyrie, went to the Goddess six years past. The children are grown men and women. My brother's son has the name Oweyn and still lives in Balbank, though it is King's Bank now, part of Lien. This house belongs to him, of course. One day—before I am gone perhaps—the house will be restored . . ."

Gael felt keenly the old woman's loneliness and tried to cheer her.

"Ah, but you had one more adventure, Captain," she said, "after you came home!"

"By the Goddess, I had!" said Old Murrin. "Riding with the Westlings by the side of Yorath Duaring and his free company. There was a mighty man and a noble heart!"

"It must be fine to be remembered," said Gael Maddoc. "To have folk bless your name, as we do the name of General Yorath."

"Psst," said Murrin. "You are young. You will have fame and fortune."

They played several games of Battle with well-worn wooden figures. Murrin was a master player; for her sake, Gael wished that she could play better. They took up the tale of Bretlow Smith's adventure far away on the shores of the Western Sea.

"These Black Sheep are newcomers," said Murrin, "but they have a strong whiff of Eriu still about them. It is a rare green island full of the beauty of the Goddess and with old harsh magic. It would surprise me if their current liege, Kelen of Lien, does at all well by them."

Gael was reluctant to leave the old woman alone, but Murrin urged her to get home.

"There's another wild night coming," she said. "I'm snug here, with Oona the Cat. I can play Battle by myself for hours together. I have much to remember."

II

The storm wind raged again all night long, but the rain had edged off to the northwest. From the top of their hill the Maddocs could see sheets of water on the plain by Hackestell. Bress had run home from Banlo Strand with news of an Eildon ship, stranded on the beach. The ship's captain and the crew were guarding their vessel, ready to get her off again when the blow was over.

There were some travelers taken from the ship coming through to the inn at Coombe in a farm cart. No, they were not hurt, not even shipwrecked, properly speaking, but they were fine folk who complained in loud voices.

Two mornings later, when the wind had dropped, there came the sound of a horse splashing through the yard and then a thunderous knocking on the door. When Mother Maddoc lifted the bar, there was a grinning, shock-headed fellow: it was Bress's boon companion, Shim Rhodd, the innkeeper's son. He stood by their fire and spoke up, full of importance. The reeve, Master Oghal, begged their pardon. Would Captain Maddoc please to ride up to Coombe without delay, in full kedran kit, ready for a journey.

"Surely," said Gael, who had been stirring Ebony's hot mash. "What does he want with me?"

"I'm not supposed to know," said Shim, "but I do. The lord and his lady, they from the ship, they will have an escort."

He winked at Bress.

"There's money in it," he said. "They are the finest folk ever in Coombe. Their man gave me two pieces of silver just for cleaning three pair of boots."

Maddoc spoke up from his place by the fire.

"Money or not, our family will be pleased to come at the reeve's call, seeing he asks so politely."

Shivorn sent all the men out of the kitchen and warmed water for a soldier's wash. She packed the saddlebags—all her daughter's kit was in good order. Gael strode out of the cottage in her rust red "dress" tunic, dark brown cloak and green riding cap with a kestrel feather. As she fed Ebony and groomed him, she thought of the summer day she had run to Lowestell behind Blayn of Pfolben's horse, Daystar.

The floodwaters were draining away on the road, but it was still heavy going in places. Shim Rhodd and Bress, both mounted on the big brown workhorse from the inn, splashed ahead. They sang for her, the kind of teasing old Chyrian song with which the folk of the coast greeted newcomers who did not understand the language.

Here comes a girl
Dressed up so fine,
Is it Queen Meb, fairest of the Shee?
Or is it the Swineherd's daughter?

So they came up the hill to Coombe, and there was Leem Oghal, the reeve, peering out of his porch, waiting. He had been reeve as long as Gael could remember, and his father before him. He was a solid, comfortably built man, with a lined face. Even those who envied his fine house and his land had to admit that his life was not easy. Now he smiled at the crofter's daughter and a boy came to hold her horse.

"Step in, Captain," said the reeve. "You must pardon my wife, she's not down yet."

They sat together at a long table in the very room where Maddoc had asked for relief from his taxes. Ronna, the reeve's daughter, brought a milk posset and new-baked bread.

"Gael Maddoc," said Reeve Oghal, fixing his eyes on her. "You must help Coombe village out of a hole."

"How can I do that, Master Oghal?"

"The shipwrecked folk over yonder in the General Yorath . . . you've heard of them? It is an Eildon nobleman, Lord Malm, his lady, and their one servant. They were taking ship to Balamut, but the storm landed them on Banlo Strand. They are traveling with little state, almost secretly, and I have no idea of their business. They will come with all possible speed to the court of King Gol. They need an escort or guide, as well as horses . . ."

He stopped short, gulped at his drink, and ran a hand over his thinning hair.

"You are the only soldier here in Coombe today who is fit to ride as their escort. We have no Westlings on leave and no riders who have had dealings with such high and mighty folk," he said. "They are giving Rhodd a terrible time."

He smiled a little, for the reeve had a running fight with the innkeeper, that other pillar of the community.

"I will do it gladly," said Gael Maddoc.

"Good girl!" said the reeve. "But hear this—the ways are cut. The road past Hackestell is under water. You must ride the high ground. Have you ridden far on the plateau?"

"I have traveled on the new roads as far as Goldgrave," she said, "with Druda Strawn and other Summer Riders, three years past."

"Of course," said the reeve, seeming relieved. "That is but a step from the city of Lort and the Palace Fortress of our king."

Gael thought of the High Plateau, home of the Shee, a fine, deserted place where one could watch the stars. It could not be chance that now took her to those heights, these nights as the storm had risen. She had been called. Strangers had come from Eildon, the magic kingdom of the west. Surely all must hang together with her quest . . .

"Now we come to the money," said the reeve bluntly. "I will hire you to serve the village of Coombe. We will provide horses and a kedran captain as guide, and I believe the Lord Malm will pay as much as twenty pieces of gold, five before setting out and the rest when the journey is done. If you please these folk they may add to this . . . a gratuity. In any case you can keep four pieces of gold for yourself when you return. All the rest is for Coombe. Rhodd may enrich himself with his inn prices, but I can do no such thing. I trust you, Gael Maddoc. You are the daughter of a crofter of Coombe . . . the Maddocs were there when the Standing Stones were set up!"

"I will not fail you, Master Oghal!"

"Finish your breakfast," he said wearily, "I must send off a reckoning."

He bustled away, and she heard him climbing stairs. Presently Ronna Oghal came in and sat down to table. She was a handsome girl, about the same age as Gael, with dark eyes and fine brown hair under her coif.

"I must thank you, Gael Maddoc," she said in a soft light voice, "for helping Bretlow—my poor Bretlow Smith."

"How is he doing?" asked Gael.

"A little better," said Ronna. "But his arm is still lame. Oh Goddess, what is this bane come upon him? Do you know? Is it this wicked Erian magic—or some other sickness?"

"Truly, I cannot tell," said Gael. "I believe he should keep on with his treatment at the Holywell . . ."

"Should we find a true adept?" whispered Ronna. "A Magician or a Wise Woman?"

"I did hear of one thing," Gael said, hesitating. "I read it in a book of old tales that Druda Strawn gave me at the Winter Feast, years past, to help my reading."

"Tell me . . ." pleaded Ronna, "or maybe send the book to me to read . . ."

"Perhaps I should do that," said Gael, feeling herself blush a little. "There was this warrior roused from a spell when his sweetheart—held him close!"

Ronna understood at once. They both heard her father, the reeve, returning. Ronna stood up, gathering dishes on to her tray, and said:

"Why yes, send me that book, if you please, Captain!"

"I'm ready, Captain Maddoc," said Reeve Oghal. "We'll seek the dragon's lair!"

The inn and the inn yard were unusually still. A decent pack horse from Rhodd's own stable stood ready and a passable charger, for the lord, from Vigo Smith's stable; two riding hacks for the lady and the servant were being brought from the Long Burn Farm. There was whispering in the hallway; Rhodd, the innkeeper, was comforting a weeping maidservant. He was a handsome man, a veteran of the Westlings and a widower. The gossips said that only gold pleased him more than the love of women. He nodded briefly to the reeve and took Gael by the hand, smiling.

"By the Goddess," he said, still keeping his voice down. "Is this our little Maddoc?"

"We'll go in," said Reeve Oghal curtly. "Will their man say our names or will you?"

"The man's upstairs seeing to the baggage," said Rhodd. "Come along."

He stepped up, knocked on the door of his best room, where the recruiting officers were entertained and the tax gatherers, and, in summer, the hunting parties. As he announced Reeve Oghal, a voice cut him short.

"We have been waiting!"

The reeve hitched at the belt of his tunic and went in with Gael at his heels. Lord Malm stood before the fire, a tall, ruddy-faced old man, broadly built and made broader by his robe of padded grey velvet trimmed with squirrel fur. His lady, somewhat younger, sat at the oaken table. She wore a thick, furred surcoat over green brocade and on her head a hood, peaked like a house gable, that showed her hair, smooth golden brown. They were both notably clear skinned, fair and well fed. But their faces were almost deformed by impatience and disgust for the situation in which they found themselves.

"Lord," said Oghal, bowing. "The horses will be ready shortly and I have a kedran captain for your guide. May I present . . ."

"No," said the lord. "Don't be a fool. I'm not *meeting* this woman, I'm hiring her services."

As the poor reeve stood openmouthed, Gael stepped into the midst of the chamber, stood to attention, and saluted. The Eildon lord paced all around her, where she stood, and put his face next to hers. His breath reeked of mint leaves.

"Name and rank!" he cried, just below the level of a parade-ground shout.

Gael did not flinch; she rapped out her reply, included her unit. She stared into the middle distance and remembered her foolish thoughts of the magic kingdom.

"Maddoc!" said Lord Malm.

His Eildon accent thinned it to *Meddoc*.

"Served in a household regiment?"

"Yes my lord!"

"Ridden escort duty?"

"Yes my lord, and personal escort service to the Lord Blayn, Heir of Pfolben!"

"How d'ye happen to be in this wild, forsaken place, Captain?"

"On my long leave, my lord."

"You *live* here?"

"At Maddoc's croft, by Holywell, my lord."

He turned on his heel, clasped his hands behind his back, and bent toward his lady.

"Malveen, my heart," he said gently. "What do you think? Seems sound enough."

"I could ask for better," drawled Lady Malm. "Are we not in Mel'Nir? Where are the giant warriors?"

The reeve began to speak, but she waved a white hand at him and said: "Let the Captain answer!"

"My lady," said Gael, "the nearest garrison of the Westmark is at Hackestell Fortress, twenty miles away."

"We must journey with all possible speed," said the lady, twisting her hands together. "We must come to the king's court. We have been cast away . . ."

"My lady," said Gael, hoping the reeve would keep silent. "We might arrange an escort of cavalrymen from Hackestell. They serve Knaar of Val'Nur, Lord of the Westmark."

Lord and Lady Malm exchanged a long look. Plainly, they had no wish for an escort of Val'Nur's troops.

"Get on," said the lord. "The captain will guide us. We must ride within the hour. Speak to the steward about our quartering!"

"The matter of payment . . ." murmured Reeve Oghal.

"Speak to the steward, man!" said Lord Malm.

He turned his back on them. They went out and found Rhodd drinking his best wine in his own parlor with the third member of the party. Master Wennle, the steward, was a thin elderly man whose faded brown eyes missed nothing. He did not bargain with Rhodd or with Reeve Oghal but opened a writing case of polished wood and noted all the expenses in a little parchment book. At last, Rhodd and the reeve went to see to horses and provisions.

"Captain," said Wennle, "tell me plainly, is this a dangerous journey?"

"No," said Gael. "The roads are good. The waystations provide shelter. The storms of autumn hardly reach the high ground."

"I cannot understand why there are no garrisons in all that wild region, the High Plateau."

"Master Wennle," she said, "have you not been told that it is the last home of the Shee, the fairy folk? It has always been treated as some kind of neutral ground. Long ago there were mining towns, Goldgrave and Silverlode, before the precious metals and jewels gave out and those towns became empty places, ghosts. Armies have marched and fought on the high ground, there are roads for travelers now, and Goldgrave is rebuilt, but a garrison would be seen as a provocation of the Shee and of the war-leaders or the king."

"Eildon folk," said Wennle with a smile, "are all cousins to the Shee. It accounts for their wayward behavior."

"Master Wennle, can you tell me the reason for this journey?"

"No," he said stiffly. "It is not my place. Put your question to Lady Malm when she knows you better."

"I think that will never be," sighed Gael. "The lady would rather have giant warriors as her escort."

"Captain Maddoc," said the steward, "were you never afraid? Can you imagine how it might be . . . cast away in a strange country?"

Gael bent her head, thinking of the endless sands.

"Yes, Master Wennle," she said humbly. "I will do my best to serve your masters well."

"Now the problem of fresh horses," said Wennle. "What was it that the reeve suggested?"

"If there are no horses at the Halfway House," said Gael, "we might hire them from Nordlin, in the Great Eastern Rift. It is no more than twenty miles from the great inn to this valley. Yet if these horses we have are strong, I think we would do better to let them rest up and go the whole journey. We are not riding as couriers, Master Wennle. I for one will not change my mount."

The innyard was full of activity all of a sudden. The sun had come out for the first time in many days and the hay piles steamed. The two horses from the Long Burn Farm were sleek and strong, and there was a lady saddle besides, but Wennle assured the reeve that Lady Malm would ride astride. As she went about checking girths, Gael Maddoc was drawn aside by a tall man with his face muffled. When Culain Raillie lowered his plaid, his eyes held a wild look.

"Gael Maddoc," he said, "help me as a friend. Who are these Eildon folk?"

"Lord Malm and his lady," she said.

"Two great nobles? Here in Coombe?"

"Stand here and you will see them ride out," she said.

"What escort do they have?"

"Only myself," she said, "and their steward. They are bound for Lort, and in a hurry."

He relaxed a little and smiled his mirthless smile.

"Good traveling, then! . . . I hope the gold they have paid is good," he added, "whoever they may be."

"They are the Malms," she said, wondering at his concern. "Bound for Lort. Depend upon it!"

"Well, I wish you a safe journey."

Her name was called, and she went to help with the packhorse. Culain Raillie slipped away, did not even stay to see his horses ridden off.

Vigo the Smith came from the forge with a lance, nicely balanced and newly tipped, on which the steward threaded a banner for the knightly order of the Hunters of Eildon, with their device, a silver bow. The yard had been cleared, but the street was lined with people as though the Westlings were mustering.

Lord Malm came and complained loud and long about the horses, then about the saddles. Lady Malm had changed her clothes . . . it struck Gael that she could hardly do this by herself, that a kedran might have to do duty as a lady's maid.

Now the lady wore a riding habit, with green breeches under a flowing brown skirt and a shaped jacket, trimmed with fur. She sat her horse well, without complaint, but she asked, angrily, why her lord was mounted on an old nag while the kedran guide rode a fine charger.

None of the Coombe folk would answer her; Gael pretended not to hear; the steward leaned across and explained: the black charger was Captain Maddoc's own property. At last Lord Malm looked over the small party and gave a shout of "*Meddoc!*" He waved his hand to her, she raised the banner and led the way.

They rode slowly through the village. Among the thin, hoarse cheering, she heard the lads, Bress and Shim, singing, in Chyrian, another jaunting verse to their song:

Who is that lord
With the shining face?
Is it King Nud, the Lord of the Lake?
Or is it a drunken tinker?

She saw Druda Strawn standing by an oak sapling where the road led downhill. He waved a sprig of the sacred plant, Mistel, that grew with the oaks, and gave them a blessing for the journey.

At the foot of the rise there was water across the road in pools, reflecting the pale color of the sky. On their right lay the roads to the south, with a distant view of Lowestell. The fortress stood out stark and grey against the trees of the Southwold; to the left the road led down through orchards to flooded fields that reached all the way to Hackestell. There was the boundary wall and a crofter and his wife, waving proudly . . . she dipped her lance to her father and mother. Then they were right down, upon the plain, almost at the crossroads.

Hackestell was visible to the north, with water spreading out before it like a moat. Ahead was the first stretch of "new road," leading directly to the cliffs of the High Plateau. Gael Maddoc spoke up as a guide should do, crying out the landmarks and calling the way they must ride. The small party of riders pressed on, and well before midday they were climbing upward.

The road was broad and comfortable, cut into the cliff in long rising tiers, shored up with stonework. There was a perceptible improvement in everyone's spirits as they came closer to the lip of the plateau. Gael thought back with sweet regret to the innocent days of the Summer Riders; the lord and his lady talked together and laughed aloud. First Wennle sang a song in a sweet cracked voice, then Malm cried out:

"Captain, give us a wild folk song for this desolate place!"

"My lord," said Gael, "I can do no better than a riding song from the Southland . . ."

So she lifted up her voice, which was tuneful enough, and sang a verse that came into her head.

In Pfolben fields I saw a maiden,
She sang this song while she harvested the grain,
"Ride on, dear heart, ride on the whole world over,
Ride home to me in Pfolben fields again!"

Lady Malm laughed again, and the lord persuaded his wife to raise up her own voice.

"Well, let us have a catch," she said. "I will begin, then Wennle, then the kedran."

It was an old song, and with one or two false starts they were able to sing it well.

Birds sing in spring,
Sweet sweet the nightingale and tawny owl . . .

"Hush!" said Lady Malm as Gael's last note died away.

Borne on the wind from overhead, there came a few sweet notes of the catch repeated.

"An echo, my lady," said Wennle. "Is it not, Captain?"

"I hope so," said Gael.

They rode on for the last hundred yards in silence and came over the crest of the road. What they saw took their breath away and kept them silent for a time. There was no sign of any living creature; the riders stood now upon a piece of higher ground, as on the lip of a great bowl, and the plateau spread out before them. It was a mighty plain, red or sandy in places, with a few stunted trees close at hand, tussock grass and dark scrubby bushes. It was afternoon and there was rain in the wind, but the weather was still holding. Cloud shadows moved over the plateau, purple and grey. Off to the east, at the descent into the Great Eastern Rift, there was mist, and mist further to the south by Rift Kyrie. Gael looked to the Larch Road in the west, where she had climbed up with the Summer Riders coming from Hackestell with Druda Strawn. She saw that they were not quite alone: one horseman, two, maybe a third were slowly descending to the flooded plains. Now those distant riders were hidden by a few larch trees.

Directly ahead, down the dark ribbon of the road, was the first waystation, a square house of yellow stone, after the fashion of Mel'Nir. It was about ten miles away, though distances were hard to judge. A little south of the waystation rose a tall standing stone, the Black Menhir.

Gael tried to prepare the travelers for the first night of the journey.

"My lord," she said, "the first waystation yonder is called Rieth's Rest, for the Prince of Mel'Nir, the King's nephew, who camped here as a child on his way to the king's court."

"Hear that, my love?" cried Lord Malm. "It is a good omen!"

"My lord," said Gael, "presently I will ride on ahead and get the fire lit."

Lady Malm at once reined in her horse and cried out in temper:

"Is there no one there? Is that what you are saying, kedran? No servants? No hot water? No beds?"

"No servants, my lady," said Gael. "The house is clean and fire is laid and there are straw palliasses for travelers. Water can be heated. It is the custom to leave food or drink in the store coffer for the next travelers. We have good provisions."

"And is it so all the way over this plateau?" demanded the lord.

"No, the Halfway House is like a true large inn," said Gael. "We will reach it tomorrow night if we ride early."

She rode off at last and came to Rieth's Rest, which to her own eyes looked snug enough, even welcoming. She got the fire to burn, swept the hearth, shook up the beds, even before she saw to Ebony in the stable.

The Malms came in and complained and at the same time said they must make the best of things. Wennle consulted with Gael over the evening meal: they stewed a chicken with onions and herbs and barley. There was plenty of applejack, and it mellowed Lord Malm a little. He took himself off to the larger chamber and soon could be heard snoring although it was an early hour. When Lady Malm rose up from her place by the fire, Gael said timidly:

"My lady, may I be helpful as a tiring woman?"

The lady looked at her with undisguised disgust.

"I hope you have washed your hands," she said.

There were forty leather buttons on the back of the noblewoman's riding habit. Gael came back to the fire and said to the steward:

"Will you sleep by the fire, Master Wennle?"

"No, Captain," he said. "Thank you kindly. I will read in my book a little by this candle then later try to sleep. Pray take the place by the fire."

She banked the fire and lay down upon the straw-padded settle, wrapped in her cloak. The way before them seemed very long and far removed from a quest. She slept and dreamed a confused happy dream of her old friends in Kestrel company riding up to the door of Rieth's Rest and greeting her.

The sight of the High Plateau at dawn next day, as she rapidly went from one task to another, was enough to cheer her. As she saw to the horses the whole eastern boundary of the plain and the rift valleys were shrouded in golden mist. Then they were all on the road again before the sun was up, and they saw it rise, burning over the cliffs by the distant Eastmark. In mid morning of a clear autumn day they came toward a crossroads, and first Gael, then the other travelers, saw two horsemen waiting in the meager shade of a thorn tree.

As they came closer, Gael saw that Lady Malm would meet two of the "giant warriors" she had desired for her escort. The riders were indeed two mighty men of Mel'Nir, dressed in link mail with surcoats of bleached cotton and mounted upon heavy chargers. At last, when the curiosity of the Malms knew no bounds, one of the men, carrying a banner upon his lance, spurred forward, and Gael rode out to meet him.

The man she met was over thirty, carrying a little too much weight even for his considerable height. He was a sergeant, by his shoulder knots, with a smiling red face and black shaggy hair marked with a white streak.

"Breckan," he said, saluting. "Badger Breckan to my friends, serving Obrist Hem Lovill, who sends greeting to those you serve, whoever they may be."

"Maddoc," she said, "of Coombe, formerly of the Kestrels in Pfolben. I serve Lord and Lady Malm, come out of Eildon, journeying to the king's court. What is your lord's garrison?"

"Godfire!" said Breckan. "What fine folk we have here! The obrist is from the King's Longhouse itself. Pray you, Captain, bring greetings to your people and bid them join my noble lord yonder for a sup of wine and fresh oatcake."

She tipped her lance to him with a smile and brought back the message.

"Ha! A local lord? Obrist, you say?" cried Lord Malm. "See now, my love, here is fit company, more or less, for a picnic on our way."

"Mortrice," said Lady Malm, "what a boy you are!"

The party rode on slowly and Hem Lovill, already dismounted, bowed low before them. He was a striking figure, even in a land where the average height for men of his race was over six feet. He was not only broad and strong but handsome, with rounded features and shining brown hair that peaked upon his clear brow.

The Malms were as pleased as Gael had ever seen them, bowing graciously and speaking very pleasantly to the young officer. The sergeant set out a picnic place with the help of Wennle, and Gael saw to the horses. There was a water trough and a hitching rail beside the thorn tree. When the horses were settled she went back and stood at the edge of the obrist's fine red blankets, which made up the picnic place, waiting to be of service.

"Dismiss, Meddoc," said Lord Malm, testily. "Don't hover. The steward will see to our needs."

As she walked back to the water trough, the Malms and Hem Lovill laughed aloud. Sergeant Breckan sat with her at the trough and brought out a leather bottle of some rough schnapps. One whiff was enough. She drank water.

"A heavy duty," he said, "serving these folk."

She did not care for the sergeant and felt a certain loyalty to the Malms.

"They are high bred," she said, "and cast away in a strange land."

He pressed her again to try the schnapps, though she doubted he took very much himself. She was restless, for it was one of the longest days before them on the road to the Halfway House. She was soothed by the view of the plateau and the cloud shadows moving over the plain.

"Were you ever in the Eastern Rift, Sergeant?" she asked.

"Not me, Captain," he grinned, "but my father was there, years ago, before the war. It is a rich corner of this land."

At that moment Wennle stepped a little away from the others and stared in her direction. Lord Malm called "Meddoc," and she ran smartly to the picnic place. The obrist had risen to his feet, and now he stood close, looking at her down his nose with a half smile. She saw how Lord

Malm watched from his place on the ground and how Lady Malm veiled her face with her headdress and turned aside impatiently.

"Captain," said Hem Lovill, "you served in the Southland. How far have you ridden upon the Plateau?"

She could not see his drift at all, but she knew that the Malms had somehow approved his right to question her.

"To the Halfway House many times," she said.

Before she could finish, Hem Lovill turned back to Lord Malm, spreading his hands.

"My lord, my lady," he said, "our meeting was a happy chance. Cut your losses!"

"And to Goldgrave," said Gael Maddoc, sudden catching his drift.

"Oh, to Goldgrave," said Hem Lovill, mocking. "How often to Goldgrave?"

"Once," she replied. "My Lord Malm, what is played out here?"

"How dare you!" snapped Lady Malm.

"Lord Malm," said Gael, "you accepted my service. Whether I have been to Goldgrave once or a hundred times, you have never been there. I am your escort!"

"No more!" blustered the old lord, climbing to his feet. "Be not so bold as to address me! Wennle . . ."

"Steward Wennle," said Gael, "tell the lord I meant no disrespect. What do you say to all this?"

"Captain," said the steward sadly, "this officer, Obrist Hem Lovill, travels clear across to our goal at the king's court. Lord Malm will end your service."

"Then I must have part of the sum agreed upon," said Gael Maddoc. "Not for myself, but for Coombe, a poor and needy village that has done its best to serve these noble folk, come by chance to our door."

"Hungry for gold!" breathed Lady Malm.

"And what of the horses?" asked Gael.

"Broken-down nags the lot of them!" said Lord Malm.

"My lord," said Wennle, "we must use the horses until we reach the Halfway House."

"Yes, yes," said the lord, "and then Lovill will fetch us some decent mounts. Meddoc, you're insubordinate, my wife doesn't like your looks, you stink of the midden, and the chicken last night was tough. You're dismissed. The steward will give you two gold pieces, quite undeserved."

She said no word. It occurred to her that Lord Malm was mad, and no one dared correct him because of his noble birth. She was bitterly resentful of the part Hem Lovill had played in her dismissal and thought he was of the breed of "bull-bocks" who hated kedran. They were few in the Southland, and she had seen no lord, not even the sly and selfish Blayn of Pfolben, fall into childish abuse of the kind Lord Malm had uttered.

She turned and walked away toward the thorn tree and the horse trough. Lady Malm's sharp voice followed her and was carried away by the wind. She saw Badger Breckan standing among the horses. Wennle, the steward, touched her arm, and when she looked back, he pressed the two gold pieces into her palm.

"This was not my doing, Captain," he said. "The horses will be left at the Halfway House. It was so arranged, was it not?"

She could only nod. The folk from Coombe planned to come to the Halfway House on the next long watch to find out if the party had obtained new mounts or ridden the old ones on over the plateau.

Then came a loud shrieking neigh and she saw Ebony rear up while the sergeant laughed and flinched back out of his reach behind the horse trough. The black horse was unhitched from the rail, and now he galloped free, bucking and twisting, to the west. Gael Maddoc ran after him as fast as she could. She ran, and Ebony galloped, far ahead, over the rough, pitted ground of the plateau. She ran and called to him and prayed to the Goddess that he would not lame himself or ride off down the cliff road to the plains.

At long last he stood still and she came closer, soothing him with her voice, but he would not yet allow himself to be caught and tossed his head and was off again. So the pair of them went on for a long time, until at last Ebony hung his head, foam flecked. She came to him, put on a leading rein, stripped off her saddle and saddlebags and wiped him down with his own special cloth. She gave him drink from her water bottle in her wooden food bowl and put on his blanket. She examined his body all over to make sure he had done himself no mischief and wondered how Breckan had caused him to misbehave. A slap or a tweak might have done it . . . Ebony was a capricious animal.

At last, under the noonday sun, they walked side by side, exhausted, back to Rieth's Rest, having run so far it was less than a mile away. She looked back down the road and could see no more than a dust cloud, far beyond the thorn tree at the crossroads. Her service with Lord and Lady Malm was ended. She had two gold pieces to bring Reeve Oghal.

She spent the whole day caring for Ebony at the waystation, going out to his stall, then coming back to the cool rooms. In the evening she lit the fire, brewed herb tea, ate the goat cheese and bacon her mother had slipped into her saddlebag. She thought of the good food from Coombe that the Malms carried upon their packhorse. She was in two minds about taking back the food she had laid in the store coffer of the waystation that same morning. Still brooding, she fell asleep very early before the fire and then woke, sometime after nightfall, and went to the door of Rieth's Rest. She was on the High Plateau, home of the Shee, and the moon was full.

The certainty of her calling, her quest, grew upon her as she went on foot to the Black Menhir. There was no sound far and wide except her own footsteps upon the road. The stillness was quite unlike the stillness of the countryside, of the woods, or of the heather. There was a quality of waiting or listening about it. She stepped off the roadway and climbed up to the stone. The turf was soft under her feet, half overgrown with downy moss.

The black stone rose like a three-sided tower, glistening faintly in the light of the full moon. She stood before the eastern face of this monolith, lifted her arms, and prayed silently to the Goddess. Then in a clear loud voice, she cried out the words that Druda Strawn had taught her for the summoning of the Shee. The words were Chyrian and some so old she could only guess their meaning. Three times she repeated the words, walking to the three faces of the towering stone.

Then, as she had been instructed, she knelt, head bent, and waited. She waited thus, kneeling on the damp moss, for a long time, and received no answer. Her magic ring flashed and sparkled all the time she was near the stone, but still nothing happened. At last she rose up, stiff and disappointed, and in that same moment a wind, coming from nowhere, whirled all around the stone, lifted the hair upon her head, then was gone.

She walked quickly back to Rieth's Rest, feeling sure that the Shee had heard her and not deigned to speak. She had been snubbed by the fairy race. She went to Ebony in the stall, laying her head against the living heat of his warm black neck, and did not know whether to laugh or cry. Before she settled down to sleep again by the banked fire, she thought suddenly of the lance that Vigo the Smith had given her. It had been stuck in the ground with the Malms' banner on the edge of their picnic place; perhaps it had been left for her or carried on to the Halfway House. She thought, too, of the next summoning place: the Green Mound on the edge of the Great Eastern Rift, where Yorath Duaring himself had once communed with the Shee.

Her dream that night was ugly and strange. She saw a woman with thick braids of golden hair crouched in a filthy cave, huddled beneath an old sheepskin. The woman's face was in shadow, but she reached out with one white hand from under the fleece and made elaborate gestures in the air. Gael knew in her dream that the woman was making magic and wondered, still in her dream, if she was a witch imprisoned to be burnt by the cruel Brotherhood of the Lame God, far away in Lien. She knew the woman and did not know her, as it was sometimes in dreams. At length she heard the woman's message, her summoning, muffled by fear:

"Forgive. Help us. Free us from demons."

CHAPTER VII

THE BRIGHT FOLK

Gael went deeper into her sleep and did not remember the cruel dream until she was riding toward the crossroads again as the sun rose.

Her lance was still there, stuck in the ground, only the banner had been removed. Gael Maddoc laughed aloud and said:

"Well rid of them!"

Yet her words had the sour taste of failure. Captain Maddoc could lead her troop of lost ones across the desert, but she could not bring two Eildon nobles over the High Plateau. As she rode on in the autumn sunshine, she found herself falling into a wish-dream: the Malms were at the Halfway House, displeased in some way with Obrist Lovill and Badger Breckan . . . they begged her to be their escort again.

Yet as the day wore on and she could see the tall inn off to the east, she hoped the party had already moved on. She needed rest for herself and her horse, but she had no wish to be under the same roof as the Malms. Her reasons for continuing to the Halfway House alone were private, although she could give out that she was seeing to the Coombe horses. She was determined to try for the Green Mound, and there to once again address the Shee as Druda Strawn had taught her.

When Gael looked toward the Eastern Rift, she always had a thought, a longing for Pearl of Andine, the wise woman who had known her destiny. Yet she believed she must not seek her out. Lady Pearl, she was sure, must have told her all that she felt able. Now Gael passed the road leading off northwest: to Silverlode, and she recalled the stirring tale of

Yorath Duaring that had been set forth for the Summer Riders by the tutor from a great Rift household—yes, Pauncehill.

Now, in the autumn weather; dark clouds were scudding toward her, filling the sky. The weather here on the High Plateau had turned at last; she rode on at a smarter pace and came to the Halfway House in darkness and drizzling rain.

It was a spreading barnlike structure, built of wood and grey stone in the style of the great houses in the Eastern Rift. Faint lights shone out into the rain: inside a fire was lit. Gael took her way to the roomy stable and knew at a glance that the Malms were not among the guests. There were only two shaggy ponies stabled, brown and white; there was no groom though the place was lit with two lanterns. She rubbed Ebony down in the best stall and heaved up her saddle and saddlebags to take them into the house. A third horse nickered anxiously, and there, at the end of the stalls, she found a horse from Coombe. It was the roan gelding with one white foot from the Long Burn Farm . . . Wennle's horse.

"What, have you gone lame?" she asked softly. "Gone lame and been left behind?"

She could see no sign of lameness, but the light was not good; she promised the roan to come again after her dinner. She wondered how the Malms meant to return the Coombe horses if they had ridden them on to the north. Had the party ridden down into the Eastern Rift to find other mounts?

Gael went up the steps and came into the Halfway House from the stable. She remembered the atmosphere of the place, which was welcoming, almost cozy, although the building was shadowy and vast, with a vaulted roof. There were two hearths, in the west and in the east, but now only the eastern fire was lit.

Well-worn settles and generous tables provided room almost for an army; overhead hung two huge round candleracks, each with a few sputtering candles. Two staircases, to the west, led to a gallery with finer rooms for noble guests. Along the southern wall there were curtained cells which contained pallet beds for other travelers.

Tonight there were two attendants in the house—a tall woman stirred a cauldron over the fire, and a young man came to take her saddle. She had seen others, years past in the summertime, and recalled that they were all of the same family, name of Cluny. The young man was short and brown as a Danasken; he smiled but did not speak and motioned her toward the fire.

"How came that roan gelding into the stable?" she asked.

He gave no answer so she walked on and repeated her question to the woman, addressing her as Mistress Cluny. The woman bore a strong likeness to the young man, but she was as tall and bony as he was short and well covered; she took a long look at Gael Maddoc.

"The horse is from Coombe," said Gael, "hired by a party bound for the king's court. Have they gone through? Why was the horse left?"

Still the woman said no word, and Gael, for the first time, began to be alarmed. Then the woman made a small gesture of resignation as if she could hold back some news no longer. Gael followed her glance to the chimney corner. An old man sat there shivering, wrapped in his cloak. His face was marked, his hand, holding the cloak, was wrapped in a bloodstained rag.

"Master Wennle!"

He stared at her with a look of shock and terror that slowly faded into recognition.

"Oh Goddess!" he whispered. "Oh Maddoc! Maddoc!"

He tried to stand, but his legs would hardly hold him. She went to his side, and the hostess, Mistress Cluny, was there offering a leather bottle, with spirit finer than applejack. Gael held it to his lips; he sipped and choked, sipped again.

"Master Wennle," she said, "in the name of the Goddess, what has brought you to this pass? Where are . . ."

"Hush!" he said. "Do not say the name! They are taken!"

He watched fearfully as Mistress Cluny took back her bottle and returned to the fire.

"I should not speak," he said, "or worse will befall. Yet the news must be brought with all possible speed . . . you can help me, Captain. You must have found your good black horse again!"

"I will help you," she said, "but what is this wild talk? Where are—your companions? How are they taken?"

"For ransom!" he said. "You saw nothing amiss? No one saw through those two brigands. Oh Maddoc, if my lord and lady are harmed, life holds nothing for me!"

She took his hands in hers. She understood all at once several things about "Hem Lovill" and "Badger Breckan." How Lovill's garrison, "The King's Longhouse," came out so pat after she innocently named the travelers and their destination. How the kedran escort with the best horse, who might give trouble or ride for help, was quickly dismissed. How Breckan deliberately sent Ebony to bolt over the plateau.

"Master Wennle," she said urgently, "you must put all your trust in me. Tell me the tale!"

Wennle drew a long, shuddering breath.

"We rode on," he said, "while you were almost out of sight, chasing your horse. The warrior who gave himself out as Obrist Hem Lovill scolded the sergeant for making your horse bolt . . . I thought it did him credit. My lord and lady were very pleased with their new companion.

"We had lost some time, so the pace was a little faster. As it was growing dark, we came to another crossroads where a track ran off to the northwest. Then of a sudden, Lovill, who rode first, with Lady Malm, seized her bridle, and Breckan, who rode behind Lord Malm and myself, leading our packhorse, uttered a long whistling cry.

"Half a dozen dark shapes rose up from behind the bushes and were all amongst us. Two seized my bridle. Breckan held a huge dagger at the lord's throat, and when I cried out and tried to break free, I was struck from my horse by one of those on the ground. Lovill swung a halter of rope about Lady Malm's neck; he called to his creatures for light, and there were torches. Then he spoke up in a loud voice and said they were his prisoners: the hostages of Tusker Lovill, the Wild Boar.

"Then Lord Malm spoke or asked to speak, and when the knife was taken from his throat, he begged this brigand to take him alone and the gold they carried and let his good lady go free, for she was on an errand of mercy. But Lovill told him to be silent, and Breckan gave the lord a blow on the head.

"Then we were all forced a short way along the track; I was made to walk with my hands tied behind, and two of the brigands rode upon my horse. I did not see plainly what happened next, but there was a little flash of light, and Lady Malm tried to escape. I believe she used a simple bit of magic, a hand movement and a spell that twisted her halter from Lovill's grasp. But her horse stumbled, and Lovill cried out again, calling her a witch and worse names. And then . . . oh Maddoc . . ."

Wennle shook his head, and his face, turned to hers, was deathly pale with staring eyes.

"What, Master Wennle? What was it?"

"There was a strange light," he whispered. "The torches burned with a strange greenish light. It played around all of them, Lovill and Breckan and their followers. They changed before our eyes—their faces—their whole bodies. Maddoc, I swear that they took on the shapes of monsters, hideous, half-human creatures! They reeked, they had slavering mouths and sharp teeth, their hands were huge, hairy, claw-like . . ."

"The Voimar . . ." Gael found herself whispering too. "Creatures from the old tales. I heard they were seen but could not bring myself to believe it."

"It was the shock!" said Wennle ruefully. "I saw Lady Malm, who is a brave woman, faint dead away and slip from her horse. Yet I swear, Maddoc, that their true shape is human, as we first saw the two warriors. This is magic!"

"What happened next?"

"We went on, the whole monster pack, with the lady slung across her saddle. After a few miles, I thought I saw the walls of a town."

"Silverlode," said Gael, "an abandoned mining town."

"I never entered it," said Wennle. "Tusker Lovill drew me aside, just as he was in this terrifying guise. He sorted me out and my horse, while the others went on into the town. A single henchman from the demon pack remained and held me. Lovill was suddenly himself again, yet very fierce.

"He shook me and swore that my lord and lady were lost forever if I tried any tricks. I must ride, he said, on to the Halfway House and on to the king's court and there find ransom for them . . ."

"Master Wennle, they must be rescued!"

The steward slumped in his chair, worn out with the mere telling of his ordeal.

"It would endanger them," he whispered hoarsely. "Who . . . who would rescue . . .?"

"There is the garrison at Hackestell," said Gael Maddoc. "There are the Rift Lords and their followers."

"I was told not to try any tricks."

"How will they fare, the lord and lady, in the hands of such creatures?" she asked. "It will take ten, twenty days, a whole moon of days, to go to the king's court and convince them of the need for ransom."

Wennle had begun to tremble in all his limbs; he could not answer her. Gael looked about for the old woman, who came anxiously to observe the sick man.

"We must put him to bed," said Gael. "See, here is gold for his lodging in one of the rooms."

Mistress Cluny blinked, did not take the money. Between them they half-carried the old man to one of the traveler's cells on the south wall and laid him on a pallet bed with clean coarse sheets. He seized Gael's hand feebly.

"Oh, kedran . . ."

"Rest, Master Wennle," she ordered. "We can undertake nothing till the morning. I will think what is best to do."

She sat by him in the small curtained cell, listening to his rattling breath. Mistress Cluny fetched a draught, which she fed to Wennle; he breathed easier and fell asleep. Gael Maddoc tiptoed away and returned to her place at the eastern hearth. She had her supper, scarcely knowing what she ate. The steward's story had awakened strange echoes of that stirring tale of the Bloody Banquet of Silverlode.

There was a name she recalled from the aftermath of this terrible feast. Huarik the Boar and some of his followers were buried in Silverlode: they had come home no more. Yes, here was the name—Huarik's young wife, mourning her fallen lord, took her infant son home to the hall of her father, Lovill of the Eastmark!

Who could doubt that Tusker Lovill, the Wild Boar, was this same child grown to manhood? Surely, at a word, the Lords of the Eastern Rift would raise a company to root out the young boar whose father had killed their fathers! Gael stirred the remains of her posset with a wooden spoon, shaking her head. This might cost the life of the hostages, Lord and Lady Malm. Perhaps, instead, the Wild Boar, entrenched in the dark underground labyrinths of Silverlode, could be taken by stealth or magic? Who would be bold enough to risk such an effort?

Gael Maddoc saw her ring flash in the firelight, and she thought of another saying of Druda Strawn. She had her answer. "Nothing passes on the High Plateau that is unknown to the Shee."

She looked toward the hostess and the young man who were seated quietly under one of the candleracks, playing Battle. Mistress Cluny came to her at the fireside, bringing drink. Gael Maddoc fixed her eyes upon the old woman and said:

"How came the old man, Master Wennle, to such a pass?"

"How should we know?" answered Mistress Cluny warily. "He told us nothing. He very nearly did not come here at all . . ."

"What do you mean?"

"The roan horse came in riderless, about noon," replied the old woman. "My son, Gwil, followed its tracks as best he could and found the old man where he had fallen and brought him back."

"Mistress," said Gael, with great urgency. "I must speak with the light folk. This is a matter of life and death."

"They will not parley," said the old woman. "Think no more of it!"

"I have words to summon them," said Gael Maddoc. "Shall I cry them out, here in this hall?"

"You are too bold, kedran," said Mistress Cluny.

Her eyes were brown, flecked with gold, and her voice was stronger than it had been.

But Gael Maddoc would not stand down before her. "I have but to ride to the Eastern Rift and tell my story . . . the old man's story . . . of two great Eildon nobles waylaid and captured by the son of their old enemy, Tusker Lovill, son of Huarik," she said. "Even their reverence for the high ground will not hold the Rift Lords. I could return with an army to dig out the Wild Boar from Silverlode!"

"This is wild talk!" said Mistress Cluny. "What have the Eilif lords of the Shee to do with old treachery?"

"Nothing passes upon the plateau without their knowledge," said Gael firmly. "Here are innocent travelers waylaid, who made no trespass. I am their guide, and I *will* have them back again!"

She sprang up then and strode into the center of the mighty hall between the two candleracks. She held out her arms to the empty air and uttered the third and most powerful of Druda Strawn's invocations. The words were old; the gist of them was: "Come scions of Tulach Hearth, come Bright Ones, heed my cry! Be seen in the dark world! Give ear to my true need! Luran, awake!"

Her voice echoed through the Halfway House and fell away into a chill silence. The old woman and her son quickly slipped away. Gael Maddoc walked back to her place by the fire, her steps loud on the wooden floor. She sat with her hands on her knees and let desolation sweep over her as the moments passed and there was no answer.

Her magic ring winked so softly that it could have been the firelight reflecting in its one green eye. She was not alone. In the settle across the hearth there lounged a young man. He wore finely-dressed russet leather, a tunic of antique cut. Gael thought of that moment in the sacred cavern when she first saw Blayn of Pfolben, perfectly handsome.

The young man had fine hard features, as if the skin were tightly stretched over his high cheekbones, his pointed chin. His hair was red-brown, fine and luxuriant, glowing in the firelight as his skin glowed, with a faint bronze luster. His eyes were light brown, very penetrating. His thin brown hand toyed with a heavy chain of gold looped about his neck. He wore rings, one with a yellow stone. He was a strange being, one of the light folk. All men and women, however beautiful, were by contrast earthy, dark, mortal.

"Well, kedran," said the newcomer in a bell-like voice. "I am awake!"

"Lord . . ." said Gael Maddoc as firmly as she could. "Lord Luran, I must ask the help of the Eilif lords of the Shee . . ."

"You have asked before," said her companion. "What is your name?"

"My name is Gael Maddoc," she replied. "Last night, by the Black Menhir, I called upon the Shee with a question of my own. Tonight I ask help for two Eildon nobles, Lord Mortrice of Malm and his wife, the Lady Malveen. They have been taken for ransom by brigands in Silverlode."

"How shall we help?" Luran waved a hand, making her ring sparkle. "This is the violence of the dark and mortal world."

"Not all, lord," she said. "Tusker Lovill, the robber chieftain, has had access to some magic. His followers go about as the Voimar to frighten travelers."

"Mother Cluny is right," said Luran with a sad laugh. "You are very bold, Gael Maddoc. Where did you get that strong summoning? 'Scions of Tulach Hearth' indeed. We had not thought to hear our dear hearth named again by a mortal. What do you know of magic?"

"I have the summoning from a holy man, the Guardian Priest of Coombe, Druda Strawn, who has spoken with you before. I have seen some magic in the Southland, where I served the Lord of Pfolben, and in the Burnt Lands. Lord, I was rescued there and helped to lead others to safety; I found a string of magical tokens that pertain to the lands of Hylor."

She drew out the gold medallions of the Hallows, threaded on their thong. They looked old and dark as she held them toward Luran, but suddenly, as he made some sound, the tokens blazed with golden fire and leaped to his hand. Stranger than all, Gael became aware of others who were present, watching unseen, crowding round. She flung up her head at a sweet, almost twittering sound in the air.

"Hush!" said Luran fondly, not addressing Gael. "It is Gwendyre's home working, for sure. Take the hallow-string . . ."

The string of coins vanished from his outstretched hand. He veiled his eyes and sat with bent head. Gael understood in him, in this Eilif lord, a kind of helpless pity; it seemed to her that there were points of likeness between the dark and the light race. Then without a sound the Hallows, on their thong, were laid gently on the arm of Gael's settle.

"That is truly an ancient token," Luran said at length. "Tell me the tale. Where did you find it? How did you come to the Burnt Lands? You are a kedran of Coombe in the Chyrian lands below the high ground . . ."

Gael cleared her throat, finding herself parched and dry at the very memory of the desert. Luran waved a hand, and Mistress Cluny was there again, wearing a blue surcoat over her workaday gown. She brought two fine goblets and a flagon of golden wine. After one sip, Gael found she could tell the story of her journey to the Burnt Lands pretty well. Nothing was lost on Luran and on those others listening. They understood the terrors of the Afreet and the sandstorm and the shortcomings of Blayn of

Pfolben. They followed Gael and her cohort all the long unknown way through the desert to Seph-al-Ara, the town of the Zebbecks.

When the tale was done, Gael was bold enough to say:

"I believe that these tokens, which Druda Strawn calls the Hallows of Hylor, will lead me on some quest."

Luran smiled.

"Perhaps you have been summoned to perform a service for—for the light folk."

"Anything within my power, lord," she said. "But only when I have freed those prisoners, the lord and his lady."

"Now you are bargaining . . ." grumbled the Eilif lord. "Come, let us see if your nerves are still good."

He rose to his feet; Gael Maddoc strung the golden tokens around her neck and took his outstretched hand. His touch was cool and invigorating: they walked from the eastern hearth to the very center of the vast, shadowy chamber as if performing a dance step. They stood under the largest candlerack, and Luran raised a hand. He uttered a single word in old Chyrian, and it seemed to be simply "Tulach!"

She felt the darkness gathering instantly, moving about her like a dark whirlpool; she was conscious of movement but could see nothing. She felt the hand of Luran still; the experience lasted only a few heartbeats. Then Luran had gone, and she had come to another place.

It was a very old lofty chamber, lined with tarnished, lovely hangings, beautiful as moonlight. The fire in the broad hearth burned green and blue: something stirred on the bearskins before the fire, and she saw that it was a very large dog—a mountain dog, still quite young, with a thick golden coat. She stiffened a little as the creature stood up. The dog came toward her, but with sounds of pleasure, wagging its tail, stretching, eager to be stroked. She dared to sit on one of the padded settles, near a low round table, and the dog laid its great head in her lap. The door of the chamber creaked open, and they came in.

There were four or five of them, and they were difficult to see; they kept flickering in and out of her sight, of her very consciousness. Their voices were like cracked bells, jangling a little, or like birdcalls, or like the sound of the sea. She made out an old man, tall as a tree, but the others were female, the Fionnar, the pale ones, the fair ladies of the Shee, consorts of the Eilif lords.

One thing was certain: all but one of these ladies were very old, as old as the hills, as old as the woods of Eildon, as old as the stones of Achamar, as old as the springs of the Chyrian lands, as old as the sands of the desert.

Gael stood up, and the dog moved back to the hearth rugs where it stood sadly sweeping its tail back and forth, as if hoping to be noticed. Gael made a bow, and the bell voices chimed. The youngest and easiest to distinguish separated from the group. A few shreds of mist swirled away, and Gael was confronted with a beautiful woman, ageless, in a broidered gown of blue and green. Her skin was drawn tightly over her bones and had the magical sheen of her race. Golden hair lay smoothly under her white coif; her eyes were grey and fathomless.

"I am Ethain of Clonagh," she said graciously. "Sit down my child. I see you have made friends with Bran. Let us take some mulled wine."

"Fion Ethain," Gael bowed and sat down again.

There were silver cups and a pottery jug of mulled wine, steaming. Ethain sat down, and two more ladies drew closer, smiling at Gael. One swiftly altered her looks by magic—now she had a round soft face and clouds of dark hair lying in long swathes upon the shoulders of her wine-red velvet gown.

"Myrruad Ap Tzurna," she said. "This is Ylmiane—or that is all the name she goes by."

The old creature wore her years; her eyes were jet black, her face impossibly wrinkled. She was swathed in creamy, silvery fabric of the Shee, a floating bed gown. She peered at Gael and laughed in a strong voice.

"Maddoc," she said, like a bird talking. "Maddoc, Maddoc, Maddoc. You were bred by the Holywell—is it not so?"

"Yes, Highness!" said Gael, bobbing her head.

"There, you see?" said Ylmiane softly to her companions. "It is the one that was to come. Now it is here."

At last the old Eilif lord approached the table by the fire. He adjusted his ancient face and was a handsome knight, enormously tall, with long greyish ringlets, a scar on his cheek, and a long surcoat, quartered with many crests.

"Captain Maddoc," he said in an echoing tone, "I am Hugh McLlyr of the Fishers."

He smiled wryly at her, lifting the corner of his mouth. Gael Maddoc sipped the warm wine and took heart.

"Good Sir Knight," she said, "You are a long way from the Sea!"

And the Eilif lord and all the Fair Ladies burst into laughter at her timid jest. The room rocked with merriment; they applauded Gael and patted her hands with a touch so light it could not be felt. Luran was with them all again, and he nodded approval at her.

"Well, Mother," he said to the Lady Ethain. "You have heard our dear Ylmiane speak. Captain Gael Maddoc could indeed serve us!"

"If we undo this foolish working at Silverlode," said Myrruad in a low voice.

"It was a rash deed," said Hugh McLlyr, "and in a dark season. Let the dark child of Coombe undo the knot. I will ride with her if it would help."

Luran sat down at the round table and his mother, the Lady Ethain, poured wine into his silver cup when it appeared.

"We accept your bargain, Captain Maddoc," she said. "We will assist you in bringing these poor Eildon souls out of Silverlode."

"In return you must ride on quests for us," said Luran. "Some would say this was an honor for one of the dark race . . ."

"Indeed I feel it as the greatest honor . . ." said Gael.

She looked as closely as she dared at the old ones and began to share with Luran feelings of helpless pity for them. All the light folk spoke a little apart in that Old Chyrian she could scarcely understand, then between one breath and the next they had swirled away, leaving only Luran to parley with her. She could not have sworn how they left the chamber—through the open door or simply by vanishing away.

"All!" said the youngest of the Eilif lords sternly, fixing Gael Maddoc with his golden eyes. "All of them, all of us . . . do you understand me? Only folk of the half-blood will remain, here and there in the lands of Hylor."

"I have heard," said Gael Maddoc, almost whispering, "of the Sea Children, and of other magic beings . . . like the Afreet and the Djinni . . ."

"True," said Luran. "And the Children of the Sea, Hugh McLlyr's close kin, are flourishing in their watery element. But the Shee are, to all intent, a lost race. Lost as surely as the unicorn and the white mountain deer, the pied winter geese, the ring adder and the great grey bears—the last one died in Nightwood by the Danmar when Yorath Duaring was still a young lad, roaming that patch of forest."

"Lord Luran," said Gael, "how may I serve the light folk?"

"There are certain tasks yet to be done," he said plainly. "The tying up of loose ends—the settling of certain debts. Enormous discretion is required and boldness and complete truthfulness, as in a good envoy.

"This wandering messenger of the Shee must go far and wide, not only riding like a kedran, but crossing larger distances in the light or magical fashion as we did to come here, to our home, that Tulach Hearth of which you were bold enough to speak in your summoning."

"I can do all this," said Gael Maddoc, "if you put your trust in me. How far have we come as the dark folk measure distance?"

"We are in the region of Goldgrave," smiled Luran.

"You will think this a foolish question," said Gael, "but can a horse and rider be transported in this way?"

"Not foolish at all," said Luran, though he smiled a little. "The magic is strong. With a grand working, one could take the Halfway House and set it down in the market place at Krail, to the stupefaction of Val'Nur and his henchmen."

There was another overtone here and Gael was careful to mark it; although Luran distanced himself from the doings of the race of men, "the dark folk," he was not altogether averse to show his leanings. He seemed not to care for the Lord of the Westmark, Knaar of Val'Nur.

"But first of all we must 'untie the knot' and rescue your Eildon visitors," he continued. "It is time for a first swearing, Gael Maddoc. What would you swear by for a binding oath?"

"Why, we swear at home, I mean in our house, 'by the Goddess and the waters of Holywell,'" she said. "We have always done so. My father and I used this form before the reeve one time . . . and he laughed and said it was very old."

"Excellent!" smiled Luran. "Lay your hand on this holy jewel, for a reminder of the Goddess and her mercy . . ."

He gestured, and there was a golden round, about the size of a small food bowl, and in it was set a huge jewel, unfacetted, glowing with a blue white light. Gael reached out and laid her right hand upon the cold surface of the jewel and repeated the words of the oath of silence that he gave her. Luran did not veil the jewel from sight again but left it in the middle of the table, allowing it to add its own light to the shadowy chamber.

"The light folk have suffered in ages past from the diggings on the high ground," he said, seeing her gaze linger upon it. "We made every allowance for the dark folk and their mining of precious metals and their search for jewels.

"Indeed we do not scorn these things ourselves and have dealt with those of every race who were gold and silversmiths, jewelers—but it was a relief, certainly, when the veins of gold and silver diminished, when the rubies were gone.

"Two years past, the ground moved up here, in our domain, not far from Silverlode, and we were afraid. Our servants told us that at least one new vein of pure silver has been revealed. We will not have it taken out, mined by the dark folk round about, until the Shee have gone . . . you understand me?"

Luran sighed deeply and sipped his wine. He waved a finger at the fire so that it burned up a little; the big vaulted chamber was cold. Bran, the hound, crept close to Luran and laid a paw on his knee, asking for comfort.

"Poor Bran would do better with dark folk," said Luran.

"Is he not one of the Huntress's Own?" asked Gael.

These hounds of legend belonged to the Shee and were as strange and contrary as their masters.

"No," said Luran, "he is a dark dog . . . aren't you, old fellow?"

He sipped wine and went on with his story.

"Before the earthquake," he said, "we had been aware that a warrior from the Eastmark, a young disaffected man, Corvin Lovill, whose true name is Corvin Huarikson of Barkdon, had brought a small company of his men to nest in the empty town, Silverlode. He is landless, for the holdings of his father, Huarik the Boar, were confiscated long ago at the time of the Great King's War. Do you know the story?"

"I do indeed," said Gael Maddoc. "It bears upon the life of our hero in Coombe, Yorath Duaring."

"A charmed life," said Luran, nodding. "I have spoken with Yorath. A man of great modesty and good sense. A worthy hero, if ever there was such a thing. At any rate, it was soon clear that Tusker Lovill, so-called, son of the Boar, was seeking wealth and revenge upon the world. His company scoured the old mine workings for tailings—that was their excuse for coming to Silverlode—and began to rob travelers. The number of travelers over the high ground has gone down, and this is to our liking. No one will go prospecting in the region about Silverlode; Lovill and his band are quite ignorant of the new lode to the west."

Gael knew this was not all, but she did not ask "What of the magic? What of the Voimar?" After a silence, Luran spoke again.

"We yielded to temptation. There are two renegades among them whom we know well. So-called witches, a man and a woman, Fyn O'Quoin and his wife, Catrin. They have taught various spells to Lovill's followers. They are of the half-blood of the Shee; they come from Aird, a village on the plateau west of Goldgrave, where there are many of the half-blood."

"What must be done, lord, to rescue the prisoners?" asked Gael.

She understood it as a small part of the problem surrounding Tusker Lovill and his henchmen. Was she to pluck away two prisoners, during some kind of magical truce, and leave the Young Boar to work his havoc as before?

"I have studied battle plans," said Luran, "and the plans of fortress and keep. This kind of thing makes me queasy. Here, Gael Maddoc, here is Silverlode . . ."

He rapped on the table top and a large irregular piece of stuff seemed to fall out of nowhere with a soft flopping sound. Gael saw that it was not paper, nor parchment nor cloth but, when she dared to touch it, a piece of vellum or other soft, treated skin. The plan of the deserted town was drawn very finely, with side pictures for all the levels underground and for the upper floors of the main buildings.

"You will take a small group of helpers," said Luran, matter-of-fact as ever, "to search the underground. You, as the leader, will be armed with spells of bidding and binding, so-called. You will all be heavily shielded against attack. One part of the quest is more difficult . . . we have spoken of 'untying the knot'; do you know what this means?"

"No, Lord Luran," Gael shook her head.

"The magic makers, the O'Quoins, have 'charmed the ground' as we call it and hidden a witch-quoyle, a large amulet of coiled rope and other things, somewhere in that ground, at Silverlode. It must be found and burnt at once, or it will hamper the rescue."

"Might we not ask the witch-pair—or one or other of them, where the quoyle is hidden?" asked Gael.

"I know what you mean," said Luran. "Put one of them to the question!"

"Not so, my lord," smiled Gael. "I thought of some magic that made a person talk, answer questions truthfully, without need of harsh measures."

"This is not a simple matter." Luran made a gesture of negation. "It is better for you and your followers to find the quoyle with a search device—your own ring might do."

"It has found treasure more than once in the Burnt Lands," admitted Gael, "and it is sensitive to magic."

"The whole venture into Silverlode will be mainly a test of courage and steadfastness," said Luran. "You will bring out the prisoners, Mortrice of Malm and his lady."

Gael said carefully: "Sir Hugh McLlyr has volunteered to come . . ."

Luran sighed again and gave the reply she had expected.

"There is no knight with more courage, but Sir Hugh must not take part. He is too old and too frail. You have acquaintance among the folk of Coombe, Captain Maddoc. Who is to be trusted for this venture?"

Gael had already been racking her brains.

"My brother, Bress Maddoc," she said firmly, "and his friend, Shim Rhodd, son of the innkeeper. I do not know the people of Coombe as well as I should, and the young men I trained with under the rule of Druda Strawn are all away with the Westlings in Krail. I would have the young man of the half-blood, Cluny, from the Halfway House, and Wennle, the Malms' steward, if he has regained his strength. Best of all I would like to seek out two kedran officers from one of the households in the Eastern Rift, if any of the Rift Lords are acceptable to the Shee. I know there is some kedran tradition in the valley."

Luran chuckled.

"This sounds well enough. I will send word to a person of trust in the household of Lord From of Nordlin. But the invitation must come from some other . . ."

"Might not Mistress Cluny of the Halfway House send a message to the kedran captain at Nordlin Grange, asking for two ensigns to ride escort on some nobles?"

"That will do very well."

"Lord Luran," she asked, "how will word come to Coombe for summoning my brother and his friend?"

"We will send to our true servant the Guardian Priest, Kilian Strawn," said Luran. "He will tell the men what they need to know and have them swear an oath of silence."

"If they are asked, they might say they are coming to fetch home the Coombe horses left by the Malms," said Gael.

"Plotting and planning!" exclaimed Luran. "And the light folk are always blamed for their devious ways!"

The fire had burned low on Tulach's hearth; the dog Bran lay sound asleep. They spoke further of the enterprise in a way which showed Gael Maddoc that Luran knew very well how to plot and plan. At last he instructed her in an offhand way in her first magical procedures. She learned words and fingersigns and practiced until she got them right: her instructor was pleased at her quickness. He added certain warnings against magical workings, as they affected "the dark folk," mortal men and women. The valuable "shielding," for instance, must be removed for a pause, after hours of use.

Luran led the way out of the chamber and down the grand staircase into the great hall: fires were banked on two wide hearths, and there a few hooded servants going about. She wondered if any were wraiths, who served those with magical powers. She followed the Eilif lord out into the moonlit courtyard and from there was able to use her new tricks to travel alone through the whirling dark back to the Halfway House, clutching the rolled map of Silverlode.

Mistress Cluny was still awake although the hour was late. She smiled at Gael and greeted her with a warm posset. Gael knew this was from her own new status as confidant of the Shee, sworn into their service. She quickly told the tale of the Malms and how they were to be rescued from Silverlode.

"We have heard of the Young Boar," said the old woman, "but no action has been taken against him by the bright folk."

Mistress Cluny was pleased that Gael had chosen her son, Gwil, to ride in her troop of rescuers. When she heard of Gael's request for two kedran, she nodded wisely.

"There are good strong girls there in Nordlin Grange," she said. "I will send Gwil with a message to their Captain Gleave, asking for two ensigns to come about noon."

She indicated a special cubicle with a soft bed made up: Gael Maddoc slept very soundly at first but then began to dream. A soft dream of flowery fields and the clear sky overhead suddenly became dark: she was plunged again into the dark cavernous place where the woman was imprisoned. Now she knelt up in the straw, flinging back her heavy braids of yellow hair; a faint ray of light caught her face as she made her summoning.

"Come soon! I know you will come! Oh, forgive us!"

And Gael was able to reply, in her dream:

"Yes! Yes! We are coming! Hold fast! You will be rescued!"

The woman was Lady Malm.

II

The day was bleak and cold, but about noon the sun struggled through. When she saw the two kedran come riding out of the last patches of mist, Gael realized how much she had missed her old comrades and the routine of kedran life. She saw that the two women were well mounted on a bay and a dapple-grey, and finely dressed, with much accoutrement, saddle leathers, leather cloaks, baldrics, all marked with the three bird crest of From of Nordlin. She stood aside, saluting, and they rode past her into the stableyard behind the Halfway House. She followed and approached the rider on the bay to help her dismount, but the ensign, who was heavily built and dark, waved her aside.

"See to the lord's daughter," she said.

Gael held the stirrup of the dapple-grey and helped down a tall pale girl with shining brown hair curling from under her cap and a curious set smile. She, too, wore an ensign's knot.

"That groom is far behind on his damned pony!" exclaimed the dark ensign. "We'll have to shift for ourselves."

"Where is the hostess?" inquired the other in a soft, drawling voice. "Are you part of the escort troop?"

"I am the leader," said Gael Maddoc firmly, "and the ranking officer. Gael Maddoc, Captain, formerly of the Kestrels of the Lord of Pfolben in the Southland, now riding escort to Lord and Lady Malm of Eildon."

She gave them a salute and received one back from the dark woman, who spoke her name:

"Ilse Bruhl, Ensign, of the first household troop of the Lord Harel From of Nordlin Grange. I ride with the Lady Ellin From, Ensign."

"Do you know of a Danasken wench named Leshnar who served with the Kingfisher company in Pfolben?" asked Ensign From bluntly.

"Indeed I do," said Gael, smiling. "Was she a member of your household troop?"

"She was a stablehand," said Ensign From. "A Danasken. I heard she was dead in the desert . . . her people were yammering, raising the keen."

"She has come safe home," said Gael, not at all liking this one's tone. "Let us go in, and I will explain this strange duty that has fallen to us."

"One word, Captain," said Ensign Bruhl, who seemed to make nothing of From's rude and haughty manner. "Who gives this duty? Is it the Eildon lord? Whom do we serve?"

"We serve the light folk," said Gael Maddoc. "We serve the Eilif lords of the Shee and their consorts, the Fionnar."

Ensign From gave a nervous splutter of laughter.

"My father's scribe, Old Padric, said as much! I think the high ground drives everyone out of their wits!" she cried. "The Shee? The Fairies? The Ghost horde? Where do you get this crazy talk?"

"Where do you get your manners, Ensign?" said Gael fiercely. "On this showing, I should order you to mount up and ride home!"

"The Lady Ellin has come just a little time past out of Lien," said Ilse Bruhl. "She has been in training for only half a year, and she knows no tradition of the high ground and the Shee."

"She must not only learn that tradition," said Gael bluntly, "but also how to address an officer. What do you say, Ensign From, shall I relieve you of this duty?"

"No, Captain. I apologize, Captain." From spoke in a singsong voice, barely civil, like a wayward child.

Gael, for now restraining herself from making further comment, led the way into the cavernous stable of the Halfway House. While they were attending to the horses, Gwil Cluny came riding up on his pony. When Ellin From ordered him to water her horse, he did so willingly, but gave Gael Maddoc a sidelong glance and a wink.

"Master Cluny will ride in our troop," said Gael, "and so will two young men from Coombe."

She led the way into the inn, where Mistress Cluny was serving an elderly couple out of Goldgrave, traveling south to Rift Kyrie for their grandson's wedding. Gael sat down with the kedran and Gwil Cluny near the eastern hearth, at a big screened table for their special use. The map of Silverlode was spread out, and she bade them all study it.

"I have visited Silverlode once in summer, about four years past," she said, "but I cannot say I know the place. Has anyone else been there?"

"I know Silverlode pretty well, Captain," said Gwil Cluny. "I ran about there as a child with my sister and brothers."

"How accurate is the map?" asked Gael.

She could see that it had been altered several times, and some of the underground levels had been scored out.

"So far as I can tell," said Gwil, "it is true right up to the present."

"Was it made by the fairies?" drawled Ensign From.

"More likely by the half-Shee, at Aird," answered Gwil, seriously, "or some human scribe at Lort, where many of the chronicles are written."

"Ensign Bruhl, Ensign From," said Gael. "Have you been sworn to secrecy in this matter?"

"Captain Gleave said it was a private matter," said Ensign Bruhl, "and we gave our word to keep it so."

"This is sufficient for me, at any rate," said Gael. "I hope the lord we serve will agree."

At this moment there came a gentle knocking at one of the screens, and Wennle joined them. He was still very pale, so that the marks upon his face stood out harshly, but he was himself again. Gael made him known to the two kedran and then said:

"You know, Master Wennle, that we have been given the power to rescue Lord and Lady Malm. Have you regained your strength? Can you tell us the tale again?"

"I can indeed!" said the old man, lifting his head. "And I will ride with you in good heart, Captain Maddoc!"

He sat at the end of the table and in his clipped, dry tones began the tale.

"My master, Lord Mortrice of Malm, of the order of the Hunters in Eildon, together with his Lady, was traveling with all possible speed to the court of King Gol, in his Palace Fortress by the Danmar. Captain Maddoc was our escort, from the village of Coombe. On the second day of our journey as we came from the waystation Rieth's Rest, we were met by two armed men of Mel'Nir. They gave themselves out as Obrist Hem Lovill of the King's Longhouse and Sergeant Breckan, his aide . . ."

Wennle convinced his hearers: even Ensign From grew very still when he told of the trap being sprung upon the innocent Malms, so pleased with these "giant warriors." When he came again to the band of brigands and their fearful transformation into the Voimar, there came a sound of voices in the great hall beyond the screen: the two new kedran jumped. Gael, who knew the sounds well, excused herself and went out to greet Bress and Shim Rhodd.

The pair of them looked the part, she was glad to see: both wore tunics of the Westlings and were accoutred with swords and round shields of wood and metal. She saluted them, and they returned the salute with no more than a trace of a grin.

"Sister!" burst out Bress in a noisy whisper. "What in the name of Old Pigger's Ghost is brewing here?"

"I told you!" said Shim, wide-eyed. "It is the bluggy Voimar. We must fight the monsters, is it not so . . . Captain?"

"More or less," she smiled. "But what we have here is a rescue. We will have magical protection, and your Voimar are nothing but a pack of rogues wearing witch masks!" She sent Bress to the servery hatch to order a round for the whole troop from Mistress Cluny and briefed the young men a little before they went in behind the screen. Wennle had finished his tale. Presently Mistress Cluny came with the light ale for which the Halfway House was well known. A pretty, dark girl, surely another Cluny, followed with platters of food; she smiled at Bress, who gave her his bold look, and served up roast meat, bread, and pickled red cabbage. Everyone was suddenly very hungry. There were comments among the adventurers about the excellence of the food and the openhanded ways of the Shee, for all this came gratis.

"Eat hearty," said Gael, drawing out her knife, "for we must learn well, all this day, and ride out upon our mission at dawn tomorrow."

"What shall we be learning, Captain?" asked Wennle.

"Magic," she said, "and how not to fear it . . ."

CHAPTER VIII

SILVERLODE

It was early morning, and the mist had not lifted. Gael had chosen an old trail with good cover, which would bring the troop out a few miles south of the road to Silverlode. They rode swiftly from tree to tree and took advantage of two small hills, old burial mounds.

Captain Maddoc was not too displeased with her troop—what they lacked in polish they made up for in quickness. Everyone had learned well: Bress and Shim had shown skill in the riding practice in the inn yard; the two kedran picked up the searching and holding cleanly and well. Wennle was strong and levelheaded, eager for the rescue. They even had a name: at supper, the two lads had sung a verse of their jesting song and translated it for Ensign From, who had only a smattering of Chyrian:

Here comes an escort
Fit for a King
In motley shirts and britches.
Are they all out hunting swine
Or are they hounding witches?

So now they were the Hounds, or the Witch-Hounds, and signaled to each other with soft barks and howls as they made their way through the scrub and the wind-twisted trees of the plateau.

The main highway over the plateau, called the King's Way farther north, was a well-made road in the manner of Mel'Nir, paved with stone, wide enough for six "giant warriors" riding abreast on large horses.

Lesser roads and tracks led off to east and west. In the south, the rescue party could see the place where Tusker Lovill had been waiting for the Malms, and the Larch Road, running west, down from the plateau.

To the north, beyond Silverlode and its slag hills, was a wider road that descended directly to Hackestell. The riders were all keyed up, underslept; when a grouse flew up from the thick grass, they shied like their horses. Gael got down and crawled with Ensign Bruhl to the top of the second mound—they looked toward the crossroads and made a summoning.

Gwil Cluny, acting as their scout, appeared beside the horse trough with his brown pony. He made a sign meaning "all clear" to the south, but then he signaled urgently to his left along the misty reaches of the highroad. A party of travelers were approaching from the north: Gael and the ensign could just pick them out beyond the turn off to Silverlode. Gael stood up and signaled "Come in, Scout."

"What'll we do with them, Captain?" asked Ilse Bruhl.

"We must ride out to meet them!" said Gael. "We must see them safely on the road to the Halfway House or at least past the turn-off to Silverlode. It would do no good for our plan if the Boar and his men held these folk for worth robbing and came out some way to seize them or lure them in."

"Captain," said Bruhl, "do you suppose the Young Boar knew that your party, with Eildon nobles, was on the way?"

Gael Maddoc had thought about this possibility.

"We were in plain view on the high ground, and we were not alone," she said. "I saw riders on the Larch Road. The Malms were richly dressed, and they rode with an escort, a servant, and a packhorse."

"That road is a good way off," said Bruhl. "Do you suppose they used magic to spy out travelers? The art of farseeing?"

"A seaman's glass would have done it," said Gael smiling.

She reached into an outer pocket of her saddlebag and brought out a small brassbound glass that she had purchased in the bazaar at Seph-al-Ara, the town of the Zebbecks.

"We must not turn everything to magic," she said.

They took turns observing the party approaching from the north: a small covered cart or traveling wagon and two riders. They were not easy to identify, though at least one could see what they were *not.*

"No men of Mel'Nir," said Bruhl. "No Giant Warriors."

They scrambled down to the others and remounted. Gael gave the news of the travelers and then gave orders.

"We will ride out upon the high road," she said, "and pass the turn off to Silverlode. Ensign From and I will ride ahead and speak with these travelers. Remember the story, Ensign?"

"Yes, Captain! We're awaiting a party from the Eastern Rift."

"Captain," asked Shim Rhodd, "does this spoil our cover for the secret action?"

"It does indeed," said Gael, "but we cannot risk an attack on these travelers just as we intend to make our play."

She led the Witch-Hounds out of cover, and they set out in good style to the north on the broad road, through the mist clouds. The road to Silverlode that they had all seen in their dreams came closer; looking back, they saw that Gwil Cluny was catching up. Nothing stirred as they passed the way to Silverlode: Gael concentrated furiously, comparing the countryside, the grass thick with dew, the twisted trees, the nearer slag heaps and old diggings, with the map they had studied.

Then they were past the mouth of the road; Gwil rode up beside her and said:

"One sentinel, I think, Captain!"

"Where?" she asked. "Thank the Goddess for a good scout, Master Gwil! I saw none!"

He tilted his head to one side and stared clear up into the whiteness of the sky: a solitary hawk or buzzard twirled overhead.

"Is that one of the witches?" she asked. "Or is it some fetch, some watching device?"

"It is both," said Gwil. "Not many folk, light or half-light, turn themselves into birds—like the famed Messengers of the Eildon Falconers. Mostly they send out their spirit in a bird's guise."

"What can we do against the watcher?"

Gwil Cluny had a small crossbow on the front of his saddle, and he patted it with a smile.

"No use taking a shot!" he smiled. "We must behave like travelers."

They went a little way farther along the road. The vehicle approaching was now clearly a carriage, with a hood of grey fabric; the outriders were soldiers, guards, with grey cloaks. Gael was suddenly full of mistrust.

"I will have Master Wennle look over these travelers," she said. "Fall back and send him up, Scout Cluny."

"Aye, Captain!"

Presently, as the carriage drew close, Wennle came to her side. It was part of the plan for him to take a good look at any they met on the roads of the plateau. He was "disguised" in clothes from the Halfway House, a cotton padded jacket of Mel'Nir, with a hood, and he rode a fresh horse.

"I'll pass the time of day," said Gael. "Master Wennle, take a keen look at all the travelers and see if any were in Huarikson's monster pack."

"I will do my best, Captain," he said firmly.

As the entourage came closer still, she saw that all the horses were very fine, with a matched pair of red roans for the carriage. This did not speak for any connection with the Wild Boar. The large crest on the carriage was in gold, red, and green, with three golden bells in one of the quarterings.

"Captain, I read the crest on the carriage!" exclaimed Ensign From.

She was alert and obedient, a good ensign, now that her interest in what they were doing had been aroused.

"Report!" said Gael.

"It is a noble family of Lien—Barry of Chantry," said From. "This will not be the duke, but the younger son, Lord Auric, or some of his household. Moon and Stars know what such folk are doing here in the wilderness of Mel'Nir!"

Gael signaled the others to clear the way, to move to the eastern edges of the road, then she rode forward, with From and Wennle after her. The ensign carried a lance with a pennant for Nordlin, the crest of three birds; now Gael took it herself and dipped the lance politely. The two riders of the escort, men at arms in blue cloaks, spoke to the coachman and crossed to the western side of the road. The carriage drew to a halt.

"Good day to you!" Gael addressed the coachman.

She saw that he was middle aged, clean shaven, with a ruddy complexion and a city look about him. He stared at her, unsmiling, holding tight to the skittish roans.

"Where are you heading, Master?" she continued.

He shook his head, would not utter a word.

"I must speak with your liege," she said in a loud voice.

The carriage was a fancy, light equipage, not entirely suitable for an autumn journey over the high ground. Now a curtain behind the coachman's high seat was whisked back. She could look right into the carriage and see the man whom she could not doubt was its owner. She heard Ensign From's excited whisper: "Lord Auric!"

He was not much older than herself and one of the most handsome men she had ever seen, though in a quite different style from Blayn of Pfolben. His features were aquiline; his full lips curled in a smile that brought boyish dimples to his cheeks. His eyes were a brilliant dark blue, the color picked up in the trimmings of his coat, in his sapphire jewelry. His hair was rich dark red, worn rather long, and it gave him the appearance of paleness.

He was not alone in the carriage: a woman in an enveloping blue cloak and hood sat on his left. On his right was an older man with a wisp of beard, who peered out through a single eyeglass on a long handle.

"Good day to you, kedran!" said Lord Auric Barry. "How is the way south?"

The voice was very smooth and resonant, almost a player's voice.

"My lord," said Gael, "the route south is not safe. May I ask where you are traveling?"

"Oh we are bound to the east, a little," said the young lord. "To the great inn—what's it called?"

"The Halfway House," said Gael. "Here lies your way . . ."

The best paved road to the Halfway House lay only a few yards distant.

"Thanks, good kedran!" said the lord.

He raised a beribboned cane and poked the coachman in the back.

"On you go, Ned!"

Gael and the others drew away; Ned, the taciturn coachman, swung the carriage expertly, and the whole party moved off down the road to the inn. As they rode back to the rest of the Witch-Hounds, Ensign From said:

"I think Lord Auric has drawn up again, yonder by the trees . . ."

"Captain Maddoc," said Wennle in a quavering voice, "I have never seen any of these men before, though the young lord himself seems strangely familiar to me. But what is one so finely dressed as this young duke's son doing out in such an equipage in this place, so out of season?"

"This was a strange meeting," Gael agreed. "Perhaps this mystery will later resolve itself to our satisfaction. Now we must go to our task with all possible speed!"

She glanced down at her right hand, resting upon Ebony's neck: her magic ring still flashed and twinkled urgently as it had done all through the brief interchange with Lord Auric.

"Form up!" she ordered, as the troop came together. "This is the time! We will put on the shields at my word!"

She was deliberately hurrying them along, not giving time to be afraid. It was, she judged, about the third hour after sunrise, called nine by the Lienish clock at the Halfway House.

"They're watching us from the carriage, yonder," said Gwil Cluny.

"We cannot delay!" she said.

They were all in place, looking surprisingly well set up and keen.

"Remember," said Gael Maddoc, "that we are in every way stronger than these brigands, because of our magic. We must not hesitate to use our power and to use the power of our arms to subdue them."

Then she returned the lance with the Nordlin banner and took from the hand of Bress her own lance, with the banner for Coombe. She raised it high and cried out:

"I ask the blessing of the Goddess and of the Eilif lords of the Shee upon our enterprise!"

Then she gave the words for the shields, and there was a crackling in the morning air: the troop gave the response. The horses nickered a little and clopped their feet upon the road. Gael led off at a good walking pace, no more, and they came quickly to the mouth of the road to Silverlode. She smartened the walking pace to a trot.

The road wound through low hillocks covered with greenish brown tussock grass: ancient slag heaps from Silverlode's mining days. As they came within sight of the walls of the town, Gael saw that they had been patched up, here and there, with piled stone and wooden stakes, like a stockade.

Once there had been two gates into Silverlode, the main gate to the south and a smaller eastern gate facing the old road over the plateau, which had run in more or less the same place as the broad new road. The eastern gate had been closed, bricked up, and marked with heavy crossed beams. It had not been used since the bodies of the Rift Lords—Strett of Cloudhill, Paunce of Pauncehill, Keddar of Keddar Grove—had been carried through on their last journey to the Eastern Rift, for burial. As Gael watched, the main gate swung open, letting out two riders.

"On the walls . . ." said Ensign Bruhl.

"Come up!" ordered Gael. "We'll meet these two and go in at the gate!"

She urged Ebony into a good canter, and the others picked it up; they bore down on the two riders. One was on a shaggy brown and white pony, a boy in green; the other was Badger Breckan, on his big troop horse. Gael raised her lance, feeling the magic run all through its length as she uttered the spell; she cried an order:

"Encircle!"

The two riders were surprised, but they let themselves be surrounded.

"Now, friends!" cried Breckan, cheery as ever. "Who have we here? Have you come to a ransom, Master Steward?"

"Oh, more than that!" replied Wennle in his strong cracked voice. "A just reward for a foul deed, eh, Captain?"

For the first time, Badger Breckan recognized the captain of the troop as Gael Maddoc, mounted on Ebony, the horse he had set running over the plateau. The merest shade of anxiety crossed the wide map of his face.

"You wouldn't think of trying any foolish tricks," he said firmly, looking Gael in the eye. "Not with the two pearls of price in our power. The man and the woman."

"We're armed against you," said Gael, loud and harsh. "Bring us into the Boar's Lair, Breckan, or by the Goddess, you will lie in earth, like a true badger!"

Breckan did not believe her, but he was a shade unnerved. He gave some order under his breath to the young lad, who began to swing his pony toward the widest gap in the circle, a space between Bress Maddoc and Shim Rhodd. Gael gave her own order:

"Strike and bind!"

The action worked like a charm indeed. Raising the wooden pole of his lance, Bress tapped the boy behind the head so that he fell forward onto his pony's neck. Together with Shim, he chanted a line, and they clashed their lances rhythmically together over the slumped figure. Horse and rider became absolutely still, bound as if frozen by the simple spell. They had all tried it on each other the previous day, and Gael recalled the cold absence of sensation, the dreamlike fading of the world. When the spell was released, some of the horses had been upset. Now Ebony stamped and snorted along with From's handsome dapple-grey gelding, as they recognized the spell again.

Badger Breckan did not keep still; he drew his sword, roared out, and tried to turn. Gael advanced; he struck at her boldly with his broadsword and could not come to her because of the magic shield. She slid the point of her lance through the invisible barrier, and brought it up under Breckan's chin.

"Rein in, Badger," she said. "Or my hand will not be steady!"

Already, with the grip of his mighty knees, he had brought the charger to a standstill.

"Lead us in to Silverlode," said Gael. "No foolish tricks!"

He croaked out some words—she let him speak.

"The boy . . . spare the boy . . ."

"He will stay here until we lift the spell," she said. "There is no danger in it unless he remains bound for too long . . . now bring us in."

The big man obeyed, wild-eyed. He led them toward the rough gateway, and Gael saw that it was in bad repair—the Wild Boar relied on magic, not on wood or stone. She questioned Breckan quietly as they rode along.

"How many in your liege Huarikson's troop?"

"Thirty or so, with the servants and helpers," he said.

He was not surly or unwilling. Gael could not tell if he had simply changed sides once cornered; she could not trust him.

"Where are the O'Quoins, man and wife?" she asked.

Badger Breckan spat convincingly into the grass.

"Oh you can have *them,* Captain!" he said. "I'll give you the pair of them!"

He turned his head and stared back, between the riders, to where the boy in green remained slumped upon his horse in the cold landscape.

"Those damned half-blood Shee have set up shop in the second lodge to the west of the Roundhouse—has a painted sign for Yorath and the men of Cloudhill who were assigned to the place years past."

"For the Bloody Banquet!" said Gael.

They had been using the common speech, but now she spoke in Chyrian, and sure enough Breckan did not understand until she quickly translated. She said to Bress and Shim Rhodd:

"First, when we're in, you two must place a triple binding around the stone hut marked for Yorath and the men of Cloudhill. You know where it stands?"

"Aye, Captain!" they chorused grimly.

Before they came too close to the gates, Gael said to Badger Breckan:

"Get down and leave your horse out here to graze."

He was unwilling, and she moved her lance, saying:

"What, are you afraid it will bolt over the high ground?"

When the big man had dismounted, Bress led away the big, docile charger to a green place. Breckan gave a brief hail, and the broken gates were opened. They rode slowly into Silverlode. The place was rather tidier than Gael had expected; the brushwood and weeds had been kept down. It had the same aura of emptiness and loss. The lofty stone Roundhouse, the Commissariat roundhouse, and the scattering of smaller buildings all cast long black shadows. Women were drawing water at a new well; there were five, six, armed guards lounging on the framework that did duty for a battlement on the south eastern wall.

Gael and her troop of Witch-Hounds rode steadily into the middle of the yard, to a water trough with a hitching rail, directly before the Roundhouse steps. One of the massive doors of the Roundhouse was open, and a man in a dark brown tunic, fancily cut, ran out on to the steps. He darted his hands, fingers extended, at the troop; then came a fearful crackling sound as his magic bounced off their shields. Gwil Cluny shouted "O'Quoin!" at the same moment as Gael raised high her lance and pronounced the Grand Bewitchment, the Stillstand, the stone hour.

She saw it work, serially, from west to east, clamping down on a party of men carrying harness, then on the women at the well, then the men on the scaffolding: one was caught off balance and fell to the ground. Only the witch, O'Quoin, was not held rigid, for he had a personal shield, but he was kept to his place on the steps. And Gael believed that he looked toward the hut for the men of Cloudhill.

"Dismount!" she ordered Bress and Shim. "Encircle that hut yonder! Triple strength. He cannot stop you."

"Master Cluny," she said. "Speak to O'Quoin, as we planned."

Gwil Cluny got down and tethered his pony. Before he could walk to the steps, men came crowding out of two of the smaller houses, ten, fifteen, twenty, some wielding swords. As they came into the yard the Bewitchment seized them, the leaders sprawled and others fell over them, and they lay in grotesque stiffened heaps, as if turned to stone. Three women, together with two young boys, came out of the Commissariat roundhouse and stood bewitched like all the rest.

"How is the count, Breckan?" she demanded. "We have at least thirty of the Young Boar's folk in the yard . . . how many are still hidden?"

The big man was sweating with fear and impatience.

"How shall I know, Captain?" he panted. "A few . . . the lord is in his headquarters, in the Roundhouse. That damnable O'Quoin hag is entrapped by your boyos there. . . ." He pointed to the Cloudhill hut.

"There is only one way you can shorten this exercise, Sergeant," said Gael Maddoc. "Where are the prisoners?"

Breckan growled and shuffled his boots in the dust.

"Are they in the underground rooms? Can we go in through the kitchens?"

He nodded sullenly.

Gwil Cluny had pressed on to the steps of the Roundhouse and Gael observed that his shield could just be seen, as a faint golden radiance, surrounding his body. He spoke to the witch, O'Quoin, and straightaway, while they parleyed, Gael went on to the next, the most difficult part of the action.

"Well, kedran," she said, "are you ready? Do you see the way?"

"Aye, Captain," chorused Bruhl and From.

"Captain Maddoc," said Wennle, "I pray you—let me go with the ensigns! I must find my lord and lady . . ."

"Of course," said Gael, "but have a care of yourself, Master Wennle!"

The two ensigns and the old steward broke off and rode at a slow walk to the Commissariat roundhouse; Shim Rhodd, on his way back from encircling the Yorath hut, followed Gael's high signs and went to attend to their horses. Bress came back to her at the horse trough and said in Chyrian:

"Other side of the Yorath hut is something we could use—I mean for the lord and his lady!"

"What's that?"

"A covered cart—almost a carriage. Not so fine as that one we just saw on the road, but I warrant the Boar himself rides in it with his fancy women. It has two good greys in the shafts, and they are bewitched, poor creatures."

"We'll have it then," said Gael, returning to the common speech. "Can you loose the greys as you were shown, bro?"

"Aye, Captain!" he said, teasing.

"For the Goddess's sake, don't make a botch!" she said. "Bring the thing over here—but not between us and the Roundhouse."

She felt exposed and endangered, despite all her magical protection, standing there with only a few horses and a prisoner. Suddenly there was a burst of movement, the pattern changed. As Bress came from behind the O'Quoins' house, driving the grey horses harnessed to the covered cart, there was a loud clattering sound from the roof of this simple Roundhouse. It took Gael a moment to realize that it was made by bricks and tiles showering from a hole in the roof.

The air was filled with a loud screaming cry, uncanny, half-human. Something moving very fast, so that it could be seen only as a blur of light, shot straight up into the blue morning sky above Silverlode.

Gael Maddoc reacted with a mad swiftness that she associated with magic itself: she directed her charged lance at the flying object and uttered a different holding spell. She saw in her mind, like a diagram or a battle plan, the domed shape of the holding spell that was presently operating in Silverlode. Luran had pointed out that there was a space above the town where the spell did not work—where a witch, for instance, or its familiar, might fly safely. But now the witch, Catrin O'Quoin, making a bid to escape, was caught and held thirty feet above the ground. She could be clearly seen as a small, dark woman, in a green gown, clutching a dark cloth bundle. She was in an awkward posture, her skirts clinging to her limbs; she was held upright as if she would dance upon the air.

Her husband, Fyn O'Quoin, who had been talking angrily with Gwil Cluny, let out another cry. He ran down from the steps of the Roundhouse, waving his hands, and cried out to Gael Maddoc.

"Captain! Captain! Hold steady!"

"Keep back, Master O'Quoin," said Gael. "I have a steady hand . . ."

"Where d'you get these tricks!" he cried. "Hold steady!"

His sharp, dark, Chyrian face was twisted with anxiety; he mistrusted her grasp of magic as well as her hold on the lance.

"You have been told the truth!" said Gael. "We come in the service of the Eilif lords of the Shee, your kinsfolk, and they have granted us these powers!"

She shifted her lance a little, knowing it was a cruel thing to do; the figure of Catrin O'Quoin moved above them, very slightly, in the empty air. Fyn O'Quoin fell on his knees and held out his hands to Gael on her tall horse.

"I implore you!" he said. "For the love of the Goddess, let me lower her to the ground."

Gael had no stomach for it, but she knew she must use this advantage. She did not look at him but at the woman above them.

"Summon your witch-quoyle to your hand, Master O'Quoin!" she said fiercely. "Abort its power and give it to Gwil Cluny, our scout. Not until then will I lower your wife to the ground!"

O'Quoin came wearily up off his knees, his eyes fixed upon the figure of Catrin, his wife. He cursed under his breath, rubbed his hands together, and made a stylish gesture that Gael recognized as that of a person truly adept in magic. He raised his left arm above his head and moved the fingers, uttering a few soft words in old Chyrian.

The dark cloth bundle that Catrin O'Quoin was clutching came away from her arms with a shower of golden sparks that hung in the air like falling stars. It dipped down, floating, to Fyn O'Quoin's hand; he held it at arm's length and said loudly in Chyrian:

"Sleep now, little heart, true helper!"

The bundle, as long as his own forearm, moved once, then was still. He flung back the cloth wrapping and revealed a piece of curved metal, like a digging tool, a length of rope dyed a brilliant red, intricately twisted around the handle. Gwil Cluny took it in his hands and said:

"It is safe, Captain!"

"Captain, have mercy—let her down!" cried O'Quoin again.

Badger Breckan swore under his breath and murmured to Gael:

"Don't trust them! Don't let them come together!"

Gael Maddoc rode out a little on the restless Ebony, holding her lance very steady, trained upon the witch in the air.

"Master O'Quoin," she said. "Your time in Silverlode is over. Fly up to your wife, take her in your arms, and bring her away yonder, to the northwest: go down from the high ground by Hackestell Fortress. Remember I can strike at you while you're within the range of my magic lance . . ."

"Thanks!" panted Fyn O'Quoin. "Thanks, Captain. We are in your debt."

He was concentrated on his wife—she could hardly doubt his sincerity. He clapped his hands to his sides and went whirling up as his wife Catrin had done; he did exactly as he was told. Gael released the binding spell from the lance, and Catrin O'Quoin went limp in her husband's arms. He carried her in a darting movement, nothing like the flight of a bird, and went over the old wall to the west of Silverlode. Gael rode out, tense and ready for tricks, but there were none. There was a clear view out of the town, and she saw the pair dip down over the edge of the high ground, hovering above one of the roads to Hackestell.

"Captain!"

Ensign From cried out behind her. She had come from the Commissariat roundhouse, from the cellars underground; she supported Lady Malm, and Shim Rhodd had left the tethered horses and come to help her. Gael was shocked by the sight of the prisoner: Lady Malm could barely speak, she was half-conscious, dirty, in disarray, all her fine clothes stripped away except for a few petticoats. Quite to Gael's surprise, none of this seemed to be the lady's greatest care. "My fleece," she whispered piteously. "Where is my fleece?"

Gael looked at Ensign From, who shrugged, and showed the Captain the richly worked piece she held under her arm, a once-white fleece that had suffered along with its mistress in the cell below Silverlode. The edges were marked by a curious branding, in a decorated Eildon script with which Gael was not familiar. "We found the lady sheltered with it," From said to Gael, in quiet aside. "Of course we did not leave it behind."

Gael now recognized this object as the fleece she had seen the first night in her dream. She was not sure what to make of the lady's fierce attachment, but now was not a time for questions.

"Put the poor lady in the carriage," she said. "Stay with her, Ensign From."

"I have the medicines and comforts Mistress Cluny made up," said From. "Captain, there'll be trouble bringing out the old lord . . ."

There was a confused roar from the Commissariat roundhouse; Ensign Bruhl came out first into the morning sunlight, then Wennle, heaving along the struggling figure of the old lord, his master. He spoke to Lord Malm, doing his best to soothe him; he was assisted by a stranger, a heavily built young man, another prisoner, who held Lord Malm by his left arm. Shim Rhodd went to help. Malm struggled fiercely, but he was weak and had some kind of leg wound. At last Gael dismounted, tied up Ebony in the charmed circle with Sergeant Breckan.

"Sergeant," she said, "this will soon be at an end. You have done what you were asked. Pray you hold out a little longer."

"Why have you done all this?" he demanded. "For that mad old man who treated his kedran escort like dirt?"

"I am his kedran escort!" she answered. "I know my duty. And I know my duty to Coombe Village, which I promised to serve well. I look to see more than the lord and lady, Sergeant Breckan!"

"What else?" he asked.

"Their horses, from Coombe, together with the Malms' saddlebags. Along with some hundred royals in gold that the lord carried."

He hung his head. Gael strode over and confronted Lord Malm, who was a fearful sight, purple in the face, his mouth flecked with foam, his eyes red and rolling.

"Lord Malm!" she said loudly. "You are rescued! Peace! Pray you be still!"

The old man checked in his struggling and stared at her, panting loudly. Then it seemed that he knew her and this set him off again.

"Med—Meddoc!" he growled. "Damned Chyrian pack . . . . Stink of the midden! Dare to lay hands on us! Awake! To arms! The Hunters to the rescue!"

Gael raised a hand and bound him into stillness where he stood.

"He should be ashamed, this lord!" burst out Ensign From. "You have woven this whole web to rescue him and his lady, Captain."

"Oh, he has had too much to bear!" cried Wennle. "My dear lord—see, you are free! I swear he will come to his right wits . . ."

"Let us have him in the carriage," said Gael. "You too, Master Wennle."

She looked at the young man, the other prisoner, who had assisted with Lord Malm. He was pale faced and his hair was black; he wore a grey tunic and over it a scholar's gown. He was looking at her strangely—with awe? with fear or admiration?—watching the blue spark that lighted her lance's tip.

"Are there other prisoners below ground?" she asked.

"No, Captain," he said. "I was being held for ransom alone, till these noble folk were brought in."

He bowed his head to her and said:

"My name is Tomas Giraud, of Lort. I am a scribe."

"You will come out with us," she said. "The old lord must be placed in the carriage . . ."

This difficult action was performed without magical assistance; Lady Malm cried out her lord's given name, "Mortrice!" in a faint high voice. Gael said to her troop, cryptically:

"Draw together for a long lifting!"

The ensigns took up positions on either side of the carriage. Bress drew his horse alongside the two greys in the shafts and soothed them;

Shim Rhodd rode close behind the carriage, leading Wennle's horse. Under the cover, the old steward and the scribe, Tomas Giraud, sat with the poor Malms, propped on pillows.

Gwil Cluny prepared to mount his pony and join the group, but Gael held up a hand to him.

"Captain!" called Ensign Bruhl. "I pray you, come out with us all!"

"Gwil and I will come a little later . . ." said Gael Maddoc.

She prepared the spell carefully and deliberately—walked right round the carriage and its attendant riders, uttering to herself the marking formula. Then she walked to the Roundhouse, went up three steps, and stood there side by side with Gwil, looking around at Silverlode. She saw all the men and women who followed the Wild Boar stock-still in strange attitudes or fallen in heaps, and she felt a deep distaste for her work. She called loudly:

"Be ready!"

Then she raised her lance and uttered the words for a long lifting. There was an immediate, loud crackling in the air overhead, and a cloud of sparkling blue mist settled over the place she had marked. It hung there for as much as thirty pulse beats; Gael thought of Luran's words about bringing the Halfway House down in the midst of the city of Krail. The mist cleared slowly; the carriage, together with eight human beings and seven horses, had gone, hopefully to the chosen field behind the Halfway House.

"I must do this!" she said to Gwil. "The Eilif lords have brought us so far and will not desert us now."

"Yours to command, Captain," said Gwil wryly.

"Then fetch Badger Breckan to me, from our charmed circle just there," she said. "Put our shield upon him. Loose the circle entirely—our two horses should stand here by the steps. We will leave quickly."

Gwil Cluny did as he was told; Gael had always a thread of anxiety for her horse, Ebony, but he was taking it all quietly. Badger Breckan stood at the foot of the steps with the shocked look of those who had seen powerful magic done.

"What more d'ye want, Captain?" he panted. "I'll do my best with the horses and the gold."

"I will go in and parley with your master," she said. "I must speak to Corvin Huarikson."

"No!" he said. "No, I'll not betray . . ."

"I will speak with him!" said Gael Maddoc. "I've harmed no one here today, have I, Breckan? Trust me! Lead us in!"

He stared into her eyes, then made his decision and walked past her, up the steps and into the Roundhouse. She and Gwil followed him closely into the old high-domed hall; a young servant boy who had been watching behind the door ran off. It was dark after the sunlit yard: the tiled roof, with its heavy beams, had been mended a little over the years. There was an arrangement of shutters letting in the yellowish daylight. Gael strode to the very midst of the round hall, taking in the shadowed gallery, the door to the old kitchens. This was the scene of the Bloody Banquet of Silverlode. A long table stood before her, with a red cloth, and she remembered bunches of evergreen set out five summers past by the Memorial League—the women of the Rift.

Gael made out two, three figures seated at the table, with food and dishes on the red cloth. She had time to single out the leader, Corvin Huarikson or "Tusker Lovill, the Wild Boar," as he called himself. Then there was a single note high in the air, like a plucked harp string, and the air burned green. The shadowy figures at the table rose up, their heads grew and writhed: instead of hands, they held up huge claws; jaws opened upon long fangs.

"Yield or you will die!" roared out the Wild Boar in his monstrous disguise. "I am empowered in this place!"

At the same moment, Badger Breckan shouted:

"Lord! Stop and parley! They're full of magic!"

His master gave a slow, thunderous sound of rage and came out over the long trestle table with a bound. Gael made a small circling movement with the tip of her lance and uttered a few short words of unbinding. The monster, with a mighty, boar-like head and sharp tusks, fell to the dusty floor of the Roundhouse. The spell was broken: a giant warrior of Mel'Nir scrambled up again: "Obrist Hem Lovill," as she had first set eyes on him by the crossroads. His fury was real enough.

"There'll be a harsh reckoning!" he growled. "Badger—?"

"Hem Lovill, speak with me!" said Gael.

"And what are you, kedran?"

"I am the one empowered here!" she said. "And by the Eilif lords of the Shee. Will you talk, or should I bind those monstrous witch masks upon the heads of your two friends, yonder, bind them so that they never come off?"

He glanced back at the two maskers behind the table, with the heads of a bull and a bear. The fight went out of him, and he turned back, saying:

"Pray you, remove the spell, as you did with me. I'll parley."

She moved the tip of her lance twice more, carefully directing it and repeating the words. The two maskers were revealed as young women, one dressed as a battlemaid.

"Hem Lovill," said Gael Maddoc, "or rather Corvin Huarikson. Years have passed since your father died in this place. I do not doubt you have suffered unjustly for his deeds—but your honor is your own. Leave this brigandry—or by the Goddess, with or without my witness, the Rift Lords and the men of Hackestell will soon fall upon you. Have you no land in the Eastmark?"

The Young Boar bitterly resented having to hear this or reply to it, but he said:

"I have a free company to feed and clothe!"

"Then put your trust in the Shee!" said Gael earnestly. "Remain in Silverlode and guard the road honestly. Ask the Eilif lords how you may serve them, at mining perhaps . . . any payment from them would be more certain than this robbers' life."

"How will I come to these lords?" he asked. "O'Quoin and his wife have flown away, so I hear."

"Ride with a few followers to the Black Menhir by Rieth's Rest," said Gael. "Or to the top of the Green Fort, further north. Ask for an audience with the Shee—I am their servant, and I will speak for you."

"Captain," said the big man reluctantly, "I have forgotten your name."

"I am Gael Maddoc, formerly in the service of Lord Maurik of Pfolben," she said.

"You are very bold," said Corvin Huarikson, smiling for the first time.

Gael saluted him and nodded to Gwil. They marched straight to the open door, but someone, whether the Boar himself or one of the women, tried some last trick. There was a noisy crackling in the air and a barrage of lights, floating flames. Badger Breckan interposed himself with a roar:

"Stop that! She can strike us down! Let it be, Tusker, for the Gods of Blood, let it be!"

Gael shouted to Gwil through the spreading chaos; they raced out and vaulted into their saddles like heroes of old time. They rode breakneck out of Silverlode, leaping over entranced soldiers, women. The rickety gates were opened wider by her shouted spell and the twitch of her lance, then slammed shut behind them. They reined in a little and Gael said, panting:

"We'll free the boy . . ."

There he was, slumped over his pony's neck. When Gael removed the spell, he blinked at her and asked sleepily:

"Da? Are you there? What's doing?"

"You must not go in to Silverlode for another half hour or so," said Gael.

"My Da!" he said fearfully. "What have you done with him? Why would he leave Goldheart, his horse, yonder?"

"What is your name then?" asked Gwil Cluny.

"I'm Alwin Breckan!" he said proudly.

"Your father has come to no harm," said Gael Maddoc, smiling a little. "I suspect he will soon come out and fetch you.

"Mind what I said," she went on, moving away. "Take my word and do not go in the gate until you hear a great commotion there in about one half hour . . . the time it takes the shadow of that tree, yonder, to move as far as the grey rock."

So they rode swiftly away from Silverlode in bright sunlight, leaving Badger Breckan's young son staring after them.

II

"We are both in good heart, my lord and I!" said Lady Malm, smiling. "Depend upon it, Gael Maddoc!"

The lineaments of the lady's proud, handsome face had not changed. It was still possible to see in her the same woman who had treated Gael and others so ill. Yet now she was smiling and pleasant. Gael thought of telling it all to Druda Strawn, one day, as a kind of miracle.

Gael looked from a high window in the Halfway House, in the special rooms kept for noble guests. Down below there lay a fair round field, where no crops were planted, where the grass grew high and green, intertwined with wild flowers. It was clearly a blest round, or a cantreyn, a place for dancing and rituals—and a place for magic. In this round field, the precious caravan had landed, by magic, just as it had been planned, carrying the Malms and the others. The carriage from Silverlode still stood there among the wild flowers: Gwil Cluny and a stable boy were just beginning to draw it away, to prepare for the final part of the journey.

In the fine room where Lady Malm had spent four days recovering from her ordeal, a slim, dark girl was going about finishing Lady Malm's packing. This was Lyse Cluny, Gwil's cousin, perhaps his sweetheart, and Gael saw that the simple addition of a lady's maid to the original party out of Coombe might have worked wonders with her ladyship's disposition. In the next door chamber, they could hear the rumble of Lord Malm's great voice and the sound of his laughter, then the sharper tones of Wennle, preparing his master for the road.

Everything, she conceded, had worked out very well. If she was still untrusting and watchful, it was because of all the magic, the stress, the responsibility. At least the money was more or less right for Coombe and for all those who had been enlisted to help in the action.

It had been a good moment, she admitted to herself, when one of the Wild Boar's men and the young lad, Alwin Breckan, rode into the stableyard on the second day after the rescue, leading the three Coombe horses and the handsome sorrel of Tomas Giraud, the scribe. All the saddlebags were full to the last thread: there was Lady Malm's jewel box, untouched, and two purses of gold . . .

There had been a fond leave-taking on the morning of the third day: Ensign From and Ensign Bruhl received ten royals from the Malms and rode off back to Nordlin at the head of the Rift.

Bress Maddoc and Shim Rhodd, true sons of Coombe, had ridden home to the village carrying gold for the reeve, plus two royals each and a personal letter from Lord Malm thanking the reeve for "the work of the special escort troop led by Captain Maddoc." Bress and Shim had the task of telling the reeve, privately, what had taken place. Gael expected a great saga would come of it. She sent fond words to her mother and father but could not tell them when she would be home again—perhaps at the year's end.

"So fine . . . fit for a prince!"

The voice of Lyse brought her back. The little maid and Lady Malm had unfolded on the bed a package wrapped in pale silk that had also come from the saddlebags. It was full of swaddling clothes and fine wrappings—fit for a royal child. For now, at last, the reason for the Malms' journey to the court of King Gol was known. The family of Malm belonged to the knightly order of the Hunters, led by Prince Borss Paldo, and Lady Malveen of Malm was a midwife.

In the Palace Fortress by the Dannermere, a young princess of Eildon was soon to give birth: Elwina Paldo Duaring, wife of Prince Rieth, the King's nephew and heir to Mel'Nir's throne. Yes, certainly, the healers and midwives of Mel'Nir would be attending the Princess; there was an element of discretion about the visit of the Malms. Perhaps Princess Elwina would like to see a familiar face. Perhaps an Eildon midwife with a knowledge of magic appropriate to her calling would be a good person for the princess to have at her bedside in a foreign court.

The Eildon fleece Lady Malm had been so loath to leave in Silverlode—it belonged to this part of her equipage. Gael had not asked, but she was sure it held some Eildon magic. It lay there on the bed, holding pride of place among the young prince-to-be's clothes, rendered snowy white and cleaned by the touch of some small spell, and marked with the Eildon script that Gael could not read. It was a fine piece, and made her wonder about the only Hallow the Druda had not properly described to her, the Fleece—of Lien, it must be, for all the other countries, save Athron, had their Hallows named, and Athron, of all the countries of Hylor, did not have a long magical history. Gael, looking at Lady Malm's fleece (which it seemed the lady had taken some care *not* to describe to her), wondered if the Hallow Fleece, like Mel'Nir's Lance, the Krac'Duar, was considered so sacred that it was wrong even to speak aloud its name. Whatever the case, it was clear that it, too, was missing, along with the Lance and the Chyrian Cup.

She dutifully admired the fine baby clothes, then excused herself and went out onto the gallery. At the foot of the stairs stood a tall, well-built young man in a dark green tunic and a decent scholar's gown, trimmed with plum velvet: Tomas Giraud in his best clothes. She was pleased to see him; he was a serious young man, and she could not doubt his honesty.

This Tomas was by his birth a Lienish man; his parents had crossed the border into Mel'Nir the year Lien had become a kingdom, almost fifteen years past now. From Lort his family had retained their Lienish connections, and done much business for their old country. Tomas had told her promptly how he had come to be imprisoned in Silverlode. He had been traveling on a private but not especially secret errand for a rich man out of Lien. In fact, for Lord Auric Barry, whom he had planned to meet at the Halfway House. His task, for which he was to be well paid, had been to purchase a book. This was a true Book of Light, an illuminated sheaf of manuscript, listed in the scrolls, and owned by a master scribe and collector, Nostris of Rift Kyrie. The original makers of the marvelous book were scribes out of Lien, and their work told of the Lands of Hylor and its rulers before the Farfaring, the coming of the Men of Mel'Nir.

The purchase had been completed and the price paid, some at once and some with a bond signed by Lord Auric and his factor, Tomas Giraud. There was no thought of robbery: but since the book was precious, Tomas had arranged not to carry it himself—a merchant caravan with a sturdy escort brought this book of light, *The Elder Kingdoms,* up to the plateau along with their other goods and were to deliver it to Tomas and to Lord Auric at the Halfway House. In fact, this last had already taken place—the young lord had received the book even before he knew the fate that had fallen upon his factor. For indeed Tomas, on his way to the meeting place, had been seized near Silverlode by ten or more of Huarikson's henchmen. They took his remaining gold and his horse and flung him into their underground prison. He had not been able to send word to the Halfway House before the Malms were brought in and imprisoned nearby.

So the book was never in danger. Gael asked if Lord Auric was a collector of such things? Tomas smiled and said that *The Elder Kingdoms* had been purchased as a gift, and Gael learned for the first time of what would take place in the spring, in one of the older kingdoms. The young Queen Tanit Am Zor, one of the paired Daindru queens of the Chameln lands, was to be married in the spring. Tomas was not even sure where the ceremony would take place—in the Chameln's fabled city of Achamar or in the beautiful city upon the plains to the south, Chernak New Town. The bridegroom, yes, it was a lord out of Eildon, only a year or two older than the bride. It was Count Liam Greddaer, great-nephew of the Duke of Greddach, far famed indeed for a collector of all kinds of rich and curious things, on his wide acres at Boskage. He was sure, Tomas confided, that the politics of the match were enlightened. Raised up as the young queen's consort, a noble from Eildon, the ancient founder of the land of Lien, would moderate the fanatic hatred of the Brotherhood for the Land of the Two Queens.

Gael was surprised. In the four years she had been deep in the Southland, she had heard little of Lien and the grimly changing style of its government. Certainly, the Druda had hinted a little of this, that day she'd ridden to his house, begging help to write the Bretlow letter, but at least in Coombe, she had seen nothing of any rising Lienish influence—indeed, Ensign From and her terrible manners had come as a complete surprise to her, a revelation, and an unpleasant one. Bruhl had since confided that Lord Harel From had set his daughter to training as a kedran in part as tonic for the dangerous manners she'd brought home from Lien's court: for she had returned not with the polish of a court lady as he had desired, well versed in the social graces, art, and poetry, but rather with a dogmatic, almost angry poise, full of lecturing and bitter words against the freedoms allowed to Mel'Nir's women—manners most unsuitable to a Rift Lady who must manage a kedran guard when she came to rule her own house, along with a household of women who had never questioned their right to work alongside the house's men.

In Lien, the power of the Brown Brotherhood was still growing. Age had settled on Lien's king's shoulders, and in his weakness, the Brown Brotherhood had found their strength.

To a Chyrian woman like Gael, it was an unwieldy puzzle. She had never thought to travel to far-off Lien. Its fine ways and abhorrence of kedran training had set her deep against it. These things were bad enough without its influence and manners penetrating Mel'Nir's borders.

Yet now, looking down the steps at Tomas Giraud—his warm, thought-filled eyes and his fine mouth—even knowing him for a man of Lien, Gael found herself thinking: *I have found a friend. One who understands . . .* A scribe and a kedran! She had to smile. No one she knew in Coombe would call it a natural pairing. Yet she went swiftly down the stairs, her heart foolishly aflutter, and she said:

"Are you ready to lead the way?"

"No," he said, with a grin. "Lord Auric is tasting a flask of white grape-of-greys from Keddar Grove."

Gael looked into the great hall of the Halfway House and beheld the party of the young Lienish lord at his midday table by the Eastern fireplace. She recalled his efforts, more or less successful, to find out all that had taken place at Silverlode: what had led up to this magical intervention?

Lord Auric had not made so bold as to approach the Malms themselves when they first were flown to the Halfway House—his henchman, Captain Tully, had approached the two kedran ensigns, Bruhl and From, making it known that he was an army healer. Then, when he did not learn enough of the rescue from the Malms, Lord Auric tried again when Gael rode into the Halfway House with Gwil Cluny. This time he used his female companion, Mistress Hestrem, one of the most worldly creatures Gael had ever met.

She had spoken very kindly to Gael Maddoc with hints of "kedran love"—and though Yolanda Hestrem was a voluptuous beauty, Gael found herself ill chosen. She remembered how she had been offered the favors, in Aghiras, of her virile guardsman, Jazeel, and decided that she must be "a lover of men," as the kedran had it. Yet she shared some food and wine with the fair Yolanda, and she proved a pleasant companion. She spoke of her home in a district of the great city of Lindriss-on-the-Laun, in Eildon, where her father had been a fencing master and her mother had run a bakery. Gael deliberately gave her a truncated account of the Malm's rescue, knowing it would be passed along to the ears of Lord Auric Barry.

Since then, the young Lienish lord had continued to decorate the Halfway House with his presence and had made forays down into the Rift. His traveling companions, Mistress Hestrem and Captain Tully, made themselves useful with the rescued travelers from Silverlode. The captain brought healing arts out of the Chameln lands, and Mistress Yolanda played sweet music upon the lute.

Now Lord Auric had offered Tomas Giraud a place in his carriage as far as Lort. Tomas had done other work for Lord Auric and said it had to do with his family. Gael had learned, in conversations over the course of days, a great deal both about Tomas and his family. His father, Frois Giraud, had been a scribe and mapmaker who did not agree with the teachings of the Brotherhood of the Lame God.

Today Lord Auric had guests: a tall fresh-faced man of Mel'Nir with thick brown curls and a quiet, well-controlled voice, and his lady, a pale beauty. This was the Rift Lord and leader of the other Rift Lords, Degan of Keddar and his wife, Perrine of Andine.

Gael settled at a table in shadow, watching the lords—half-hoping she might draw the Lady Perrine's attention—while Tomas fetched beer from the scullery hatch. Yes, she said as he returned, there was a distinct likeness between Lady Keddar and her sister, Annhad of Pfolben. She kept it to herself that she saw an even stronger likeness to the lady who had foretold her own destiny—and she deliberately asked Tomas what he knew of the unmarried Strett daughter, Pearl of Andine. Tomas Giraud knew so many things of this sort that she had teased him about it, saying *scribe* was another word for *gossip*.

Tomas had a serious way with him. Gael found herself sharply aware of the deep tone of his voice and the way his thick dark hair fell over his broad forehead. He seemed pleased to seek out her company; yet somehow he was not like Jazeel or Lady Hestrem, who, despite their pleasantness as companions, had sought for information *through* rather than *of* her.

"Pearl of Andine is unmarried," he said, "and occupies the family home, Cannford Old House, in the center of the Rift. Some say this lady, Mistress Pearl, is the most beautiful of the three sisters. She is a teacher to the daughters of the Rift Lords. She is a healer, and it has always been rumored that she is versed in magic."

"I felt sure you would know!" said Gael, smiling. "How would one learn magic, Tomas? Yes, I know I have had to learn a smattering of the art for this 'Silverlode Incident.' But I wonder how anyone, even a lady of a landowning family, could truly become an adept."

"First requirement," he said cheerfully, "is another adept, a teacher. That could be a member of the fairy race, or a half-Shee, like the O'Quoins. The story is that Lady Pearl went into Eildon for several years as a young girl, in the aftermath of the Great King's War."

Presently Gwil Cluny came in: the carriage from Silverlode was ready, with its own greys hitched up. Lord Malm had asked the day before if this was war booty from the Boar's Lair, but Wennle had explained that it was not. After consultation with Gael, the steward had returned a certain amount of silver to Huarikson's trooper, who had brought back the horses—as payment for the simple carriage and the two greys. A bargain, certainly, and an offer the Boar could not refuse, but the Malms' party, to Gael's mind, had come in peace and did not gather booty.

Up above, on the gallery, Wennle and Lyse began moving out the Malms' baggage and bringing it down the stairs. Gael, a little disappointed that there would be no chance for her to tender her respects to the third of Strett's daughters, indeed disappointed that Lady Perrine, unlike the Lady Annhad, had not singled her out and reached out to her, went into her own small room under the stairs and fetched her saddlebags and her lance. Where was destiny in this? But then Tomas the scribe drew her down to sit at the table again, and she was of sudden brought to the moment.

"Gael—Gael Maddoc," he said with sudden urgency. "You will leave ahead of us. Lord Auric will take some time for his talk with Keddar. You have said that your service with the Malms lasts only until you bring them safely to the king's court—the Palace Fortress."

"Then I am at liberty again," said Gael, "until the spring."

It seemed a long time until her next meeting with the Shee; she must journey to the village of Aird in the Willowmoon and there wait for instruction.

"Winter over in the city of Lort!" said Tomas. "Let me secure you a good room in the Swan Inn, with our Landlord Rolf Beck, together with his family. There are scribes, like myself—you will have good talk, old tales, sweet music, games of Battle . . ."

"Yes," she said, feeling a rush of warmth and friendship. "Yes, I will do it, Tomas! The Swan Inn?"

"By the ancient Ox Gate."

Then it was time for Lord and Lady Malm to descend the stairs, the old lord going ahead and reaching a hand up to his wife. Gael, standing at attention with her lance and banner at the foot of the stairs, thought she had never seen Mortrice of Malm looking more sensible. His bluster had all gone. He returned her salute with a smile:

"Meddoc! Ready for the road?"

"All ready, m'lord!"

Everyone had come to see the Malms take their leave: Mistress Cluny and all the extra help came from the kitchens. Lord Auric stood up and spread his hands, beckoning the Malms to his table. Mistress Hestrem, a fine lutanist, played her sweet music.

"Too short a meeting with such illustrious company!" said Lord Auric. "Let us send you all safely on your way to the king's court!"

His smile was sincere and charming: he could command all the world to be happy. Lady Malm beamed and nodded:

"We are all in good heart for the last part of the journey!" she said.

"Permit me to present to you . . ." continued young Auric.

Lord and Lady Malm were presented to Keddar of Keddar Grove—one day, perhaps, Keddar, Lord of the Eastmark, returning the Marches of Mel'Nir to their proper balance. It was no more than a brief exchange of greetings: Lord Malm tossed off a stirrup cup.

Gael Maddoc, standing well back from the nobles, was glad she had no part in this palaver. She felt a profound uneasiness in the presence of Lord Auric and trusted him very little. Even as she readied herself for the departure, she was trying to give Tomas Giraud some kind of magical protection against the wiles of this handsome lord—silently repeating a protective spell in his name: part of her new, small arsenal of magic.

Out in the yard, Gael thought of the first leave-taking from Coombe, the beginning of the journey. This time the Malms were good as gold in the carriage from Silverlode—it was not half so elegant as Lord Auric's equipage, but it was as comfortable. Lyse, the waiting maid, rode with the Malms. Now Gael, on Ebony, and Wennle, on his same horse from Coombe, led off; Gwil Cluny, as coachman, swung the greys out of the inn yard to a few cheers. They took to a good road that led them past the Green Fort, a sacred place of the Shee; it was a fair, warm autumn day, not long after noon.

Before they had joined the King's Way, north of Silverlode, Wennle said to Gael Maddoc:

"Captain, I have remembered something!"

"Yes, Master Wennle?"

"This young man, Auric Barry—he is not entirely unfamiliar to me. I saw him—years past—in Eildon. He was then a page, in service to the envoy sent from the Lienish court."

It could hardly surprise her that Lord Auric was so highly placed in Lien; still, this information made it all the more strange to her that he had traveled all this distance into Mel'Nir's rough interior.

Now they were on the King's Way, and it was not so rough and wild as the way they had passed. The party made a halt at a look out, and all gazed down from the western rim of the plateau. They could look back to the south at the fortress of Hackestell, manned by the soldiery of Val'Nur. Near at hand, they could see the river Demmis. It sprang up in the Bens of Deme, on the steep sides of the high ground, and made its way across the plain to flow through the golden city of Krail, where Knaar, Lord of the Westmark, would not hear of magic.

At the first waystation, there was a kedran company of good King Gol's royal garrison—the unit called Golden Ash—who helped travelers. Then, before Goldgrave, there was another inn, a smaller version of the Halfway House, new since the time that Gael had ridden through with Druda Strawn and the other recruits. Here Gwil Cluny changed the carriage horses, leaving the good greys from Silverlode to be collected on his return.

The Malms and their party had time to take their ease and enjoy the autumn beauty of the high ground. Gael was busy with her charts and maps, including a new map, printed in the Lienish fashion, the gift of Tomas the scribe. She saw the way that led to the west, to the village of Aird, home of many half-Shee. Near it there existed on its own magical plane the fair palace of Tulach, where she had been received by the Eilif ladies and lords.

So at last they came to the town of Goldgrave, where gold and precious metals had been taken from the surrounding land in the early years of the Farfaring. Goldgrave, once abandoned like Silverlode, was now a market town with a tannery and a mill, standing on the western edge of the great plateau. It was famous now for battles during the Great King's War.

Rooms were taken at a renowned hostelry, the Heroes of Goldgrave. The travelers had been nine days on the road, but only one long day more would bring them to the Palace Fortress of King Gol. Lady Malm had prepared letters and, now a courier was found to ride at once to the court and bring the news of her arrival to Princess Elwina. So the party rested, like old campaigners, at the Heroes, talking of the dangers they had passed.

On the third morning, there was a commotion in the inn yard. Gael, having her breakfast, looked out and sent Lyse to wake the Malms at once. An escort troop of the royal guard, with the prancing horse of the Duarings upon their golden tabards, had just arrived. She sprang up and went out to greet the officer—Captain Hem Carra, a lord's son indeed, suitable for the Malms' escort. He was a giant warrior with golden hair tied in a knot and a certain cool, almost languid manner she later learned to associate with the men of the king's court.

"Trouble on the journey, Captain Maddoc?" he asked, raising a golden eyebrow. "B-brigands?"

"Things were put in order," said Gael.

"And before that, a shipwreck, in the wild Chyrian Lands?"

"Well, not quite," smiled Gael. "Wild Chyrians like myself would call it a ship beached by a storm.

"But, indeed," she added, "Lord and Lady Malm have not had an easy journey."

Besides the ten men of the escort, there was a new carriage, with a coachman and two liveried servants up behind. Princess Elwina had sent a waiting woman to attend Lady Malm. There was a great fuss and bustle of preparation; the Malms came down in tremendous spirits. When all the baggage had been stowed, Wennle paid off Gwil Cluny and Lyse. Their service had ended. They would drive the old carriage back to the Halfway House, leading the last horse from Coombe, Wennle's own bay; the steward would ride with the coachman.

The old lord, standing in the inn's finest room, looked much as Gael had first seen him, in his fur-trimmed gown. Lady Malm stood by the window, where she could gaze at her escort of giant warriors forming up in their splendid uniforms. A new young waiting woman was helping with her traveling cloak.

"Well, well, Meddoc!" cried Mortrice of Malm. "End of the journey for you—now we have a proper escort at last! Wish ye well, Captain . . ."

Gael would hardly admit to herself that with the arrival of the royal escort the Malms had simply "changed back"; they had returned to the world they wished to inhabit. Now Mortrice of Malm had failed some test that Gael could hardly put into words. What understanding could be expected from this stiff old Eildon lord? She had been handsomely paid off by Wennle as long ago as the Halfway House. She said firmly:

"If it please your lordship, I will ride along behind. My duty is not ended until you and your lady come to the Palace Fortress."

"As you will," he said, with a wave of his hand.

Gael gave him her best salute, then bowed and bade farewell. Lady Malm turned from the window, and Gael had a moment of hope. The proud noblewoman who had summoned her from the dungeon in Silverlode would remember and make all well. But Lady Malm simply nodded her golden head, accepting the kedran captain's last bow kindly enough.

The procession went out of Goldgrave at dawn and came down from the high ground into fair hill country with clear streams in the valleys. They passed an old ruined tower alone on a hilltop and continued up and down on the King's Way. The pace was fast—at noon they were already climbing up to the city of Lort. Gael rode alone behind the Malms' carriage, keeping a good length from the two men in livery on their hard seats. She stared to the east and saw in the distance ranks of dark trees. This was the enchanted forest of Nightwood, where Yorath Duaring had roamed as a boy.

The procession thundered into Lort through the southern gate; they were awaited in another inn called the Good King Gol. The Malms were taken up to their chambers, but only for food and a short rest. Captain Carra, who always took care to give Captain Maddoc a seat at his own table, explained that the visitors would be brought straight on.

"We will have them to the palace this evening," he said. "How is your horse, Captain Maddoc?"

"Ebony is doing well," she said. "He is as tough as a camel!"

They talked then of the Burnt Lands and the Royal Hunt—yes, Prince Kirris Paldo had been along, the brother of Princess Elwina. Then, since Captain Carra must know Lort pretty well, Gael ventured to ask him the way to the Swan Inn, where she planned to pass the winter.

"Aha!" said Mihal Carra. "That place is a scribes' pit, an ink bottle! Do you not know what they cook up in the Swan, Maddoc my friend?"

Gael laughed and shook her head.

"Why, the blessed scrolls!" he said, in a stage whisper. "A nest of archivists live at the Swan and work on *The Book of the Farfaring*, the Dathsa, the Scroll of Vil, and the so-called *New Chronicles.*"

"Well, I did not believe the scrolls were God given," she said, "but I thought of greybeard scholars working in the Palace Fortress itself . . ."

"The actual writing is done here in the city at the Old Almshouse," he said airily, "and the scribes come in all shapes and sizes."

"Hem Carra," asked Gael, "do you know anyone who works on the scrolls?"

She felt sure she knew one scribe already who did.

"Yes," said Carra. "An old fellow called Brother Robard—a former tutor in Carrahall, my father's house. He is a military expert and still comes to the King's Longhouse to lecture the young ensigns. The rest of the time he works on the Scroll of Vil, the most warlike of the scrolls."

"I'll keep a look out for him," said Gael.

"One does hear tell of royal persons lending a hand—and of female scribes!"

"What next!" she grinned.

Captain Carra had a writing case fetched and drew a sketch map on the back of one of Gael's charts, showing the way to the Ox Gate. She sighed inwardly for her own lack of various skills—her writing lagged behind her reading. But she thought comfortably of lessons in the wintertime at the Swan Inn, of learning from Tomas Giraud and his fellow archivists who worked on the scrolls—learning from those who made the records of Mel'Nir's history.

So, at the fourth hour after noon, the procession formed up for the last time—the Malms were rested, as well as the horses, and the guard had been very moderate at lunch. They rode out in good heart, and Gael, bringing up the rear, saw that Lort was a spreading town, filled with new buildings in a handsome Lienish style. It was not so much of a city as Pfolben or Aghiras or even, by repute, Krail in the Westmark, but it was a pleasant place. Down a long vista of houses and public buildings in yellow stone, she glimpsed the mighty Ox Gate, built in old time, before the Farfaring.

Beyond the northern gate, the King's Way was wider than ever and marked out with fine avenues of trees. The weather had altered a little, giving way to fine sun-showers coming in from the east. The escort went up one more hill, and there before her Gael beheld the end of the Malms' journey. There, spread out like a picture from the scrolls, was the inland sea, the Dannermere. Directly ahead, amid an array of gardens and flowering trees, there rose the walls and towers and bastions of the Palace Fortress of the Kings of Mel'Nir.

Gael Maddoc could see the way the procession must take, even to the open gates at the end of the last avenue. She beheld men and women of every degree going about near the gates and could make out a group of ladies and lords who might be waiting to receive the Malms.

She considered her two charges—how she had thought to speak to them, bid farewell, at the last inn, the Good King Gol, but had simply lacked courage. She wanted the Malms to remain in her memory as more or less humane and thoughtful, in the end. Deliberately, she reined in her horse on the crest of this last hill and let the fine gold carriage draw away. The two "runners" mounted behind waved to her, and, as she lifted a hand in salute, a curtain of misty rain blew across from the east, hiding the escort and the carriage from view. Her duty had ended; she had brought the Lord Malm and his lady to the king's court.

Suddenly the afternoon sun came shining through the misty rain and, a magnificent rainbow sprang up, arching over the green hills; the procession passed under its mighty arch. Gael Maddoc was not alone on her hilltop—they stood all about her. There was Sir Hugh McLlyr, mounted upon a tall grey horse; Ebony shied away from this wraith. There were Myrruad and Ylmiane, seated in a small bronze carriage, drawn by two more ghost greys, while the Lady Ethain was mounted upon a real horse, a dainty roan. Luran stood in the grass by the roadside, with the great dog Bran on a leash.

"Well done!" cried Sir Hugh of the Fishers in a ringing tone. "Well done, Captain Maddoc! You have brought these poor dark folk to the king's court!"

Then all the ladies of the Shee applauded and cheered, like a peal of sweet bells.

"Corvin Huarikson has come to heel," said Luran. "All in all a rescue most skillfully carried forward!"

Gael could only nod and smile, like an old lady of the Shee. She felt tears on her face among the soft raindrops.

Appendix 904 (Marvels and Wonders, witnessed and unwitnessed) of that compendium of ancient writings in Chyrian and other tongues known as *The Book of Sooth* or, more commonly, THE DATHSA:

> Then, as Lord Mortrice of Malm, knight of the Hunters, and his Lady Malveena were brought to the Court of King Gol of Mel'Nir, their servants and the men of the escort cried out loudly. The escort and the royal coach were halted, and all looked back the way they had come. There upon the brow of the last hill, under the arch of a mighty rainbow, there was a tall kedran upon a black horse. Horse and rider were outlined in golden fire. There were those who understood that this person, whose name was known, the woman who had saved the Malms from a cruel fate, was none other than THE WANDERER. And this was made clear to all by the figures of five or six lords and ladies, Ruadan and Fionnar together, of the Eilif race, the Shee. This was the largest showing of the Bright Folk since the days of Ankar Duaring, the so-called Wizard King, father of Ghanor, the so-called Great King, and grandsire of Good King Gol. There they stood on the hilltop, bearing witness to the deeds of their true servant . . .

CHAPTER IX

THE SWAN IN WINTER

The inn was a spacious old building of yellow stone, built in the plain manner of Mel'Nir; it reared up and spread along the city wall within sight of the mighty Ox Gate. Besides the splendid inn sign, some attempt had been made to beautify the Swan with hanging plants and bright metal swans on the iron balconies.

Gael dismounted in the misty rainbow weather and looked for the entry to the innyard. As she led Ebony under an archway, a groom in tan livery came running up and said he was Daken, at her service.

"Is your place kept, Captain?" he cried. "The old Bird is filling up this time of year!"

She assured him that her place was kept, by Tomas Giraud.

"Good! Good!" said the young fellow. "Now come, my beauty—"

He had a way with horses as well as a handy piece of carrot, and Ebony allowed himself to be led into a good stall.

"How far have you traveled, Captain?"

"All told," she said, smiling, "it sounds a longish way. We have ridden from Coombe, a village in the Chyrian lands—between Lowestell and Hackestell."

"Coooombe?"

It was a loud hooting cry in a strange resonant voice, and it seemed to come from the gallery of the stable.

"Coombe, did ye say, good Captain?"

Gael could hardly believe what she saw: a tiny man, with a shock of snow white hair and a body gravely twisted, was perched on the gallery rail.

"I did indeed," she replied. "Do you know Coombe, good sir?"

She had seen one or two dwarfs in Pfolben and more at the court of the Dhey at Aghiras, but none so cruelly deformed as this old man. Now he waved a hand at the groom, Daken, who said:

"Right you are, Master Forbian!"

He stood under the gallery, holding out his arms, and when the little man swung down on a rope, he caught and steadied him.

"Set me on my saddle, good Daken," he said, "so I may talk to this brave kedran!"

Sure enough there was a child-sized saddle fastened upon a stall rail. The groom gave Gael a wink as he set the dwarf in place.

"My name is Forbian Flink," said the dwarf when he was comfortably settled. "I am a scribe, and I once served a young master, a hero of Mel'Nir, who did great things during the Great King's War in the village of Coombe."

"What?" said Gael. "You served General Yorath?"

Forbian Flink laughed so hard he nearly tumbled off his perch, and the horses were set off whinnying and stamping.

"There!" he said. "There! His name is still well-known?"

"Truly," said Gael, "he is well-remembered. The whole Chyrian coast blesses the name of the founder of the Westlings of Val'Nur."

"Have you served in Krail, Captain? Should I know your name from the lists of the Sword Lilies, Lord Knaar's famed kedran troop?"

It was a remarkably polite way of asking her name and that of her troop.

"I am Gael Maddoc, Master Flink," she said. "I have never served in Krail, but I trained and served in Kestrel Company, first household troop of the Lord of Pfolben in the Southland."

"Aha!" said the little old man. "Then you will surely know who is the captain-general of the palace guard . . ."

"Why, it is Eugen Florus," said Gael promptly.

She did not quite understand his questioning—later she learned it was more than the simple testing of her own story, and it was a common practice at the Swan Inn, she was to find. The scribes and archivists checked their information whenever they could.

"Good, good!" said Forbian Flink. "Now I recall another very strange tale from the Southland—and from the Burnt Lands. Many are anxious to come to the true gist of this tale. A troop of kedran were given up for lost in the desert wastes after some kind of seasonal hunt—but there was among them a remarkably stubborn officer who brought the poor gals home again after many hardships . . ."

"Who has spoken of this?" asked Gael warily.

"Why, I had it from a man of Eildon," he said. "An esquire name of Merflyn, serving now at the court of King Gol. Do you know anything of this magic cohort and their leader?"

"Yes, Master Flink," she replied, catching his eye. "I do indeed. They were all good hearts and with my officers I brought them home!"

He took it in with his old bluish brown eyes widening until they shone in the dim light of the big stable.

"Psst!" he said, looking about to see that Daken, the groom, had not heard them. "Not a word, Captain Maddoc! Who else hereabouts knows of your part in this adventure?"

"Why, I have told the story only to my friend, Tomas Giraud, a scribe, whom I met on the way to the king's court," she said. "But it is no secret that I served in the Burnt Lands."

She deliberately omitted the fact that she had told all to the Shee, who surely did not count in this context of telling news or passing on tales. But then Gael felt a stab of pain, or at least disappointment. Had Tomas asked her to the Swan only because of her adventure in the Burnt Lands? It did sound to her just the kind of stuff that might be written up into a tale—like those in the paper Lienbooks she had exchanged with Druda Strawn.

"Aha!" said Forbian Flink. Perhaps the dwarf sensed a little of her hurt, for his matter gentled, he reined in a little his scholar's enthusiasm. "A good man, a reliable archivist, and one who can be trusted. Tell no one else! Let good Tomas know that Old Flink is in on the secret and will write it all up fair for him with illuminations and without extra charge! This is only right for a kedran from Coombe!"

"I will do all that you ask," laughed Gael, "if you will tell me true tales of the life of our hero, General Yorath."

"I may surprise you," said Forbian Flink.

He flicked back his shock of white hair and laid a crooked finger alongside his crooked nose. Then he climbed down from the rail, scuttled to his rope, and scrambled up again into the stable loft. Gael called for Daken and gave him a silver piece—she wanted to ensure good treatment for Ebony. He thanked her warmly, and she struck out across the damp yard, carrying her saddlebags.

There was a small, dark entry, then a large comfortable room, more like the hall of a large private house than anything else. A low fire burned on the hearth, and the settles were filled with guests, none of them very fine, but all remarkably relaxed. Mainly men, she must allow, but there were women and girls there, too, even some in kedran dress. A woman in a dark red gown, who had been serving tankards of ale from a tray, came up to her now, smiling.

"Yes, Captain?"

She was a striking figure, sturdy but not fat, with slanting dark eyes and straight coarse black hair done in thick braids, twined with colored threads. Her skin was a clear yellow brown.

"I am called Maddoc," said Gael. "Tomas Giraud will have taken a room for me . . ."

"So he has! I am Demira Beck, the host's wife. Come into the taproom, and we'll write you down in the book!"

She waved a hand, and two young boys ran up. They were short and sturdy, so it was hard to tell their age—perhaps as much as eleven years. They were identical twins, with the same slanting black eyes as Mistress Beck, skin of a light olive hue, and heads of dark brown curls. They were a natural wonder, and it was impossible not to smile at them.

"Yes, yes!" said Mistress Beck, not really hiding her mother's pride. "Double the trouble, I can tell you, Captain. My sons, Kay and Marek."

She clapped her hands at the twins:

"Now you can bring the captain's saddlebags to the turret east."

Gael followed Mistress Beck into the taproom. It was even larger than the outer hall, and the talk was just as intense and lively. In one corner, four dark-clad older men had their heads down, checking sheaves of pages, while a fifth man read aloud. Then she noticed that there was written work going on everywhere, in a more relaxed fashion, punctuated with laughter, food, and draughts of ale. She signed her name and rank in a huge black book, and suddenly a cry went up:

"Chyrian? Knowledge of idiomatic Chyrian?"

The speaker was a thin, bearded man, who looked indeed like a scholar—he wore eyeglasses and a shabby green gown. His voice was strong and penetrating. No one came forward, but a younger fellow cried out:

"Damn you with your outlandish tongues, Robard!"

Gael set down her pen and held up her hand. She made her way to Brother Robard's table.

"Chyrian," she said timidly.

"Aha!" said the scholar eagerly. "Captain . . . ?"

She gave her name and was greeted by an older woman, Terza, and a young lad, Hannes, who were working on an untidy pile of parchment. She sat down and accepted the offer of a pot of ale and was plunged into the struggle with an account of a battle on the Chyrian coast in old time.

She knew the story: it was part of the life and legends of King Baradd O'Doon, Baradd of the Golden Throat.

The original parchment was mainly written in Low Lienish, which she soon gathered was an early form of the common speech and easy for these folk to decipher. There were several passages, however, in the original Chyrian, as spoken by the handsome young king, Baradd O'Doon, and his adversary Leem Dhu. This rogue had the habit of turning into a monstrous water serpent who hid his hideous coils in a lake near Tuana, the old capital of the Chyrians, north of Banlo but south of the Westmark proper.

Gael wondered if she had been too rash in her offer of help, but in fact she was able to deliver exactly what her new companions wanted. King Baradd, in this written version of the tale, used a very quaint sort of Chyrian, with many homely turns of phrase. She was able to explain that "the one who empties" was the first person to get up in the morning, who must, as a rule of hospitality, empty the chamber pots. It became clear that burnable or black cut were words for peat, the burnable turf that had spread out around Tuana lake. The peat marshes were almost worked out, but the custom was still remembered. Also, Taran's Kelch, the ancient Hallow of the Chyrian people, was used for a large measure of mead for thirsty warriors, and a *binlennie bride* was a fancy woman, a singing girl—named for a vanished village where women could be brides for a night. She mentioned little of the Hallow; Robard, she was intrigued to note, seemed hardly to mark its name.

The team of scribes worked well together and easily: they all wrote down their work or made notes, but Terza was the scribe who wrote all out fair on a new parchment, in a beautiful, clear straight letter and in the common speech. But she also contributed many thoughts and turns of phrase and knew where they had been used. The boy, Hannes, was very sharp and learned, and Brother Robard guided them all firmly but with kindness and good humor.

Time passed, and they took ale and then a platter of fresh bread and cold meat. Her new colleagues were pleased to have found her, and she believed she did the right thing in waving aside an offer of payment. Now Hannes brought up a vexed question.

"Captain Maddoc," he said. "Those entertainers at the courts of the Chyrian Kings—we have seen them called clowns and fools and even satirists. The Chyrian word, or one of them, is Atharn. What is the best translation for this?"

"This name is borrowed from a singer of ancient times," she said. "Athairn or Atharn, a bard of the old Tuana 'court.' An atharn, such as

King Baradd's Riggan May, was always a skilled musician and singer."

"He was a bard, then?" put in Terza.

"No, the atharns had a different way with them," said Gael. "They could indeed sing and play the harp or the bagpipe, but mostly they made up certain verses on the spot."

"They improvised!" exclaimed Brother Robard. "Aha! Yes, I've heard something of this . . . part of the mighty oral tradition of ancient times, now withered away."

"Not quite," said Gael, smiling. "It goes on to this very day . . . I know two young men in the village of Coombe who are well known for their squint-singing or rigganoi."

"And these village boys sing in Chyrian?" pursued Brother Robard.

"Yes," she said, "but it is simple stuff and can be done easily into the common speech."

"Example!" said all three of her new friends in one voice.

Gael explained that it might be considered bad form or bad luck to sing again an improvised verse, but in the interests of scholarship, she gave forth with two that she remembered, first in Chyrian, then in the common speech.

Here comes a girl
Dressed up so fine,
Is it Queen Meb, fairest of the Shee?
Or is it the Swineherd's daughter?

One for a kedran in dress uniform, then one for a visiting lord:

Who is that lord
With the shining face?
Is it King Nud, the Lord of the Lake?
Or is it a drunken tinker?

"Remarkable!" said Brother Robard, as Terza and Hannes clapped their hands. And Gael, for the honor of the art of squint-singing, was inspired to continue.

"But the heart of the thing is to make a new verse every time," she said. "As if one might sing like this . . ."

Here stands a man
In a scholar's gown,

Is it Robard, the first at Beck's bar?
Or is it the Carrahall tutor?

Terza and Hannes laughed and cheered so loudly that the other denizens of the taproom noticed them. Brother Robard chuckled and shook his head—he was plainly delighted to be teased in this fashion, and in two languages.

Then the others smiled as a hand fell on her shoulder, and it was Tomas Giraud.

"Well, you see I did not lie!" he said. "The Swan is a fine place in winter!"

"Sit down, Tomas!" said Brother Robard. "Trust you to summon an expert in Chyrian to cheer our evenings! I hear that the Dathsa 'soothsayers' are still searching for the origins of that marvelous tale from the Burnt Lands . . ."

Tomas had slipped into a place close beside her, and she found she enjoyed his closeness. Their eyes met, challenging, and she brought out:

"Do I know that tale, Tomas?"

"Well, if you do, Gael, keep it to yourself in this house of scribes!" and the way he spoke, Gael knew she trusted him, could not help but trust him, and she knew as well, she would certainly come to tell him the secret of the hallow-string she had found in the Burnt Lands. Perhaps even, because he was a scholar of the scrolls, he would help her learn the meaning of her quest, and all that had fallen to her since that golden afternoon when Lady Pearl had read her fortune and seen Mel'Nir's lost Lance within her palm—along with all that other tumble of images.

So they all sat together, making foolish jokes in all the languages they knew, and Gael had not felt so happy for many moons. She asked if any knew the languages of the Burnt Lands, and, sure enough, young Hannes had a smattering of them. She held her magic ring beneath the tabletop, but when it sparkled, Tomas covered it with his hand and changed the subject. He went off to buy another round for the company, and while he was at the bar, Terza leaned close and said to Gael, woman to woman:

"So now we see our good Tomas smitten with a kedran captain."

"Oh, go along with you!" whispered Gael, feeling herself blush.

"No," said Terza, wisely. "You are his winter guest. It has come to mean a partner, a sweetheart."

"Have you such a guest?" asked Gael.

"I have no need of one," said Terza. "I am here all year round with my true love. There are certain brotherhoods who do not demand celibacy."

She smiled in the direction of Brother Robard, who was busy playing some puzzle game on paper with Hannes, the scribe apprentice.

"I know that well," said Gael. "It has been so with the Chyrian Guardian Priests, like our good Druda Strawn from Coombe village."

"By the Goddess," said Terza, her eyes alight now with the zeal of the scholar. "I will pick your brains all winter long, Gael Maddoc! You are a goldmine for my book of Chyrian words and customs!"

"Look there, Captain!" put in the boy, Hannes. "Master Giraud is beckoning you!"

Indeed, Tomas stood at the bar of the inner room, with a solid-looking man who must be the host himself, Rolf Beck. Gael went to them and was introduced. The innkeeper had a plump, handsome face, a head of unruly grey curls and a rim of grey-brown beard; his eyes were blue-green. Gael saw her ring flashing with a strange pearly light; perhaps the man was wearing a powerful amulet.

He greeted the new guest heartily and said:

"Now we were speaking here, Captain Maddoc, of a certain doubtful character, a man named Tully . . ."

"I have told Master Beck what I made of this rogue," said Tomas, "but we would value your opinion, Gael Maddoc."

"He gave himself out as an army healer," said Gael, "and indeed he did know something of this work. But he was plainly an adventurer. I believe he had been hired by Lord Auric Barry, of Lien, mainly as a bodyguard. He seemed to me a dangerous fellow to attack—with strength and combat training and magical tricks besides."

"And which land of Hylor was his home?" inquired Beck softly.

"He claimed to come from Chameln Achamar," said Gael, "and though I could not tell it from his speech, he seemed to know that city. He described it very fondly, as if it were indeed his home, and mentioned a district called the old town, where there was once a playhouse."

"You have a gift for this kind of observation," smiled Tomas. "Did I not say so, Master Beck?"

"Tully . . ." said the host thoughtfully. "The old town, indeed."

He heaved a sigh, and then his face brightened. A beautiful young girl of perhaps fourteen summers came by with fresh glasses, and he presented to the guests his eldest child, Zarah Beck. She had the same slanting black eyes as her mother, the hostess, and the twins, but her hair was straight shining black, and her skin was pale, only touched with gold.

Master Beck had asked Gael and Tomas to join him in a special drink, so Zarah brought the drinks and a free round of sweet pastry back to

Brother Robard's table. Then the host drew them both aside to a table beside the bar where Mistress Beck had set out a little supper, with more pastries and bowls of salad.

Rolf Beck sat down with them, and he was indeed a genial host, but Gael felt that what was played out here was somehow critically important to him.

"Tomas knows I value news of certain kinds," he said. "It has to do with old battles, old treachery, old enemies. Anything that comes from the Chameln lands—certain intelligence out of the noble houses of Lien."

Gael said hesitantly, looking at Tomas:

"Should we talk of Mistress Hestrem?"

Tomas shook his head from side to side—she noticed again his thick and shining dark hair—then said slowly:

"Well, I have undertaken some work—the purchase of rare books, for instance—for Lord Auric Barry of Chantry in Lien in the past, and he always pays well. But I must say his two companions who came with him into Mel'Nir were intriguers, creatures of the half-world. First this Tully, the bodyguard, then that proud beauty, Yolanda Hestrem."

"I will not judge her harshly," Gael said. "She could be called a courtesan, or perhaps an adventuress, a woman who lives by her wits. She is very accomplished and can be a pleasant companion. She has the common touch. It seems that she must be Lord Auric's mistress, but perhaps this is too simple. An important task for her must simply be to gather information. She is Auric's spy, his agent. She comes out of Eildon."

"Note it all down for my own scrolls, good Tomas," said Rolf Beck.

Then he smiled at Gael and added:

"I am delighted to have you winter in our house, Captain Maddoc! Welcome to the Swan!"

Her ring still sparkled and flashed below the tabletop; the host moved away smiling, but she had a strong impression of seriousness, even sadness, about this jovial-looking man. She murmured some of this to Tomas as they finished their wine. He nodded wisely and cast a glance back into the taproom. The crowd was thinning a little. Some of the lodgers were going to stay up much longer, not to royster but simply to read and scribble and argue.

"Come," said Tomas. "Let me show you to your fine tower room!"

Their eyes met, and she was shy, felt herself blushing. But when she raised her eyes, Tomas was flushed too and a little awkward. He went to the bar again, paid part of their score, she guessed, and came back with a flagon of the golden wine.

Her room in the east tower was indeed spacious and fine, with a fire in the grate behind a metal guard. Two mullioned windows looked out over the city of Lort, to the west, then, up a little winding stair, there was a small tower room with a balcony. They went up and gazed out through the night at Nightwood and the inland sea, the Dannermere.

Tomas had pointed out his own two rooms on the way to the east tower. They sat by her fire and drank more of the golden wine. She reported her conversation with Forbian Flink in the stable.

"Of course!" cried Tomas. "He'll do much for a captain from Coombe, his master Yorath's old hunting ground!"

"Will you take his offer, then?" she asked warily. "Did you get me to winter over at the Swan because I belong in your collections of strange tales?" She thought of the Hallows, and wondered again if she could trust him with this part of her story.

But Tomas Giraud only smiled slowly.

"Yes," he said. "I will certainly take his offer! We will spend the winter writing up your Journey to the Burnt Lands. Flink the Scribe knows more secrets than the Moon Sisters—he will say no word out of place. But that is not why I asked you to be my winter guest . . ."

She looked at him again, and he set his goblet down upon the stones of the hearth.

"I have a great desire to lie with you," he said, reaching out a hand to her. His voice was a little roughened with his feelings. "I think you know that . . ."

They stood up now, very close, and she felt her heart pound and wound her arms about his neck. Their kisses were long and deep.

"Winter," she whispered, against his neck. "Winter at the Swan!"

Tomas inquired in his scholarly way about the tale that kedran, battle-maids, knew of certain herbs. She laughed and brought out the pouch from her saddlebag with the rolled pellets of a substance called Kedran Shield or Maid's Friend. There were thick curtains round the wide, warm bed, but they left them partly open, to watch the firelight.

II

The winter was mild, with only light snow flurries at the time of the Winter Feast, which Beck, the innkeeper, celebrated in the manner of the Chameln Lands. There was a mighty Winter Man, a scribe of Mel'Nir called Gereth, in a robe covered in pine and tannen twigs, and a headdress of gilded branches like antlers and a gilded mask. He was an older fellow, a fatherly partner for lovely Zarah Beck as the Green Woman, the Goddess in her forest dress. The young scribe apprentice Hannes Trun was the Moonchild; he rode a white pony that drew in a tall fir tree on a sleigh, together with sweetmeats and gifts for all.

The scribes and archivists at the Swan, Gael found, were diligent, not to say obsessed with their work and kept it up steadily all through the feast days. They were also the receivers of news of all kinds and were among the first to hear the joyful tidings from the Palace Fortress of Good King Gol that Princess Elwina Paldo, the fair young wife of Rieth, the King's nephew, Heir of Mel'Nir, had been safely delivered of a son. There was much speculation among the genealogists at the Swan about the naming of the child, and when the names were given out as Kirris Rieth Elwin, it was agreed that the Duarings had taken a good moderate course, using names from all the royal families involved. Gael thought often of the Malms and their strange adventure in Mel'Nir and the part she had played in it. She was becoming restless in the confines of the inn and the town of Lort, in spite of the love she felt for Tomas and the lovemaking and the closeness they enjoyed.

Now she had told Tomas of the hallow-string, and even shown him; Tomas had been very excited and promised to bring pieces from the scrolls to her that had bearing on the lands' ancient treasures, but little had come of this yet, though he had been able to confirm that, yes, the sixth Hallow was indeed the Fleece of Lien, just as she had guessed, and it too had been missing, from before the time Kelen of Lien had taken a king's crown—indeed, it had been missing from the early years of the archmage Rosmer's rise to power.

Since the weather continued mild, Tomas conspired with Forbian Flink, who did much of his copying in the room at the top of Gael's tower. To satisfy Gael's restlessness, they took her out riding soon after New Year, at the end of the Tannenmoon.

They came out of Lort not long after the winter sun rose; ahead lay the gardens of the Palace Fortress, and to the north there was a fine clear view all the way down to the banks of the River Bal—Mel'Nir's border with the Kingdom of Lien. Far away to the west, between the river and the High Plateau, she caught a misty glimpse of the green hills that were the edge of King's Bank—now the domain of the Kingdom of Lien, formerly Balbank of Mel'Nir. There was a border clearly marked around the Lienish lands, with trees and in places a wall or a barrier. Gael could see the guard posts where kedran were turned back, forbidden to enter the lands of Lien—unless perhaps they disguised themselves in skirts and wimples.

This morning, Forbian directed Gael toward the east. Ebony was glad of the exercise. Forbian rode before Tomas on his tall sorrel, called Valko. Almost at once Gael could guess where they were going.

"Nightwood!" she cried. "You tricksters! You are taking me to see General Yorath's old haunts in the magic forest!"

Forbian laughed aloud, and Tomas reached out a hand to her. They had spoken of her admiration for the hero of the Chyrian coast.

"The life and death of General Yorath is a protected subject at the king's court," Tomas explained. "We know he was the legitimate son of Prince Gol, as our good King was known then, and Princess Elvédegran of Lien, but Yorath was indeed a 'marked child'—his grandfather, Old Ghanor, the so-called Great King, would surely have had him killed because of his twisted shoulder. Hagnild, the healer at the court, saved the child's life by spiriting him away. I am sure King Gol suffers pangs of regret—Yorath was his only child."

"Would he have acknowledged Yorath as his heir?" asked Gael. "If our great General had not been driven over the cliffs at Selkray, protecting Knaar of Val'Nur, his brother in arms, during that ambush?"

"There is more to be known about Yorath's death," said Tomas. "The King attaches some blame or lack of care to the Lord of Val'Nur. Perhaps you have not heard this in the south, for the Chyrian Coast is guarded from much news by the Westmark Lords in Krail, but the true story is rumored to be part of the reason Knaar of Val'Nur has remained so quiet under Gol's strictures, even twenty years following Yorath's great sacrifice. The one who knows all is Forbian Flink, our copyist. Perhaps he will tell you."

Gael was shocked, for she had been taught that General Yorath and Knaar of Val'Nur had been boon comrades, but when she looked at the dwarf, the little man simply shrugged and bowed his head, as if to say, "patience, and the story will unfold." There was no comfort to be found in this; Tomas's dark hints could only point to a hidden—ugly—truth.

Now Forbian had arranged this journey. Ahead lay the dark trees and thickets of ancient Nightwood, east of the Palace Fortress, with its own bit of coast on the shining waters of the Dannermere. They rode downhill from the city walls and went some way along a fine "King's Road." Then Forbian directed them into narrower roads on the fringes of the wood. They followed these broad, pleasant trails and came to a clearing with a dolmen of grey stone—two uprights and a crosspiece, like a lintel. Not far away grew a single tree, leafless now, but Gael knew it for a golden ash, one of the most beautiful of all trees. There was a grey stone, a tombstone, at the base of this tree.

"We must get down," said Forbian, "and pay our respects . . ."

She exchanged a questioning glance with Tomas, who surely knew who had been buried in this place, but he only gave a sad smile and helped her dismount. On the stone there was a name carved in the common speech:

HAGNILD RAIZ
HEALER

Gael drew a sobbing breath. Here lay the great Magician Hagnild, healer to the court of King Ghanor, who had spirited the child Yorath away and raised him secretly in Nightwood. On a patch of trimmed grass before the stone, there were smooth pebbles, clay dishes, birds and animals molded from clay or carved from wood or stone. These votive offerings had been left at the grave of this wise man with a prayer or a request, perhaps as dedication for a child or thanks for some blessing, some wish fulfilled.

She felt in the pocket of her tunic and found a good luck charm of her own, a plain, smooth pebble with a hole in it, a natural amulet that Bress had found on Banlo Strand. Stepping up to Hagnild's grave, she laid her offering among the others.

She whispered: "When the spring comes, let me serve the light folk well and bravely! And bless as well my dear love Tomas Giraud, the scribe."

This grave was set at the edge of a dense outcrop of Nightwood proper, and from here they had to go some way on foot, leading the two horses down the leafy road, Forbian still riding on the pommel of brown Valko's saddle.

"I have heard," said Tomas, "that Master Hagnild chose this place to be buried because it was halfway between the palace and his own house, deep in Nightwood. These were the two places where he did his work and lived out his life."

Presently they were able to mount up again and ride on to the village of Finnmarsh, which lay between Nightwood and the old marsh, its land mostly drained now and used for farming. There were houses clustered round a small alehouse, and there stood the old smithy, with its fine yard. Gael saw that the inn was called the Bear, and its sign showed a great grey bear of the sort that once roamed in all the forests of Mel'Nir. She remembered the words of red Luran, the Eilif lord: the last of these noble creatures had died when Yorath roamed Nightwood as a boy.

They rode into the yard of the smithy, where a sturdy, handsome woman was helping a soldier of the guard to mount his new-shod horse. A mighty man worked at the forge with two or three helpers, young men and women.

"A New Year Greeting, Mistress Finn!" cried Forbian, above the din of the forge.

"Why Master Flink—the year's best to you too, my dear!" was the cheerful reply. "Can we serve your friends' horses any way?"

Then Forbian did the honors, naming Gael and Tomas as scribes and travelers from the Swan's winter sessions in Lort.

"Step in for a sup of mead with Uncle Dane!" said Mistress Finn.

As they dismounted, Gael took the opportunity to check Ebony's shoes and have a small stone removed. Marta Finn, wife of Tam Finn, the smith, praised Ebony and found out his provenance in the Southland.

"I served as a Sword Lily, in far off Krail," she said, "but my good man Tam Finn found me out on a visit to his uncle, Arn Swordmaker. I like the life better here."

Gael was impressed. She thought of saying the name General Yorath, but decided to wait until Forbian spoke. They went into the handsome old house and were made welcome by servants and an old man, Uncle Dane, the eldest surviving son of Old Finn, the Smith, who had taught Yorath to fight as a young lad. He was pleased to talk of this hero, remembered him well, and he was led on by Forbian to tell of a great fight in the stableyard when Yorath and Old Finn defeated a bunch of Danasken mercenaries. An ambush it was, against Strett of Cloudhill and his wife, who fought boldly at her own lord's heel as his esquire, by the Goddess.

Forbian then asked: "Is Mistress Vanna in the brown house, Master Finn?"

"Oh yes," said the old man, slyly. "Will ye take the captain from Coombe for a walk in the woods?"

Tomas explained softly to Gael: Mistress Vanna was a widowed daughter of Finn the Smith, who had cared for Hagnild in his latter years, after he left the service of the Palace Fortress. A young woman who was the cook gave Gael and Tomas fresh food to carry to the brown house: milk, greens, fruit, cooked ham, and fresh eggs. They went off with Forbian riding on the shoulders of Tomas, but the path was easy and well worn, so he often jumped down and skipped on ahead.

Nightwood was a moody place, with the ancient trees and the thickets between them dark in some places and almost shining with their own light in others. They went in silently, pretty deep, and heard only a few bird calls. The path faded, and then there was a brake of holly and other thorny trees, clear across the way. Forbian Flink ran up to this barrier, gestured, and uttered some password. Then there was, by magic, a path through the brake, with soft leaves and fronds in place of the thorns. Before them in a spacious clearing, roofed overhead by the forest, stood a brown house.

It was old but solid and reminded Gael of certain houses in Coombe, even her own home by the Holywell. Forbian Flink knocked politely at the heavy door and it was opened by a tall woman, perhaps fifty years of age, perhaps older. She exclaimed with pleasure at her visitor, and the little man presented his two friends to Mistress Vanna Am Taarn, Guardian of Hagnild's House.

So they came into a warm brown room with a fire glowing gold and green on the broad hearth and two large cats, one striped grey brown, one golden and spotted like the skins of the leopard that Gael had seen in the Burnt Lands. There were settles covered in hides and on the wall some trophies—a shield, a bow—so that the place put her in mind a little of Old Emeris Murrin's quarters in Ardven House by the Cresset Burn.

Mistress Vanna called her granddaughter, a young maid called Erith, and they were both very pleased at the fresh supplies brought along by Gael and Tomas. So they all sat down and Erith served them warmed applewine with spices and fruity bread for the winter season. There was talk straightaway of Yorath Duaring—it was almost a prepared speech that Vanna gave to visitors. Yes, here he had lived and grown and sat with Hagnild over the books and hunted in Nightwood with his friend, Arn, ninth child of Finn the Smith, who later became Arn Swordmaker in Krail.

Then, as they had their cups refilled and took some excellent honeycakes, Forbian said suddenly:

"Do you hear or scry anything of the great wall that is being built in the land of the Inchevin, Mistress Vanna?"

"Indeed," replied the wise woman, her brown eyes catching the firelight. "This wall has been well planned, and the far eastern border of the wide Chameln has never been held stronger. Great leaders press ahead with the work!"

"I will go there in the spring," said Forbian Flink. "My old comrade, Arn Swordmaker, will come out of Krail to carry me." The little man spoke these words with such conviction that Gael was quite astonished.

She had heard only the faintest smatterings from Tomas of the wild tribes of the Eastern Chameln. She could only wonder that lame, town-bound Forbian should conceive such an expedition!

Tomas joined the conversation—the great wall was to keep back the wildest of the tribes, the Skivari and their like, who made brutal, bounty-seeking incursions into the Chameln lands, the realm of the two queens, the Daindru. The talk flowed freely, but Gael was more and more conscious of an undercurrent, something unspoken between Forbian and Vanna Am Taarn. At length, Vanna said directly to Gael:

"Captain Maddoc, I have heard from a friend in the palace that you rode escort to Lady Malm, the royal midwife, and her lord."

"Yes," said Gael. "Their ship was beached on Banlo Strand in the autumn gales, and the Malms came through to Coombe and traveled overland to the king's court."

"You are very discreet," smiled the older woman. "There has been talk of a great adventure and a bold magical rescue, near the Halfway House."

"I had good helpers!" said Gael. She smiled at Tomas and took his hand.

"I was among those rescued," Tomas offered, "and I can bear witness to Gael's courage, if she will not—such magical workings I never saw!"

Vanna's dark eyes were thoughtful. "There was word also of a showing of the Fionnar and the Ruadan, the day Lord and Lady Malm came to the Palace Fortress."

The woman pressed too far. "Why do you ask these things?" Gael said, as politely as she was able.

Vanna stared a moment longer, then seemingly came to a decision. "Come!" she said, and rose up from her place on the settle. "I will show you."

She gave Forbian a nod and a wink and beckoned Gael to follow her. "I think a visitor from Coombe will be interested in seeing some further memorials of Master Hagnild and his pupil, Yorath Duaring."

Gael was suspicious, but she got up to follow her.

"Remember my words, Captain!" piped up Forbian, seizing another cake. "I said, even on that day we met in the Swan's stable, I would surprise you!"

Tomas gave Gael a solemn look, but he made no move to follow her.

The guardian of Hagnild's house led Gael into another comfortable room along the passage; she explained that it had been the Healer's study—there were a number of his books and scrolls. Gael's ring sparkled at her side for the presence of magic, magical objects. Mistress Vanna beheld this and smiled.

"I don't doubt that you can work magic, Captain, for I know the ones you serve—the light folk, blessings upon the poor souls."

"Truly, I do serve them," Gael admitted, staring around at the room and all its contents. "But how has this come to be known?"

"At least one person versed in magic was watching at the gates of the Palace Fortress when the Malms and their escort drove in. That great showing of the Eilif lords beneath the rainbow arch upon the crest of that last hill—you were seen, as well as the marvelous presence of your companions. Great heavens, child, there were the Fionnar—Myrruad and Ilmane in a carriage! I do not know when a mortal, one of the dark folk, has been so honored!"

Gael felt herself blushing.

"I feel myself deeply honored by the chance to serve such folk!" she said. "I have the spirit for the tasks they will set me when I return to them in spring."

"Yes, and you are in love with Tomas the Scribe," said Vanna, smiling in a motherly fashion, "and that has given you even more courage. But now I will change your view of the world, and again for the better."

She whisked aside a fine silken cloth embroidered in green and gold that lay across a table and revealed two large jewels—they could only be Hagnild's scrying stones.

"See here," she said. "This is the Great Wall that is being built in the far northeast of the Chameln lands. Here are the builders and their leaders."

As Gael stepped up to the table, wondering at all this interest in the Great Wall, she heard Tomas give a cry in the outer room.

"There now!" said Mistress Vanna. "Forbian has told the secret to your friend . . ."

Gael looked into the left-hand stone, and in its bluish depths there grew a scene, very clear and natural, like the reflection in a fine mirror or a mountain pool. In the jewel-world there were dark trees and a work place with bricks, mortar, and blocks of stone. At a rough trestle in the open air, there were young men, finely dressed, and a small escort of kedran in uniform. Plans on parchment or vellum were spread out on the trestle, and further back she could see the wall itself, half-made. There was no sound in the world of the stone, but suddenly all heads turned as two men, one old, one younger, came walking into the work yard.

The old man was a giant. He overtopped all those present, he overtopped the world. His long hair was white with a few reddish strands, and he had a strong, cheerful face, ruddy with exertion. The younger man seemed to be his son, almost as tall, and as broadly built—with bright auburn hair and moustaches—clearly these were both Melniros.

"This cannot be!" breathed Gael Maddoc.

"Yet it is so!" whispered Vanna. "The ambush, years past, on the cliffs at Selkray did not kill Yorath Duaring."

"The Great General lives!" said Gael. "And surely that is his son by his side!"

"Yes," said Vanna, "that is Yorath Yorathson, but he has taken the name of his mother—he calls himself Chawn Yorathson."

"And Yorath's lady, the beautiful Owlwife?" asked Gael. Gundril Chawn, Yorath's leman, had never been in Coombe, but Druda Strawn had seen her once in Krail, and she was a part of the old stories.

"Why, she is as beautiful as ever, despite her years," smiled Vanna, "and that gossip, Forbian, has it that she will visit Chiel Hall, to the southeast."

Gael shook her head, for this last name was not familiar to her.

"You have never heard the story of Lien's swans?" Vanna looked surprised.

Gael did not know how to answer. She thought she knew the story, but then, she had thought she had known the history of Yorath at the cliffs of Selkray! Vanna saw this, and took mercy. "Princess Merilla Am Chiel, third in line to the Chameln Zor throne, is Yorath's cousin. As you must know, the Swans of Lien were the daughters of Guenna, the last woman of Lien to rule as Markgrafin—and the mother as well of King Kelen. Guenna's daughters were all married to Hylor's Kings—not that it served to protect any of them from the archmage Rosmer, to whom Kelen had fallen sway."

"Elvédegran of Lien was Yorath's mother!" Gael said.

"That is correct," Vanna replied, "just as Hedris of Lien was Queen Aidris Am Firn's mother, and Aravel, the last swan, mother to that other Daindru King, Sharn Am Zor, the reigning Zor Queen's father."

"But the Witch-Queen is a dwarf!" Gael protested. "How can she and the giant Yorath be cousins?"

"What has the south been teaching you?" Vanna laughed. "The Firn people are short, but they are no dwarves. I suppose you must be a true Melniro, to consider her so!"

Gael blushed, for she considered herself of good Chyrian stock, and she had never thought of herself in this light, despite her fiery hair and long legs. But Vanna had never been to Coombe—perhaps it was not surprising that she should say this.

Then Vanna gave a sigh and went on:

"The Princess Merilla is widowed now—like so many of us. Esher Am Chiel has gone—the good lady manages her property with the help of her two sons. I can guess what the princess and the Owlwife spoke about . . ."

"What is that?" asked Gael.

"The princess still hopes for news, good or ill, of her younger brother, Carel Am Zor, who was never found after the cruel death of King Sharn—what, it must be more than fifteen years ago now. Have you not heard of the Lost Prince?"

"I have," said Gael. The story was very romantic, tied as it was to the ritualistic death of the last Chameln king at the hands of the wild eastern tribes. Following a great betrayal, King Sharn Am Zor had sacrificed himself for his family, for the land . . . and Carel, for whom a brother had died, had slipped away from history's pages. "That story I certainly have heard—they are always mulling over old tales, the secrets of Hylor, at the Swan Inn!"

This news of the Lien cousins was unsettling, for Gael Maddoc had always thought of Hylor's lands as separate nations, each with their own treasures, customs, and ways. To think now how the ruling families were so closely tied together . . . "But Matten, Heir of Lien, must also be a cousin," Gael said aloud, somewhat startled.

"Yes," said Vanna, her manner darkening. "Though it took Kelen years longer than his sisters to get himself a child, young Matten is cousin still to old Aidris and the others. Perhaps that is the reason the Brown Brotherhood feels so threatened by the Land of the Two Queens. Despite all the hand they have had in young Matten's upbringing, they fear to see this tie renewed."

Gael looked again into old Hagnild's scrying stones, now darkened. She was uneasy at the thought of so much hidden in the chronicles of the lands, but at least the secret revealed to her today was not a cause for sorrow.

"I am glad to think that Forbian Flink, a master scribe and a keeper of secrets, will be able to see his old comrade once again!" she said softly.

"He must wait until spring," said Vanna, hiding Hagnild's stones as she pulled the embroidered cloth once again over the table.

Gael gave a sigh. "So must we all," she said. "I have asked a blessing for my enterprise—my service with the light folk—at Hagnild's resting place."

"This spring should be a time of rejoicing," said the guardian of Hagnild's house. "There will be a great celebration in the Chameln lands—Queen Tanit am Zor will wed the young Count Liam Greddaer of Greddach, and many visitors will come out of Eildon. It is said that an Eildon marriage will bridge the angry gap that has opened between the Chameln and Lien—but sadly, I fear the politics of this marriage may have an effect opposite to that which is intended. There are those who do not desire to see the gap between Lien and the Chameln lessened . . ."

"Why does the Brotherhood of the Lame God hate women so?" asked Gael. "Why should they challenge the rights of the double queens?"

Vanna Am Taarn passed a weary hand across her face. "Is that all you have heard in the south? No—it is not that simple. It is not just women the Brown Brotherhood hates. To them, the world is a foul and ugly place. Life, the very senses of the body, is a mud that clouds the spirit. Ah, it is a strange fate indeed that brought sensual, life-loving Lien to their control, that brought Fideth of Wirth, who worshipped at the Lame God's altar, to be Kelen's bride."

This talk was strange to Gael. "In the south we have heard only that Kelen is weak, Fideth's will is strong, and that their heir the young Matten wavers," she said.

Vanna nodded. "In that, they have not heard wrong. Kelen weakens by the year, and now a new zealot has risen at Fideth's side: it is the Witchfinder, Brother Sebald. Pray the Goddess that this cruel hunt dies down!"

Gael had already heard this name at the Swan, spoken among the scribes, but she had given it little attention. Now she marked it. She would ask Tomas more of this later—Lien was her lover's country, and he must have some deep opinions regarding these matters.

They went out into the main room, where Forbian sat on a settle petting Stripe, the great tabby cat, and looking himself like the cat who got the cream. Gael and Tomas exchanged rueful smiles.

"Well, we have been surprised," he said. "Yorath lives! And I may not even hint at it in my work on the New Chronicles."

Late at night they sat by the fire in Gael's tower room. The milder weather had gone—a winter storm had come up, with harsh gusts of wind striking against the narrow windows of the tower room. Tomas poked at the glowing logs and said:

"Do you recall that old scribe I mentioned as a byword?"

"Yes," she said, "what was it again—'No one knows more than Brother Less.'"

"That's the man. He knows as much as Forbian—and now even more, I warrant."

"I thought he was dead," smiled Gael, "a part of history like Valko Firehammer, or Ghanor the Great King, or Fair Felnifarr, the lost bride of Rift Kyrie."

"Well, I've always considered the lost bride pure invention, a tale from the hand of some high-born lady in the Southland," Tomas said, "but Brother Less is very much alive. He was a great scribe and a great one for collecting tales and gossip—he traveled about as a follower of Inokoi, trained at one of their houses in Lien, near Cayl. He told me once that he had spoken to Yorath Duaring in Selkray, before the General's unfortunate death. Now I feel that he helped uncover the truth of the General's 'accident,' and must have known that he survived."

"Where is he now—in a haven of the Brotherhood?"

"Somewhere much more interesting," said Tomas. "Years ago he became the house priest, the chaplain of a noble lady. He claims to have found his enlightenment. I read this in a dispatch from a scribe in Lien. Now Brother Less has formed the Followers of Truth, a reformed group of the Brotherhood."

"He lives dangerously," said Gael. "The king and queen and even the young prince, are guided by the Brotherhood. And now this fanatical Brother Sebald has a witch hunt sweeping the Kingdom." She spoke shyly, almost tentatively, for her knowledge of these things felt new to her, but Tomas only nodded, as though she spoke accepted truth.

"That hunt is directed against the Chameln lands, I think," said Tomas. "The idea of the Land of the Two Queens is unholy to Lien, not least because the tie of blood those queens have to their own heir might serve to lessen their own influence."

"So Brother Less is not in danger?"

"Brother Less is protected—he serves the mother of the powerful Duke Fernan of Chantry, the Dowager Duchess."

"But that must be . . ."

"Yes!" grinned Tomas. "Zelline of Chantry had two sons. The younger one is our curious acquaintance, Lord Auric Barry."

"Oh, Lienish ways are all so strange!" cried Gael, suddenly. She thought of Auric Barry and his mistress Yolanda Hestrem, and could not quell a sour suspicion that the strictures on the common women of the land must be harsher than those which governed the folk born to a higher estate. "I am weary after today's magic. I long for the spring to come, but I am afraid of my employment with the Shee. I wish I could return to this tower, where we have been so happy through the winter."

He drew her down to his side—she sat on the sheepskin rug and leaned her head on his knee.

"I have had the same thoughts," he said in a low voice, stroking her hair. "The spring will come, and you will ride out bravely—I have asked Mistress Beck, and the tower room will be ours. As a betrothed pair . . ."

He drew out a small coffer from his sleeve pocket, and in it lay two silver rings in a simple plaited design; the larger ring was plain and the other set with three small moonstones. Gael caught her breath; they exchanged the rings in the firelight. Outside the storm howled about Lort and flurries of sleet were flung against the sturdy walls of the Swan, where lights still burned in many of the windows.

INTERLUDE:

THE REALM OF THE TWO QUEENS

I
The Hidden Rooms

There were hidden rooms high up in Chernak New Palace. Queen Tanit Am Zor, she whose heart was called cold, spent much time there in secret, when she was believed to be asleep, at prayer, having fittings for her clothes, or visiting some other great house. The young queen had never enjoyed reading, but now, at last, she read hungrily in books of history and magic. No other person had been told of the rooms, but she thought it likely that some of her closest attendants knew of them and guessed where she kept hidden. She kept watch stones all about the entrance to the rooms, ready to flash a warning and to show who was approaching.

Once Tanit saw a young page, a handsome boy called Dene, wandering about in the chapel outside the rooms. How would it be if she let him in—swore him to secrecy—teased him. Or better still, she thought harshly, when Dene, all innocent, had simply gone away through the corridors, she could have used a spell to strike him dumb.

Then there came a dream. At night in her sumptuous bedchamber, she dreamed that she stood in the largest of the hidden rooms, excited, half clothed. Dene the page was dead. He lay on a carpet and shriveled and divided until he was no more than a basketful of dead leaves, which she scattered from the mouth of a gargoyle onto the gardens below.

Of course the queen was well guarded; there was a palace guard of tall foot soldiers, the Tall Oaks, and two companies of kedran, who ran the palace and its stables. Besides this, there was the queen's personal bodyguard, the Companions. Ten chosen soldiers, five kerns, five kedran, who lurked about discreetly in dark clothes. They knew the location of the Hidden Rooms but did not come too close. Tanit did not like being guarded: the Companions were not her friends.

She commanded many persons, but there was no one she loved and trusted. Ishbel Seyl, daughter of her Chancellor, had been a kind of 'best friend.' Ishbel was a beauty, a simple girl, lost without her domineering mother. Now she was married to young Lord Barr and lived in a great mansion by the Danmar, the inland sea.

Tanit was full of an angry guilt because of her own mother, whom she could see as the best, most kind and worthy person in the world. Yet she could not love her mother as she should. The young queen's heart was a hidden room, a cold room, full of old tales, of voices, even, which told of treachery and death.

On an old hanging shelf near one slitted window she had set up two portraits, larger than miniatures, but coming from the school of the great portrait painter Emyas Bill, famed for the delicacy of his small work. There was a young woman with dark hair and blue eyes, wearing a simple blue and white gown and a single great yellow jewel at her throat, on silver chains. She was not too much taken with the portrait and had been pleased when Lord Seyl looked quizzical and said perhaps it was too bland.

The other portrait showed a young man—another young man, one of Emyas Bill's trusted pupils, had traveled to Eildon to do this work. Prince Liam Greddaer of Greddach had rich brown black hair and taut, aquiline features. Yet his expression was sweet and pleasant; he wore a half smile, and it was for a spaniel, black and white, which sat on a hassock before his tall chair.

She had found a way to exchange informal letters with the prince. His formal letters, including the announcement of his suit and the declaration of his Troth Gift, were written in a fine, straight letter, by a secretary. The informal letters, which were carried by the wife of an envoy, Lady Fayne, were in a fluent Merchant's Script, which she judged to be more childish than her own:

I hope you will not blame me if I say that I have read every word I could find about your late father, King Sharn Am Zor and his time in Eildon and all of his life and his most tragic and noble death. I have a few works by me of the great poet Robillan Hazard, your father's friend, and I have my factors searching for more of his work. Perhaps these are to be found in Chameln Achamar, where the poet died, at a good age, not many years past.

Tanit herself was not sure if she cared for Hazard. They had met a few times; he had dedicated several of his last works to her. Perhaps she envied all those who had known her father, the king. She had done her best for years at the classes on history and government that Lord Seyl tried to arrange, with and without fellow schoolmates. The most agreeable and sensible schoolfellow was Hal of Denwick, son of old Zilly, another of her father's friends.

There was a dreadful suitability about him as a prospective suitor. She was absolutely cold and cruel to him from the time she was twelve years old, and tormented him in the classes with her waywardness. But even with her growing beauty as a lure, he was too sensible to persevere—to her surprise, he left the Chameln lands and traveled into the Kingdom of Lien, to his family holdings at Denwicktown and elsewhere. Then he was off to Eildon, had purchased new estates, and was studying with a tutor from the household of Prince Ross Tramarn, soon to become Eildon's new Priest-King.

Then there were two outlandish suitors, one a King of the Milgo who lived beyond the mountains in the southeast. He pointed out that Queen Tanit would be permitted to spend half a year in her own lands and that she would be his number one wife. The other was a distant cousin, a connection of her paternal grandmother's father's family, the Pendarks of Eildon—the great-grandfather who had been married to Guenna of Lien. Tanit's suitor, Eorl Kimber, was one of the seven eorls of Eildon, and he held estates of moderate size in the northernmost reaches of the Pendark lands, almost touching the lands of Paldo, in the center of Eildon. His Troth Gift, a present, an earnest to prove a suitor's worth, had to equal or exceed in value, tradition, beauty, and so forth a named piece of the bride's own lands. In this case, she and Lord Seyl and her mother had settled upon the Royal Memorial Park by the river Chind. It contained the hunting lodge called Greybear, where King Sharn in past days had gone in summer, all the wide acres surrounding the lodge, and the Valley of the Stones, a sacred place, a place of pilgrimage for Queen Tanit.

Kimber was ill-advised: he offered a hunting revier in the north famed not for anything sacred but for a country fair. The queen and her court were insulted, even those who held Tanit Am Zor for cold and half-mad.

She knew they were right; since the day of her father's foul murder they had been right; secretly she prayed to the Goddess that if she was granted a true love, she would be healed, that the hidden rooms of her soul would be filled with peace and soft light.

In this hidden correspondence with Liam of Greddaer of Greddach, she had been relieved to perceive in herself a sort of lightening—she could only pray this was an omen of better things to follow.

Count Liam's Troth Gift was in perfect taste: it was a sacred island in a lake in the northwest of Eildon, the lake isle of Elsmere, on which there was an ancient shrine to a pair of lovers, Mavair and Aengus, from the times before the Holy College and the Priest-Kings.

She made sure that all of Hazard's works were sent at once to Count Liam. They wrote, through Lady Fayne. His distrust of those about him echoed her own—perhaps it was at the very heart of their connection. *My half-brother is in the Sacred College of the Druda, but like many priests, he has worldly ambitions. I think we must let him perform the ceremony, together with your good cousin Gradja. O, when we are together in Chernak, in your Kingdom, how great my happiness will be. Are you certain of the spells that protect our letters?* And she was able to reply: *Yes, I am sure, my dear. The letters are safe even from Fayne herself.*

Tanit very nearly confided something else. Her paraphernalia of watch-stones and protective spells told her that *someone* was trying to get through, to communicate with her, in her secret retreat. A boy—no a man—with dark eyes and a ragged brown robe, though the rings on his fingers were fine and golden. She could not tell what he wanted; she began to spend less time in the hidden rooms—it went about that the queen's cold heart was warmed by her handsome Eildon count.

Seyl spoke frankly about the groom's terrible old great-uncle, the Duke of Greddach, who had once exhibited captured folk of the Tulgai, the small race who inhabited the Chameln's great border forest, in his park at Boskage in the south of Eildon. Now the present duke was renowned a collector as bad or worse—he kept the notorious Museum in the extended park. Rumor had it he'd displayed a sacred Chyrian treasure, the Star Kelch of the Nymph Taran. Now it had been stolen—taken back by some loyal Chyrian. But then, the duke treated all around him like toys for his collection. Her betrothed, who had lost both his parents as a child, confided he had felt himself part of that collection, a bartered toy, until the day—upwards of five years past now—he had gained his own inheritance.

Tanit Am Zor still slipped away to the hidden rooms, but she allowed them to become lighter, more comfortable; she had daydreams of bringing

Liam to her secret places. But as the guests from Eildon began their progress into the Chameln lands, she had one last dream that threw again a shadow on her thoughts. She saw a portrait upon the wall of her throne room, and it was veiled. As she watched, filled with a strange lassitude she knew to associate with magic, a hand lifted aside the veil. The boy she had seen sometimes before was seated under an oak tree. He had straight features and long, dark blond curls: now he had shed his ragged robe for rich, almost kingly dress. He was frowning, holding in his lap a richly bound book. When it seemed he knew she was watching, he opened the book to her. There on the first leaf was a picture of three silver swans upon azure water, a black swan watching from the land. She was intrigued. In her dream the boy turned the page, and there was yet another picture, this time a more formal portrait, of an older man. He might have been forty, but it was hard to tell his age. He was handsome, if a little aged, with thick, ash-colored hair: he wore a clipped brown beard. This man, the picture within the picture, was shown smiling; he held in his hand two oak twigs crossed, sign of the Daindru thrones, complete with spring-budded leaves. The boy closed the book on this portrait and frowned; Tanit thought he gave her warning.

As this picture faded, she thought the portrait of the man within the book had a look of King Sharn Am Zor, her beloved father, the last person on earth for whom she had felt the true warmth of love . . .

II
Aidris Am Firn

Aidris Am Firn was glad that her health remained good. She had been blessed with her heir, Sasko, serious minded and certain to make a good king. Now he was wed to his wild northern girl from the Nureshen, and Micha, her elder daughter, had married a man from the central highlands, Rigan of Nevgrod Heights. The queen had been gifted with six grandchildren—two from Sasko, boy and girl, and four—count them—three girls and a boy, from Micha. Maren, the youngest, had always confided in her mother; she did not marry and at the age of sixteen was professed as a Moon Sister, in the service of the Goddess, with the sisterhood who had formerly lived in Benna, near the pass that led into Athron. Aidris had since given the Sisters a country estate nearer the city of Achamar—Benna was too close to the Kingdom of Lien, governed in part by the Brotherhood of Lame Inokoi.

Aidris was praised as a wise woman and a good mother, but she took little heed of the praise directed at a queen. She knew that she had failed in the matter of Tanit Am Zor, her co-ruler; she was stricken with grief and pain by this failure, as if she had failed Sharn himself, a man so golden and beloved all had called him Summer's King.

It was simply too easy to date this failure. Aidris had always been close to Lorn, the bereaved wife of Sharn Am Zor—in fact the quiet kedran girl, sent into her service by Old Gilyan, one of her Torch Bearers, had been her choice as a possible bride for Sharn. But Tanit—her beautiful niece had much in her blood that had come from her glorious, passionately headstrong father. The Heir of the Zor had never been close to anyone since the day of her father's death.

Aidris prayed to the Goddess that her niece's coming marriage might finally bring a healing; she recognized in Tanit's demeanor a wild, almost desperate eagerness that this should take place. Yet this very wildness concerned the old queen, made her wonder again what lay at the rooted heart of Tanit's chill. Was there some hidden magic here? Aidris might have suspected the Brown Brotherhood, but for the fact that these folk eschewed the magic arts, punished those who were thought to use them. If Rosmer had been alive, she would have known her answer—Rosmer, the fearful sorcerer, the eater of souls, had hounded every descendant of Guenna of Lien, wracked by greedy hunger to maintain his power over Lien's throne.

Though of course, if her best guess was right, Rosmer in truth was in some way at the problem's root . . .

In her deepest heart, Aidris feared Tanit's coldness was a mark of King Sharn Am Zor's last, his only, spell, the *Hunting of the Dark*, the *Harkmor*, the ox-felling. If so—nothing so simple as a marriage would heal it, all hope must be lost. Yet this marriage might at least bring another generation, a renewal . . .

Tanit had been nine years old when her father was murdered—just two years younger than Aidris had been on the day she witnessed her own father's assassination, back in the days when the Melniros had seized control of the Chameln. But there were differences, important differences. Racha Am Firn's death had come from a clean killing blow, however deeply steeped in betrayal and Old King Ghanor's martial ambitions. Sharn Am Zor's death had been surrounded by magic and familial betrayals that, even now, Aidris was loath to remember.

And of course it had been Rosmer of Lien, hounding the Swans of Lien and their heirs, who had orchestrated Sharn's death. He had cast his web of magic over Sharn's disaffected and willing cousins, the Inchevins, along with the king's boon companion Tazlo Am Ahrosh. Some even went so far as to say that Carel Am Zor, Sharn's younger brother, now called "the Lost Prince," had fallen under Rosmer's influence, though others, including Merilla Am Chiel, Sharn and Carel's sister, swore this could not be so.

But whatsoever the case, whoever it was in the circle around him who had made the betrayals, Sharn had been lured to his death on the Chameln's eastern border, and in his last hours, he had known—he had cursed—the spider hand that had brought him there. He was a true King, and the power in him, going willing to his death, was strong. Dying, he called down the *Harkmor*, the spell of vengeance, and his strength was such indeed that he carried Rosmer with him through death's portal. The day Sharn Am Zor fell was the day his uncle Kelen was crowned Lien's king; but the spider Vizier who had raised Kelen to this height had not lived to enjoy his liege lord's victory.

No. That had been left to the Brown Brotherhood. Those carrion had swooped to fill the vacuum left by Rosmer's death, and those men—to Lien, they had proved worse tyrants than Rosmer. For the folk who were not of Guenna of Lien's blood, those who were not potential heirs of Lien, living—oh, unbearable!—outside of his control . . . despite all her family's suffering, Aidris recognized that the misery Rosmer spread had been contained. But the Brown men—with the Brown men in power, the suffering in Lien had spread to the land's every corner.

The old queen sighed. A sad fate indeed had fallen on her mother's country. But it was the Chameln, not Lien, that must be Aidris's concern.

This *Harkmor* Sharn had called . . . in her deepest heart, Aidris knew it had left its dark mark also on Tanit.

Tanit's upcoming marriage—the old queen had done her best for her young co-ruler. Liam Greddaer was young and handsome, an Eildon marriage would bring Tanit much prestige . . . and perhaps the new Zor consort would bring a smoothening of the Chameln's relations with Lien, in the last years grown so rancorous. It was hard for Aidris to hold onto the hope, though as queen, it was a hope she *must* hold on to. The Brotherhood of the Lame God were unreasoning fanatics, but with Kelen of Lien aging and disabled, Aidris had come to understand that among Inokoi's cult there were extreme and even more dangerous factions, wrestling for power as the king reluctantly loosened life's hold.

In her scrying stones, she had seen her young cousin Matten, Kelen's heir, and she could see that he was not all his mother's son, dedicated to sackcloth and scouring. There were days when he slipped over the palace walls, broke free, if only for a short hours' grace. Would this be enough?

What would happen, in just one year, when Matten reached his majority? She thought of the boy, with his dark eyes and the ragged brown robe his mother and her counselors so often forced upon him—a drab shell in a land where the nobles still jaunted free, still wore their garb of silk and velvet. Would Matten revolt against his mother and her counselors, or would he turn his spleen against the nobles of Lien, those shining folk who had brought him so much humiliation in his youth, even as he shared his mother's gowns?

Aidris sighed. She thought she knew at least the next intrigue that would be forced upon the Chameln—she had heard its stirrings. If she was right, Tanit's marriage would flush it forth.

The queen-haters in Lien—perhaps in a conspiracy with some faction of those in treacherous, ever self-serving Eildon—would attempt to establish a rival to the throne of Zor, would attempt to upset the succession. Aidris had begun to hear murmurs of "the Lost Prince"—as if the Zor had *ever* been without an heir. For a thousand years, the Daindru, the twin oaks, in lines unbroken, had ruled the Chameln. But now there were murmurs out of Lien: Tanit was not the true heir, her Uncle Carel, banished by those who would set Tanit up in his place, should be called home. Tanit must be taken down—her marriage to Liam Greddaer of Greddach must not take place, or perhaps it could be voided, if only she could be proved a pretender to the Zor throne.

These thoughts made Aidris gnash her teeth. Tanit was indeed the first ruling Zor queen in seven generations, but that was a chance of birth, no ordered exclusion of women from the line of rule. And if not Tanit—Merilla, the child between Sharn and Carel, would have held the throne. But not for the Brown Brotherhood was this reasoning. They followed their own logic, not caring of the pain they brought to families, their desecrations against the bonds of love.

Her real sadness—whatever man was brought forth in Carel's name would prove a pretender. For Carel had certainly not been banished—in the chaos following Sharn's death, he had simply disappeared. His role in Sharn's death, his own fate—whether dead at Skivari hands, in treasonous retreat among their company, or taken as a hostage—had never been determined.

Like Merilla, Aidris was inclined to a trusting view of Carel. She knew the prince, since the day of his arrival in the Chameln Lands with his sister Merilla, a pair of runaways from the court of Lien, where they had been held as gilded-cage captives.

Prince Carel? He was eager and innocent and a little too young to easily make a place for himself in his homeland, a country estranged to him by seven years of exile at Lien's courts. Carel was anxious to have a brother again, to please his brother, to join in his life; but Sharn, busy learning to be a king and a man, could not become close to Carel—certainly, Carel had felt swept aside. Soon it was too late—though Aidris preferred to believe "too late" meant their separation by Sharn's death, not Carel's proving traitor.

Reason said Carel had simply died in the battles that followed the king's capture. It was well-known that Derda Am Inchevin, daughter of the mad old traitor who had led the uprising, had ridden off with Rugal of the Skivari, the Terror of the North. She had become one of his lesser wives and died in childbirth.

Ah, but this "Lost Prince" nonsense. Lost princes were a threat. Even Merilla, who had spent much time trying to find the truth, by magic and with the help of trusted searchers, now hoped for proof of death. Aidris knew this would not satisfy those who longed for wonders and the return of the long lost. There would be pretenders as there had been for hundreds of years, set up, usually, to benefit noble families politically. There had been pretenders when the Chameln Lands were in the grip of Ghanor of Mel'Nir. A poor young actress, befuddled by spells, had been given a false life, the imagined life of Aidris the Queen. Even now, through the years, Aidris could still feel the shock of confronting that benighted creature face to face.

Another pretender, the False Sharn, had acted more deliberately—he had rallied the southern lords and helped drive out the Melniros. Aidris was able to smile now, remembering. She had once, before she wed Bajan, given her heart to another, then taken it back again. Now, widowed for years, she walked in her gardens with a seafaring man, a merchant, with long grey moustachios, who went on trading ventures to the Lands Below the World. A man much given to role-playing, even, an *actor* . . .

"Do not fret, my brave Queen," said Raff Masura, as the spring came closer. "Poor Tanit Am Zor surely loves this Eildon boy, Count Greddach. All the reports, from the people and from your own watchers, say that she is happier . . ."

"You mean less mad," sighed Aidris.

"There is madness in all of us," he replied seriously. "She is less cold. The ice is melting in her heart. Speak to her a year after she has wed."

"Mark my words," she said, smiling a little. "If she and Liam prove too warm, there will be a pretender or two."

"Some have their reasons." He pressed her hand, and she could not help but feel a pang at all the sacrifices this man—lover, pretender, the first rolling stone on the slope that had made the Chameln lands free from Mel'Nir—all the sacrifices this man had made for her.

"There is someone else, in the scrying stones," she said. "A woman, a kedran. From the past or the future or one foretold. Have you heard of a battlemaid who rides on errands for the Shee, the last remnants of the poor souls, in mighty Tulach Hall . . .?"

"No, by all the Gods, I have not," said Raff Masura. "You can find her out!"

"Grandmother Guenna has passed into the sunset herself," said Aidris. She made a small gesture with her hand, negating him. "She had a much stronger power than I do. Everyone has passed on . . . Lingrit has gone and Sabeth and your father, Jalmar . . . Poor Iliane Seyl and old Zilly of Denwick."

"Here comes one who is still going strong!" he said, to cheer her.

And there, striding down the archery lawn from the mighty wooden palace of the Firn, was a tall, sturdy old woman in kedran dress.

"My Queen," cried Ortwen Cash, who had ridden in Athron with the queen. "Have you ever heard of a town on the Chyrian coast called Coombe?"

"I don't think so," said Aidris. "But wait—yes, I have it . . ."

They sat at the round table under a spreading ash, and the servants nearby came at once to serve the queen and her friends.

"Yorath Duaring was in Coombe during the civil wars in Mel'Nir," said Aidris, "fighting for Krail. He raised a horde of Chyrians to relieve the besieged garrison at Hackestell Fortress. They became the Westlings—part of the army of the Westmark."

"There is a Holy Spring in Coombe," said Ortwen. "I have this from your own friend, Mistress Vanna, in Hagnild's house by Nightwood. The *Wanderer,* this maid of destiny, comes from Coombe. She is of Chyrian blood, yet she is also almost one of the 'great warriors' of Mel'Nir, a tall lusty lass capped with tresses of red; they say she has visited the Shee in Tulach Hall."

"They are lost," said Aidris sadly. "A lost race, fading one by one: aged ladies, the Fionnar, fading into the sunset."

"Will you find the battlemaid?" asked Raff Masura, with a grin. "I do not think anyone can hide from the pair of you!"

"Go along with you, Seafarer!" said old Ortwen, giving him a push.

Aidris watched their interchange and smiled, trying to keep a face of calm, though inwardly she felt new excitement rising. Perhaps—perhaps her fears for Tanit would prove unfounded. Perhaps the girl would be healed . . . "No," she said. "If this *Wanderer* is the one I seek, she will journey this way on her own account."

III
The Lightening

The days before the wedding were trying—they would not let her see him, and she did not know if the last ice would abate. She grew querulous, and all around her drew back, dark with fear, and her anger rose in its turn, to know they imagined the coldness had returned to her. *Just let me see him,* her heart was keening. *I must know, finally, if I will ever be free of this chill.*

The court of Zor was desperate to improve her mood. Every effort was made to distract her, all of it serving the wrong turn. To soothe her, the aged keeper of the treasures, the ancient serving woman Riane Am Rhanar, even brought her so far as the Gift Treasury, but the sight of all the precious treasures stored up against her wedding day only drove Tanit into a fury.

"These cold stones!" she cried. "These cold stones are not what I seek from my marriage-pledge!" The piles were all around her, stifling her heart: jewels and gold, encrusted hunting weapons and saddles and cloth-of-gold and everything imaginable for this blessed wedding. She thought—in the one small corner of her mind that was not tied up in all her selfish, frantic passions—of the honor this marriage would bring the Daindru thrones. Then she felt cold and small, and even more diminished.

Lady Riane, her features still fine beneath the soft wrinkles—as a young girl she had come from Lien to the Chameln, a serving woman to so distant a figure as Aidris's long-dead mother—in her age and wisdom, she understood a little of Tanit's despair, and she tried to comfort her.

"Dan Tanit," she said, "my beloved Queen. Not all of these are gifts for statesmanship. There is love here also. See—look here, my lady, at this—" She held up a tarnished bronze box, beautifully hammered with leaves and flowers. "This will be stones, perhaps, but as a gift it holds a meaning more lively. They say it is a present from Prince Beren Pendark and his mother, the Lady Merigaun. She is the aunt of your betrothed, I believe—the woman who made suit to free him of the old duke, when his parents so untimely were taken. Surely this is a gift of love?"

Almost against her will, Tanit found herself looking at the bronze box.

She should not have touched it—in a matter of safety, to keep her free from spells, she should have had Mekkin Am Rann, her taster and bodyguard, be the first to hold it in her hands. But Mekkin was not here—she would not stop to have her called, yes, she would open the box—

It was a shining necklace of graduated blue white stones, uncut but highly polished. They were ice, they were a blue fire that melted ice . . . Tanit realized she was shaking. There was magic here, a power, a purity. A risk.

"This gift is mine from this moment," she proclaimed.

Riane drew back, alarmed, and glanced anxiously toward the doorway. "Dan Tanit, I did not mean . . ." She shrank before Tanit's imperial gaze. "My Queen, these gifts are for presentation after the wedding."

"No," Tanit said, sudden queenly. "The rest can wait. This I take charge of from this moment."

The stones were cold to the touch—colder than nature, but Tanit would not fear them. She placed the necklace in Riane's hands, and her poor lady of treasures, her age-softened fingers trembling, undid the clasp and placed it around Tanit's lovely young throat.

"There you are, my Queen."

Tanit's smile, as Riane brought a mirror, was warm. "There I am indeed," she said softly. "Think you not I will make a beautiful bride?"

As Tanit turned, and the old woman looked into her face, the breath caught in her throat; she dropped to her knees before her lady. Tanit, shining with newfound wonder and rushing joy, placed her hands on the old woman's shoulders and raised her up. *More than this,* the young queen thought, feeling the shudder of the old woman's heart against her own breast. She felt herself transformed, felt a fresh freeness running all through her, as though she had come, at long last, to the end of an old, cold dream. She looked over Riane's shoulder into the glass of the mirror and smiled at her own reflection. *I will put my childish pain behind me, and I will rule with Aidris as equal queen, upon the Daindru thrones.*

The formalities of their meeting were trying, but they had looked and loved with one burning glance. When Liam took her hand, she was filled with longing. Now that Kirstin, Lady Fayne, the queen's true friend, was here in person and the watchers, the holy stones, all set in place, Tanit was bold.

Of course Liam had his own familiar, a valet called Mack who helped him come to the hidden rooms. And there, without more ado, they made love, eagerly, warmly, perfectly, upon an old soft bed, covered with glowing silks and soft linen. Tanit cried out once, very softly, and Liam kissed away her tears, her slightest wounds. She felt wonderfully serene—no one knew their secret—at least not for certain. But then, at one of the ongoing ceremonies she caught her brother, Gerd, looking at her in surprise, and she blushed.

So it went on, her charmed wedding feast, and sure enough, there came the portrait she had been shown in her dream. Now that the portrait had arrived, she told Liam about her warning dream of the swans and the dark-eyed boy. Tanit kept the picture in their bedchamber until all the revels and ceremonies were done and the vast array of guests and their escorts swarmed away, down the Bal, through Athron, even a few impatient guests from Eildon or the Southland who were carried home by magic.

Then, in this nowhere time before the life of the court had settled, Tanit and Liam brought the portrait to a small retreat, their smallest audience room, and propped it upon a desk. They sat staring at it. The frame—this much at least they knew—was out of Eildon.

"Does it look like Prince Carel?" asked Liam.

"Yes," she said, "but it is a family likeness. I suppose the age is more or less right. It looks like my father, wearing a beard. Perhaps some Pendark cousin?"

"I swear it is not Carel, nor a cousin," said Liam angrily. "Some fellow with a chance resemblance, maybe from the Pendark lands. They have a festival in the east, near that Oakhill, in the picture, where there are players in a pageant, picked for their likeness to golden Shennazar, to your royal father." Shennazar, Tanit had learned without amusement, was the Eildon pronunciation of her father's name. It said much for her newfound love that she had not corrected him—she already accepted he was trying for her sake to repair this "fault."

"Old Aidris is fussing about a pretender—there have been many of them over the years," said Tanit. "She is sending for Emyas Bill, the old Master Painter, to see the portrait before we see the subject himself."

"You will have this man come here?"

"We will have him in our power, to observe him," said Tanit, clenching her hands. "What d'ye think the plan would be if the man was acknowledged as Carel, my father's brother, the Lost Prince?"

"Disruption," said Liam. "At the very least, a watcher at court, who sends reports to his master. At worst . . ."

He suddenly caught her in his arms, where they sat on a velvet settle.

"I know, I know who would do such a thing," he whispered. "And you know him, too, and it fills me with shame! I fear it is my priestly half-brother himself. He would break our marriage, my uncle has been working on him. He would not see me raised to power, or to joy—"

Tanit, who had always believed that she knew the ways of the world, did her best to conceal her shock. Druda Aengus had been one of their marriage celebrants! He had taken his leave very promptly after the ceremony—perhaps this was why. But she thought about the warning the dark-eyed boy had given her in her dreams—the swans, the boy's brown robes—and she did not think Eildon alone was to blame here.

Next day, they waited for a visitor in the same room, with the portrait. In she came, a tall, well-made older woman, burning with mad anxiety and the hope of many years.

"Dear Goddess!" cried Merilla Am Zor. "Bless you Tanit! Bless you too, Count Liam!"

She gave them each a firm embrace and a kiss, flung down a magnificent sheaf of flowers on the table.

"Where is the thing? Ah—"

She sat on a brocade chair and surveyed the portrait. Tears stole down her cheeks, and she wiped them away with her kerchief. At length she said:

"No. It is a marvelous portrait, but not of Carel. I wonder who on earth it might be?"

"Aidris posits some distant Pendark connection," said Tanit. "She will send old Emyas Bill to look over the picture. Aunt Merilla, have you heard of a magic battlemaid, called the *Wanderer*?"

"Yes," said Merilla, "she comes from Coombe, in the Chyrian lands of Mel'Nir, where our cousin Yorath Duaring did great things. Now this Captain Maddoc rides about doing good and going errands for the Shee."

"She was here, in the escort of Merigaun Pendark," said Tanit. "A tall, strong red-haired kedran. One of the wedding guides, Auric Barry, suggested I might enlist her services to find out more of this pretender."

"Good idea!" said Merilla, in her blunt way. "Maybe she could go into Eildon!"

She turned away reluctantly from the portrait and said:

"Did Gerd see the picture before he went off on this study tour to Mel'Nir with my boys?"

"No," said Tanit, "they all went rushing away—it is the kind of thing they enjoy!"

Then both women laughed fondly in a motherly fashion.

"Nay, come," laughed Liam, "I have been on many tours—to see ancient monuments, to see my beautiful lake—your lake now, my love, for it is the Troth Gift. Would you have young men all roystering and fighting?"

"Alas," said Princess Merilla Am Chiel. "We have had some of that in Old Achamar. My dear Carel ran about the streets with young rogues called the Salamanders—even Sasko, heir of the Firn, joined them on a few escapades."

"The Inchevin," said Tanit bitterly. "A bad branch of the royal houses. And that evil man from the north, Tazlo Am Ahrosh . . ."

She reached for the hand of Count Liam, and her deep blue eyes filled with tears.

"Ah Goddess," cried Merilla. "We must not mourn over old times and all those who are lost! Come, sweet niece, dearest Queen. Come with your true sweetheart into the gardens, and we will drink kaffee from the lands below the world!"

She turned back, gathered up her bundle of flowers, and rang the bell for a servant, who carried them away to arrange. Then, stealing another glance at the portrait, Merilla said:

"Did you read the lettering on the saddle in the portrait?"

"Yes indeed," said Liam. "It seems to say A Y V . . ."

"For Ayvid," Merilla said with a rueful smile. "Carel's horse, which was never found. These tricksters have been very thorough."

BOOK III

CHAPTER X

THE FIRST TASK

Ebony was restless, throwing up his head to snuff the spring breezes. It was the appointed time—the twelfth day of the Willowmoon, the Month of Planting, about midday, and they were on the main street of Aird, the village of the Shee, home of changelings of both kinds. Aird was one of the prettiest places Gael had ever seen, not so dear to her as Coombe or the villages in Pfolben fields, but rich with flowers and trees. The houses and cottages rambled a little, as did the roses. She passed an inn called the Two Unicorns and came to her trysting place, the inn called Tzurn's Haven.

She tried to ride into the innyard, under an arch twined with reddish leaves, but Ebony started back and would not go into the neat, old yard. No other horses were to be seen in the yard, although there was a heavy old grey with plumed hooves and a plaited tail hitched to a rail outside the inn door. She got down, looking toward a man in brown with the air of a groom, who stood chewing a juicy apple just outside the archway. He made no move to help her, to hold Ebony while she removed her saddlebags. Choosing to ignore him, she led Ebony to the other end of the hitching rail, fed him some apple of her own and urged him in whispers, with her own firm stroking of his shining neck, to stand firm. Then she took her saddlebags and her good lance and went into the inn.

It was dark after the spring sunshine, but she soon beheld a spacious room with only a few customers. A party of travelers in bright clothes were taking a midday meal at a round table. She set down her load at a smaller table by a window; a man's voice called harshly:

"Don't sit there, kedran! And y'can bring no weapons in here!"

Gael had not expected a rude reception in Aird—she counted it as an anteroom to Tulach Hearth, the abode of the light folk. Now she sat down deliberately and waited until a heavy dark man came striding across to her table.

"Are you deaf, soldier?"

"My name is Maddoc," she said coldly. "Captain Maddoc, and I am awaited at this inn, on this day. I will sit here, where I can see my horse. Bring me a small ale and buttered bread, if you have it."

"*Awaited* are you?" sneered the dark man. "Get out before you are hurled down the high street! This is Aird you're in, and you must fear our uses! Awaited indeed!"

Gael was more puzzled than ever and wondered if this was some kind of test of her resolve or her patience. Could the Shee have all vanished away, forgotten their compact with her? Was it a reaction to the strange comings and goings on the River Bal and in Lienish Balbank—the Eildon Princes coming to the Chameln lands for the royal wedding? She tried to temporize, knowing she had no advantage—she could not name those who awaited her.

"Good sir," she said. "I understand your uses well and will not offend any in Aird. In the name of the Goddess, let me wait here and bring a little sustenance for a traveler."

She stripped off a gauntlet and let her right hand rest on the table's edge: her ring flashed in a rainbow of colors. The dark man, far from being soothed, became more angry than ever.

"You and your trumpery ring! Think you know magic, d'ye? Think you can partake of our heritage, here in Aird! Try one tithe of a working here in Tzurn's Haven, and you'll know all about it! Outside, I say! If anyone *awaits* you they can find you on the bench under the next window. Go quickly! I'll send out your small ale if I don't change my mind!"

"I think you'll regret being so rude," said Gael.

She got up, loaded up her saddlebags and her lance. As she trailed out again, the guests at the round table laughed and questioned the host. He waved his arms and complained. Some folk never listened. This was Aird, not the kedran barracks.

Outside she set down her belongings on the bench: Aird was as comely as ever; the sun was shining and the air was full of the scent of flowers. She went to soothe Ebony and saw a carriage in the innyard that had been closed to her, or at least to her horse. She waited as patiently as she could, and presently a buxom young girl with bright brown eyes came out with her ale and bread. Gael found out the name of the host, Master Galdo, and the girl's name, Bergit.

"Who's your tryst, kedran?" the girl said boldly. "A maid or a man?"

"A fire-breathing dragon from the Burnt Lands!" grinned Gael sourly. She paid her score and added a small tip.

"There, now," said Bergit, giving advice. "That's the kind of reply that puts Master Galdo in a rage. Joking of magic and dragons because this is Aird, supposed to be a magic place. We've had too much of it, Captain, in these days before the Chameln wedding!"

"Bergit," said Gael, "Master Galdo was harsh and rude. I am a stranger in your beautiful village, and I can say no word of the people who bade me wait at this inn on this day. Please try and soothe your master."

Then she was made alert by a stinging from her magic ring and a single bell note that rang faintly in her head. Far away, at the end of the neat white street and its cobbled squares, a figure on a white horse had appeared. The rider wore a pale homespun cloak and a black hood, on which she could soon pick out bands of green. The young girl, Bergit, thumbed her forehead, in a gesture of protection and said in a low voice:

"O Blessed Huntress . . . !"

She ran back inside the inn. Gael barely had time to load Ebony with her saddlebags and couch her lance in its traveling bands before the rider came up to the small fountain in the cobbled square before Tzurn's Haven. Now she took the rider for a man and wondered if it might be Luran in person. She read the hood as a mark of mourning and was afraid for the last of the Shee. The rider held a lance now, with wisps of drapery upon it, and he beckoned her with this weapon. She mounted up on Ebony, who was pleased to be moving again, and walked him sedately toward the rider on the white horse.

She saw with wonder that the horse was real enough, but the rider was stranger to behold than the Shee themselves. He was a wraith—his long gaunt face under the hood half-transparent, with bright burning eyes that glowed like a cat's eyes in darkness. When she came up, he said in a low voice, penetrating as winter wind:

"Captain Maddoc—I am called *Waltan*—I have been sent to fetch you!"

It was the name of a mythic figure, one of the shades who fetched the dead to the heaven of the warriors or to other heavenly abodes. Gael could see him as a warrior himself, a ghost, a man who had once lived. She saluted and gave a polite greeting. He bade her take one of the misty pennants from the tip of his lance and lined up Ebony close beside the patient white mare. Then he set the tip of his lance on the cobblestones before him, and a circle of blue fire sprang to life, ringing the two horses. That cloud of mist Gael recalled from the rescue at Silverlode settled down as he uttered the spell. The sensation was not precisely one of flying, and the journey was very short, for Tulach, the hall of the Shee, was not more than a few hours ride from Aird.

When she arrived all was as before, with lights burning inside the ancient hall although outdoors it was a sunlit afternoon; servants came to take the horses, and Waltan led her in. He brought her as far as a hearth in the west, then excused himself and was gone, fading swiftly behind an arras. Then down the staircase came bright Lady Ethain, holding out her hands and smiling:

"So here is our messenger! Come, Gael Maddoc; we will go to Little Hearth again!"

Before they reached the head of the stairs, there came the sound of deep, excited barking. There up above them was the great dog, Bran, and he came galloping down and leaped to welcome Gael Maddoc, waving his plume of a tail. She made much of him, and the Lady Ethain sighed and said:

"There now! What a fuss he makes!"

They came into Little Hearth again, the same chamber where she had first met the Shee, and settled before a small spring fire. Bran crowded against Gael's feet. Lady Ethain rapped upon the tabletop, then turned aside, listening.

"My son will come, and we will instruct you in this first task. It is a happy occasion . . ."

"My lady," said Gael warily, "I hope I may send greeting to all those I saw on the hill, near the Palace Fortress . . ."

"You are a good child," said Ethain. "Yes, we continue well and happy in our retreat."

Then all at once Luran was with them, smiling, and he greeted Gael in his own serious fashion. He spoke of an easy task, a time of rejoicing, and she felt the smallest twinge of regret. Yet she knew that adventure was not a thing she should crave, let alone danger of any kind.

"You will bring a wedding gift into the Chameln lands," announced Luran, "a gift for the young queen, Tanit Am Zor."

Lady Ethain waved her hand gently over the table, and there stood a bronze case, gleaming darkly and decorated with leaves and flowers and bird shapes. Gael knew that it must contain jewels. When Luran turned its key and opened the lid, there they lay, giving off their own serene light. The coffer was lined with blue velvet, and the necklace was of graduated blue white stones, uncut but highly polished.

"This is a work so perfect that it has a name," said Luran. In a dark-born man, Gael would have called his manner reverent. "It is called Moon of Erris—the work of a master craftsman of Eildon, completed not so long ago by our reckoning."

Lady Ethain brushed the necklace with her hand, excused herself, and was gone. Luran went on, very matter-of-fact, about the journey. Gael must travel by magic to the Dannermere and ride into the Chameln land near Nesbath, through the historic pass at Adderneck.

There she would meet two officers from Eildon, part of the escort of a noble guest. She would give her precious gift to the ranking officer and go along with them to Chernak New Palace, where the feast would be celebrated.

"From Eildon?" she asked, intrigued.

"From the Knightly Order of the Fishers—Prince Beren Pendark and his wife, Princess Nairne of the Wells, will also be attending the wedding, together with the Princess Dowager, Merigaun—a born cousin of Sir Hugh McLlyr. These noble folk will come with a great company out of Eildon, bringing in the bridegroom, Count Liam Greddaer of Greddach," continued Luran. "Your two companions are the Princess Merigaun's personal retainers."

"The Eildon princes have already come into the Chameln lands?" she said. "Did they sail up the River Bal?"

"Yes indeed," Luran smiled. "The Kingdom of Lien, however set against magic and influenced by the Brothers who serve the Lame God, still has a duty toward its old liege land. Kelen and Fideth must grant the knightly orders safe passage—there is always a busy traffic of traders upon the river. Rulers and governors of the dark folk and the light keep up some relations, however chilly, with lands who do not share their views." Luran smiled again.

"It was a sight to behold—the caravels of Eildon left the ship at Lesfurth Strand and were escorted through the territory of old Balbank, in a grand progress. Kerns, kedran and their horses, the carriages and palanquins of the princes. This was not long past, in the first days of the Willowmoon. There were some folk there who were known to you—Lord Auric Barry led the wedding guests, along with his henchwoman, Yolanda Hestrem. Then, at the Adderneck Pass, they were greeted by King Gol himself."

"Our good king is far gone in years," put in Gael timidly. "How is he faring, Lord?"

"Yes," smiled Luran, who seemed determined to be cheerful. "By dark standards he is old, but the Duarings are tough and long lived. The king was there with Queen Nimoné, along with his heir, Prince Rieth, and a few members of his household. He accompanied the noble guests through the pass into the Chameln lands. The wedding will be celebrated, of course, at Chernak New Palace, in the lands of Queen Tanit Am Zor."

"We have heard something of all this in Lort city," said Gael. "Is there nothing more in this task? Must the jewels be guarded?"

"We expect no treachery!"

"And where shall I say I come from? Not from the Southland . . .?"

"Tell the truth," he smiled. "You served in Pfolben and have ridden escort duty as a free lance, bringing visitors from Eildon over the high ground. You can be recruited at the Halfway House."

"Will my comrades know that I serve the light folk?"

"You all serve the light folk, more or less," he smiled. "Be more trusting and cheerful, Gael Maddoc. Learn the ways of Eildon—enjoy the beauty of the Chameln. See—here is gold for you, for your soldier's pay. Your uniform, all your new accoutrements, waits in another chamber. The women will see to it!"

Gael had one more question.

"Will there be guests from Pfolben? From the Southland?"

Luran gave her a questioning look.

"I long to see my old companions again," she said. "Riding escort duty, perhaps . . ."

"It is possible," Luran said. "For the dark folk, it is a long journey from the Southland, and I feel sure they will have joined the ships of Eildon."

After the wedding duty, she would have a furlough. She could return to Lort until she was summoned to make a report or perform a new task. Luran finished his instructions and was gone. An old woman came bustling in with a tray of food—roast meat, salad, new bread, a flagon of wine, and a jug of water. She spoke very cheerfully and pointed out, from the door of Little Hearth, the bedchamber where Gael would spend the night. And yes, her clothes were there—very handsome—and she should try them on before bed. But her measure had been taken, the old woman smiled, and they would fit perfectly.

"I am the Widow Menn," she said. "My son was a soldier in the service of the old dark King, Ghanor . . . and my daughter was a kedran, far off in the city of Krail, in the Westmark. Ah, Captain, it is good to see young folk ride out, finely clad, from an ancient hidden place like poor Tulach . . ."

So Gael and Bran sat very comfortably by the fire, and she gave the big dog meat and drink from her own plate. She peered from an unglazed window in the corridor and saw that the sun had already set; she found herself tired, though she had had little exertion. After preparing her lessons in writing and in reading given by Tomas, she simply bade the fire burn low. Later, Bran took his run down an ancient outside staircase near her bedchamber. There was another fire burning in the pleasant room; her saddlebags were there and, on a tall rack, her new clothes.

They were certainly very fine—two tunics, a tabard, extra sleeves, tight trews, all in black and silver, together with blue-green. The swirling patterns woven into the clothes came from the sea waves; there were decorations of pearly shell and buckles of silver, with coral. This was not all—she found something she took to be a nightshirt, undershirts, breast binders, and underdrawers, finely sewn. There was a spacious new set of saddlebags with a crest, the waves and silver-green fishes of the house of Pendark.

Gael tried on several garments and looked at herself in a long glass, very old, its silver backing worn thin. In the soft light of the candles, the room in the mirror was another place, a magic place, where she might see some other figure, not the kedran in her new clothes. On the wall hangings of the bedchamber, there were scenes of men and women dancing, together with tame beasts—lions, leopards, unicorns.

Gael had that persistent feeling of strangeness that was part of all her dealings with the Shee. She told herself that this was partly the contrast with her simple origins in the cottage by the Holywell. Perhaps this night, with her lessons and her room, was like the life of any young pupil, new to a great household.

Bran lay down on the hearthrug, and Gael, when she had washed in the small tiring room, dowsed her candles and climbed into the small soft bed. She fell asleep and dreamed a long kind dream of dining with Tomas and others and even Bran, the dog, in a house, as it was in dreams, that she knew yet could not recognize.

Then it was daylight—Widow Menn had just flung back the hangings at a window to show a bright spring morning. There was her breakfast, with a milk posset and fried bacon and apple pancakes. The old woman led Bran away; he swept his tail unhappily from side to side and looked back at Gael.

Later she was to remember this first leave-taking as the best and brightest she ever had out of Tulach and the strange world of the Shee. The Fionnar were grouped on a balcony overhead, in the sunshine—sadly, ancient Myrruad had kept to her bed. Sir Hugh, with Luran and Ethain, led Gael, now garbed as a kedran captain of the Fishers, into a grassy round before the hall. It was another blessed cantreyn field; within already stood Ebony, arrayed in magnificent trappings of blue and silver and green. A groom stood by, holding a full head covering, and a wreath of silk flowers—Ebony, he said, would not wear these things. Gael, while she checked the girths and set on the new saddlebags, laughed aloud.

"We must let him have his way," she told the groom.

Luran shrugged and nodded to the groom, consenting to this omission. When she had mounted, he handed her the leather traveling pouch with the wedding gift, the jewels of Erris, and she slotted it into the holding place before her on the great saddle. Lady Ethain made a finger sign, and the case became invisible, though Gael could feel it still and knew this handy scrap of magic herself. Then, unexpectedly, old Sir Hugh stepped up with a small soft package wrapped in silken cloth.

"There now, brave Captain," he rumbled. "My gift for my cousin, Merigaun."

Soon everything was stowed—she took her own leather cloak on the back of her saddle and wore a plain black riding hat without a plume. The groom couched her lance in its carrying straps. Then the whole company began to wave, and the ladies upon the balcony threw bright leaves and flowers. Gael turned the restless Ebony about, and Luran, speaking the ritual for the landing place, drew the line of light all about them in the blessed meadow. The mist gathered; horse and rider were taken up and moved, in the way they knew, toward the borders of the Chameln.

The landing place, behind three birch trees in bright leaf, was on the Nesbath road, not a hundred yards before the Adderneck pass. There was the Dannermere, the inland sea, calm and still in the spring sunshine. She could glimpse the peninsula of Nesbath, with its fine old mansions. To the west, beyond the wide grassy verge of the road, was the border with Lien. For years now it had been an actual wall of grey stone, with an ingenious fence of piles and dressed logs blocking the waterway, the confluence of the two Lienish rivers, the Bal and the Ringist, where they flowed out of the inland sea.

Gael's landing place was beyond this bridge. She came out from behind the trees and praised Ebony and rode on smartly into the shadow of the high cliffs that enclosed the Adderneck pass.

The chronicles she had read over the past winter with Tomas made much of the historic ambush in this place. The Red Hundreds of Ghanor, the Great King, led by the General Kirris Hanran, had ridden into the pass, unsuspecting, with martial music and insufficient scouts. For all they had known, the main part of the Chameln army was safely bottled up on the shores of the Dannermere, their tribal reinforcements delayed, far in the north. Yet, on the wooded heights and in the narrow way, there lurked the Morrigar—the Giant Killers. The troops of Mel'Nir had been given up to the Chameln by the lost race of the Kelshin, the kin of that other small race, the Tulgai.

These small folk had guided an army through the border forest, and Aidris the queen had gone with them, to drive the invaders from her land. The strategy of the ambush was good: its success not only severed the Melniros' Supply lines, it also allowed the divided armies of the Chameln to rejoin. Soon the main force of Mel'Nir had had no choice but to fall back into its own country.

Legends had grown up around this disaster for Mel'Nir. At home, the few surviving warriors had been ill treated, disgraced; Ghanor the Great King fell into a long fit of violent rage from which the healer Hagnild must rescue him.

In the chronicles had been gathered the many tales of signs and wonders that foretold the ambush or accompanied it. Black-clad women wept in the heavens. After the battle, the death-sendings of many of the doomed Hundreds were seen throughout all Mel'Nir's lands.

On the anniversary of Adderneck, in the middle days of autumn during the Aldermoon, milder on the Chameln border than in the lowlands of Mel'Nir, memorial services were held in both countries. Ladies from the court of Good King Gol walked into the pass with baskets of red flowers.

Today, in spring, thirty years or more after the Great Ambush, Gael Maddoc rode on into the pass and could feel nothing dreadful. The pines on the towering slopes of the pass showed tufts of tender green on the tips of their dark shaggy branches, sweet birdsong trilled through the air. The foresters had not been at work: dead trees lay where they had fallen or piled in heaps beside the road. The place teemed with birds and small animals: perhaps no hunters dared to come here. She rode on, and Ebony's hoofbeats echoed through the narrow way. He gave a signal, pulling back a little. She saw that there was an old man ahead of them in the pass.

He was short and slight, and he wore a long grey blue robe, a priest's garb, and carried a staff. Now he stood up and waited for her to draw level.

"Good morning, Captain!"

He had a long, bony face, lined with age; he bobbed his head in greeting.

"Good morning to you, sir," said Gael. "My name is Gael Maddoc. Can I be of service to you?"

"You serve the Knights of the Fishers," said the old man. "I think you must be bound for the wedding of the young queen."

"Indeed I am," said Gael. "It will be a great festival!"

She saw the badge or crest that he wore over his heart, and it showed three golden bells. She knew at once who he was.

"Good sir," she said humbly. "I have been working with certain scribes of Mel'Nir in the town of Lort. I believe your name—your fame—is known there."

He smiled a little. "My fame?"

"No one knows more than Brother Less!"

He gave a wry smile. "The scribes do me too much honor."

Gael had seen that there was an arrangements of smooth rocks behind him, against the eastern wall of the pass. It was a well, not so big as the Holywell, of course, but still a blessed place, with a rough trough hewn into the stone of the pass's side and an empty altarstone beside it.

"Good Brother Less," she said. "Will you do me the honor of breaking bread and taking a sup of water?"

He nodded his agreement; she dismounted and took down her small sack of provisions. She removed the heavy saddlebags, and Ebony, in his finery, was able to nibble the soft grass on the roadside. They settled on the rocks; rays of sunshine still found their way down into this part of the Adderneck though the narrowed pass ahead was dark. As she signed the Goddess's blessing over the cup she gave him, an ironic gleam came to the old scribe's eye—she knew Brother Less to be a follower of Inokoi—but he accepted the cup from her hand with good grace.

"I have been thinking of the grandmother of Queen Tanit Am Zor," said the old man. "Aravel Vauguens Pendark, a Princess of Lien . . . her tragic history."

"I have heard that she was not in her right wits," said Gael.

"For a time she was truly mad," he said bluntly. "And it was the work of a cruel sorcerer, acting upon her frail wits and nervous disposition. Yet she was healed completely! Yes, good Captain—I saw it myself!"

"Perhaps this was a kind magic?" She wondered at the identity of the princess's healer—for surely the cruel sorcerer was Rosmer, the deceitful vizier, Lien's Kingmaker.

"Yes, there you have it," Less said. "A kind magic and kindly sent from a young man with a noble heart. He sent the poor mad queen half of a magic fruit, and it restored her reason." The old brother gave her a look—a testing look—and she remembered what Tomas had told her about Less knowing the secrets of Yorath's supposed last hours. Perhaps this "noble heart" was Coombe's hero? Gael Maddoc looked Less squarely in the eye and saw that this must be so. Knowing her task today—to bring a present to this madwoman Aravel's granddaughter, she wondered why the old man should bring up this old history. Did he mean to warn her? This encounter must have been deliberately arranged. She wondered how much he truly knew of her purpose. The young queen also was rumored touched by madness—had this fallen to Tanit from her grandmother? And could this madness also, by kindness, be cured? She wondered if the Shee had thought of that when they had chosen their present.

"Good Brother Less," she said. "A wedding feast is meant as a happy occasion, a festival—especially where the bride is a beautiful young queen—but I have some foreboding. What might go wrong in the days ahead?"

"Oh, there will be a good deal of intrigue," he said coolly, "but that is to be expected in court circles. My own land—have no doubt of that—would revel to see the Land of Two Queens overcome by sadness and dissent. I see the hint of some sending—from the past—or *pretending* to be from the past. It is a vision, a face in a glass—perhaps a portrait. Bring this notion of mine to Princess Merigaun herself, if this is convenient."

He brushed the crumbs from his robe and stood. They talked a little longer—Gael tried not to show the anxiety she felt at the old man's words. She drew Ebony away from the sweet grass, made ready again, and mounted up. They bade farewell, and she gave Brother Less a smart salute. Then she rode on at a trot through the Adderneck pass, marking the carved stones along the way. The narrowest part of the way was old and dark; Ebony hated the place, and she let him canter through.

Then, suddenly, she was out upon the plains in bright sunshine. A broad road lay straight ahead; heading north and off to the east was an older road leading to ancient Radroch Keep, upon the plain. Tall oak trees grew not far from its gates, planted in pairs so close they had grown together over the years and joined, like wrestling, leaf-covered giants. Gael urged Ebony to keep up a good pace and rode on, as she had been instructed, beyond old Radroch, to the town of Folgry. Before she came to the gates of the town, all hung with garlands of white flowers, a rider wearing the same colors she wore, the sea colors of Pendark, came riding out to meet her. She made out that the horse was grey, though all the caparison that shrouded it made it hard even to tell the creature's color.

She breathed deeply, thought of her dear love Tomas and of all her family and friends at the Holywell, and prayed to the Goddess to lift her spirits. The rider drew rein. It was a man, past middle age, with a neat brown beard streaked with grey and thick shoulder-length hair under his plumed riding hat. He carried no marks of rank, but she believed she knew what this must mean. As they came close, she drew rein and saluted smartly.

"Maddoc," she said. "Joining the Pendark Escort."

"Captain Maddoc," he nodded. "I am Lemaine. Have you ridden far? Is your horse fresh?"

She took a chance of getting things wrong and replied:

"Yes, we are quite fresh, m'lord."

"That is a splendid black you have there," said Lord Lemaine. "Bred in Mel'Nir?"

"Ebony was bred in the Southland," she replied, "where I served the Lord of Pfolben."

"I'll have the gift box, I think, Captain," he said, "and we'll ride into the town a little way."

Gael, a little reluctant, let the jewel box show itself in the special carrying place on the front of her saddle. The lord urged his old grey charger closer so she could hand over the precious gift.

"Shall I mount the banner, my lord?" she asked.

"No—no," said Lemaine. "Simply ride ahead."

She set off at a decent walking pace and rode in through the flower-decked gates of Folgry. Escort duty—when had it last been light hearted for her? She thought of the time when she rode proudly through the lands of Aghiras before Blayn of Pfolben, glorying in her young lord's beauty and his seeming matchless grace. Such innocent days—they seemed so long departed, though it was not yet one full turn of the seasons since she had trod on the Burnt Lands' sand!

Adrift in these musings, she paid little heed to the lie of the land around her, but presently, as they crossed a wide strip of greensward inside the gates, there was a hail from the right—a kedran in the now-familiar Pendark garb was riding toward them on a bay.

The second officer sent to meet her was a sturdy woman. Past forty, Gael decided, and she wore stars of rank that were somewhat rare. A guerdon general, retired from her regimental duties. Gael saluted and said her name.

"Annwyn Sallis," said the general in return, cracking a smile. "Handed over the last of the presents, Captain? Good. Shall we go? Have to report back to the Grand Array before too long! We'll take the Festal Way across the plain to the left."

"General," said Gael. "I must raise the banner!"

The pair seemed a little impatient with this punctilio, but Gael, despite their superior rank, ignored them, knowing it to be her right. It was a matter of dismounting, taking her lance from its carrying sling, then threading the long pennant for the Fishers, carried by Lord Lemaine. The spring breeze caught it well as they turned in good order and went out of the gates of Folgry. The Festal Way was beautiful, decorated along its whole length with white flowers, planted in tubs or in beds on the roadside, twined in long garlands overhead. Men and women were still working on the long display—they waved and cheered as the three riders went by.

Gael Maddoc, looking to left and right, beyond the white flowers, understood at last the nature of the Chameln, the vastness of the plains, the scattered groves of trees, the rolling hills and distant mountains. She thought of that distant work camp in the wild northeast where an old man, a hero, still lived and labored. She had come out of the realm of the ancient King Gol of Mel'Nir, and now she was in the same country as his trueborn son!

Behind her, General Sallis and Lord Lemaine rode side by side and kept up a lively commentary not only on the countryside but on groups of liveried servants and escort troops and the finer folk whom they served. Now they were in sight of Chernak New Town, a large town, unwalled and spreading. Gael knew and now was informed again, by Lord Lemaine, that the place had first grown up to house the builders of Chernak Palace, constructed at the whim of the one they called Summer's King, Sharn Am Zor. General Sallis had the tale that the town reeve and his council had petitioned the young queen for a change of name. King's Town, was it? Or Summer Town? At any rate Queen Tanit had refused the request. Now the general called directions, and they swung past the town and came to a great field below the royal gardens, which rose up in tiers, crowned on the heights with the long, glistening windows of the palace.

The broad meadow was like a new town itself, with three groups of pavilions, structures between a tent and a longhouse, bearing the crests of the orders of Eildon. The general pointed out that Gael had a place allotted in the Pendark pavilion. They walked their horses slowly across the field, crowded with visitors and with hucksters selling food and tokens of the wedding. They were hailed and saluted by other men and women in the colors of the Fishers. Gael saw the pavilions of the Hunters and wondered if Lord and Lady Malm might be among the wedding guests. Well, thank the Goddess, they would have their own Eildon escort this time!

"Let us go first to the Gift Treasury," said Lord Lemaine. "This Moon of Erris weighs upon me. You can lead up the paved path at the end of the lower terrace, Captain."

As they passed along toward this white path, Gael thought of Sir Hugh McLlyr's gift for the Princess Merigaun. She felt sure that if she mentioned it, her companions would quietly take it from her and deliver it in private to the Princess in some fine room, away in the palace. Yet she longed to behold Merigaun, one of the Lyreth, the sea folk; it might be better to hand the gift over in person. Who could say it was not her duty to do this? She thought then of the warning, the warning from Brother Less, and his particular wish that his words should be brought to Merigaun Pendark, and she decided to keep her peace.

The Gift Treasury was a solid stone building—perhaps a storehouse for the gardeners in winter. Now it was decorated, like everything else, but also guarded with a muster of fierce kerns from the northern tribes. It stood at the extreme western edge of the palace grounds, and there were marvelous vistas in every direction. Fountains were playing—behind a screen of trees, there was a lake with swimmers; the glazed windows on the wings and towers of the palace were flung wide and glistened as they caught the sun.

"Is it the finest palace you have seen, Captain?" inquired Lord Lemaine, smiling.

Gael was conscious she had indeed gazed with wonder.

"It is very fine, m'Lord," she replied. "I think it is in the style of Lien, where I have never traveled. But I have seen fine palaces of a different sort, in other lands."

"What, in Eildon?" asked General Sallis.

"In the Burnt Lands, General."

There was a burst of shouting, wild cries, from the dark building behind them, the Gift Treasury. From some door that Gael could not see, in the east, burst a rout of the footguards, tribesmen in leather bucklers and fur hats. They were wrestling and shouting, trying to seize and hold three men in curious tight fitting green trews and short jackets. These fellows were very nimble; the shortest one, not more than a boy, carried a hank of bright green rope. Now, as his comrades raced away across the lawns, this boy fell, and the guards began to beat him with the handles of their spears.

Gael gave a cry to the general, as if to ask her leave, but already she was urging Ebony across the grass to the mêlée. She cried out for the guards to halt and backed up her cry with a single, focused working—a mere whiff of the Stillstand but enough to tumble a pair of guards onto their backs.

"Hold!" she cried. "Don't kill the boy! What has he done?"

The officer, whose rank she could not read, cried out:

"Is he from the Pendarks of Eildon? Is that it, Captain?"

His grasp of the common speech was good, his accent strange.

"No," she said, panting. "But hold a moment—allow him to declare himself!"

The boy scrambled up painfully, holding his left side; there was blood on his face.

"Captain—save me from these wild men!" he said clearly. "Look where my brothers are returning. We are the acrobats, the Fareos, and we came with the Athron guests!"

Sure enough, the two older men in green were returning across the lawns.

"Ach!" The officer of the guard cursed under his breath in another speech. "It's a mistake," he said, in the common tongue. "We found them coming through a side entrance, took them for robbers. There's a mort of fine treasures in the Gift House."

"If the boy could be brought to a healer," said Gael. "My name is Gael Maddoc—"

"I'm Han Harka of the Durgashen, chief of this troop, Ferrad's Own." He returned her salute, showing white teeth under his dark moustachios. "We've been sent from Dan Aidris Am Firn for this special duty to the Daindru." Dan, she remembered as he spoke, was the Chameln style of address for their rulers.

"Chief Harka," she said, "I'll see that the boy is taken care off. Do you see two high-ranking Pendark officers yonder? They truly have a rich gift to deposit in the Treasure House. They would value an escort!"

"At Pendark's service, then!" said Harka.

He rounded up the men who had run out with him, sent five back to the side entry, then marched smartly down the slope of greensward with the remaining seven. She saw the escort collect Lord Lemaine and General Sallis, then approach the entry to the Gift Treasury.

The two elder Fareos were lithe and well muscled. They had brushed off their brother and were feeling him for broken bones. The second eldest was the spokesman: he gave their names as Tane, Trim, and the youngest, Tell. He thanked the good captain for saving the boy. He assured her that the Athron guests had a healer and a healer's tent to serve their people. She watched them climb up toward the eastern wing of the palace. The boy was riding on Tane's shoulders.

She was conscious of an emptiness, a glibness about this exchange; it was as if one rode among an army of other troops, hardly known to each other. There was no spirit of welcome, of expectation—she thought again of the Royal Hunt of the Lakes of Dawn in the Burnt Lands and the joyous spirit that had prevailed, despite all that afterward went wrong there.

She saw that the guards had escorted her companions right into the Treasury. She was tempted to seize this moment and ride off alone to the palace—search for the Princess of Pendark or perhaps for the headquarters of the palace guard, for some kind of soldier's mess and a stable where she could groom Ebony. Instead, she rode dutifully down again to the entry of the Gift Treasury, that frowning box of dressed stone, and waited for the officers of Eildon to return and meet her. Remembering the day she and the other Kestrels had laid the treasures of the Burnt Lands before Lord Maurik, defiant and proud as they declared their resurrection, she felt a pang of emotion, something like grief, that the gift of the Shee, the Moon of Erris, had been taken from her hands so ungratefully, as such a simple matter of course. Where was the hand of destiny upon her in *this*?

The Pendark officers reemerged presently with four of the palace kedran, who assisted at the display of precious gifts. Lemaine was in high good humor, noting that the Pendark gifts from Prince Beren and Princess Nairne were very fine, and assuring Gael that the gift from Princess Merigaun also took pride of place—yes, this last was how he described the Eilif lords' lovely necklace! General Sallis passed a scolding remark about the captain's interference with the guards' duty.

There was a silvery trumpet call from the palace, echoed by the strange hooting sounds of the wooden trumpets of the Firn—it was the changing of the watch. Gael and her companions had been riding for hours without rest or refreshment. It was time for their watch to change too.

"We will attend the princess, then," said General Sallis, dismissing her. "You won't be required until the morning call, Captain, when the Eildon orders bring in the bridegroom before the Hall of Mirrors."

Gael saluted unenthusiastically and watched them ride up the lawn toward the east wing. She turned aside with some relief and went on down to the Pendark pavilion on the fields below. The sun was casting long shadows through the trees, and the place had the familiar air of a camp. There were spacious stable tents; kedran and kerns went about their duties. She handed Ebony over to a young groom and was directed to the half of the pavilion that housed the kedran. She tramped in wearily; the light within the pavilion was blue green, as if they were all under the sea, like the Lyreth folk. After a trip to the wash place, she went to quarters.

There was some kind of bustle running ahead of her—when she entered the big chamber, there were some twenty Pendark kedran, clustered together, smiling.

"Captain Maddoc?" an ensign spoke up. "We know who you are!" Another kedran took Gael's saddlebags and a third her lance.

"We know how it was in the Burnt Lands!"

Then the ranks parted, and there stood two tall kedran, one with dark hair, a captain, and one a red-headed ensign.

"By the Goddess!" breathed Gael. "Kerry-Red and Kerry-Black!"

"We changed our duty, Captain!" said Kerry-Black. "And Ensign Dirck—remember him?—is with us in the Pendark lands."

Then the old companions all embraced, and the others cheered and laughed, and Gael Maddoc began to think that a wedding duty might be a happy time after all.

II

The grand array of the wedding guests flowed over the lower lawns and rose up to the palace like a silver tide. The Falconers of Eildon were first, led by their patron, Eorl Leffert, for their former patron, Prince Ross, was now the Priest-King, far away in holy seclusion. Next came the powerful order of the Hunters, led by Prince Borss Paldo, then the order of the Fishers, led by Prince Beren and his bride, daughter of one of the seven eorls. Only Prince Borss and his son Kirris were mounted—the Falconers and the Pendarks, including the ageless beauty Princess Merigaun, walked over the greensward. Princes and nobles from other lands walked with the orders of Eildon. King Gol of Mel'Nir and his queen, Nimoné, rode in a small bronze open carriage, drawn by two Chameln grey horses. Prince Joris and his consort, Princess Imelda Am Kerrick, came from Athron, and from the distant Southland came Hem Blayn of Pfolben and his new wife, Ella of Wier, in Rift Kyrie. The kedran escorts had left their horses down in the pavilions, all but a few who were chosen to stand behind the array.

When all had settled to rest, music sounded—harps and flutes and sweet voices came from the palace itself. In a wide crescent of the lawn, covered with splendid carpets, doors opened. From the eastern door came the young queen, beautiful as the morning, her long dark hair unbound, reaching past the waist of her white and blue gown. A necklace of graduated blue white stones, uncut but highly polished, sparkled upon her neck, seeming to drawn all light in toward her. From the western door came the bridegroom, tall, handsome, his hair also dark; he strode out smiling, and cheers sounded from the whole array. Count Liam extended his hand and walked toward his bride—Tanit Am Zor reached out and took his hand. They stood at arm's length, and at last the queen smiled. It was as if the sun had come out.

On a balcony just above the young pair stood the old queen, Aidris Am Firn, straight and regal, in Chameln dress: white doeskin breeches and a long tunic of white velvet, thickly embroidered in gold. On her right was Prince Sasko, Heir of the Firn, and his consort, Danu Rema Am Nuresh; on her left was a tall stately woman in a blue robe, the dowager, Lorn Am Zor, mother of the reigning queen. Beside Danu Lorn stood a young man, well built but not tall—this was Prince Gerd Am Zor, her son, the queen's younger brother. He was of considerable interest at the court because it was rumored he was a Seer, born full of natural magic. If this were true, he might have heard the sad thoughts of Aidris, the Old Queen, herself gifted in this way: "So many dead, so many gone from us! O Bajan, my love, O Sharn . . . O Sabeth, my friend . . . O Jalmar and Pinga—true servants—O Hazard, great minstrel . . ."

Then Dan Aidris and Lorn Am Zor moved aside, making way for the Chancellor of the Zor, Lord Seyl of Hodd, a handsome man, his dark hair barely streaked with grey. He spoke out in the common speech:

"Behold the Celebrants for this holy rite!"

It had been a subject for speculation: a marriage ceremony could be performed by a shaman or by a priestess or priest of any religion, also by a man or woman of high rank. Now Seyl led forth an older woman in a robe of blue, covered by a healer's cloak, and it was Gradja Am Gilyan, the cousin of Danu Lorn and the young queen. Then he led forth a man from Eildon, in the dress of a Druda, from the college of Priests. His name, Druda Aengus of Wencaer, was whispered about—he was the half-brother of the bridegroom, Count Liam. The choice was very seemly and pleasing—these two would perform the rite next day. There was a discreet ripple of applause throughout the large array . . .

Gael Maddoc was in the line of seven mounted kedran captains who stood behind the massed array of the princes from Eildon and other lands. They were on a small strip of lawn, and it was trying for some of the riders—a captain of the Falconers on a high-strung roan had nearly gone down the bank. Ebony, despite his skittishness, knew how to stand, and Gael rewarded him with tidbits. Far away, before the Hall of Mirrors, the young pair stood hand in hand, too far for Gael to see more than the blue and white of the queen's flowing dress, the smudge of burnished orange that was the color of Liam of Greddach's house. At long last, when the horses were past restless, the music changed. Doors opened behind the bridal couple, and the queen led her betrothed into the banqueting hall.

Now was the time for a long leisurely feast for the noble guests—they began to drift indoors while their escorts waited to leave the field. Gael picked out a number of persons she knew—there was Blayn of Pfolben, handsome as ever, with his bride from Rift Kyrie. Was that Lord Malm, looking jolly and in his right wits? She saw that her old comrade Wennle was not in attendance on the master he had served so faithfully, and she believed that his service had ended one way or another. But there was one person at least that she could call a friend, Yolanda Hestrem, assisting an aged lady of the Falconers, and there was Lord Auric Barry, one of the few attendees from Lien.

A beautiful woman, richly dressed in sea green and black, with a coronet of pearls, came out alone from the nearby group of the Fishers and walked directly to Gael Maddoc. Gael could see this was a magic being: her hair ash blond, her eyes deep grey, her skin almost shining silver in the day's dying light, and silver in her voice. This was the Princess Merigaun, a child of the Lyreth Lords of the Sea. Gael gave her best salute.

"Captain Maddoc . . ."

"Highness!"

"You have something from my cousin Sir Hugh McLlyr!"

With these magic beings, it seemed to Gael, such things never came as surprises. She reached into the place for gifts on the front of Ebony's saddle and handed the princess the small soft package Sir Hugh had trusted to her.

"Highness," she said in Chyrian, *"I have something else! A message from a great scribe who serves in the household of the duchess of Chantry!"*

Her guess that the princess would understand Chyrian was correct.

"You must mean Brother Less!" said Merigaun. *"Tell me . . ."*

"He had a foreboding about this wedding—it concerned a portrait, pretending to show a face from the past."

"I will consider this message," said the princess, returning to common speech. "My dear nephew's happiness—" Gael knew she meant Liam Greddaer, Queen Tanit's new husband. "It is precious to me. I will not see it lightly set asunder. Thank you, Captain Maddoc. My greetings to those you serve at beloved Tulach."

With this last salute, she went off to join her retainers, Lemaine and Sallis, in the measured approach to the banqueting hall.

The mounted captains, set free from a troublesome duty, rode down from the upper lawn in good spirits. The horses, also set free, were provided with hot horse apples. Down among the pavilions, trestles were set up and the ale was flowing. Gael sat down with the Kerry sisters and with another friend who had come home from the Burnt Lands, Ensign Dirck, the good kern now a captain with the Fishers' infantry.

Gael learned first of all what soldiers of Chernak had duties at the palace—she had seen the Tall Oaks of the Palace Guard and some of the household kedran. All finely drilled but friendly enough to the visiting escorts. But beware of the Companions! The queen's "personal bodyguard," were hard as rock—seldom mounted but lurking about, tall as Melniros, even the kedran, and dressed in dark clothes . . .

There was plenty of other comment and gossip, which Gael saved up for Tomas: Who was *not* at the wedding? Why *not* the bride's aunt, the widowed Princess Merilla Am Chiel, and her handsome, lordly-grown twin sons? It was said the young willow-boned queen, Tanit Am Zor, was in a fair way to bear twins herself, poor lass—they ran in the family of the Zor—or was it the Vauguens of Lien? Gael listened for anything concerning a picture or portrait but heard nothing. She took care not to get drunk—though there was no duty for her until the morrow.

After seeing to Ebony in the Pavilion stable, she went early to bed and enjoyed a long kind sleep, with dreams of the Chameln lands, stretching to the horizon. Next day the young queen was married to Count Liam on the balcony over the Hall of Mirrors, in view of noble guests and the folk from Chernak. There was a certain amount of crowd control for the kedran; after the ceremony, the folk and some visitors went westward to another green meadow to watch acrobats—including the Fareos—jugglers, minstrels, perform.

There were more exacting duties on the day following, when the bride and groom did their marriage walk, first in front of the palace, then down to the lower lawns. There, fine open carriages were waiting; the marriage walk became the royal progress. With the personal escorts of the princes riding before and behind, the procession drove to Chernak New Town to receive the greetings of the reeve or attaman, then on down the White Way, almost to Folgry. There were one or two incidents when citizens tried to get close to the royal pair with presents or flowers; they were intercepted by tall Companions in dark clothes, who flung them to the ground.

This was the wedding celebration. Many nobles had dispersed already.

After two more days helping to dismantle the Pendark pavilion, Gael bade farewell to the Pendark delegation and to her friends. She retraced her steps—first to Folgry town, then to the Adderneck Pass, now full of horse and foot traffic, going both ways. She rested and made camp twice on the way and came at last to the Palace Fortress of the Kings of Mel'Nir, where banners showed that the king and his queen had already come home. Then she rode on to the city of Lort, and home to the Swan Inn. Ebony was pleased to come home to his stablemate, an old mule; she asked a new groom after Master Forbian Flink, and the boy pointed up to the loft.

"He is sleeping, Captain—after long nights in his tower with scribe work!"

It was afternoon of a Midweek, as the days were counted in Mel'Nir. The Swan was quiet—she received a warm welcome from Demira Beck and gave out small gifts and tokens from the Chameln lands. Rolf Beck was off at the markets—she knew he would want a good report on the wedding of Queen Tanit Am Zor. Tomas was at his archives in the city; she waited in the dear and familiar tower room until he returned. When she saw him come in, wearing his dusty scholar's gown, Gael Maddoc was filled at last with the happiness she had been promised everywhere, for the wedding duty. "And how was your task?" he asked her.

She replied from the shelter of his strong arms.

"It was a fiddling, uncomfortable escort duty. But on my way I met a friend from Lien!"

"Do we have many friends there?" asked Tomas.

"We have Brother Less!"

He gave a whoop—showing what pleased a scribe.

So, free from care at last, she slept late, made reports to Tomas and Innkeeper Beck and to Brother Robard and his wife Terza. It turned out that Forbian Flink was poorly with a chest rheum. Mistress Beck had brought him indoors and was feeding him possets. Gael visited him once, and he seemed bright eyed and cheerful already, but she gave him only a few snippets of the wedding at Chernak. There was no talk of Yorath Duaring in the northeast, where the great wall was being built.

Only a few days into the Birchmoon, the second moon of spring, Gael was summoned to return in haste to Tulach. The old servant Hurlas arrived by magic on his horse, just outside the ancient Ox Gate, one fair morning. He rode into the yard of the Swan, and Gael was brought down to him at once.

"Thanks to the Goddess, Captain," he panted. "Here—here is the summoning."

In the leather bag he pressed into her hands was a mirror. When she held it up, Luran looked out of the glass.

"Come at once, Gael Maddoc," he said. "Hurlas will show you the place to stand, near the Ox Gate. Fion Myrruad cannot stay . . . she has a task for you!"

CHAPTER XI

LIFTING A CURSE

When they alighted in the courtyard Luran and Ethain were waiting, their faces grave. Gael had arrived in the brightness of a beautiful spring morning, but Tulach was shadowed and dark.

"My Lady—my Lord Luran . . .?" cried Gael.

"Come, Gael Maddoc," said Ethain, taking her sleeve and moving swiftly with her toward the inner hall. "Myrruad's light is fading."

Other servants were in the courtyard, attending to Ebony. As they went through the mighty oaken doors, Luran said:

"Myrruad will pass into the sunset. Yet before she goes, she will speak with you and give you a special task."

Only a few candles were burning in all the reaches of the great hall and the corridors. At the grand staircase Luran touched her arm before she set foot upon the first step. Ethain made an impatient gesture, and they were transported with a rapid gliding motion up and along to a vast shadowy chamber where Myrruad lay in a bed with golden hangings.

Gael hardly marked the other ladies and Sir Hugh McLlyr, who sat in the shadowy reaches of the chamber. She hurried to the bedside where Myrruad lay in a cloud of draperies. Her face seemed to glow with its own golden light and her eyes, very old and bluish green, burned like flames. She held out a hand and clasped the hand of Gael Maddoc.

"Thank the Goddess of us all, light and dark, who has sent me a messenger!" she said in a cracked voice.

"Fion Myrruad," said Gael, "I will serve you faithfully!"

"It is an old tale," said the lady of the Shee. "I will tell you, and then Luran can give you further instruction."

She gestured feebly, and Ethain gave her drink from a jade goblet. Her voice was stronger—she had become a storyteller:

"It seems but yesterday to one of my race," said Myrruad, "though the dark folk will have found it longer. I was a young maid in the distant fields and woods of beloved Eildon and in the beautiful island of Eriu before I was betrothed to my Lord Eilas of Tzurn, in a bonding of two Eilif families, the Helevelin and the Tzurn, I led a carefree life, and I fell in love with a mortal, one of the dark folk, a man of Eriu so handsome and strong he was like a godson. I will not say his name—he is long dead.

"In that far off springtime of my life, I bore a lovechild, a daughter. I have heard that the dark folk set great store by maidenhood and ill treat children born out of so-called wedlock. With the Shee it is not so, especially if the child is of the half-blood. I went off with my ladies to the kingdom of the princes, to Athron, and there bore my daughter, sweet Veelian. I loved her with all my heart, but I did not remain with her after I had nursed her—it is so in great houses—children are not always reared close to their parents. Veelian remained in the care of a true companion of mine, a woman of the half-blood who raised her as her own, in her own great house at Wennsford, not far from Varda. Athron was not a rich or magical land in those days, but the manor houses and domains of the great families were places of peace and protection.

"I returned to Eildon and was married to my dear Lord. I bore him two sons and a daughter. My sweet Veelian was their elder half-sister, who came to visit us very often in our house on the Grantoch Burn, among the border mountains.

"Alas, time has passed, and now I am the last of all my line, the Helevelin, and of my Lord's house, the Tzurnu. Yes, it is hard to be rid of the light folk, but there were battles in those days with the Eildon clans, and magic was used, and my eldest son fell victim to a bolt of magic. My other children lived on and wedded and had children themselves. I never thought to outlive them all—some were taken in battle, others by that melancholy which sometimes afflicts our kind.

"My dear lord and I lived on as comfortably as we might, being of the Eilif folk, and the move to this high ground made our many years easier. But I must speak to you tonight, Gael Maddoc, of the fate of my daughter of the half-blood, lovely Veelian. She lived in Athron, that was her true home, and in time she was betrothed to an Athron knight, a great lord in his own land. Then we were parted by a time of battles and unrest in

Eildon—finally, I went to Athron myself and was faced with another dreadful sorrow. My dear friend, Veelian's foster mother, had hardly dared to tell me what had happened in what for her had been the year since I had sent troth gifts and blessings for my dear child.

"She was the third wife of the Athron lord, though he was still in the prime of life—it seemed that his two young wives had died in childbirth. Now Veelian was dead, not a year after her wedding day. But her foster family, being of the half-blood themselves, had some magic—some ways of finding out the truth. Her lord was a cruel tyrant, who took pleasure in women's pain; I cannot speak of the torture my sweet child had suffered in his keeping.

"I was filled with rage and sorrow. I remember it very clearly even now. I went out alone under the crescent moon and stood on a wooded hilltop, above the river Wenz. I summoned up all the magic I had learned and the most intense power of my own nature. I cursed the man who had killed my daughter, I set a powerful curse upon his house for all succeeding generations. I cried out for these folk to beware their marrying and giving in marriage; their happiness would be blasted and their lands barren.

"I know that the cruel tyrant himself died mad, but I did not follow all the working out of the curse—Luran may be able to tell you more. All that I can say is this: now that I must pass into the sunset like so many others of my race and my family, I will remove this grievous curse. There are some of this family who still live. You, Gael Maddoc, must journey into Athron, to the far northeast beyond the Ettling Hills, and remove the curse that I, Myrruad, placed upon the Wilds of Wildrode. Do you accept this charge?"

"I accept the charge, Fion Myrruad," said Gael firmly.

"Then it is well—" said the ancient lady. Her voice sank to a dry whisper.

She released Gael's hand and fell back upon her pillows. At a glance from Ethain, Gael rose up and left the bed chamber. She saw all the others draw in closely about the bed. She knew the way through the corridors to Little Hearth, the room for her briefing. The dog Bran rose up from the hearthrug, overjoyed to see her again, but even he was subdued by the sad time.

Presently Luran joined her and summoned to the table a huge map of Athron worked upon ancient leather, like the map of Silverlode. He was very brisk, like an officer instructing his troops.

"By the reckoning of your people, the Curse was set down by Myrruad some one hundred and sixty years past," he said, "but the land has changed since then. Athron will always be a rustic kingdom, but now it has its own magic, and it remains always at peace."

They concentrated upon the town marked Wennsford, to the west of the city of Varda. There was a hill where the river Wenz rose up from a spring and curled around the base of the hill; Luran traced its course southwest to the sea by the harbor called Westport. He explained that the river, once no more than a stream, had been widened, with a canal system and a river haven near the town of Wennsford. Further north, the river Flume flowed down to the Western Sea through sea-oaks and salty marshes; there was a picture of the wild white horses, the Shallir, who roamed there.

Luran moved his hands over the map familiarly and said that he knew Athron well.

"There are true friends of the Shee in that land," he said. "Some of the half-blood, some dark folk—you might call them our watchers, who send us intelligence of the sort that still interest the folk in Tulach Hearth.

"The family called Wenns were nobles in Athron," he went on. "Veelian Ap Helevell, Myrruad's daughter, was raised there in the great house and given the name of Wenns. Myrruad's friend of the half-blood was the Lady Elfridda of Wenns, who did not marry and remained head of the house. Later the estates passed to a male cousin, but there has always been a strong tradition of women who ruled this domain—much later there was a battlemaid, Frieda of Wenns, who fought against the troops of King Ghanor of Mel'Nir, in the Chameln lands.

"There is a sacred grove with a Carach tree, the magic tree of Athron, on the top of this hill . . . I think this is where Myrruad uttered the curse—it would be a fitting place for you and your good Ebony to set yourselves down."

The magic trees, each with its own blessed piece of ground, were marked upon the map. Luran pointed out that the curse had best be lifted at dawn or at dusk, and the ritual should be done in the presence of someone who still lived in the old keep.

To the northeast of Wennsford, Gael traced with her hand more hills, the Ettling Hills, and a barren, brownish expanse marked like the Burnt Lands. The estates of the Wilds of Wildrode ran right up to the mountain border with the Chameln, although there were no passes marked through the mountains.

"There is another Carach," she pointed out, "very close to the Wildrode lands. Suppose I went on at once to that place in the dawn and waited until dusk, surveying the territory?"

Luran agreed that this would do very well. He seemed ironical, as if this was a typical ploy of the dark folk, but Gael could not ask him how one of the Shee might behave.

There was a certain urgency about her mission, and there was always secrecy. If anyone asked questions, she could say she was riding to the nearby town of Hatch.

"Erran's Eve, the spring festival in Athron, has passed," said Luran. "But there is a tourney between spring and summer in this town. You may give it out that you are going there for training, as many knights and kedran do. Or you might say you are riding to consult a Shaman in the Black Plains, beyond the northern border of Athron."

Gael asked for a name she might give for her liege or names for herself and her home.

"Just as before, in your first happy task," said Luran. "Give your true name and your home village of Coombe. Say that you serve at the Halfway House and ride escort for travelers."

He summoned by rapping on the tabletop a thin tablet of dark wood on a silver chain, which he handed to Gael. It lay on her hand very lightly and reached from the base of her palm almost to the tips of her fingers. The words for the lifting of the curse were written out fair in Chyrian and the common speech on one side of the tablet. There were small drawings of the appropriate gestures to be used with the words.

Luran took her carefully through the ritual, then for the first time he smiled, turned the tablet over, and rubbed his thumb across the smooth dark wood. He handed it to Gael, and it had become a kind of mirror. She saw first of all the chamber where Myrruad lay in her golden bed, surrounded by the last of the Shee. Now Ethain gave the ailing Fionar her drink again, from the jade goblet. Then Gael beheld a certain place in the great hall of Tulach, a kind of inglenook by the eastern hearth, where Sir Hugh was seated, playing a solitary game of Battle. The ancient knight became aware of her watching and uttered a word of greeting. Luran indicated that she should thumb the wood as he had done, and the picture was gone at once.

"We have absolute trust," said Luran, "but the dark world is full of chance and strange turns of fate—you can use this device to call upon us." Then he added with a half smile:

"With this tablet you can summon whoever you will—if you know the room in which they stand. They will behold you in a mirror or perhaps a pane of glass . . ."

It was afternoon, and she had her instructions; Luran went away. Without asking leave, she took Bran down into the wild gardens of Tulach and walked with him until evening. Then, after their supper, she spent time going over the ritual to remove the curse. Gael was beginning to feel lonely and bereft, not exactly fearful, at the prospect of flying off alone, with only Ebony for a companion.

Tomas was never far from her thoughts, and she knew she would try to speak with him in his room at the Swan. Now she thought wistfully of the gallant company of the Witch-Hounds, who had done so well at Silverlode. Yet she told herself that these were foolish thoughts—this was not only a soft duty but a worthy mission, to remove the curse from this family, members of the dark folk as she was herself, for all that they were of a noble house.

Then she and Bran went to her room again; she sent up a prayer for Fion Myrruad, going into the sunset. She slept soundly as before, but her dreams were of Coombe, clear as day, the house by the Holywell, and the grotto itself, with its flowing basin, lit by a single shaft of moonlight from above.

She awoke to a room lit with candles. Mistress Menn, the housekeeper, had just flung back the hangings at a window, to show the first streaks of dawn in the sky. Ethain stood beside the bed with food and drink to break Gael's fast. She wore a white robe and draperies of black and green, colors of mourning.

"It is finished," she said. "You must be on your way to Athron."

"Fion Ethain," whispered Gael. "I must wish you comfort in your sorrow."

"You are a good child," said Ethain with a sad smile.

Bran the poor dark dog was led away as before, with sorrowful glances at Gael Maddoc. The old woman helped her dress—there were new clothes in solemn dark greens and blues, not in the Pendark wave patterns—and told of the food and drink in her saddlebags. Gael went down into the courtyard, as before, and the steward, Hurlas, led her to the blessed round of grass, the cantreyn of Tulach, where a groom held Ebony. While the horse was laden, she wondered if she must set up her magic flight without further farewell.

But then she saw the steward and the groom looking up at the balcony, just above the great hall. Luran stood there and old Sir Hugh. Luran made gestures, showing that she should mount up; the spring morning was cold, she was glad of her cloak. A few long pale rays from the newly risen sun crossed the grass. When she was in position, with her lance slung on her right and Ebony facing to the northwest, the magic circle was set down around them. As the mist rose, the clear voices of the two

Ruaden could be heard bidding her farewell; then Gael and Ebony were being transported to Athron.

It was the longest journey she and Ebony had yet made, but it passed swiftly, like a dream. They set down lightly, still shrouded in the magic mist, upon a patch of soft grass on the chosen hilltop, behind two slender young poplar trees, green for the spring. The hilltop was deserted—Gael rode out from behind the poplars and beheld the Carach tree.

It soared up in the midst of its circle of clipped grass, beautiful as any tree she had ever seen: golden ash, oak, sea-oak, the tall elms of Pfolben and the tamarisk groves, the shimmering water-willows of the Burnt Lands. It was forty feet high, with a straight trunk of whitish green and a rounded shape that was the very pattern of a tree in a tapestry or ancient book. Its leaves were large, almost five-fingered, of a dazzling green gold; she fancied it was alert, listening, and it radiated serene power.

She rode around the low black wooden fence that enclosed the Carach and dismounted, whispering to Ebony to stand firm. He was docile and began to nibble the Athron grass. She was eager to take in more of the river below the hill and the bright town of Wennsford, but she knew she must first pay her respects to the noble tree. She went back, stepped over the railing, and knelt at the tree's base.

"Blessed Carach," she said in a low voice. "You will know I have come to this fair land of Athron on an errand of mercy. My name is Gael Maddoc."

Then there was a whispering among all the leaves over her head, and the tree replied:

"*Wanderer*—the chosen servant of the light folk . . ."

The voice was low and deep, like the purring of a huge cat.

"Return here . . ." said the Carach tree. "Will you return from Wildrode?"

"Yes," said Gael, surprised, "I could return."

The Carach spoke no more; its presence had been withdrawn. All at once, four of the new leaves fell down before her from a lower bough. Knowing the Carach never shed its leaves lightly, she gathered them up, then went back to Ebony and tucked them safely away, in among the saddlebags.

Down below, the river flowed round the base of the hill, silver in the early morning sunlight. The town of Wennsford was small and compact, with the remains of a town wall. There was a tall stone keep with two towers built into the northeast corner of this wall.

The wooden houses were gabled with roofs red and brown, and there was more than one building half of stone; there seemed to be a statue in the town square. Gael drew out her sailor's glass from Seph-el-Ara and saw it was the figure of a woman in a flowing gown, her hair bound round her head. She guessed that this might be Elfridda of Wenns, who had ruled her own domain and fostered Veelian, the daughter of Fion Myrruad.

She did not delay but mounted up again, in case people from the town came to visit their sacred grove. Gael cast a last glance down at the river haven and the wharf, where a vessel lay at anchor. It was a small, solid vessel, finer than a trader but not the pleasure boat of a noble. Above its furled grey sail was an azure banner with the device of a silver swan—it was a ship out of Lien.

Then she brought Ebony to the place behind the young poplar trees, concentrated firmly, and set down the magic circle with the point of her lance. The mist swirled about them; they were carried to the northwest and soon descended beside a second Carach.

It was later in the day now, and Gael was wary, letting the curtain of magic mist linger while she peered through the rifts at a new grove of trees, a new part of the Athron countryside. She sent the mist away and rode out from behind a clump of gnarled oaks. The land was farmed, with a sheepfold, a good number of sheep grazing, and, far to the south, a few cottages. She looked to the northwest, and the land changed; it was wild, with sparse green among dry tussocks. This was the edge of the lands of Wildrode.

The second Carach was as handsome and serene as the first, yet with its own character. When she had dismounted, she went to pay her respects, hiding a disrespectful thought—paying homage to a tree, again, what next? Then, before she could step into the tree's enclosure, a voice said loudly:

"Great Goddess—where did you spring from, kedran?"

An old man, a shepherd with a crook and a thick cloak down to his heels, had come from behind a hedge on the other side of the Carach.

"I will kneel before the Carach tree, Master Shepherd," she said mildly.

"What land do you come from?" he asked.

"From the Chyrian coast of Mel'Nir," she said, "but I have traveled a little, as a kedran."

She drew out her sailor's glass and looked through it toward the Ettling Hills, to the northeast.

"What is the way to the town of Hatch, good sir?"

"Ah, so you are going to the Tourney!" he said. "There is a high road leading past the Aulthill Keep yonder."

She found it easily and handed the old man the glass.

"It is plain to see!" she said.

He was delighted and looked all over the place—to his sheepfold, up to the sky, out to his sheep in the pasture.

"There now!" he said. "I thought Athron had plenty of magic!"

"Well, I do not hold this glass for magic," she grinned. "It is a kind of instrument made for far seeing, as eyeglasses are made for scholars."

"True. True," said the old man. "Thank ye kindly. My name is Dutten, Old Nal Dutten—would you care to come back to the fold with me and share a bite to eat with me and my lads?"

"Thank you most kindly, Master Dutten," she said, retrieving her glass. "My name is Gael Maddoc. I hope you will not take it ill if I stay here with my good horse Ebony: he has been a bit colicky. I have food, and I thought to rest now in the shade yonder and eat a bite and go on later in the day."

"Fine, fine!" he said. "And good luck at the Tourney!"

"Master Dutten," said Gael. "What is that old keep toward the east?"

"Ah," said the old man, shaking his head. "That is Wildrode Hall. Some say it is an accursed spot, best avoided. Certainly no place for travelers."

"Accursed?" echoed Gael. "Does anyone live in that dark pile?"

"Oh yes," he said. "The poor old knight tarries there still, with one or two of his followers."

They took leave of each other, and she watched him return to the sheepfold, which had a kind of longhouse beside it, with a smoking chimney. Before anything else, she did kneel before the second Carach tree.

"*Wanderer,*" purred the new tree. "You bring us a blessing. When will it be done?"

"Early evening," she said. "Just as the dusk comes down."

She went back to Ebony, and together they settled comfortably in the place behind the gnarled oaks. Gael warmed some food for herself in a small fire she made in a circle of stones, and she gave Ebony some oats, his favorite food. By the position of the sun, she believed it was a little after noon. She was sleepy, although not much had been done. She removed his saddle and bridle and suggested to Ebony that he take the order to lie down. The big black horse gave a whinny of pleasure and lay down at once in the soft grass. Soon they both fell fast asleep.

I I

The evening was cool and beautiful, with the first stars to be seen in the northern sky. The bulk of the old keep came nearer. Gael had her gauntlets off; her magic ring gave off a strange dark glitter as they closed in on Wildrode. She had seen riders on the highroad to Hatch in the distance but passed no one else. The setting sun, at her back, was reddening the sky in long streaks, which might have been a shepherd's good omen.

Wildrode Hall was a massive old keep, built all of stone that had darkened with age; its walls and buttresses and towers were streaked with damp and overgrown with mosses. It looked like the lair of a robber baron from some fanciful tale in the scrolls of Mel'Nir. Gael had never seen such a place inhabited by a family—it recalled Hackestell Fortress more than anything else.

The keep faced northwest, so she rode a little further until she was not a hundred yards from the main entry. The portcullis was raised and rusted in place; a broad path swept right up to the main doors, and a gateway between had fallen down. There was an air of sadness and neglect about the place, although the grass had been cut in a few places. The faintest glow of light, perhaps a reflection of the fading day, was to be seen in a high turret.

She felt a certain shyness now and was unwilling to begin her task, to break the silence of the dusk. Yet the dusk was not completely noiseless—birds were calling; somewhere a dog barked. She thought she glimpsed a movement under an old oak growing against a buttress tree and called softly:

"In the name of the Goddess—come forth from Wildrode Keep!"

Now she was sure a dark figure stood beneath the tree. Gael knew she must delay no further—perhaps those left in the hall might be unfriendly. She raised her lance in the first sign of the ritual, standing before the ancient keep like a Knight Questor. As she spoke the first words, a call for attention, she and Ebony were outlined in a glimmer of bluish light.

At once there was a loud cry: a tall old man came staggering from beneath the tree and stood upon the path. Gael could see that he wore a knightly surcoat and supported himself with a lance bearing a tattered pennant.

"Is it you?" cried the aged knight. "Is it you, Jessamy, my dear heart, my true companion . . .?"

"Good Sir knight," said Gael, "I am the servant of the Eilif Lords of the Shee! Pray you hear what I must speak!"

"Ah Goddess!" cried the old knight, "I thought—I thought—a kedran, all ringed with light? Good Kedran—what will the Shee with the poor Wilds of Wildrode . . .?"

He came closer, and she saw that he had ragged white elf locks and wore a white patch over his left eye.

"If there is any bad working, any ill fortune," he boomed, "let it fall upon myself alone and not on any others of my house. I am Jared Wild of Wildrode, and I will bear anything the Shee may send upon me!"

Gael knew that she must go on, she could not explain or comfort the old gentleman. She flung up her arms, holding high the lance in her right, then with the magic tablet to prompt her in her left hand, she cried out the first lines for the lifting of the curse, in Chyrian and then in the common speech:

"In the name of Fion Myrruad, who set down the bane and bann, let all be lifted from the Wilds of Wildrode, wherever they be, in all the lands of Hylor and the Lands Below the World. Tulach will bless and no longer curse this ancient house! Now will come light instead of dark, life instead of death, no marriages will be accursed, no children of this house! So shall it be!"

Then she made three passes with the lance, first toward the keep itself, then to the right and left, holding the lance flat and moving it in a sweeping motion as she had been instructed. Before she was done with this, there was that crackling in the air overhead. It came lower and was almost like chords of music played upon a lute, waves of sound passing over the fields and hills, over the grey keep and its buildings. It echoed away behind the hall into all the distant reaches of the lands of Wildrode, even to the mountains that divided Athron from the Chameln lands, the realm of the Two Queens.

"Kedran," whispered Sir Jared, "what have you done?"

"Oh, be of good cheer, Sir Knight," said Gael. "I have fulfilled my task—the Curse is lifted from your house."

"Oh heaven and earth!" It was a cry of anguish as well as relief.

The old man slumped down on to a crumbling wall beside the path, and his body was racked with shuddering sobs. There were voices now, and lights. To left and right, torches bobbed in the fresh darkness: a young lad came running, and an older woman who set her torch in the ground and comforted Sir Jared.

"Kedran!" cried the boy. "Who are you? What has happened? What was that sound in the air?"

"Have no fear," said Gael, getting down from her horse at last. "My name is Gael Maddoc. I have come to do a service for Sir Jared and for all in Wildrode Hall. You may truly be of good cheer."

"A service?" the boy echoed. "Tell me, then! I am Abel Roon, and this is my mother, Mistress Neva Roon, and our family has served the Wilds for many years . . ."

"I will tell you," said Gael. "I have lifted the curse from the Wilds of Wildrode in the name of the Eilif lords of the Shee, the light folk, and first of all in the name of Fion Myrruad, who has passed into the sunset."

"It is the truth," said Sir Jared, who was quiet again. "Pray you, good Captain—Maddoc was it?—step into our poor hall and sit a moment by our fire. Abel here will see to your fine horse—our stable is well kept."

Then Mistress Roon came forward and clasped Gael's hand.

"Oh Captain!" she said, tears streaming down her cheeks. "Oh my dear, you have done a great work of charity, pleasing to the Goddess and to all the poor dark folk. Come in, come in . . ."

Gael was glad to see that the boy led Ebony ahead of them and right into the hall itself before crossing to an open door for the stables. There was a living space lit by candles next to a small fire upon a large hearth. Mistress Roon carefully dowsed her torch. When Gael had set aside her lance, she gave her food satchel, from the saddlebags, to Mistress Roon, and asked her to use what she pleased—the chickens, the terrine, the salads—for supper. The good woman was delighted and went off, not to the kitchens of the keep but to a small kitchen alcove in one of the window embrasures.

"It is a time of magic and the settling of old debts," said Sir Jared. "Who knows what else will befall in the lands of Hylor before Midsummer? We have heard of the great wedding feast for the young queen of the Zor, long may she reign. But there are dark rumors, Captain—sad and bitter tales out of Lien have reached us, even in this part of the world . . ."

"Out of Lien?" prompted Gael.

"The Brown Brothers. Ah, Captain—why would men with a God be so cruel? Witch-burning! This new young firebrand . . ."

He broke off when Abel Roon came back and sat down with them, saying that Ebony was a fine fellow—and no, he had given no trouble. He seemed to like the old white mare who was stablemate to Sir Jared's charger—which Gael guessed might be rather old too.

"I sent them all away to safety!" burst out the old knight, following always his own thoughts. "I mean my dear wife Corlin and our two grown children, the ones who lived . . ."

"Where are they now, Sir Jared?" asked Gael.

"In Achamar," he said, "in the care of Queen Aidris Am Firn. She is a great queen and a friend to all in need. I fought for her cause, long ago, and before that she spent a little time in this very keep, during her exile . . ."

"Ah, I have read the scrolls!" said Gael. "Queen Aidris served as a kedran seven years long at Kerrick Hall, near the river Flume and the town of Garth!"

Then Mistress Roon brought their fine supper and stoups of water and of plain red wine. They ate and drank with good appetite, then Sir Jared bade them good night and was helped to his bed, still in the hall, with thick hangings.

When the old knight had left them, Gael began to question Abel and his mother a little about the family. Abel fetched from a chest a sheaf of paper and parchment and showed her some old pedigrees and some new work that he had done, written out fair.

"This is good work," she said. "It should be seen by an archivist."

"Ah, that is his dream, Captain," said Mistress Roon. "To be a scribe and to work upon the history of this family and of others."

"Oh, it could be done!" said Gael. "I have spent the winter in the town of Lort in Mel'Nir, where scribes and apprentices from many lands work upon the scrolls. Now that your fortunes have changed here in Wildrode, I do believe that Abel might join these scribes!"

She was rewarded by the look of eagerness and hope on the face of the young lad.

Presently, Mistress Roon showed Gael a comfortable pallet made up in a small room leading off the hall, that might have once been a bower for ladies. There were mirrors, a washing place, and even a green-cushioned privy. In the bed was a warming pan. She accepted all this luxury with a smile, but it could not mask the poverty and the wretchedness that still lingered about the Wilds of Wildrode. She sent out only her thoughts to Tulach Hearth—"It is done! The Curse is lifted! Pray heaven it was not too late!" She saw the mirrors and thought of her dear Tomas in his room at the Swan, but decided that she would speak to him from some happier place on her travels, perhaps from Wennsford.

She slept and began to dream a little, and a voice began to call her name. She answered in her dream, and suddenly it was no dream . . .

She was awake, and there was a soft light in her "bower." She said softly, "Who is it?" Then she saw that in the largest mirror, clearly visible from her bed, another room was reflected, and in this room sat the woman who had called her.

"Captain Maddoc . . ." said the woman, "I hope I did not startle you!"

She was seated by a fire in a room richly furnished; there were books on her table and a large jewel, like a scrying stone, and some children's toys, carved animals of painted wood. She was almost an old woman, though spry and active; on her tunic, she wore the silver locket of a widow. She had tightly curled hair of grey and black; her face was alert, fine boned, and her eyes were a striking green.

Gael Maddoc knew her at once. She had last seen her upon the balcony of Chernak Palace, richly dressed.

"Queen Aidris," she said. "How may I be of service to you?"

"You served Merigaun at the wedding!" smiled Aidris Am Firn. "And my beloved niece besides. I know your name and some of your deeds from a friend of the Daindru, we rulers of the Chameln lands—Mistress Vanna Am Taarn, the Guardian of Hagnild's House in Nightwood.

"I am eternally grateful to you and to the Eilif Lords and the Fionnar for the lifting of the curse upon the poor Wilds of Wildrode."

"Good Queen, I have heard that you visited this keep," said Gael.

"I came as part of an escort, bringing a gift of horses to Sir Jared, at the time of his wedding," said the old Queen. "I had a friend in the keep, poor Jessamy Quaid, Jared's esquire as a knight questor. They could not marry. It is a sad tale. But he had a good marriage with Corlin Aula, though they lived always in fear of the curse. They made sure there was no marrying nor were any children born in the keep. Now Lady Corlin and her son and daughter live here in Chameln Achamar."

Aidris Am Firn laid her hand on her scrying stone and continued.

"I have news of evil deeds that are to be done very soon—in a day, no more—beginning in Wennsford, not far from Wildrode."

"In Wennsford?"

"A ship has come up the river, the canal system of the Wenz, from Westport—a ship out of Lien!"

"I saw it, good Queen," breathed Gael. "The silver swan . . ."

"The emblem of my mother's house," said Aidris Am Firn bitterly. "On the ship are a troop of deluded men, with a prisoner. They mean to take advantage of a friendly agreement with Prince Joris and march their prisoner from Wennsford, to Varda, and so on over the pass into Cayl at the town of Benna."

"Good Queen, who are these men?"

"Their leaders are Brother Sebald, the so-called Witchfinder, and a senior Brother Advocate. Sebald and his followers are bringing a poor woman into the Kingdom of Lien, where she will be put to the question and burnt alive!"

"Dear Goddess, no!" cried Gael Maddoc, incensed to think of Lien's madness, reaching into this quiet country. "This must not be!"

"It is a long way from Wennsford to Benna," said Aidris Am Firn. "Brother Sebald is too bold! He takes this way so that he can preach in Varda and try to win people of Athron for his vile witch hunt."

"Could this march be . . . prevented?" asked Gael cautiously.

"You had good success with a rescue at the town of Silverlode!" said the old queen.

"I had brave comrades," said Gael, hardly daring to accept what was being asked of her, here in the night, in Wildrode keep. The thought of a woman on a forced march through this gentle land, trending always toward a burning stake, turned her stomach. Yet she was quite sure that the Shee did not mean her to intervene here, would not want her to turn the gifts they had given her of magic to other purposes . . .

If the old queen saw Gael's hesitation, she did not heed it. "I do not ask you to go alone," Aidris Am Firn said. "There are some others who keep a vigil near the roundhouse, in the old walls at Wennsford. They do not expect your coming, but one at least is known to you . . ."

"The Carach tree on the hilltop," said Gael. "It bade me return . . ."

"There, you see . . ."

Aidris Am Firn gave the warm and friendly smile of a grandmother and vanished as the mirror filled with a sparkling mist. Gael was excited, shivering a little, not sure what she should do, yet already resolved within herself.

She reflected that Aidris Am Firn was not called Witch-Queen for nothing.

CHAPTER XII

RESCUE IN ATHRON

The town of Wennsford was still decorated for Erran's Eve, the Spring Festival. Thick garlands of flowers and leaves, woven in the courtyards, were strung along the balconies of the houses. Gael had not gone to the Carach on the hilltop after all, but ridden on a well-worn track round the hill and come to the river crossing, a ford in old times but now a solid causeway, well above the moorings where the Lienish ship and other craft had been made fast.

Over the causeway, there was a livery stable at a busy crossroads, with market stalls, a pen for fowls and the first lambs. One road led to the north past a gate to the town. The other joined the high road that led through the meadows and on to the handsome main gates of Wennsford, never shut in these peaceful times.

Gael rode this way, beside a fine grove of trees, with ash and apple and a tall larch, all green for the spring. She observed the old roundhouse across the highroad. There was plenty of cover in the roadside meadows for those watching: she saw a place where a great tun of ale had been tapped, and drinkers sat on tavern benches.

She turned back and went to the livery stable at the crossroads. A gaunt old woman called the Widow Craine led Ebony to a stall and let Gael lock up his saddle and her own saddlebags in a numbered chest. She asked cheerfully where Gael was traveling—ah, yes, the tourney in the town of Hatch.

Gael strolled across to the tavern benches, carrying her lance at the trail. She sat in the shade of a tree with her small ale, watching.

Talking to trees, she thought, and now on a wild goose chase—or "herding the cloud sheep" as they said in Coombe—for the Witch-Queen of the Chameln. *O Tomas, when will I see you again?*

She was scanning the crowd for "someone known to her," as the queen had said—for some reason she thought of Gwil Cluny and of her old comrades Amarah and Mev Arun from Pfolben. Then she saw them—a man and his wife, both strongly built, good folk for a rescue indeed. She caught the woman's eye and waved.

"Here you are then!" said Marta Finn in a hushed excited tone. "Look, Tam—"

Tam Finn, of Finnmarsh by Nightwood, smiled and gripped Gael's hand.

"By the Goddess, Captain," he said in his rich, rumbling voice, "this is a work of mercy we will do—and I'm glad to see you come to our aid."

Then, before she could ask anything else—the plan, the other rescuers—where was the poor prisoner, where was the Witchfinder?—she was hailed aloud and truly surprised.

"Captain Maddoc! Gael, my dear friend!" cried a rich sweet voice.

There stood none other than Yolanda Hestrem, Lord Auric Barry's henchwoman, last seen serving the nobles at the wedding of Queen Tanit Am Zor. She was beautiful as ever and arrayed in a kind of kedran dress, with trews and a long tunic. Of course—it was her fencing costume; Gael recalled that Yolanda excelled in the art of the thin blade. Now she sat down at their rustic table, and it was clear that Yolanda was known to the Finns—in fact the leader of the whole enterprise. She quickly found out how much Gael knew and filled in the rest.

"The poor old woman is pent up in the old castello, yonder, but we have two women there who can send us word how she does and when the procession will begin," said Yolanda. "These Brothers have guards but not close to the prisoner herself, lest they be 'defiled.' There was no way we could go in and take her from her cell."

"They will make a procession through the town?" asked Gael.

"I would guess at the hour of noon," said Tam Finn, squinting up at the sun. "We've time in hand!"

By this time another kedran, a young ensign, had joined the group. Then there came two young men in sailors' dress, with long striped tunics and tall sea boots of purple leather.

"What is played out here?" Gael asked. "Where have the Brothers found this poor soul? What is this cruel campaign against witches?"

There were witches indeed in all the lands of Hylor, and there were many women and men who used magic in everyday life. But charges of bewitchment or evil workings were dealt with by law or by custom—outbursts against a particular witch, wizard, or sorcerer were not common. Witches like the O'Quoins at Silverlode, who had aided the renegade Huarickson, might demand harsher measures, magic against magic. But to strike out against a woman for owning witchcraft, in and of itself—this was new.

"She is a woman of the Merwin, or the River Tribe," said Yolanda Hestrem. "She had long since left the sea but was sailing with her kin, to celebrate the Holy Days. When their ship put in at Westport, the largest port of this land, Athron, she went ashore to buy supplies from the market. She was seized by a party of Lienish soldiers and the Brothers serving Sebald, the Witchfinder, and placed upon their ship, the *Sacred Fire*."

"How did these men know the woman for a witch?" asked Gael.

She had heard tales of the River Tribe, a strange band of wanderers who roved up and down the rivers that flowed into the western sea.

"The woman was wearing a Merwin cloak, with a pattern of sea creatures," said Yolanda. "Was it not so?"

"Aye-aye, Yolandee," one of the sailors murmured his reply, revealing his origins as a Merwin. In this interchange, Gael became aware of a great anxiety and unrest in Yolanda herself, though the woman fought bravely to keep up a face of calm.

"Then this Lienish ship was brought up the River Wenz to the river haven, yonder," Yolanda went on, "and Brother Sebald sent word to Prince Joris in Varda, with a treaty claim, a right of way for travelers returning to Lien. They plan to bring the prisoner through Wennsford, then overland through Varda, and so on to the pass into Lienish Cayl, at Benna. We have heard that Brother Sebald will display the old woman along the way and preach against witchcraft."

"There are those in Athron who will cry out at this!" said the ensign, whose name was Bly. "And the consort of Prince Joris, Princess Imelda of Zerrah, in the Chameln lands, is known to be strongly against the passing of the Witchfinders!"

"Ah, 'tis all wretched spite," said Tam Finn. "It is the Brotherhood in Lien working against the Chameln lands because they are now the Land of the Two Queens! They would draw the Chameln into open conflict against them!"

"How do the Witchfinders mean to travel?" asked Gael. "They will surely not walk every step of the way!"

"They've two wagons hired from the Widow Craine's livery stable," said Marta Finn. "Got them set out ready at the other end of the town, on the Varda road."

Gael got up from her seat and stared through the gates at the broad street curving down through Wennsford toward the square in the center of the town, with the statue of the Lady Elfridda of Wenns. The place was not crowded as it would have been on Erran's Eve. She returned to her place and said quietly to Yolanda Hestrem:

"What was your plan?"

"Magic!" said Yolanda. "A version of the bloodless rescue at Silverlode, though we lack the skills you were given for that task. We would have tried the Grand Bewitchment, but we are not sure of the shielding spells."

"And the escape with the poor prisoner?" asked Gael, pleased that they had not planned to meet violence with violence in their own turn. "Would you use one of Sebald's wagons?"

"We have our own small cart behind the trees," said Yolanda, pointing.

"Better than that!" said the older of the two sailors—Gael never learned their names. "We've our own good boat, the *River Queen,* in the first lock of the Wenz canals, just astern of that accursed Lien boat!" Yolanda gave Gael a look that had a little of amusement in it, as if she had not intended to reveal her plans so far, but was unwilling to curb these sailingmen's enthusiasm.

Bells overhead, perhaps in the roundhouse itself, played a little round and then two single chimes.

"Our good kerrick clock," smiled Ensign Bly, "from Lord Niall—the Wizard of Kerrick!"

A young girl carrying a washing basket came to Yolanda at the table and whispered urgently, then went on into the meadow.

"Aha!" said Yolanda. "The Brothers are astir—they will pass through the town sooner than we thought! The guards in the roundhouse have spoken with the prisoner's women."

"Look there!" whispered the young sailor. "The devils have slept on their ship."

A party of Brown Brothers in robes and raised hoods were coming round the trees from the harbor; at their center was a pale man in a black hood. Guardsmen in the blue and silver tunics of the Kingdom of Lien led the way to the high road and through the city gates. The team of rescuers watched in grim silence as these men turned to approach the roundhouse.

"I have heard they use no magic," said Gael, coming quickly to a decision. "But Lien is known to have as much magic as anywhere in Hylor. We must put on shields. You and I will perform the Grand Bewitchment at the center of the town, Mistress Yolanda!"

She remembered how she had "donned the shields" in the mounted troop of Witch-Hounds before Silverlode. Now there was a witch to be rescued, and a somewhat different shielding must be used. She bade them all draw in closely and said:

"We must concentrate our minds for this working—it will be done with good Athron magic!"

Then she drew out the four green gold leaves shed for her by the Carach tree on the hill above them. The leaves were divided into seven pieces and moved around and into a circle in the center of the table. They all whispered the words of the shielding ritual after Gael, using the common speech, then tucked away their Carach fragments. She repeated the words in Chyrian: uttering the final words of binding, she held her lance upright. A large spark of blue fire shone out for a moment upon its point.

"Come, then!" said Gael. "We'll get into position!"

Tam Finn paid their score, and they wandered away to the second gate into the city on the west road. There was a good clear street leading down into the square with the statue of the Lady Elfridda, a tall woman with bound hair and a look of the Goddess in a sacred grove. Gael and Yolanda took up places on either side of the statue, in the midst of the square. The roundhouse was out of sight, up a hill. Now the kerrick clock struck the hour of eleven, and soon afterward there was a trumpet call. The people in the streets, men and women going about their business—marketing, carting, taking garlands down from balconies—turned to the curb to see what was going on. Gael was glad to see that not many were lining the streets. The rescuers were placed beyond the statue, ready to spring into action when the hour was at hand.

Now the procession could be seen approaching, led by a duty escort of two Athron guardsmen in green uniforms with the device of a golden stag's head for Prince Joris Menvir, the ruler. The Athron folk were law abiding, and they were puzzled by the procession. Yet some understood and were bold enough to protest and cry out to the guardsmen. The shouts of "For shame!" and "Set her free!" increased as the prisoner came into sight. Still some way off by the statue, Yolanda Hestrem drew forth her long sabre.

The old woman was guarded by three tall soldiers in the uniform of the Royal Guard of Lien, all in bright blue with the emblem of the silver swan. One went ahead, with a rope strung around the prisoner's throat. Her face was down bent; the way the rope was tied, if she tried to hold her head proudly, she would choke. The two other guards held her on either side, tightly by the arms; they wore mailed gauntlets.

The prisoner was a tall old woman; even now in a filthy, ragged kirtle of reddish drugget, she retained some marks of what must have been a formerly striking beauty. Behind the old woman walked three members of the Brotherhood of the Lame God Inokoi; two were in the familiar brown habits, with their hood raised; they carried scourges, cats of more than nine tails. In the center, directly behind the prisoner, strode a young man with a long black and silver tabard over his brown robe, his face shielded from the sun by his black hood. This was Brother Sebald, at present Queen Fideth of Lien's most favored counselor, known in his own land as Hagbane and everywhere else as the Witchfinder. Gael thought his thin young face had the look of harsh determination she had seen in certain officers, both male and female.

The procession came on, step-by-step, at an orderly rate; Gael had her hand raised to Yolanda across the square. Now the prisoner was near the statue and the Lienish soldiers led her to the right a little, and now the Witchfinder himself was behind the statue and she let her hand fall. Working in perfect unison with Yolanda she raised her lance and pronounced in a loud voice the hour of Stillstand, the Grand Bewitchment.

There came that crackling in the upper air as the spell took hold, and it seemed louder in the clear air of Athron. The Witchfinder, the brothers, the soldiers, the prisoner herself, all stood like statues now. The spell had grasped and held everyone in the high street and a few were off balance: children and their mothers, an old man before the inn, tumbled down and remained still. Already, Yolanda had run to the prisoner, unbuckled her halter, and loosed the chains at her wrists with a spell of unbinding. In a few pulse beats, she had thumbed the old woman's forehead with another spell. Thus released, the former prisoner began to move her limbs and cry out feebly in the eerie half-silence of Wennsford town.

Marta Finn ran to help, and they hurried the old woman between them and led her up the empty street to the west gate. A few townsfolk stood and leaned, or lay about in frozen attitudes; their faces were blank, and, though Gael knew they felt no pain, she was sorry for them. She waited, watching closely, halfway up the street, and sure enough there was a loud, angry shout from beyond the statue. Tam and the sailors had hold of one of the Lienish guards—he had escaped the Bewitchment. This could only mean that he was shielded himself—that the Witchfinder, after all his spew of vile hate, did himself use magical protection. Yet the young guard with the shield was simply unequal to three men shielded like himself.

"Bring him here!" called Gael.

They marched the guard up the street, and he stared at her fixedly—she saw that he was not a guard but an adept. He said in a low voice:

"The Grand Bewitchment!"

Gael looked into his flushed young face. Something in him seemed relieved, perhaps even afire with joy for this unlooked-for rescue, but she only said:

"Be still!"

She slid her lance point through his shield and it became visible, an aura of blue green light all around him. He said bravely, looking squarely into her eyes: "You must be witches indeed!"

Gael, ignoring this bravado, recited her charm. He shut his eyes and fell asleep. She considered carrying him off for questioning, but time was short—they set him down in a great tub of planted flowers and went racing out of Wennsford town.

Up ahead, Yolanda and Marta, with the old woman, were disappearing behind the grove of trees, and when the others came up, there was the little pony cart, already moving off down the western bank of the river. Gael and the three men slackened their pace a little, but then the sailors could stand it no longer.

"Captain," said the older seadog, "ye've surely done a great deed here today! We'll go now to our ship yonder and prepare to sail off with Mistress Elnora."

Off they went, and Gael walked on alone with Tam Finn. They passed the harbor where a few folk were going about their business; everyone was quite ignorant of what had taken place in the town. There seemed to be some activity aboard the ship from Lien, the *Sacred Fire*. It was canted a little in the waters of the dock, and crewmen were peering over the side. Tam Finn chuckled.

"The Merwin lads have some magic of their own," he said. "They've hexed the Lien vessel some way, I'll swear."

"I hope this works for the best," said Gael. "Now the brothers will *have* to go through Varda and on to the pass at Benna without a prisoner."

Now they had come to the next lock in the canals of the Wenz, and there was the *River Queen,* a homely, full-bottomed ketch with pinkish sails and two great oars on either side, for use upriver. Nearby Marta Finn had drawn the pony cart to a halt. Gael saw the prisoner more clearly.

The old woman lay half-slumped on the bench of the cart, and Yolanda sat beside her, wiping her face tenderly with a damp cloth. Then she drew out a brush from a velvet traveling bag and began to smooth the old woman's long thick hair. They were speaking together, and the prisoner already seemed to have recovered a little from her ordeal.

"Yolanda?" said Gael softly.

"Praise the Goddess!" said Yolanda, her proud face near weeping—but for gladness. "Oh see what you have done, Gael! Mother—this is our brave kedran captain, Gael Maddoc. Gael, this is my mother, Elnora Hestrem of Hythe-on-Laun, in Eildon!"

Gael understood at last. "A former sea wanderer"—had Yolanda said this to her at the Halfway House when they became friends? Now the old woman fixed Gael with her fine dark eyes and held out her two pale, wrinkled hands. Gael laid her own hands in those of Elnora Hestrem.

"O child, child," said the old woman. "It is you. From the Chyrian coast, from the sacred ground of Lost Tuana, where the Merwin sailed in times past! You are indeed the *Wanderer*, the servant of the Shee, the one who goes about by sea and land . . ."

Tears coursed down her cheeks, and Gael answered in a choked voice, trying to smile:

"Dear Mistress Hestrem—I—I am proud to have helped Yolanda and the other brave rescuers!"

"One word before I join the bonny boys on the *River Queen*," said Elnora in a lower voice. "I see now the Goddess's hand; I must be here to give this news to you: there was a treasure taken by ship to Banlo Strand a year or so ago—it was stolen from Eildon. But true Chyrians would tell the story that it was saved, brought home again . . ."

Then, following the loud cries of the crew of the *River Queen*, Yolanda embraced Gael and all the other helpers. Elnora Hestrem gave Gael one more sharp look from her dark eyes and said:

"You and I—my daughter, too—will meet again in Eildon!"

Then Yolanda crossed the gangplank, supporting her mother before her. The pink sails filled so suddenly with wind that Gael suspected another piece of Merwin magic. The vessel moved through two locks and into the main stream of the Wenz, bearing away swiftly toward Westport and the sea.

Now, the last three rescuers stood there with Gael, and the kerrick clock chimed the half hour.

"How long yet?" asked Bly, the Athron ensign.

"Nearly another half of Lord Kerrick's hours," said Gael. "Master Finn, I must fetch my good horse. Shall we bring the wagon into the yard of the Widow Craine's stable up by the harbor and lift ourselves back to Finnmarsh from there?"

"As you say, Captain!"

They all climbed into the cart, and Marta Finn drove the pony smartly back to the crossroads. There was a shade of unrest in the people round about, and Gael thought she saw a crowd at the north gate. She made sure that Ensign Bly knew how to remove her magic shield before they all bade her farewell.

"Go to the gate yonder, where we came in and out," Gael said. "I think the folk are all staring into the town, but know enough not to step inside the circle of bewitchment. Say that you have heard that the spell will be lifted when the clock strikes the hour of noon."

"I'll do that," said the ensign, who was very young, a bright-eyed Athron maid. "But Captain, what will I do later, if anyone knows that I took part?"

"Make no secret of it, Ensign, unless you think that you'll be punished. Go to the town reeve and say you were asked to help in this rescue by folk from the land of Mel'Nir! Don't give names. I am simply a kedran captain called the *Wanderer*. Together with Mistress Hestrem and these good folk, we will be the Friends of Tuana, or the Tuannan, in the ancient Chyrian tongue!"

They all accepted the names eagerly and laughed aloud at their own boldness. Ensign Bly ran off, and Gael hurried in to fetch Ebony and her saddlebags, while Marta brought the pony cart into the yard. The Widow Craine was waiting for Gael with a gleam in her eye.

"Stillstand, indeed!" she cried. "You were one of that mad lot rescuing the poor witchwoman! How long will you keep the Witchfinder stiff as a board, eh?"

"Watch the sun, good mother, and listen for the noon bells!" grinned Gael, paying her score and adding a tip.

"Do you have names, then?" asked the widow. "Are you from the Land of the Two Queens?"

"No, we are not!" said Gael, mounting up on the skittish Ebony.

She gave the name again, Friends of Tuana, directing attention to the Chyrian coast of Mel'Nir—far enough from Lort and Nightwood—and also, she hoped, keeping this matter free of her Shee business. Then she rode into the stableyard and lined up beside the pony cart. A few words from the Finns about their destination, and she was able to lower her lance to the cobbles and send out the circle of blue fire for a long lift. They were carried away, swiftly and silently, to the yard of Finn's smithy, in the village by Nightwood.

11

Gael stayed with her friends and fellow Tuannan long enough to feed and rub down the horses and take a bite to eat in the smith's house. Word would be sent to Vanna Am Taarn—Marta and Tam Finn would give her a report on the rescue, which would be sent to Queen Aidris Am Firn. Gael asked to be sent any news that came from Athron in the aftermath of their escapade.

She rode home to the Swan through the forest, past Hagnild's grave, and it was there that she first admitted her fear. What would this venture of mercy bring her from Luran, from all of the light folk, her taskmasters for the present? She knew well that Luran had watchers in Athron; she had thought of them as friendly powers, guarding the interests of the Shee. But they and those they served were distant from the affairs of the dark folk, the politics of princes and kings. Her intervention in the dance between Kelen of Lien—or the Brown Brotherhood, acting in Kelen's name—and Joris of Athron . . . There was no reason for her to believe her acts would be welcome to those whose touch had already so far faded in Hylor.

She put aside her fear—the spring seemed to have advanced here in the north of Mel'Nir. Nightwood and the old marshlands were looking wonderfully green. Seen from the highroad, the Palace Fortress was like a great tiered garden. She galloped along to the ancient Ox Gate, thinking of Tomas. She did not even take Ebony to the stable herself but paid a young stable boy to do it—she told herself the spirited black horse was already fed and rested. Then she staggered into the inn with her saddle-bags and her lance.

The strange atmosphere swept over Gael at once—everything was as easy and pleasant as before, though the front parlor and the taproom were not full in the early afternoon. But Mistress Beck gave her a secretive nod; she was alone at the counter. Her glance indicated a table by the hearth, filled with leaves and flowers for the spring. At the table, three young men were drinking wine. She recognized one of them at once—a solid, fair young man whom she had seen upon the balcony of the palace at Chernak. Here was Prince Gerd Am Zor, brother of the new-wed Queen Tanit. His two companions were darker, and they were twins. She guessed at once who they must be—Prince Gerd's cousins Till and Tomas Am Chiel, the sons of Princess Merilla, who had not been seen at the wedding. All three of the young men were well dressed, though without display, and clearly enjoying their visit to Mel'Nir.

"Goddess keep you, Captain," said Demira Beck. "Your own Tomas will be full of joy to see you again!"

"Is he at work in the city?" asked Gael, foolishly disappointed.

"That's right! Home for dinner." The older woman smiled to see the young kedran's dissatisfaction, but there was something cautious in her manner, something that dampened her friendly teasing.

Mistress Beck had brought out the inn's book for Gael to sign, and now she bent over the big leather-bound volume and whispered, very low:

"I beg you, slip off your ring, Gael Maddoc. We must have no spark of magic showing!"

Gael did as she was told, and the hostess held out her hand.

"I have an agate cup under here," she said, just as softly, moving her hand under the counter. "It forms a shield."

Then, raising her head she said loudly and cheerfully.

"Yes, my goodman Beck has taken the children to the Spring Fair at Goldgrave!"

Gael slid the precious ring into Mistress Beck's palm and read the names of the guests written in the book. Till am Chiel—Mistress Beck indicated the twin with lighter hair—had written, as many travelers did, the reason for their visit.

We are seeking the wisdom of Brother Robard for our studies of the history of the land of Mel'Nir.

In other words they were a group of callants, probably traveling to battle sites and joining the lectures of Brother Robard at the King's Longhouse, where the young officers were trained.

A servant, called Sawyer, had also signed in the book and one called a guard, with the name of Garm Am Rhanar. One of the inn servants pointed out this fellow as he carried up her baggage. Garm Am Rhanar was a Giant Warrior whose father, most probably, came from Mel'Nir. Gael had heard of the Changelings. When the Ghanor's armies failed to conquer the Chameln lands, there were some men of Mel'Nir who swore allegiance to the rulers of this wild wide country where they had wives and established estates.

To Gael, it was clear without telling that Rolf Beck, the innkeeper, who had taken his three children, beautiful Zarah and the twin boys, to a spring fair, was hiding from these Chameln royals. Especially from Prince Gerd, the one rumored to be a Seer. It was all too much—she felt sick and tired of mystery, magic, and old tales.

In the friendly tower room, with Tomas's scrolls and papers and a candle set on the wide sill of the window, to be lit for her return, she was overcome with weariness. When she had washed and slipped on her loose blue robe from the press, she lay in the dear curtained bed under a counterpane and fell fast asleep.

The low hills of her dream had turned green for the spring, and she saw a bridge over a small river, and on a green cantreyn by the river, a familiar group of standing stones. She was home, outside Coombe village, riding on the high road nearing the Holywell. There was a handsome carriage ahead of her, and it passed over the river by another bridge and drove up long, grassy approaches toward the big farmhouse. She had reined in Ebony, and there was a tall woman beside her on the road: she was dressed in a brown robe embroidered in gold and dark red, and the skin of her face shone with light. In her dream they spoke without speaking, as if they only needed to think the words between them.

"So it has come home again!" said the woman. "It is lost no more . . ."

Then Gael understood and thought the woman's name, and the woman smiled and said aloud:

"Yes, my daughter, I am Taran!"

There was music, harp and flute. They beheld six maidens dancing in place of the standing stones. The woman went back among them, her feet, in red leather boots, scarcely touching the ground. As she was taken into the circle, the dream swirled away and Gael sat up with a loud cry:

"It is the Cup!"

The lamp was lit and several candles, and Tomas was standing by his desk. He came and took her in his arms, and they clung together as if she had been absent for a long time, instead of for only two nights.

"I must report," she said. "Dear love, I must report all from the first to the last and tell it to you."

"Before telling the Shee—the Lord Luran?" asked Tomas.

"Yes!" she insisted. "I—I may have displeased the light folk. I must record all that happened. Can you take it down in your beloved shortscript and write it up for me?"

"Of course," he smiled. "Come now, dear heart, sit before this spring fire—"

So Gael wrapped a shawl over her blue bedgown and sat before the small brazier on the hearth, for the tower room was cool as the night came on. Tomas sat in his writing chair, with a platten attached to one of the arms, and scribbled on new Lienish paper in a little book. They brewed herb tea and sipped it like two old gossips, and Gael told on and on.

Tomas laughed and sighed and shook his head at all her adventures. He had heard and read of the Wilds of Wildrode—the possibility of a curse upon that Athron house had long been suspected. He was keenly interested in her summoning by Queen Aidris Am Firn, in Achamar, but obviously in close touch with Vanna Am Taarn, the Guardian of Hagnild's house, in Nightwood.

"Aidris is often called the Witch-Queen," he said. "As well as the Old Queen. Would you say she is a sorceress, like her grandmother, Guenna of Lien?"

"It is her nature," said Gael. "It is her own natural magic that she makes. I do not know too much about Queen Guenna, but it seems she was a sorceress indeed. Queen Aidris uses magic more simply."

"No, my sweetness," Tomas reminded her. "Remember always that Guenna was Markgrafin of Lien, never Queen. Those were the days before Rosmer laid his hand upon the land, when Lien was beloved as the lush and lovely land of roses." Looking into his eyes then, and seeing the melancholy there, Gael was reminded that for all he made his home in Lort, Tomas was born of Lien, and because of this felt a deeper gladness for the evil she and the Finns had turned aside, enacted in his country's name. But it was Aidris of whom Tomas spoke next:

"Does she keep watch over all the lands as some powerful magicians are supposed to have done—Rosmer of Lien, for example?"

"No," said Gael. "It is Vanna Am Taarn who does that!" But she was grinning, for she did not really believe this.

Then they went over the rescue of Elnora Hestrem from the Witchfinder in some detail.

"I could do no other," cried Gael. "O Tomas—do you understand? I could not see any woman or any man made a spectacle of by this Lienish fanatic, hater of women and of the Land of the Two Queens . . ."

"Hush," said Tomas, "I see it very plain, and I wish I had been there to lend the strength of my arm. Gael—if there is reproach from Lord Luran, you can remind him that you are one of the dark folk and must go about in the dark world, the world of everyday in the lands of Hylor. You have your own knowledge of right and wrong, your own duty to the Goddess . . ."

"I must remember your words," she said, "to use them in my defense."

Then they spoke of the words of Mistress Elnora—a treasure brought into the Chyrian lands? Gael smiled, remembered her dream, and would not tell him more. She had some ideas concerning that treasure . . .

"Oh sweetheart," said Tomas, "I have sad news. It happened just hours after you rode away."

"What is it?" she said, afraid, thinking of her family in Coombe.

"Forbian Flink is dead," said Tomas. "He passed on from his chest rheum, night before last—word has not even been brought to Finnmarsh. Mistress Beck cared for him—did she not tell you?"

"He will not come to his old comrade, Yorath Duaring," said Gael sadly.

So they mourned for the scribe, Forbian, who was even now being taken back to his own city of Krail, in the Westmark, where Arn Swordmaker would see to his last rites. Tomas said that his history would be written up by none other than Brother Less himself.

They spoke of the Chameln visitors, Prince Gerd Am Zor and his cousins.

"Tomas," she said. "Is our host, Rolf Beck, hiding from these young fellows?"

"I have some ideas about that," he grinned. "The young prince, Gerd Am Zor, has strong powers, the sort of natural magic you saw in Queen Aidris Am Firn. He could break through any magical protection—find out secrets."

"How do you know this?" asked Gael. "From a scribe?"

"From their bodyguard, young Garm," said Tomas. "I have often wondered how our Master Beck came to wed a woman from the eastern tribes beyond the mountains—the Ettlizan, the Milgo, and the Skivari, that Prince Yorath helps to shut out with his wall. I believe poor Beck may be some high-ranked deserter from the Chameln wars with these tribes—his oldest daughter is the right age to match that explanation. We have heard of others who were trapped beyond the mountains."

"You have such good ideas!" she said, cradling his hands in her own.

Soon after, he went off and returned with their supper of lamb stew, with fine bread and greens, and a flagon of their favorite golden wine. As they ate and drank and lovingly jostled each other on their shared settle, Tomas offered to leave his scrolls in the morning and ride with her to Tulach Hearth to confront the Shee. Gael was tempted to accept his support, but she did not.

"I have a few days grace," she said, "before I am expected to return to Tulach. I have asked for Mistress Vanna's report on the Rescue—what has become of Brother Sebald and his fellow brothers and the Lienish guards? Will they yet attempt their progress overland through Athron?"

"With the prime object of display lost to them, I fancy not," said Tomas. "This attempt, at least, to convert Athron to their beliefs is lost to them. But when you have this news, do let me come with you to Tulach . . ."

"Whether Lord Luran is angry or not," said Gael, "I must beg leave of him to travel to Coombe, after I have seen him—I know something that will make him agree. I want to see my family as well, and you must come with me! I can send for you through my magic slip of wood from Tulach."

It was still not too late when they went eagerly to their bed.

She was the better part of a week in Nightwood, conferring with Mistress Vanna and observing, through Hagnild's stones, the progress of Brother Sebald. His fury was hard for Gael to bear, his wrath at suffering such "humiliation" all too evident. From what they saw, it was clear Sebald and the others had intended this venture as a sort of marching triumph of their ways. Their route had been made public to some of those who would support them. Now they progressed only to a chorus of catcalls and ridicule, for the story of the bird plucked free of their clutches in Wennsford spread swiftly on before them.

Sebald and his companions crossed at last the Adz and back into Lien—from there Vanna Am Taarn did not have the power to closely follow his movements. Gael rode home alone toward evening time, disturbed in her thoughts. Tomas welcomed her with open arms, and they fell quickly into bed together, eager for the warmth and comfort of a loving embrace.

In the night, while they were sleeping, a liveried servant rode in and left a message for Scribe Tomas Giraud, sealed with a ring that bore the crest of three bells. They read it over breakfast in the parlor of the Swan. Part was a request for common services—part was in a cipher only Tomas could read. He copied the words out for Gael on a wax tablet before he erased them and burnt the letter.

Good Tomas, I send greeting to yourself and to your betrothed, Captain Gael Maddoc. I have heard something of the rescue that was lately carried out in Wennsford, and I delight in the news that my helper Mistress Hestrem and her lady, Mother Mistress Elnora, are safe and unharmed.

The Chaplain of our house, Brother Less, has spoken to me of a foreshadowing concerning a portrait. I will speak urgently to Captain Maddoc of this matter, as I have by my side one who can shed light upon it. We will be at Aird, the town of the half-Shee, at noon today.

The signature on the message proper was elegant but without curlicues.

Auric Barry

"He is bold to speak of this rescue," Tomas told her. "In Lien, the Witchfinder carries great power. Even one so high born as a scion of the house of Chantry must watch his words."

"Even here in Mel'Nir?" Gael was surprised.

"The Witchfinder has been aggressive in the spread of his agents," Tomas said seriously. "Even within Mel'Nir, one such as Auric Barry must be circumspect."

"It had seemed to me," Gael said, "that in Lien, a high title was proof against the Brown Brothers' dictates."

Tomas smiled, a little grimly. "You should tell that to the wild Lord Garvis of Grays," he said. "He is the last survivor of Lien's highest noble house, but these past fifteen years, he has lived as an outlaw, and all because he would not bow his head to the Council of the Brother-Advocates."

Gael raised her brows—she had not heard this story. "Who is Garvis of Grays?"

Tomas shook his head and sighed. "He is not well-known outside of Lien in these days. Garvis is the example one such as Lord Auric must look to when he stands against the Brown Brotherhood's ways. He was stripped of his lands—of all his titles and riches—when he would not bow his head to accept the Brotherhood's rise. He made a plea to his fellow land-holders—but they were cowed, they would not support him. The Brotherhood keeps the people of Lien quiet; it commands obedience and order. There are few lords who will stand against that—not least because it keeps their own people tame, where they retain many of their privileges."

Gael held the wax tablet in her hand, read over again Lord Auric's message. Perhaps she felt more sympathetic to this young lord, now she knew he risked something to treat with her.

There was no question—of course she would go to this meeting. Gael knew that she was putting off her confrontation with Lord Luran for perhaps another day. Tomas showed that he understood her anxiety—all they could do was promise a swift meeting when she sent for him.

She rode into Aird not long after midday; the town was serene and beautiful as ever in the sunshine. As she came to the center of town, where the chestnut tree was in full bloom, a man came running up, followed by several others. He cried out in a troubled voice:

"Captain! Captain Maddoc!"

She was alarmed at first and reined in Ebony.

"Captain Maddoc, forgive me—"

She saw that the man was dark, middle aged, stockily built; it was

Galdo, the innkeeper at Tzurn's Haven, who had been so rude at their first meeting.

"Yes," she said. "Of course I forgive you, Master Galdo!"

"I behaved very ill, when we first met," he panted. "Then we understood that you served the Eilif lords—the hero Waltan himself came and bore you away. . . . Now we know you are the *Wanderer* . . ."

"Hush," said Gael. "I have no wish to be known . . ."

"You are awaited in Tzurn's Haven," he said humbly. "Please to step in."

She dismounted and gave Ebony to the servants, then walked with him toward the inn.

"I was so rough when you were last here, Captain," he said, "because I was half-mad with the stress of so many passing through the town on the way to the wedding at Chernak. Goddess bless us! The news we hear is that that all goes well for the young queen and her consort!"

Gael had heard something of the same news from Mistress Vanna: in marriage, it seemed the ice that had sheathed young Tanit's heart had been broken; all was well in the Chameln. Thinking on this, she touched at the hallow-string, which she had taken to wearing at her throat. The Chameln rulers had kept *their* Hallow safe—the Stone of the Daindru was cemented into the foundation wall in Achamar city. In Chernak, she had learned that the rulers performed a ceremonial "Honoring of the Stone" every year in the Aldermoon, the Moon of Death. Maintaining such reverence for their Hallow—was this how the Chameln lands managed to shrug off the trials that passed over them so lightly, while lands like the ancient Chyrian coast, so poor and impoverished, and Mel'Nir and Lien themselves, so embattled and full of rancor, could not find their peace?

Athron, where she had just been, had no Hallow to hold or lose. Perhaps this was why that land lived so well in quiet peace, lacking glory or fire perhaps, but also disruption and sorrow—save perhaps for a curdled curse of old, like Myrraud's bane on the Wilds, or an aggressive venture such as that so recently put forward, so unsuccessfully, by Brother Sebald.

Ahead of her, Galdo flung open the door and bowed; in the darkness after the bright sunlight, she saw Lord Auric, handsome as ever, spring up eagerly. She put thoughts of the Hallows hastily away—here was one whose course lay deep within the distresses of his country, high born enough to serve close to court, yet nourishing, through his mother's chaplain Brother Less, a fire that flared counter to the ruling Brotherhood's purposes. Her eyes became accustomed to the shade, and she saw that his companion at the table was an older man in Chameln dress—long full trousers of fine dressed leather and a long tunic of plum colored velvet.

"Captain Maddoc," said Auric Barry earnestly, "tell me how my friends are faring after this daring rescue! How does it stand with Yolanda Hestrem and her mother?"

"They are both well, my lord," she said. "Yolanda took no harm at all, and though her poor mother, Mistress Elnora, had been mishandled by the Witchfinder's men, she was recovering quickly in her daughter's care. They have sailed off in a Merwin ship, home to Lindriss in Eildon."

It struck her that Lord Auric had asked for this news as he would for a friend, a helper—he did not regard Yolanda as a lover, as it had seemed at first.

"What will the Witchfinder, that fanatical young Sebald, do now?" he asked. "What will his bear-leader, old Justian, the Brother-Advocate, do?"

"They are both back in Lien," said Gael, wondering that Lord Auric did not already know this. "My Tomas tells me this is a more serious matter than even I have understood."

A shadow fell across the young lord's handsome face. Gael could see he was a little disgusted, although reluctant to show such feelings. "Our queen will not delight to see her favorite humiliated—and by a pack of women out of skirts!"

Gael did not see why this should make any difference, though she knew it was the case in Lien, so she only shrugged. "They mocked him all through Athron," she said. "Whatever triumphal procession he had planned came to naught."

Lord Auric shook his head. "He is a clever man, and very stubborn. It would surprise me if he did not find some means to twist this defeat to his advantage. That is not beyond him, you must know. Some in Lien have counseled the queen against aggressive outcursions. Sebald may use this chance to bring them low."

"I wonder at Lien's lords," Gael said boldly, for she suspected Lord Auric's family might have led the outcry against those "outcursions." "It seems you feel the priesthood to be an excellent thing when it comes to promoting order among your people. It is only when its powers nip at your own heels that you begin to grow wary."

Lord Auric gave her a sharp look. "Perhaps that *has* been so," he said. "But now the Brown Brotherhood *is* nipping at our heels, and we have indeed grown wary. Which brings me to my introduction." He made a flourish with his hands, calling attention to the old man who had waited, with an air of patience and benign amusement, while the two had spoken.

"Now I will present one whose name is well-known," said Auric. "I am sure you have heard of the famed painter, Emyas Bill."

The old man had a rather pale face with a slight tuft of beard; his hair was long and grey brown.

"I know Master Bill's fame indeed!" Gael said, impressed and delighted together.

Emyas Bill smiled at her like a kindly uncle.

"Have you seen any miniatures or portraits of my school?" he asked.

"Oh, I have seen a marvelous collection of your original work!" she burst out.

Then she told of Cannford Old House in the Eastern Rift, where the Lady Pearl of Andine kept her school for the daughters of noble families.

"Praise the Goddess, yes!" cried Emyas Bill. "So the Andine-Strett miniatures have survived! Pray tell me, dear child, are they all intact? How are they displayed?"

So she went on and described something of the ambience of Lady Pearl, her magic and fortune-telling and the room where the paintings took pride of place. There they stood on a silver stand, among other family treasures.

"Excellent!" said the artist. "Oh, to think of the changes of fate and fortune that have stricken the fair girl children I painted long ago . . ."

"They have settled down," said Lord Auric, a little coldly. "Now the eldest daughter, Lady Annhad, is wed to the Lord of the Southland; the Lady Pearl is an adept, having studied in Eildon; and the Lady Perrine is wed to Degan Keddar, who will soon be known as the Lord of the Eastmark. Fine fortunes to a trio of daughters whose bastard-born father was lost to civil conflict."

Gael guessed he compared Strett of Cloudhill's daughters to the Swans of Lien, whose fate had been more harsh. Still, she did not like his manner. "Our ladies of Cloudhill had no Rosmer to haunt them, my lord," she said. "And, it is true, no one ever called them 'Princess.' But that is no reason to deny them their misfortunes!"

Lord Auric flushed a little, and it seemed to Gael that Emyas Bill hid a smile in his sleeve, suppressing amused approval. She realized as she was talking that her years with Blayn of Pfolben now served her well. She did not entirely understand the role Auric Barry sought to play in Lien's service, but she would not defer to this handsome Lord of Chantry until he had better proved his merit to her.

Timely for their tempers, Bergit the serving wench came by with a flagon of fine red wine and fresh oatcakes and greeted Gael as a friend.

"Enough of these matters." Auric Barry swirled his wine within his cup, swift recovering his mood. "I have asked you to meet me here today to speak of another strange affair: Brother Less, my mother's chaplain and a master scribe, had a foreshadowing—a portrait which somehow told a lie, pretended to be what it was not. Sure enough, this portrait soon after appeared among Tanit Am Zor's wedding presents."

"I have heard of this," Gael said. She could not tell whether or not Lord Auric knew of her strange meeting with Brother Less in the Adderneck. "Was it set out in the fortified garden house where the gifts were displayed?"

"No, it appeared at a private dinner for the young queen, the day after the wedding. It was a simple act of magic—a silk-wrapped package appeared suddenly upon the table, with broidered lettering which showed the names and crests of the young queen. Nothing bad was expected, but of course the package was not opened by Queen Tanit herself, but her taster and bodyguard, Mekkin Am Rann, who also uses magical protection."

Emyas Bill took up the tale:

"I have been shown the portrait that was in this package. One of the new style, not a miniature—they are painted in our school in the Old Town at Chameln Achamar and at many other workshops and schools of painting in the lands of Hylor. This painting showed a man seated under an oak tree and surrounded by symbols of the Chameln lands."

"There was a message to the young queen with the portrait—written out fair upon a piece of vellum . . ." continued Auric.

"A message?" Gael asked.

"Trust me!" he smiled.

He drew out from the sleeve of his cambric shirt a folded piece of Lien paper with the message hastily scrawled with a stick of charcoal, reading it aloud in his voice so silken fine:

To Queen Tanit Sharn Aravel Am Zor, who shares the double throne, greeting!

Behold the likeness of one who was deemed lost or dead but who has returned to the world to proclaim his innocence of any treachery toward his royal brother and to greet in love his niece. This is Prince Carel Esher Kelen Am Zor, the so-called Lost Prince, brother of your lamented father, King Sharn, the Summer's King, beloved throughout the lands of Hylor. Highness Carel, who is now in Eildon, humbly begs you and your advisors to give a sign that you will meet with him and hear his story, that all might be happily reconciled.

"And this was a false portrait?" asked Gael, looking from one man to the other. She was not sure she understood how this could be a threat.

"I can't doubt that this was the portrait in the foreshadowing of Brother Less," said Auric Barry. "A pretender."

"Well chosen for looks," said Emyas Bill sadly, "and carefully coached or even enchanted, as such persons have been in the past. The work done in Eildon, certainly, I recognize the tinctures used."

"Master Bill," she said earnestly, "I pray you—could you use your great gifts to make a sketch of this portrait, a copy of the face of this man?"

Emyas Bill smiled, he was flattered, and Gael knew it was because she trusted his talent. He took thick paper and a charcoal stylus from his satchel and set to work.

"Lord Auric," she went on, "what would be the sense behind this? If the pretender did convince the queen—"

"He would have a place in the court," said Lord Auric, "and might influence the government of the Two Queens. But there are greater problems here than this. Sharn's younger brother . . . some would whisper that this man would better serve the Chameln than a woman so rapt within her feelings that she could not hide the coldness of her heart."

"What did Queen Aidris have to say to this?"

"She would say only that she had grave doubts that the man in the portrait was Prince Carel—she believed this was a pretender. But Queen Tanit was intrigued—she will summon this man to Chernak, at least to observe him covertly and have him shown to those who knew Prince Carel."

"Queen Aidris is right," broke in Emyas Bill.

He was sketching with furious concentration. Then he would pause to add little patches of dry powder color to his copy of the picture. He went on:

"This is indeed a portrait of a man resembling Sharn Am Zor and his younger brother, but there is something wrong. I would swear the age is not right—I would have said this fellow was being painted as older than he really is. That clipped beard, the weathering of the skin—these are techniques we use to make a young subject appear more worthy and solid."

"This speaks for a chance likeness," said Lord Auric. "Perhaps some distant connection of Edgar Pendark, grandfather of King Sharn and Prince Carel. The sort of person who has served as a pretender in the past."

"Lord Auric, how can I serve the Daindru in this matter?" she asked.

"I had hoped you might question the Eilif lords of the Shee," he said. "They know many secrets of Hylor—perhaps they know what became of Carel Am Zor. Did he die in battle with others who seized the king—the mad Lord Inchevin and his son and daughter and the wild tribe of the Aroshen?"

Gael bowed her head. The young lord said nothing of service to his own land, Lien. She wondered what she should make of this.

She had begun to understand, a very little, the role she had been set to. Her pride of service to Hem Blayn, the bond between ruler and lifeguard that he had broken, her scouring passage through the desert . . . and now this recent disobedience to the Shee. She was the *Wanderer* in truth, with the hallow-string to serve as sigil of her service. She was not bound to a single rule or command, but to the lands and their peoples. This arrogant young lord—did he imagine her trust would fall sway to him, simply because he was a handsome man, and knew the manners a great lord called "the Common Touch"?

"Lord Auric," she said at length. "I truly do not know if I can obtain answers from the light folk."

"There is more," said Emyas Bill, in a placatory tone. She guessed from his manner that he at least had penetrated to the heart of her reluctance. "When I was summoned to Chernak to view this portrait, I gathered together some miniatures of the two families, Am Firn and Am Zor . . ."

He reached into his tapestry satchel and brought out a package wrapped in cloth and parchment. He laid out upon the table before them five, six, of his exquisite miniatures. He slid the small portraits about—the younger Aidris, her co-ruler Sharn Am Zor, Sasko, the heir of the Firn, a double portrait of his sisters, Micha and Maren, Princess Merilla Am Chiel, and finally, the young prince himself, Carel Am Zor, as a boy.

Gael and the old master exchanged a searching glance, and she believed she understood his intentions in carrying this great trove of art to display to her. Here were the faces of a fine family, cast for rule, yet loving and full of interest. Yes, this was a family. A pretender among them could tear at those natural bonds, even create a sad rift. She thought of Old Aidris as she had seen her in her private bower, the toys of her grandchildren strewn about her. Yes, perhaps for *this,* she would risk the ire of the Shee.

"I believe I know the artist who made the fake," said the old man softly, closely watching the play of Gael's expressions. "He is a young man of Achamar who worked in our school in the Old Town. Many of the school move away and begin their own school or workshop. There is in Lindriss city, in Eildon, a district called Oakhill, and there a large workroom and shop for all manner of mementos of the Chameln lands. It is called Shennazar, the Eildon name for Sharn Am Zor, who is a hero in Eildon."

"Would this painter be part of this deception?" asked Gael.

"Alas, I feel he must be," said Emyas Bill. "His name is Chion Am Varr. He has talent . . ."

"My Lord," said Gael, turning to Auric Barry, "why are you doing this?"

"For the honor of the Land of Lien," he said ruefully. "My country will not always lie under the yoke of a fanatical brotherhood. The religion will be reformed—that movement has already begun. Further than this, I trust the good sense of King Kelen's heir, Prince Matten."

"You know him?" Gael asked.

"We have been companions from our youth," he said, meeting Gael's eyes steadily. "He has been much surrounded by counselors of the Brown Brotherhood in all that time. But he is a true swan of Lien—as he comes into his manhood, he will put aside his drab brown feathers!"

There was surprising force in this image for Gael, a force that much surprised her. "If it will serve this cause," she said, as steadily as she was able, "I will travel into Eildon. For I am indeed the *Wanderer,* and it is my destiny to find out the secrets of Hylor!"

Soon afterward, when Emyas Bill had done his work and slipped it into a folder, they parted. He pressed her hand. She gave Lord Auric a salute. The host, Master Galdo, bowed them out, and they stood in the sunshine on the steps of Tzurn's Haven until Ebony was brought from the stable. Lord Auric's parting thoughts were again of the Brotherhood in Lien and the actions that might be taken by Brother Sebald and his entourage in the wake of the daring rescue of Elnora Hestrem. Gael was able to reply, but she felt her head whirl a little, with fear for her next encounter with Luran, the Eilif Lord, and with a strange exaltation.

For now that she had seen Emyas Bill's Chameln miniatures, she knew the true whereabouts of the Lost Prince, Carel Am Zor.

She mounted up and was on her way. Thinking on Lord Auric and his careless arrogance, his assumption of right and power, she found herself smiling, if a little thinly.

Perhaps it might yet be proved that Auric Barry was a right-minded young fellow, but he had allowed the glaze of his privilege to partly blind him.

Indeed, if the good Lord of Chantry had ever deigned to visit her Tomas in his quarters at the all-welcoming Swan, dispensing with the lordly formality of messengers, she had no doubt but that he too would have penetrated the Lost Prince's secret.

CHAPTER XIII

LIGHT AND DARK RECKONINGS

Gael rode off from Aird in the direction of Tulach Hearth about three hours after noon. The tall, gloomy edifice was not to be seen in the wilderness, but she knew its boundaries from her own ring, which she had reclaimed from Mistress Beck. Before she was halfway through her special summoning, there came sounds in the upper air, and the mighty gates began to appear. They swung open and she rode in, but none came to greet her. She rode slowly up the avenue between the tall elms and felt a sudden fear that the place would be empty, the last remaining Shee passed into the sunset . . . the old, fine rooms hidden under falls of dust . . . Luran and Ethain flown to their Eildon lands with the house servants . . .

Then she and Ebony stood at the portal, and before she could knock or call, Luran was suddenly beside them. He stood hand on hip as she dismounted, and she felt at once his sharp disapproval. The servant who led Ebony away was a wraith.

"You have had many adventures, Captain Maddoc!" he said, in hard bell-like tones.

Gael said humbly:

"Lord Luran, let me report on my journey!"

"Oh, I know well all you have done!" he said sharply. "The magical gossip of the dark folk speaks of nothing else! Playing politics! And on *our* sworn errand!"

She had known, as she put it to Tomas, that the light folk were well informed of human affairs "that were of interest to them."

"I completed the task!" she said, struggling not to speak defiantly. "The curse is lifted from Wild of Wildrode!"

Luran softened a very little; the doors of the hall had opened, and she saw within the candles that burned day and night.

"Go in," he said, "and tell me the rest of your adventures . . ."

They came into the great Hall itself, and he led her toward the hearth where she had once seen Sir Hugh McLlyr sitting. The air was chill—no fire burned on the huge hearth today, not even a brazier. There was a wreath of laurel leaves tied up with knots of black and green silk; Gael was full of dread. Had another of the poor remaining ones passed on? She put the question very timidly, but Luran shook his head.

They sat in silence by the cold hearth, and presently Hurlas, the old steward, brought in light ale and bread. She imagined that he looked at her reproachfully as well, and she was filled with the sadness of rejection. When they were alone again, she burst out at once:

"I could do no other, Lord Luran! You all knew well when you bound me to your service that I was one of the human race, whom you call the dark folk! I live in the world—if its rulers desire from me some boon, I must give it serious consideration! And this incident—I cannot see anyone, woman or man, used as a spectacle by a fanatical Brother from Lien and then be carried away for a slow death! Could you watch that, my lord—could you see one of the dark folk burned alive?"

Then the fine features of the Eilif lord took on a hard, pinched look and she knew he was more angry than before. She did not know, she was never to know the true answer to her question—how much compassion did the Shee bear toward humankind?

"What *rulers* do you mean, Gael Maddoc?" demanded Luran.

She took a sup of the ale and told her story from the time she came into Athron quite simply, leaving nothing out. Luran questioned a little from time to time, showing that he knew the land there very well—its towns and roads and the tamed and peaceful countryside. He listened keenly when she came to the encounter with the old knight, Sir Jared Wild of Wildrode, and all his servants. Then she described her summoning by Queen Aidris Am Firn.

"Are you sure this was indeed the queen?" he asked. "Not some spirit or magical imposter?"

"I am certain it was the queen!" said Gael. "I saw her only a short time past, at the wedding of the young queen in Chernak!"

"She is called the Witch-Queen . . ." he said, almost teasing.

"In the Kingdom of Lien this is mere insult!" Gael retorted, not much amused. "Queen Aidris uses her own strong powers of natural magic. She is not a great sorceress like her grandmother, Guenna of Lien. When she appealed for help to save this poor woman, Elnora Hestrem of Lindriss, the queen asked for my help quite simply. She made no effort to ensnare me to her will."

"As you will," said the lord diffidently, though something within him seemed a little soothed. "Go on with the story."

So she went on, and he made no more comments but laughed once or twice during the account of the rescue in Wennsford town. When her tale was done, she looked about in the dimly lit hall and felt it was already late at night though she knew that outside it was early evening.

"Much as we thought," said Luran, frowning. "You are a kedran, after all, trained in military exercises. Perhaps you are not suited to our tasks."

"I had thought to request a furlough," she said. "I would beg leave to go home to Coombe and visit my family at Holywell Croft."

"Well, we have no more use for you at present," he said coldly.

She thought of the great day when she had stood with all the Shee looking down the last hill toward the Palace Fortress—how she loved and honored them at that moment. Her eyes were filled with tears again, and she wiped them away angrily.

"Lord Luran," she said. "How do you stand with the so-called Hallows of Hylor? For another one is found!"

"What—have you heard from your dark friends the secret of the Lance?" he asked—and there was menace, true disdain, in his voice. "It is known to *us*."

"No," she said, a chill shivering through her. Luran had never before hinted that the Shee might be privy to such secrets. Did they not care that the land was out of balance, Mel'Nir's proud marches set one against the other, only held in check by Good King Gol's even temper and wisdom? "Not Mel'Nir's Lance. I speak of the Chyrian treasure."

Then he stared at her, his golden eyes alight with curiosity.

"Do not speak lightly of these holy things, Gael Maddoc!" he said softly. "The Cup, Taran's Kelch, was in Eildon, dishonored, among a collection of wonders . . . then it was stolen a second time . . ."

"It has come home to the Chyrian lands," she said. "I could send you word!"

"As you will," he said, still coldly.

"My lord," she said earnestly. She felt she was stumbling into waters beyond her depth, yet she must go forward . . . "Please let me tell you of the foreshadowing of a great scribe, Brother Less, of the house of Chantry in Lien. There is an attempt afoot to foist a pretender on the new-wed Queen Tanit and her consort, Count Liam. Those who would prevent this want peace between Lien and the Chameln lands. May I ask what the Eilif folk, what *you* know of the Lost Prince—Carel Am Zor?"

"You are more sunken into the swamp of dark politics than I thought!" said Luran, raising his voice so the sound hurt her ears. Yet his very anger seemed to tell that he knew nothing of the Lost Prince, that he had not received her own enlightenment.

They sat for a moment, deadlocked, in silence. Then there came a wild sound of barking, howling, and snuffling, with the pad of bounding feet. The great dog Bran came racing down the staircase and flung himself on Gael with signs of joy. She embraced him and wept into his golden fur until he was soothed and sat by her chair sweeping his tail across the stones of the hall.

"O Lord Luran!" she cried. "Dark and light do not always bide so well together. I pray you, set him free—let him go with me to Coombe! Perhaps you will end my service. I never looked for any reward from the Eilif Lords and Ladies of the Shee, but let it be Bran's freedom, to live in my care."

Then Luran gave a wry smile, as if he thought all the dark folk, dogs included, were wayward children.

"You are very bold, Gael Maddoc," he said. "Take your dog, then. Go to Coombe and send word of the sacred Kelch, if you can find it. Your friend Tomas the Scribe will soon tell you of a suitable place for this holy vessel . . ."

He vanished, unreconciled. She and Bran went up the long staircase and came first to the room called Little Hearth. Presently, the brazier burned on the hearth, the candles came alight. She hoped for one of the servants, but even their supper simply appeared upon the table. Bran was perfectly happy to sit beside her, and after supper, they went off in the direction of their humble bedroom nearby. Bran took his run down the ancient stairway that led out of doors, then returned to lie on the hearth rug, close by her. Gael sat on the bed in her sleeping shirt and spoke to Tomas with the aid of her magic oval of cedarwood.

The morrow was a fine spring day, and Tomas arrived most punctually at the hour of noon and rode to meet her at the open gates of Tulach. Gael had been given her breakfast by the servants—though she saw none of the Shee before leaving. Ebony was brought out in fine fettle, and the dog

Bran was overjoyed when he understood that he was going too. Tomas got down from his horse, Valko, and made much of their new companion. He had brought along, of all things, an old banner for Coombe, and Gael threaded it on to her lance.

So they rode out in the bright spring weather on the western border of the High Plateau and were far from the roads and pathways that Gael had taken in autumn with Lord Mortrice of Malm and his lady. They took a wide road leading down from the heights, and in mid afternoon they were down upon the plain. They came to the banks of the river Demmis, as close as Gail had ever come to Krail, the golden city, and she recalled the scribe, Forbian Flink, who had known so many secrets, yet passed so quietly away.

Presently they crossed the river at Tolbrig and rode on south until they came in sight of Hackestell Fortress. They spoke of the Foundation Day and of the attempt upon the life of Knaar of Val'Nur. What of the Black Sheep?

"I think I can guess their new lands," Gael said. "I saw a map before I rode home to Coombe from the Southland—and then there was the strange fight on the sea coast of the Westmark . . ."

"Have you heard any word of new settlers further south?" asked Tomas.

"I remember a few words spoken at an inn and then again in Lowestell, where I spent a night with the kedran of the garrison," she said. "The New Shepherds or the Erian Herders have taken large tracts of fallow land on the western coast. A place known as Blackmarsh . . ."

"Very suitable," said Tomas. He sighed. "There they will be well clear of the laws of Lien, I should think, and able to practice their own folkways."

They gazed at Hackestell and began to speak of the heroic past. Here Yorath Duaring had raised the siege for Valko Firehammer, Lord of the Westmark, during the Great King's War. A thousand Chyrians had risen from the heather—the first muster of the Westlings.

It was hard to reconstruct the scene, for the countryside had since been farmed and tamed by settlers from Krail. Others had come south, from King's Bank—folk of Mel'Nir who would not be ruled by Lien. Now sheep were grazing in the heathery downs where Yorath and his scouts had crept to spy on the besiegers.

They rode into Hackestell town as the sun was turning the high ground to gold; now they needed a room for the night, where travelers might take a dog, as well as good stabling for the horses. They had dismounted before the largest inn, called the Garrison Arms, when a hearty voice cried out.

"By the Goddess, it must be! The brave kedran Maddoc who saved our Lord Knaar three, four years past! *Captain Maddoc,* by all that's holy!"

It was a tall old man in a handsome robe—Huw Mentle, the reeve of Hackestell Town. She gave him a salute and presented her betrothed.

"Ah Captain," said Reeve Mentle, "I believe I know who you are."

He bent down to make much of Bran the dog.

"There was one who came by with magic, so he said, and amulets and ballad sheets for sale," went on the reeve, "and he said a great Chyrian Battlemaid would happen along, and her mythic name is the *Wanderer* . . ."

Gael pointed her lance at the ground and felt her cheeks burn. Tomas came to the rescue.

"Good Master Mentle," he said. "My betrothed is indeed the *Wanderer,* but it seems better to us not to make a show of it!"

"I understand," said old Mentle, "but I think you will be happy to meet with the kerns and kedran of the garrison—some you met during that curious Enquiry, and some friends from Coombe."

They spoke of a room for the night, and the reeve had barely time to assure them of a splendid place before a bunch of young garrison soldiers came out of the inn.

A captain cried out her name, and she knew him.

"Prys! Prys Oghal!" she cried, just as heartily.

It was indeed the reeve's son from Coombe—one of the Summer Riders. She had known him all her life and remembered him how kindly he had helped her with her reading during training. They clasped hands in a soldier's handshake, and he marked that she had made captain.

"My father thinks the world of you!" said Prys. "You brought those Eildon nobles over the high ground."

"It was a hard duty," she grinned.

She introduced Tomas as a scribe from Lort and as her betrothed.

"By heaven," said Prys, "we must drink to that!"

He introduced his fellow officers, and one of them was Stivven, a captain now, who as ensign had led Jehane and Gael about when they bore witness at the Enquiry. Several of Prys's comrades wore the device of a green tree—they were Westlings, like himself, from the Chyrian lands. Everyone rallied round—patted the dog Bran, praised Ebony and Valko, and sent them off with a groom. Yes, the host of the Garrison Arms agreed that rooms were to be made ready for Captain Maddoc and Master Giraud.

Meanwhile, Prys took leave of the officers, saying he must have some words with his old comrade, and they sat down inside, in the large comfortable public room of the inn.

"I have not seen you for almost five years," said Gael. "I hope all goes well in Coombe!"

"To tell the truth," said Prys Oghal, "things have been going so well, I have heard our good Druda say he believed we were 'under a blessing'—the way some poor folk are under a curse."

As the jovial young captain from Coombe began to explain, Tomas exchanged a long glance with her, as if to say *as we thought* . . . After Gael's departure with the Malms, Coombe had had a spell of fine weather, called a Hallowed Summer, for autumn and its storms had been set to bay; then the winter had been the mildest any of the old folks could remember. And speaking of old folks, there was a new almshouse built in Morrow Lane, back of the General Yorath, and a few cottages refurbished for the heartier elder citizens. Then, as for building, there were so many plans that Gael would hardly know the place. Did she recall the Cresset Burn? Well, it had been turned about and a dam and a dike built—Ardven House had been completely rebuilt, as fine as it was in the olden days.

"And Emeris Murrin?" broke in Gael. "Is my old comrade well?"

"Fit as a foal," Prys answered her. "While the house was rebuilt, she took one of the new cottages overlooking the burn. Her sister's children came to visit from Rift Kyrie and left a good woman, Matilda, to care for her."

"Oh, that is good news!" said Gael. "And how is my companion Jehane Vey?"

"Already chosen for the Sword Lilies!" said Prys.

Then she asked a little more cautiously how Bress and his friend Shim Rhodd were faring in the Westling barracks at Krail.

"Doing very well, the pair of them," grinned the captain. "They will both make ensign by the summer, though it seems to me, I heard whisper, your brother was thinking of finishing out his service and coming home! Perhaps he has his eye on some young filly, and your parents, back at the Well, are doing so well now . . ."

And talking of the Rhodd clan, there was news of the innkeeper himself.

"Yes," laughed Prys, "Old Alvin Rhodd has taken a third wife! A rich widow! Can you guess who that might be?"

Gael shook her head.

"Why, it is Mistress Raillie from the Long Burn Farm, mother of Master Culain Raillie, Coombe's new town fiscal. Now they say Culain himself is courting a young wife in Tuana and will bring her home soon."

"Truly," said Gael, smiling. "Coombe is going up in the world. A town fiscal!"

Then she and Prys explained to Tomas. Yes, he knew well enough that town fiscal was the local title for a treasurer or cofferer for a town or village. And it was usually a rich man so that he would not be tempted to dishonesty. But, as Prys explained, poor old Coombe had had so many lean years that there had been no place for a fiscal—his father, Reeve Oghal, had got along with a pair of scribes and kept the books himself.

There was more news of Coombe, all of it pleasant and good. Then Captain Oghal went back to quarters in Hackestell and took Gael with him to pay her respects to Obrist Wellach. The fortress was as fine and forbidding as ever—she was brought to the kedran quarters, their common room, where they sat playing battle or mending their gear as kedran did everywhere in Hylor. She knew none of these kedran from Krail, but their senior officer, Captain Black, asked if she had served in the Southland. There were twenty-five kedran in the fortress and more than seventy kerns, not including kitchen servants—sometimes the wives of the garrison.

Then she returned to the Garrison Arms, and the host showed her to a fine room on the ground floor of the inn, where Tomas was waiting: it had a garden door so Bran could go in and out. Everyone had agreed that Bran, Captain Maddoc's dog, was a fine fellow—docile and good humored. Now he took a second supper and chewed a mutton bone on the hearthrug—a dog in heaven, among his own dark folk at last.

Tomas put an arm around Gael's shoulders as they stared out into the twilight at the banks of the river Demmis and the distant lights of the city of Krail.

"This Culain Raillie," he said, "is in a fair way to become a leading citizen of Coombe. You believe he can be trusted?"

"He was chosen by the Goddess," said Gael firmly. "That will make him an honest man."

11

They rode into Coombe in easy stages, and Gael recalled how it had looked back in early autumn, when she had led out the Malms to ride on the High Plateau. Now the fields south of Hackestell were green with young oats, and the bare brown hills were a market garden. There were oats, early peas, yellow reps flowers and beds of onion, beet, turnip, and several kinds of kale. Among the fields were women in bright headscarves and men in straw hats, working.

They came to the crossroads and gazed down and away to Lowestell fortress, standing out against the dark forest of the southwold. Tomas confessed he would like to visit this keep one day and compare it with old maps he had seen. They turned west at the boundary wall and rode up a fine new road, heading for the town. Gael showed him the way to the Holywell—newly cleared, the ancient white pavingstones she remembered from her earliest days freshly scoured, and mended in places with coarse, newer stone. Then it was time: they were at the gate of Holywell farm, and she cried out in surprise and began to laugh aloud. Bran bounded back and forth in front of them, and Gael got down, calling him to heel.

The Maddocs had "come to a house" indeed. Another story had been raised, with a covered staircase to reach it; a barn had risen behind the house. The yard was covered with green turf, and ivy grew over the new canopy of the well. The old lean-to was a stable. A pathway in the grounds led down toward the Holywell. A thin dark man, getting to be old, was sitting at a rustic table under the apple tree, and a dark woman in a handsome green gown was serving him with drink and a platter of food. It was like a tapestry picture of "The Good Crofters," not anything Gael could relate to her memories of the little old house and the ways of her childhood. She thought wryly that every time she went away, the lives of her parents were changed for the better.

"Gael! Gael, dear child!"

Her mother uttered a joyous cry, and Gael remembered the puzzled, almost suspicious welcome she had received on her return from the Southland. Her father stood up with his sturdy ash staff, and her mother opened the new green gates, making much of Bran and crying out:

"A dog! Oh yes, yes, he is a *good* dog then . . ."

Gael kissed her mother's worn cheek and introduced Tomas Giraud, who took Shivorn Maddoc's hand.

Her father had called a name: "Evan!" and now a young lad came from the barn. As the family clustered under the tree, he led away first Valko, the sorrel, and then Ebony, who knew the place and gave no trouble.

"Mother—Father—" said Gael, suddenly shy, "Tomas is my true love. We are betrothed . . ."

"Master Maddoc," said Tomas, meeting her father's eye firmly, "in other times I would have asked for your daughter's hand. I do so now, most humbly, and will answer any questions you care to put to me."

"Well said!" brought out Rab Maddoc, also shy. "Come, come now, Tomas. We know who you are from our son Bress. A scribe, no less, from the city of Lort . . . is it not so? Sit down with me while my goodwife and daughter take those saddlebags into the house . . ."

Gael went with her mother and exclaimed at all the changes in the humble cottage and its grounds. But she marked that her mother already took many things for granted, good fortune having changed her as well. Mostly, Shivorn was anxious to hear about Tomas and about how and where they lived. Together, mother and daughter carried the saddlebags into the back bedroom, no longer a storeroom. Yes, said Mother Maddoc proudly, the upper rooms had been done out for Bress, his own quarters.

Shivorn Maddoc sat on the bed while Gael stowed her gear and Kenit, the sleek brown cat, came to sit by her side. "Soldiering," she said, "or being chosen a messenger for the light folk. It is a kedran's life, child, and it seems to become you. But this has to do with love, with loving—he is a tall, handsome fellow, your Tomas. Will you nibble that magic kedran herb all your life, or will you one day settle and bear us a grandchild?"

"One day!" said Gael. "Will Bress take himself a wife?"

"I'll be bound!" her mother answered, though it seemed she had heard nothing of this "filly" Prys Oghal had mentioned—did not believe in her!

When they came out into the sunshine again, the two men were playing Battle together on the board that Rab Maddoc had inlaid into the tabletop.

"By the Well!" he exclaimed. "Young Tomas here could match Old Murrin herself at this game!"

"I know it!" said Gael. "He is a master player!" She looked across to her betrothed, his elbows folded on the rustic table, his attention sharp upon the board, and an arrow of joy pierced through her that this active intelligence, this handsome, thinking man, would one day be her husband, might one day fill her womb with child. Then she was embarrassed and clasped his hand under the table, too shy to meet his inquiring look as he glanced up at this distraction.

They sat all together for a short time; it was about mid afternoon, and the spring day was very mild.

"Well," said Gael Maddoc, reluctantly rising from her seat. "I will go into this fine new Coombe and speak to the reeve and to Druda Strawn—and others."

"Yes," said Tomas. "It would be best." They had agreed that she must complete this 'other' business without him.

She changed her boots and put on her hat with the kestrel feather, then she called Bran and set off walking. They went happily along together, and she exchanged cheerful greetings with the folk they passed. Gael thought how quiet Coombe village had been when she rode in, months before—now the new town was bustling, full of life. When she reached the reeve's house—which had been enlarged and refurbished like everything else—she guessed that Reeve Oghal would be busy in his public rooms. Gael had put Bran on his leash and found out the way, up a wide staircase. She went directly to the chambers of the town fiscal.

There were scribes in the outer rooms and citizens doing business, but she had no trouble getting through. In a fine, airy chamber, there sat Culain Raillie, hemmed in among his ledgers, looking more than ever like a merchant in his counting house. His long dark face had filled out a little, his color was better; but when he saw Gael come in, his manner became wary, almost fearful.

"Captain Maddoc!" he said. "My friend . . .?"

"Master Raillie!" she answered, smiling. "What great things have been doing, here in Coombe!"

"I see you have a dog," he went on. "Is it dark or light, I wonder?"

"Oh, Bran is a dark dog," she said. "Aren't you old fellow?"

So first she asked after Reeve Oghal, who lived a little retired these days—it was certain he would be succeeded by his daughter's husband, Bretlow Smith, now completely recovered from the skirmish on the coast. Then they spoke of Ardven House restored and Captain Murrin in good health and spirits. "Her folk from Rift Kyrie are pleasant people," Culain told her. "Of course, we are expecting Ardven's true heir, Oweyn Murrin of King's Bank, later in the summer. Then Ardven will truly come back into its own!"

Gael rejoiced at all this good news. She bent and stroked Bran's head, hesitating a little before she broached her true business.

"Master Raillie," she said at last. "I think we must understand each other, as we have done in the past. It is time for plain speaking."

The fiscal nodded to his young scribe, who left the room, then he gestured her to a fine chair and sat down again behind his massive table.

"Coombe has been blessed," she said directly, "and I know the cause of this blessing."

"A certain magic," said Culain, hesitating. "You saw—you saw the blessed stone . . ."

Gael changed the subject—she wanted to come to the truth gently. "A short time past, I went into Athron," she said, "on an errand for the light folk, the Shee. Afterward I helped to rescue a poor woman who was the prisoner of a Witchfinder, the fanatical Brother Sebald, out of Lien."

"Was that you then, Gael Maddoc? There has been an echo of this business even in Coombe!" said Culain, smiling.

"The name of the old woman we rescued was Elnora Hestrem," she said quietly, not meeting his eyes. "She is one of the Merwin folk, the sea rovers . . ."

She heard his sharp intake of breath.

"What is this truth you know?" he asked in an altered voice. "Speak plainly . . ."

"In the Long Burn Farm," she said, "you hold a sacred treasure, one of the so-called Hallows of Hylor. It was stolen long past from Tuana and brought into Eildon, where it was put on show. You rescued this precious thing and brought it into the Chyrian lands with the help of the Merwin seafarers. You brought home *Taran's Kelch,* the Cup of Blessing, which has its image set among the stars!"

Culain Raillie sprang up and strode about the room. He twisted his hands together.

"I—I could not bear it!" he said. "I am a Chyrian, indeed, born in Tuana, but I lived and worked in other parts of the world—in Athron, in Lien, in Cayl, and in Eildon. I am a trader and a merchant, like my father before me. Yet when I saw the Cup in that trumpery museum on the Gred-daer estates, I could not bear it. The Goddess laid her hand upon my shoulder that bright morning: I knew I would cast away all my wealth, my good connections, in order to bring this sacred vessel home again, at least to the Chyrian lands . . ."

He paused and smiled a little and said:

"You will know, of course, why my mother and I chose Coombe . . ."

"Yes, I know that too," said Gael quietly. "You were seeking out the Holywell, where the sacred Cup could be put under the protection of the Goddess . . ."

"And so it must be!" cried Culain.

"Yes, and it will all be done before witnesses!" echoed Gael Maddoc.

"I do not come alone but with a scribe from the scrolls—my betrothed, Tomas Giraud. He knows how the ceremony must be done—and seen by all those who can see it, magically, and set down in the scrolls for a memorial!"

"Goddess be praised," whispered Culain. "I have—I have not known how to properly reveal and share my burden. Is this known to your present masters—to the Eilif folk?"

"They await my word," Gael said. "Even in their darkening days upon this soil, the Cup's recovery will be a joy to them. I will go now and consult with Druda Strawn—he will surely know the best time for the ceremony to be performed in the sacred cavern!"

"Oh, this is surely part of Coombe's Blessing!" said Culain Raillie. "I know you and your betrothed will have planned to stay at the Holywell House—but pray, do us a greater service! I offer you the Long Burn Farm for your home, as long as you care to stay!"

"If you need us," said Gael. "It is a fine house!"

"I keep some trusty kedran and kerns at the Long Burn, to guard the treasure," said Culain, and she thought he smiled a little.

"I must tell this all to the Druda," she said. "Though I feel he may know the truth already."

"Bless you for a true friend, Gael Maddoc . . ."

"You have brought a blessing to Coombe," she said. "The greatest blessing since Coombe began—greater even than the founding of the Westlings by Yorath Duaring!"

She sent congratulations to Culain's mother, now Mistress Rhodd, and led Bran down the stairs. She still felt very strange in this new, prosperous town of Coombe, but the sight of Druda Strawn's house, beyond the new smithy and the livery stable, reassured her. It had changed very little: under the great oak tree, green for the spring, there was a table inlaid with a Battle board, like the one at Holywell croft. She divined suddenly that her father, Rab Maddoc, had made this table—a gift for the Druda who had given them so much over the years.

Bran went bounding suddenly into the yard, and she called him sharply to heel—but not before a large black and white cat had sprung up from the grass and climbed the tree. Druda Strawn came to the door of his aged cottage, and he was smiling, touched by the blessing of Coombe:

"Ah—you know it all, Gael Maddoc!" he cried, spreading his arms and gesturing with the staff he carried. "A source of great magic . . ."

"My dog has sent your cat up the tree," she said. "You never had a cat before, Druda!"

"Oh but I did," he said softly, as they took their places at the new table. "We had cats when we were first wed, my dear wife and I, after the Great King's War. Perhaps I have let myself remember that happy time . . ."

"Druda," she reached out her hands to him, "my true love, Tomas Giraud, the scribe, is here with me, and we have been offered the Long Burn Farm while we are in Coombe. I have spoken freely with Culain Raillie, whom I hold for an honest man and a good Chyrian. All that is left for Coombe and its sacred treasure is a ceremony at the Holywell, for all the lands of Hylor to behold and know . . ."

"Oh, it will be done!" he said, smiling. "I have already rehearsed the form of this *Unveiling*. But it was for the *Wanderer* to confront Master Culain, not an aging village priest . . ."

He broke off and looked into her face.

"But child, you are still troubled . . ."

She shook her head, not knowing why any foreboding had fallen upon her. "I can hope that so much good fortune will not corrupt the good folk of Coombe, after years of simple living—and some years of hardship . . ."

"I believe that they will remain like themselves," he said, seriously.

"Did you hear of the Witchfinder of Lien?" she asked timidly. "And of the rescue in which I played a part—the old woman in Athron?"

"Yes, I have heard of this bold deed," said Druda Strawn, with a taut smile of approval.

"It may have cost me the trust and good opinion of the light folk . . ." said Gael.

She gave a deep sigh, and it was echoed strangely by the dog, Bran, who uttered a whimpering howl and moved close to her.

"Have no fear," said Druda Strawn, softly. He looked up at the door of his cottage: Luran strode out into the small yard. He wore a grey tunic with a russet hood thrown back; his jewels were very fine. She thought of the first time he appeared to her at the fireside in the Halfway House and of the difference between the light folk and the dark.

"It is as you said, Gael Maddoc," he said with a half smile. "I cannot disapprove of what you have discovered in Coombe."

Bran whimpered again and Luran bent toward him.

"Foolish fellow!" he said. "No, I have *not* come to take you back to Tulach! You are Maddoc's dog now!"

Gael soothed Bran and said the same things, and he seemed to understand. The black and white cat took the opportunity to descend the oak tree and march into the cottage.

"In two days we have the new moon," said Druda Strawn, "and at the *next* turning of the moon it is the Young Men's Month, the Elmmoon, and this is when the ceremony must take place at the Holywell. Tomas Giraud has the exact way of it from the scrolls, and some noble guests will wish to attend, I am sure. I believe Lord Luran will honor us with his presence."

It was a time of preparation and excitement. To be sure, Mother Maddoc fussed a little when Tomas and Gael moved into Long Burn Farm two mornings later, but she saw the honor of it. Mistress Raillie, now Mistress Rhodd, was still her good friend, and she had often visited the Long Burn. So Gael and Tomas rode out with Bran two hours before noon; it was another perfect day, spring shading into summer. They crossed twice over the burn and looked down upon the Maidens, the standing stones, in their everlasting dance for the nymph Taran.

They passed below Ardven house—Gael was warmed to see the fresh stone facing on the main building, the gay pennants rapping in the breeze, and on through the red rolling hills until the turning for Long Burn. As they came toward the Railles' handsome stone house, there seemed to be movement, but when they came into the yard, it was empty and quiet. They got down, and Gael went up to the great door and knocked loudly with the end of her lance. Suddenly there was the sound of shouting, singing, someone played a bag-pipe—grooms rushed out of the stables. There upon the doorstep, crying out her welcome, were a sturdy kedran captain and a dark ensign, Mev Arun and Amarah, Gael's true companions from her four years' service in the Kestrel Company of Pfolben, in the Southland.

So often during her journeys, Gael had dreamed that these good friends had come to her door or that she rode with them again; now the dream was truth. More than that, Mev Arun cried out that there was another old comrade, a captain of the kern guard from Lowestell—and there stood Hadrik, who had traveled with her through the Burnt Lands. Then they all embraced, and she and Tomas were taken into the house. The housekeeper welcomed them, and Gael remembered her as Bethne, who had served Mistress Raillie as a maidservant when she first came to visit the Long Burn Farm.

Appendix 903 (Gatherings and Ceremonies, fully witnessed) as recorded in The Book of Sooth, also called The DATHSA.

At this time, on the Chyrian coast of Mel'Nir, in the town of Coombe, an ancient treasure, recovered and brought home to its native shore, was *held up* and shown to the Goddess and to the Gods of the Far Faring and to the people, in a rare ceremony known as *The Unveiling*. This was done at the Holywell, within its sacred cavern and in the precinct of the Goddess, and a priest, Druda Kilian Strawn, together with an old woman of Tuana, known as Aroneth, the last surviving priestess from the Sacred Grove in the old Chyrian capital, performed the ritual. Six young maids of Coombe, in raiment of white and yellow, assisted in the ceremony.

The treasure, enclosed in a gilded chest, was carried to the Holywell from the Long Burn Farm, beyond the village, by an honor guard of kerns and kedran; the way was lined with citizens cheering and crying out and waving lilies and branches of green willow.

Inside the cavern, the ceremony was witnessed by the Reeve of Coombe Leem Oghal and the Town Fiscal, Culain Raillie, by Emeris Murrin, the chatelaine of Ardven Old House, together with Rab and Shivorn Maddoc, keepers of the Holywell, and their daughter, Captain Gael Maddoc, a freelance kedran who had done service for Coombe village. Other honored guests at *The Unveiling* included Captain Hadrik of the guard and kedran Captain Arun from duty in Lowestell Fortress at the Southwold border, with other members of Kestrel Company, serving the house of Pfolben. A nobleman from Lien, Lord Auric Barry, was also present, having conveyed to this ceremony a great scribe, now well advanced in years, Brother Less, the chaplain of the Dowager Duchess of Chantry.

The most august personage of all was hardly to be beheld, yet near the spring, in a niche of the cavern's wall, stood Luran of Clonagh, an Eilif lord of the Shee, come down from Tulach Hearth for the ceremony.

When the time came, the golden chest was opened and the treasure brought forth, and the Priestess Aroneth held it up above the holy spring and drew aside its veil of fine black gauze. It was seen to be a tall goblet of metal, decorated in ancient style, dull looking at first but then shining with an inward light. Rays of the sun came through the fretted roof of the cavern and blazed upon the sacred Vessel. Then Druda Strawn cried out in a strong voice, saying that this was *Taran's Kelch*, a bowl of plenty for the Chyrian lands and for all the lands of Mel'Nir. It had been stolen away, but now it had been brought home. So all the folk of all the Lands of Hylor and the Lands Below the World must know that it was in its rightful place again, here at the Holywell.

Tomas Giraud has writ this, Scribe of Lort, in the year of Farfaring 355.

". . . who will come next?" said Gael. "An army of wraiths from Lake Nimnothal?"

Tomas was changing his boots. They had settled most comfortably into the largest bedroom of the Long Burn Farm. This was the celebration night, which promised to be a long one. Gael's old comrades, Mev Arun and Amarah, were in the second parlor with Hadrik and some kern officers; Bran the dog sat with them. Soon they would all ride out to Coombe, where there was dancing in the streets.

Yet there was more afoot. Gael held onto Tomas and said:

"You understand that I must make this journey into Eildon?" Auric Barry had not come to Coombe just to witness the unveiling ceremony—though it was true that there were not many who would not have found themselves deeply moved by that ceremony, not to say impressed by its parade of magic. He had come to propose a journey into Eildon—there had been new letters from this supposed "Lost Prince" of the Chameln, with private details from Carel and his brother Sharn's early days as exiles in Lien. Now even Queen Aidris was intrigued—and Auric Barry all the more concerned, for these letters were either proof of the Lost Prince's true identity, or evidence that some Lien-man had provided this information, was taking part in what could only be meant for a sad betrayal. The *Wanderer* could go where folk of the Chameln—and one so noted as Auric Barry of Lien—could not, perhaps she could find out, at least, the conspirators who had set this "Lost Prince" on the road to Achamar City.

Gael did not know why—but the Shee had agreed that it was right for her to go. Luran had even given her a band, a heavy gold bracer she was to wear on her upper arm over her sleeve, and bid her fast and safe travel.

"Truly," Tomas said. "I believe you are the one to uncover these answers—and you have your old comrades to help with the work." Hadrick, Mev Arun, and Amarah would be accompanying her—good plain Melniro folk with no connection to Lien, nor to the Chameln either. Also Gwil Cluny, called down from the High Plateau—though his heritage, being half-Shee, was not quite so a plain one! "How does Druda Strawn go with arranging the boat?"

"His wife's people own the great inn, Strandgard, with its own anchorage, at Banlo. Between them, he and Culain Raillie have a vessel of the right kind waiting. My father will drive us there in a cart from Long Burn

Farm—he has some business on the coast, so it will not be inconvenient for him."

"Three young women, traveling to Eildon," grinned Tomas. "I'd like to see the three of you in skirts . . ."

"We will have our portraits painted," she said primly, "at *Shennazar,* in Oakhill, in the city of Lindriss on the Laun!"

CHAPTER XIV

A VOYAGE TO EILDON

As their vessel, a sturdy cog called* Banlo Hope, *moved carefully under the tall white cliffs on the final leg of the approach to Eildon, they saw men and women in strange clothes working upon the precipitous paths above them. The land was the same as anywhere else; but no, it was not. There was a softness to the wind that brushed their sails here, curious effects of mist and sunlight, sparking off the white face of the rock. The skipper was a young man from the Strandgard anchorage called Alun Treyn, and they carried Hadrik, who knew sailing, and another Kestrel, Imala, Amarah's friend. Eildon, Captain Treyn told them, ever presented this face of shining light and dancing mist; it was like no other country.

The weather in the Oakmoon had been splendid for sailing, and they'd been brought at a steady, good pace to the coast of old Eildon, where they passed their way beneath the tall white cliffs to the mouth of the great river Laun. The city of Lindriss, half-shrouded by drifts of magical mist and light, lay across the Laun's ancient sprawling estuary, with its own character in every quarter: ancient, magical, bright and dark at once.

Down in the largest cabin, the three adventurers primped and paraded before a long glass—Gael had made magic that turned one door of a press into a mirror. Wearing traditional female dress instead of kedran gear was a difficult and frustrating task for them—Gael had had some experience of loose robes from her happy hours with Tomas in their tower at the Swan, but never of ladies' garb, tightly laced. The gowns they wore were simple but of fine quality—mostly the property of Culain Raillie's mother, with a few culled from Mistress Oghal and her daughter, Ronna Smith, wife of

Bretlow. Luckily, these were taller women, and their clothes fit even Gael well enough. There had been a problem with hair. Mev Arun simply added a dark brown tress to her own shoulder-length hair, drawn back. Amarah, who played the role of the Bride in their story, wore a longer black fall of hair woven into her own hair and covered with a veil.

Gael, with a dashing kedran cut of distinctive red, had to wear a full wig, ordered over from Krail, and dressed by the personal maid of the new Mistress Rhodd. The color was well chosen, she supposed, a red gold, and Tomas had been kind when she tried it on. She hardly knew the woman in the glass—long hair she associated with her callow girl-child's years, and she could not see herself as much improved. At least, all agreed, they passed well for three maidens of the Southland, dressed in well-cut gowns that bespoke a certain wealth. Dark blue, pale blue and white, pale gold and soft green; head coverings, cloaks if needed, shoes firmly heeled, of soft leather, over pale, thin trunk hose: they drew the line at stockings and garters. The hemlines of their gowns brushed the instep and bore a slight train at the back. Gael struggled not to curse as, again and again, she trod her train underfoot.

Imala, their "attendant," was allowed to keep her kedran dress, and they envied her. So they came at last to their mooring place and stepped daintily down the gangplank into the crowded, colorful port of Hythe. A carriage, surely—Hadrik and Imala let Captain Treyn brush aside the hawkers and the guides; the ladies were driven up and down the misty hills of the great city to an inn called the Stone Men. The sign showed a ring of tall grey figures, like standing stones, yet cleverly wrought by some ancient stonemason (or at least the signboard's painter!) so that each one had a special attitude, a hand lifted, a head turned, a striding step.

Inside, the arrangements were noticeably quiet and respectable; the hostess curtsied and sent two wenches up the staircase to usher them into their rooms. They fell about and complained loudly in the large bedchamber, then joined Hadrik in their parlor, for cordials and a light repast.

Word had been left with the hostess that a factor would ask for Captain Hadrik's party. Sure enough, at the appointed hour, their prime helper in Eildon made his appearance—Gwil Cluny came to the door.

"Don't laugh, old comrade," said Gael.

"You look splendid," he said, grinning. "I'll tell my Mam how well long golden hair becomes our *Wanderer*."

She made him known to all the others; he accepted a tankard of the ale that Hadrik was drinking and made his report.

"It is as we thought, the workshop of Chion Am Varr at Shennazar in

Oakhill is busy, but a place can be gained with a little extra gold. They use a 'school' system, like Emyas Bill and many others—a portrait is drafted by the master, then finished by the assistants, save perhaps for details of the face and hands. A list of all those men and women who sat for their portraits can be obtained for more gold and by magic."

"And this pretender," said Mev Arun, "surely he was not painted by anyone but this Master Chion himself."

"Yes, Mistress," said Gwil. "That fact has narrowed our search. In the last two years, Chion Am Varr has done only seven private sittings. Most often he traveled to a noble house to do some notable among the gentry. Once, twice, he went off with his requisites, and perhaps one friend, as if it were a holiday." He brought out a rough map of Eildon's demesnes, to show the routes the painting master had taken.

"It is a puzzle," Gwil continued, turning to Gael. "Think of this—someone in Eildon has set up this pretender, paid for the portrait, perhaps schooled or instructed the fellow. What better cover for this portrait than a family sitting in a great house? Chion Am Varr paints Lady Thus and So, but also paints the Lost Prince, so-called.

"Before this morning of your arrival, I have been through the four nearest mansions," said Gwil. "There is always a need for a fortune teller or a seller of fancy goods among the servants of these houses."

"Do we have any promising candidates then?" asked Gael.

"One or two," he grinned. "Do you not have some sort of copy of the famous portrait, sent to the new-wed queen?"

"You first," said Gael, bringing out a large folded parchment.

"There was a tale in one country house of the Paldo clan, the Knightly Hunters," said Gwil, "of a man from the Pendark lands who worked over the summer and had his portrait done by Chion Am Varr for an inn sign, somewhere in the south."

"And the other?"

"There is a young man who has a herb garden not far from Oakhill. He joined in the Summer Pageant several years past—though not this most recent year—because he bore a likeness to Shennazar himself. To Sharn Am Zor, the Summer's King—a handsome, golden-haired man."

"But now he has grown old," said Gael. Something in Gwil's description—she knew this must be the man from the painting that had been sent to the Chameln court.

She unfolded the copy Emyas Bill had done from memory and dusted with tinted chalks here and there to give a hint of the man's coloring. They all gazed at the sketch, and Gwil Cluny said softly:

"Yes, it could be a match for Dan Royl, the herb gardener," said Gwil. "It was always held that his name is a kind of stage name, from his days playing Shennazar."

"The first part of his name is the Chameln word for a king or queen," Gael said softly. "If this man is indeed our Lost Prince, he has not done so much to hide himself."

"So where is this royal fellow?" asked Hadrik. "Gone yet? Away learning his story?"

"I can hardly believe . . ." Gwil Cluny frowned. "From what little I have seen, in some ways he might be a good man, in others not. I think he is still there, over at Thornlee Herb Farm."

"Remember what I asked," said Gael, "about the tenure of the land, here at Oakhill."

"Eildon tenure is a maze," said Gwil. "All the land belongs by custom to the three princely families, Tramarn, Paldo and Pendark, and to the seven Eorls and the Barons. There are adjustments of tenure by deed, marriage, and inheritance. There are a few earlier rights still recognized and some later changes, as when land comes 'under the cowl'—into the possession of the priestly colleges of the Druda and the white sisters, the Dagdaren. The very place we were speaking of—Thornlee and the countryside round about—is 'under the cowl,' and it is worked by tenant farmers, including Master Dan Royl. There is a steward who lives not far away and watches over all the priestly land in the name of the college."

"Tomorrow is a testing day," said Amarah. "First we meet Master Chion at Shennazar, but then it is the Pageant and we see more of Oakhill."

"The Pageant now," said Mev Arun craftily, "fancy dress and merriment. Any chance we could get out of these clothes?"

"You know my plan," said Gael. "Forgive me, sisters, but at some time during this parade, I will slip away with our Captain Hadrik. We will meet Gwil Cluny and prowl about a certain herb garden. I can't prowl in a gown."

"I have an idea," put in Ensign Imala. "Don't you ladies have riding habits?"

The idea was welcomed—the habits had trews under a wide buttoned skirt that could be thrown back or removed. Hadrik knew of a livery stable and suggested a ride on the downs after the pageant: the kedran missed their horses, missed riding.

The carriage drove to the west, through the city, crossing handsome bridges over tributary streams—Waybrook, Falconet—of the great river

Laun. The district of Oakhill was northwest of the fine Tramarn estates—they were not well tended; parts of the gardens near the mansion were overgrown. Prince Gwalchai, great-nephew of Ross, the Priest-King, was held to be the last of his line.

There had been a sad time after the Tramarn prince, when young, married Princess Moinagh Pendark, courted by so many, including King Sharn Am Zor. Moinagh became wayward after the birth of a daughter and ran off with the child to join the Children of the Sea, her mother's kin. Gwalchai lived many years alone and now had gone to a distant strand in the northwest, where he sat watching the sea. The story was a melancholy one. Remembering the dowager princess, Merigaun Pendark, Moinagh's mother, Gael could only wonder what that gentle lady had made of her daughter's wildness, and guess that her tender feelings toward her nephew, Liam Greddaer of Greddach, owed some of their strength to that earlier abandonment by her own child.

She shook herself, staring out over Prince Gwalchai's hills. As a child in Coombe, she would never have believed she would come to know so much of these princely lives—so much so that she could share and almost feel their sadness and their pain, their hopes and joys. Fine fate for the crofter's girl of the Holywell!

She touched for a moment the cool gold band upon her upper arm—Lord Luran's gift—and wondered again at his change of heart, allowing—nay encouraging—her to come here. The metal of the bracer held an unnatural chill; Lady Annhad's ring confirmed that strong magic ran within. She had sensed in Luran's manners that something in this matter was not for Gael yet to be told—a touch of dread went through her, but her trust was in the Shee. Luran must have some reason for keeping the Shee's purpose hidden. Something to protect the delicate Fionnar, perhaps, or frail old Sir Hugh.

Up ahead, there was a bustle of preparation in the streets and in four great pavilions where the carnival floats were being assembled. The three visitors and their kedran attendant stepped down from the carriage behind the grandstand, where their seats were waiting. Captain Hadrik stayed with the carriage, and the women went off in the direction of Shennazar.

Oakhill was a fine place, open and fresh with much greenery and wide streets decorated for the Pageant. Gael felt the morning sun on her face and looked up at the hill itself, crowned with a ring of great oak trees. The bright shops and stalls recalled the market near Goldgrave where, years past now, she had spent her reward from Hem Duro on gifts for the Winter

Feast. The Shennazar art workshop had a golden sign and beautiful things laid out for sale behind its mullioned glass panes. They stepped inside and were greeted by a young man, who led them up and up the broad stairs to a room full of light.

A woman in a kind of kedran dress led "Mistress Amarah Habrin," the chosen bride of a rich Danasken Lord, into a tiring room, where both the lady and her attendants were put to rights. Then they came out, and there was the Master Painter holding out his hands to Amarah and smiling. Chion Am Varr was not much over thirty, a good-looking, brown-haired fellow, muscular and strong but well covered with flesh. He wore Chameln dress, with the sleeves of his fine summer tunic rolled up.

He led them first to a wall in the workroom full of portraits and painted groups; the light was adjusted to perfectly illuminate this grouping.

"Now, what can we choose?" cried Chion. "Where will you sit—indoors or out? I believe you would do well, Mistress Amarah, in this plain setting, with flowers in the urns and your two ladies one up, one down."

There was a man with his wife and their young son in the painting upon the wall, and the background was a simple hanging, half-covering a window. They passed into another well-lit room, and there was the setting they had just seen, even to the curtain and the window behind it, showing the clear blue sky and a branch of apple tree, white with blossom. They took their places on the chair and the velvet settle and looked at themselves in a large wall mirror while Chion and his assistants moved them about, adjusted their limbs and skirts, made chalk marks. The master painter discussed the colors of the gowns they were to wear—no, of course, no riding habits. Then, with an appointment for the next day, they went on their way—the Pageant was beginning.

As they made their way back to their grandstand seats, Amarah was cast down by the role they were all playing. Chion did not seem a bad fellow, yet he was not going to get his fee. Was it certain that he was involved in this Lost Prince charade?

"Yes," said Gael. "He is. The best we can say for him is that he is an artist who does not understand intrigue, who has this great love for light and color and so on."

"You are tender hearted," said Mev Arun to Amarah. "Remember how it will end. You will fall ill, and he will receive a quit fee."

They settled into the stands with Hadrik just as the first wheeled platforms came by, to gusty cheers. There were the Hunters, the Falconers, and the Fishers, the princely houses of Eildon, and the scenes on the floats were teasing, full of foolery. Old Borss Paldo was a boozy old prince with his coronet askew; Princess Merigaun was a sorceress with a wand that turned stones into sweetmeats, which her servants threw at the crowd. Then, on the Falconer's tower were strange messengers: an old man, a woman, and a young man dressed as a bird, serving the Eorl Leffert, the patron of the order. A Mermaid, swinging overhead in a golden net—Princess Moinagh, with a little merchild in her arms—a bold reference to the house of Tramarn, family of the Priest-King. To the party out of Mel'Nir, it was almost overwhelming. In Eildon there was no disposition against the use of magic: half the pageantry figures they saw, the sweetmeats that had showed as stone—these were cloaked with glittering illusions, magic, borne as lightly as the decorations of crepe or gauze that were worn by many in the crowd.

In the second group of scenes, there came that year's Shennazar, "The Summer's King," handsome and golden-haired; clad in golden armor, carrying a great black bow. At his side rode a beautiful dark girl, wearing a crown, and her handsome partner—the king's daughter, the new-wed Queen Tanit and her new husband Count Liam.

Then there came a group of riders—knights, kedran, a pair of lovers sharing a single saddle, three dwarfs together on another—were they Tulgai from the border forests over the sea? The scene had passed before any among their little group could decide.

"By the Goddess!" cried Mev Arun. "Gael, look there!"

They laughed and cheered. The party of riders was led by: a tall kedran with a mop of bright red hair and the banner mounted on her lance proclaimed *The Wanderer*.

"Time I took to the saddle," said Gael, disturbed. Eildon was indeed a land more than passing strange, glutted upon magic. How else could whisper of her own doings have reached these shores?

She left the stand with Hadrik, and he led the way to a park; there were two horses being held by a groom from the livery stable. Gael stripped off the skirt of her riding habit and laid it with her cloak across the back of her saddle. She kept her long wig, tied back, and the smart, blue green riding cap that went with the habit. She carried no lance but wore instead her longsword, slung on a baldric. Gwil had procured her a nice, neat-footed brown mare called Sparrow, while Hadrik's mount was a big black steed who made her pine for Ebony. Was he getting good exercise at the Long Burn Farm?

They rode out of Oakhill and followed the high road, which they had traced carefully on their guide maps to Lindriss. The bright sun was darkened now and then by patches of mist in the valleys between the hills. There, some way to the west, was the great Paldo fortress. Gael told Hadrik of the wedding at Chernak New Palace and of the princes and nobles who had been there, along with her happy meeting with Kerry-Red, Kerry-Black, and their other old comrade from the desert, Ensign Dirck.

Yes, admitted Nils Hadrik, he had it in mind to quit Pfolben with his sweetheart, who served Lady Annhad, and take service in Eildon, in the Pendark lands, as the others had done. In Pfolben, Lord Maurik was ailing. Some said Blayn seemed to have settled since his marriage, but Hadrik thought him still a little swine, whatever the Southlanders' hopes. And, yes, who should visit Pfolben in a trading galley from Seph-el-Ara, but a certain rich merchant—barely beginning to grow his first moustaches! It was Ali el Bakim, formerly a camel boy who came upon a troop of magic women warriors in the Burnt Lands' shifting sands. He had asked after Gael, and they told him what news they could, and he sent his love and duty.

"There lies the way," said Gael, looking ahead, even as she smiled at these memories.

They turned off the highroad and rode east, through a village, until they saw the herb farm of Dan Royl. A country fellow in a pancake hat was strolling along the farm boundary, and, yes, it was Gwil Cluny.

"Our man is there," said Gwil, coming up to them, "and I believe he is alone except for his cat and his dog. He talks to them and a little to himself."

The farmhouse was old and solid, finer even than the Long Burn Farm. Gwil bade them leave the horses in a grove of willows by a stream and approach on foot with woven baskets, as if they came to buy herbs. At the beginning of the path that led up the hill, Gael was warned sharply by her ring; there was magic all around the house and in the garden.

"Is it a spell?" asked Gwil, "or do we have guards here?"

"Maybe guards as well," said Gael, "and the spell is far stronger than a mere working to keep thieves out of the gardens."

"How would it be," asked Hadrik, "if Master Gwil here went a longer way round and checked the back of the house?"

"Very good," said Gwil.

He ambled off, chewing a straw. Gael and Hadrik both had their shields up; they climbed the gentle slope, admiring the beds of thyme and sage, the pots of basil displayed before the greenhouses. On a terrace in the midst of the garden was an enormous garden god of some kind, in stone, with a vine that grew over him, surrounded by smaller figures.

They went into the yard through wide double gates with one side half open for customers, and took a comfortable brick path edged with lavender and rosemary and some low-growing border plants. In a shaded place under a lemon tree was a small water trough that had splashed upon the path. There on the red bricks were several large, misshapen footprints. Gardeners—or guards?

Everything went on like an ordinary visit—they came into a large open room with counters covered with potted herbs and dried sheaves. Far back under the house, there was a wide counter where a man and his wife served them cheerfully and helped them make their choice. The man was a veteran soldier with a game leg who spoke to Hadrik as an old comrade and said he had served in Lien and in the outer isles. He asked Gael if she might be a kedran, and she agreed that she was. It was friendly talk, not suspicious questioning—Hadrik mentioned the pageant. Gael paid in Eildon silver, and they carried out their baskets. They had seen no one else, and it was easy to walk around a corner to the back of the house, out of sight of the selling room. The back of the house was old but orderly, with its own small garden. Hadrik sat with their baskets in the shade of a yew; Gael tried the back door. It was open; she slipped through into the house.

There was a large hallway, dark at first. When her eyes were accustomed to the dim light, Gael saw a suit of armor—Shennazar's carnival body armor, perhaps left over from Dan Royl's participation in years past, complete with a plumed helmet and a golden lance. She tested the weapon, and it was firm and good, not a pageant property. The rooms nearby were open and empty—kitchen, dining room, all darkly paneled, unused, she would have said. Upstairs she heard the sound of a man's voice.

"Bad cat!" he said fondly. "Oh, bad Auntie Parn! You too, Tazlo, old comrade—you've had enough of the mutton!"

A dog gave a sleepy bark. The man—Dan Royl, no doubt—went on talking to his friends; he fell into a kind of chant. It was a list of names: "Derda, Ilmar, Engist, Huw Kerrick, Old Inchevin, Lady Sarah, no, wrong, Lady Zarah. Aram Nerriot, good old Nerry, came from Wencaer, city of Wencaer in Eildon land . . . ."

It was almost too good to be true. Here was the pretender learning his lines, the names of those close to Prince Carel Am Zor. Then, from outside, there was a sudden blast of a hunting horn, and Hadrik uttered a loud cry. Gael felt for the sword at her side, then changed her mind and snatched up the lance, Shennazar's golden lance. She charged out into the sunshine.

A man on a red roan charger was prodding at Hadrik with his own lance. The captain, protected by his shield, had rolled away from the attack. Gael muttered strengthening words and directed her lance at the rider. There was a familiar crackling in the air as the spell took hold: horse and rider were struck to the ground and remained in frozen attitudes. Gael rushed to check them both, while Hadrik scrambled up. They spoke in low voices—any others? No, nothing seen. The rider had ridden uphill, then suddenly blown a blast from the hunting horn slung across his chest and charged at Hadrik—at a man with his herb baskets, seated peacefully under the yew tree.

"He knew I was an observer, at least," said Hadrik.

The horse was not harmed by the fall, so far as Gael could see; the man was a stranger, past forty, well dressed—a landowner more than a soldier. He bore no crest, but Gael opened his shirt to see if he bore an amulet, and there was a brass ear of wheat. Gael, for one hot, angry moment, almost let the man's head fall hard on the flags; the man was a follower of Inokoi, the Lame God. She knew from Tomas that for the Brown Brotherhood, the holy wheat ear symbolized the six orders of creation—where farmworkers and handworkers, women and beasts, fell irredeemably into the lowest castes. But then there came a sharp pang of pain from the ring upon her finger—this wheat ear amulet was magic, some kind of collar or leash. Snapping the little piece of brass from its cord, she hid it away, safe within her tunic sleeve, then laid the man gently onto the flagstones.

"No sign of Gwil Cluny!" said Hadrik.

Gael drew out her wooden tablet and thumbed its surface briskly. Gwil's anxious face appeared; he was moving swiftly, with leaves and branches passing before him as he hurried along.

"Front of the house," he panted. "Use the other way around, and if needed, the Cloak of Air. When I come, it will be time for Stillstand!"

"The guards are showing themselves," said Gael. "Come, we must take this way—"

They went stealthily around the northern side of the farmhouse just as a strange roaring sound began to fill the air. There were, two, three, *four* monstrous shapes in the center of the sloping herb garden. Stone Men, grown from the garden figures, who stamped and flexed their arms as they danced around the graven statue of the god. Then the tall statue itself came to life, ripping aside the vines that grew around it and lifting its arms to heaven while its strange companions uttered a shrill, harsh roar.

Gael and Hadrik stared so hard they were almost overthrown. In spite of her shield, Gael was seized clumsily, crushed in a harsh embrace, and flung sideways to the ground. A fifth Stone Man had come from behind a half-grown oak. Now he was at Hadrik, his shielding pressed, burning under the pressure, so that the loyal kern was surrounded with blue fire. Unable to draw his sword, Hadrik caught up a long board of undressed pine from the edge of a garden bed and hacked at the legs of his attacker. Gael half-slipped, then took hold of her lance again, and she thrust at their adversary and shouted aloud:

"I name you for a Man, no Stone Man!" she called in Chyrian.

The other Stone Men, still stomping and chanting below them on the slope, it was too far off to see what they were, but the creature they were fighting was indeed a man. The stony covering was a carnival costume, plastered with some kind of greyish mortar; there were joins and joints in the suit. Now Gael drove at the shoulder joint, and her new lance struck home; a low sound of pain issued from the head of the Stone Man. Still he did not fall but turned to strike at Hadrik with his own pine plank.

The captain threw his assailant down by tangling his stony legs; he fell heavily within his awkward suit and lay still, senseless. Gael flicked the pine board out of his hand just as Gwil came rushing up, right across the front of the farmhouse. Down the slope the Stone Men began to move up toward them, with a louder sound. Gwil Cluny had his sword drawn, and he shouted to Gael:

"Stillstand! Stillstand!"

They faced each other across a bush of rosemary, going straight into the familiar ritual. The herb sellers rushed out at last from a cellar far under the house as the Grand Bewitchment took hold, but they were not in its path. The noise from below by the fountain grew even louder, then stopped; the Stone Men remained in frozen attitudes. It was indeed the Hour of Stone.

"Who is the rider at the back of the house?" asked Gael. "He must be seen to, with his poor horse!"

"It is Steward Nevil," said Gwil. "We'll see to him . . ."

The woman from the herb counter came toward them, holding out her hands to Gael:

"Oh kedran, kedran," she cried. "Have mercy on our poor Master Royl!"

Gael took her hands; she saw a middle-aged woman, fair and fresh faced, and thought of her own mother, older now, going about at the Holywell.

"Have no fear, good Mistress," she said. "We will help and protect Master Royl. This strange thing with the Stone Men has been done by others—do you know who might have done it?"

The woman's husband had limped over to them, using a stick, and they said their names, Lockyer, Han and Jean, from down the valley.

"Our good Dan has some work with incomers," said Han Lockyer, "and they use magic, like the lords and ladies at a ball who will not 'wear their years.' What is your name, Captain?"

"I am Gael Maddoc," said Gael.

"She is the *Wanderer*!" put in Hadrik and Gwil in one voice.

Gael looked at them in surprise. She felt like a child who gets a sudden word of praise from her parents or teachers. The Lockyers stared and smiled, and Mistress Jean made a sign of blessing on her forehead.

"I think all these Stone Men are not more than true men in mortared suits," said Gael. "Gwil?"

They went swiftly down the hill among the herb beds, and from the very edge of the spell, the Stillstand, which Gael carefully outlined now in blue light; from outside its bounds, they stood and examined the Stone Men. Three had fallen on their backs, but one was standing. It was easy to see they were in costume; there was even a patch of blood on the stony arm of one of the fallen. Gael wondered about their breathing, in these suits, but the openings on the heads, for nose and mouth, were large. The Stillstand would last something under an hour, and she almost wished to stay on, to see how these fellows took themselves away.

Now Gwil Cluny had gone down further and was examining the statue of the giant garden god, who stood stiffly with his arms flung up. She heard him chuckle as she came closer. The back of the statue, tangled with vines, was flowing now with water, and there were pipes and wheels to be seen. Gwil was at a set of long handles in the grass. He pulled one back and the god lowered his arms with a moist creaking. Gael laughed aloud.

"Yet it was a frightening show," she said, as they walked back up the hill.

She assured the Lockyers that these were real men, not men of stone, and they would not wake for some time. Everyone trooped round to the back of the house except Han Lockyer, who promised to call if anything changed. Once they came to the fallen steward and his horse, Gael quickly unbound them, and they were raised up.

"Master Nevil," said Gael. "I think you will stay here while we look inside the house."

"What are you then, kedran?" growled the steward. "What are you doing on this land?" Coming free of the Stillstand, he seemed dazed, his voice rising and falling like there was a weakness in his chest.

"You are a man of Eildon, yet you wear tokens of Lien," she said. "The land is closely and magically watched and guarded. You must know this!"

"It is all the priests!" he said, confusion clouding his aged features. "I am only their servant. Is poor Artus hurt then?" he went on vaguely, holding his head, but seeming of a sudden truly concerned. "To cast down a horse . . ."

Artus, the big roan, seemed to be doing very well; Jean was feeding him apple, while Gwil rubbed him down with a wad of hay.

"Master Nevil," said Gael, concerned at his fading manner. If, as she suspected, the wheat ear had in truth been a leash, perhaps this man was innocent of harmful intent. "I will go up and speak to Dan Royl. These folk will bring you to the kitchen—perhaps there is an ale or cider . . ."

Hadrik and Gwil came to help the steward, and he went with them easily—Gael thought he was indeed sick and troubled in his wits. Jean took charge of the big kitchen and was making up the fire under the stockpot, serving bread and ale. Gael took a sup of the brew herself but decided not to question Steward Nevil any further. She signaled Hadrik to take a turn round the farmhouse; then she went back into the cool shadowy hall and walked softly up the stairs, still carrying the golden lance.

The voice began again as she came to the turn of the stair.

"Oh cat, Oh Parn, my dear, they will be the death of me! Even little dog Tazlo will not save your poor master . . ."

Gael came to a handsome dusty landing and tapped upon the door of the largest room, straight ahead.

"Come in!"

The voice was strong and full.

She went into a beautiful room, full of light and shadow, from the half-drawn hangings that covered the old wooden slatted windows and the few narrower openings mullioned with bluish glass. The original of the portrait sketch, the man who had played the king, Dan Royl, sat at a table piled with books. A large orange cat lay at full length on a heap of parchment; the small black and white dog, Tazlo, yapped at Gael but fell silent when she turned toward him.

"So you have come," said Dan Royl. "A courier from other lands!"

"Do you know me, Master Royl?" she asked.

"Not very well," he smiled, and she thought she saw something in him like hope. "Have you worked your magic with my good lance from happier times? I think you may be the one who dealt so well with the Witchfinder of Lien!"

"I am the one called the *Wanderer,*" she admitted, "and I have come here in search of truth, and in the service of Queen Tanit Am Zor of the Chameln lands and her consort Count Liam."

"I pray you, sit down with me," said Dan Royl humbly.

He rose up from the table and shook up the cushions on a settle. She saw that he was well built and supple under his simple robe—it was hard to guess his age. His eyes were hazel, a greenish brown.

"Have you had your portrait painted recently, Master Royl?" she asked softly.

"Oh yes," he laughed. "I have entered into the spirit of the thing. They will be disappointed if the plan falls through now."

"You are not the Lost Prince!" she said.

"No," he said. "I am something quite other."

He returned to his table and felt among the books, then paused and stroked his golden cat.

"I want to come into the Chameln, to the court," he said. "I see now—this must be the safest, the best thing for me. I will do no harm to the queen and her young man." He stroked again the cat. "I have been promised," he said, "and beyond that, if the promises that have been made to me are broken, only a bond of magic could force me to act against the Chameln, and I am not afraid of that. You must know, Eildon has its code of honor, and a promise straight made will never be dishonored." He smiled, and seemed almost amused. "Of course, it is another thing if a Eildon noble *writes* you a contract. That, you should know, must be proper copied in triplicate, or your purpose would be foiled."

Gael knew he was speaking of the illusory magics for which Eildon was famous, but she could not understand the man's air of confidence, his seeming lack of fear. "Who has made you these promises, Master Royl?" she demanded. "What was the pretender supposed to do if the rulers of the Chameln accepted him?"

"I was told I would be more fully informed of that in Lien," Dan Royl said flatly. "Come autumn, I will spend a month there, within the Swangard tower, being taught to parrot words that have as yet no meaning to me. What am I to do? Spy on the royal house of the Zor, I suppose, and on Old Queen Aidris too, if I can." He loosed a melancholy sigh, and Gael saw, beneath the glamor of his golden good looks, a deep sadness in him. "If you have good advisers," he said, "you might easily come to the name of the man behind all this. I should not be surprised if young Count Liam might have guessed the answer himself."

"Before I came to Eildon, I knew you for a fraud," Gael told him. "It is that name—or names—I have come to find out. Now—what would you have me do? These conspirators, and even their pretended Stone Men, are carefully directed—they would frighten simple folk."

"Give me your hand," said Dan Royl, moving to the end of his table and reaching out. "I have not heard your name."

"Gael Maddoc," she said, clasping his strong, well-shaped hand.

"I swear to you, O *Wanderer*," he said, looking into her eyes, "that I will not harm any in the Chameln lands and, further, that I will reveal as little as I can of your visit here. But you, Gael Maddoc, you yourself must beware. I foresaw your visit coming—I prayed for it—the visit that may yet loosen the noose that lies upon me. Yet I think—I fear—I am more of a danger to *you* than to anyone in the Chameln."

She saw in his eyes that this man believed he was telling the truth, but could not come to the heart of his secret. Why should this man be a danger to *her*? "You are telling me very little," she complained. "You have not even told me the name of your master."

"I will give you my book, my journal, which reveals all," he said, "if you will leave here at once."

He moved papers on the table, exposing a book, a well-made leather covered volume, filled with parchment, like a book for a counting house.

"I will take the offer, Master Royl," she said, coming quickly to the decision. "Bind up the book for my saddlebag. I'll carry it away from your farm in a herb basket!"

"One question, Captain Maddoc." Dan Royl paused after they had made up the bundle, and she was turning for the door. "If you will. How did you know I was not Prince Carel Am Zor?"

"Because the riddle of the Lost Prince has been solved!" she grinned at him. Despite the circumstances, she found herself in sympathy with this melancholy-tainted, handsome man, with his garden-hardened hands and steady gaze, and she could not resist sharing a little of her secret. "Master Royl, are you sure you are in no danger from these bear-leaders of yours?"

"I swear it!" he said.

"Perhaps not here," she said. "But what about in Lien? The Brown Brothers claim to disdain magic, but I have seen them use it where it suits their cause. Do you not fear some magic bond to addle your wits and perhaps even send you like a dagger among the Chameln?"

"In that," he said, "I am in the Goddess's hands. I know she will not forsake me."

His confidence was eerie; she found that she believed him.

They clasped hands in farewell, and he smiled again his wonderfully charismatic smile.

"Goddess grant me that this short meeting itself does not prove a danger to you!" he said.

Unsettled, she went down the stairs quickly, gathered together her two helpers, Gwil Cluny and Nils Hadrik, then led them swiftly down toward the foot of the hill, where their horses were tied among the willows. They rode away toward the high road, but as they came to a quiet place, Gael decided to go more swiftly still. They drew together, and she cast a magic line about them, and they were carried to the cantreyn, the blessed round, which Hadrik had found hard by their grandstand seats for the Pageant. Amarah, Mev, and Imala were still off galloping about on the downs nearby, so they simply rode on home to their inn and carried their herb baskets up to their own parlor.

CHAPTER XV

JOURNAL OF A PRETENDER

Gael opened the sturdy book and was pleased to see that Dan Royl wrote in a clear large Merchants' Script. After reading the first lines, she read them again, aloud to Gwil Cluny and Hadrik. They took turns reading the strange document. Presently the others came in, Mev Arun and Amarah still in their riding habits, together with Imala. They were told what the strange document contained and joined the reading circle:

This is a history of my life. I write it here with no hope it will come to the hands of those who may timely release me from the coil within which I find myself; only with the faint hope that it may be found after all this business has played its course, and then perhaps play some purpose to illuminate matters that are yet unclear to me. If fortune smiles upon me, it will serve as notice to my innocence—at least at the start of these ventures—in many strange actions. If fortune frowns . . . I have lived so far a humble life. I thought that would always be my fate, but I see now that the roots of this life were shallow. For better or for ill, I have been plucked forth from this pretty garden I have made here in Eildon. My only hope now is that there may yet prove to be a place for me on Chameln soil, though I hold this hope for a small one.

I am the bastard son of King Sharn Am Zor. I was born before his marriage, got in my mother's belly before even his journey to Eildon to seek the hand of Moinagh Pendark. My mother was Ellen Thorn, daughter of an herb grower of Lien. She had trained as a seamstress in Balufir. She came to serve Lady Iliane Seyl, wife of the King's friend and adviser, Jevon Seyl of Hodd; all three were friends together in their young days in Lien. The Seyls came with King Sharn when he reclaimed his throne from the so-called Great King, Ghanor of Mel'Nir, and the Daindru were restored.

The life of a seamstress was sheer drudgery, and Lady Seyl was a heedless, cruel mistress. She was also the King's lover. All the women of the court worshipped Sharn, the Summer King. He was the picture of manly beauty. It is certain that he lay with other ladies and waiting women at the court in Achamar, though less commonly with the servants. He was headstrong as well as charming, but Sharn Am Zor could not truly be described as depraved or lecherous. I believe I am the only child he sired out of wedlock—the herb Ebmorin, called Maid's Friend, was widely used, and not only by the kedran.

In the year 1172, from the laying of the stones in Achamar's city walls, as time is reckoned in the Chameln lands, Princess Merilla Am Zor, the King's sister and heir, together with his younger brother, Prince Carel, rode out of Lien and came to their own country. On their long journey to Achamar, they met up with a young chieftain of the northern tribes, Tazlo Am Ahrosh, chosen by the King to ride out and bring them safely home.

Tazlo, as reward for the completion of this task, became the boon companion of the King, though it seems this man had little else to recommend him. He encouraged the King in much foolishness and folly. They hunted together out of season, played foolish pranks at festivals, spent nights roystering in secret places. No one knows whether it was the King's expressed wish or simply a thing he took for granted, but sometimes Tazlo found a pretty girl or two for their long nights.

One day Tazlo met my mother in a quiet corridor of the Seyl's town house and asked her if she might come to supper at a certain house, hardly an inn, certainly not a house of assignation. It was called Three Trees and stood outside the old city of Achamar. A carriage brought her to the meeting, together with a young page who played the lute.

My mother and I had no secrets from each other on this count, and I have heard the story of this night at Three Trees many times. As she had expected, the King was at this supper, with Tazlo and a dark-haired, dark-eyed beauty whom she never saw again, who gave her name as Emerald. My mother gave her name as Goldine. The King gave no name. They enjoyed a magnificent supper of pheasant, baked fish, sorbets, fruit, fine wines. The lights burned low, and there was music and singing coming from a gallery. At last, she and the King were alone together in another chamber, and they lay together. My mother was not a maid; she had had one lover, a boy in Lien. She admired and loved the King, and the experience of being loved by him she could only describe as the kind of ecstasy felt by mortals wooed by a Goddess or a God. She had no hopes or illusions about this happening again—before she came home alone in the carriage by the light of dawn, a servant brought her a box wrapped in silk. Inside she found a bag of golden royals—she was not insulted. Out of caution, she kept the money hidden, did not spend one gold piece. This turned out to be a caution well warranted.

My mother had already taken a good dose of the required herb Maid's Friend, and she had the notion that Tazlo had slipped her a second dose. To me, she has always denied firmly that she had deliberately set out to bear the King's child—her first care, she said, was for *him*, for Sharn Am Zor, the golden King of Summer. She would have done nothing to embarrass or deceive him. But despite all, she became pregnant.

She recognized her trouble very swiftly. This pregnancy could hardly have been welcome in the Lady Seyl's house—this lady tolerated the King's roaming ways, but to share him with one of her own servants—never! Gathering her things together, my mother made off into Lien, to her father's herb garden, near Hodd. No one heeded the loss of a seamstress in Achamar—she made some excuse about illness in her family.

Here I must make a note, speaking on my own circumstances, for it seems that I must play the part of King Sharn's brother, my own Uncle, the Prince Carel, and I want to record the small circumstance of the slight way in which his story has touched mine. After she had fled to Lien, my mother thought long and hard of any person at the court who might have known or suspected that she had met in this way with King Sharn. She had certain friends among the other servants in the Seyl household, but she confided in none of these women. Yet there was one person, a mere youth, who often spied upon the King and his friends, as if he yearned to join them. This was, of course, Carel Am Zor, the King's brother, the Lost Prince.

My mother and I have always believed that this man is long dead, caught up, innocent or guilty, in the fighting that followed the treacherous killing of King Sharn Am Zor. At any rate, this Lost Prince never proved a danger to my mother and to me, never revealed my mother's secret.

Still, in those days, my mother was eager to keep the truth of my parentage hidden. She told her father a plausible tale of losing her place through the ill humor of Iliane Seyl and a ripped seam. Then she gathered up some fine, fragrant plants and took ship for this place, Thornlee, near Oakhill in Eildon. Here was the herb garden of her Uncle Elias and his wife Phylla.

It was all swiftly accomplished for a young maid, and she accounted her success in this to the mercy of the Goddess. To bear the King's child was to be her destiny. When time came for her pregnancy to show, she confided this part of her plight to her Aunt Phylla and claimed that a young man in the guard at Achamar had taken advantage of her. She begged the good woman not to tell her widowed father in Lien, and in fact he never knew that his daughter had been with child. Then, when the time came, my mother nearly lost her life giving birth: she bore twin sons, and one could not live. This child is buried by a stream that runs through the herb farm at Thornlee. It was given no name. I was strong from the first, and my mother gave me the name of Dannell; shortened to Dan, it is a royal title in the Chameln lands, the only indulgence made to hint at the origin of the poor sewing girl's son.

Now we were approaching the Chameln year 1174; my mother took a long time to recover her strength, but I was never put out to nurse. At this time, King Sharn Am Zor came into Eildon in his quest for the hand of his cousin, Moinagh Pendark. My mother made no secret of her love and admiration for "Shennazar: the King of Kemmelond," as he was called, so Uncle Elias joined some of his companions in a visit to the Tournament of All Trees, at the Hall of the Kings, not far from here, on the northwest border of Lindriss.

He told his niece Ellen of the fine figure cut by King Sharn and how he became Grand Champion of the Bow. He brought back the so-called Emyan pictures of "Shennazar," sold as mementos at the Tourney of All Trees. These and a few other things were treasured by my mother—our only relics of the King, the god who had descended to her for one night.

I grew happily in Eildon at Thornlee, and I was so forward with studying his books that my Uncle Elias thought I might be apprenticed to an apothecary, his old friend, in the city of Yerrick, to the northwest.

My mother knew that she must build herself a new life and she was still young and beautiful—she had several suitors, from the farmers and herb growers and their sons. She came close to marriage with a young man called Curren, Raben Curren, who, taking her troth-promise, sailed off to visit the Lands Below the World, buy rare plants, and make his fortune.

I was eight years old when he set sail, enjoying myself with my books and my pony and the outdoors. My mother, my aunt and uncle were the ones I loved, and I had friends, tree-climbing companions. Then in the summer of my eleventh year, there came a strange message out of the Chameln lands; the truth of it we found out slowly. King Sharn Am Zor was dead, treacherously struck down by conspirators who betrayed their land by making a compact with the Skivari, the northeastern barbarians. My mother was stricken with sadness and mourned her King, but then so did all the world. She made sure that I knew everything concerning the King, the Daindru, the history of the Chameln lands. It was in these days that the gallery and workrooms called *Shennazar* were set up in Oakhill as a memorial to the Summer's King.

When I was thirteen years old and ready to be an apprentice in the town of Yerrick, my mother told me of my parentage. I was amazed, but I believed every word she told me. It was our own deep, close secret; no one else would ever know; there must be nothing to connect Dan Thorn and his mother Ellen with the Chameln lands.

So I went off to my Uncle's friend in Yerrick and did very well, up to a point. Yes, surely, I enjoyed Yerrick, which is a fine city; I liked the studies and the time spent with the other lads, but my master encountered a strange difficulty.

There are parts of the study of an apothecary that have to do with magic. It is barely possible to grasp certain branches of learning without magic—and to his astonishment, my teacher found that I was a *brandhul,* one locked out from magic. It is a rare form of disorder that leaves one impervious to magical workings. Indeed the spells, even simple ones needed for mixing potions, bounce off a brandhul and seize upon some other person or thing. My hopes of a full apprenticeship, a future as an apothecary, could not be fulfilled. After a year and a half, I returned to Thornlee, with the suggestion that I visit a healer or a magical adept to learn more of my affliction. But then my mother seized upon my news with an almost unreasoning excitement: she told me that this strange affliction, being a brandhul, was unexpected proof that the story of my parentage was true.

For King Sharn Am Zor himself had been a brandhul, proof against all magic and proof against even the dark powers of the dreadful Skelow tree, which grew for a time only in the garden of the Zor palace at Achamar. This tree was a mystic tree, sacred to the Dark Huntress; it is also known as Harts Bane or Wanderers Bane or Blackthorn, Killing Thorn; in some tales it is the Morrichar, the tree under which unwanted children were exposed. When we found out the tale that the King had sent a young plant of this dark tree to Eildon, in the care of the messengers of the Falconers, I was determined to see it.

There beyond the Hall of the Kings lay the White Tower, a sacred place, near the priestly colleges of the Druda and the priestesses, the Dagdaren. Before the White Tower is a garden of the rarest trees from all the lands of Hylor and from distant countries, even the "Lands Below the World." As an herbalist, I found it easy to come to the gardeners and their apprentices who tended this garden.

I beheld the beautiful Carach tree, the magic tree of Athron—the story went that it actually spoke to certain mortals. The first Carach in the garden had been stolen away and returned to Athron by an old Wizard, Nimothen. But another seedling was swiftly obtained. I saw the Larch and the Raintree and the Black Elm and the Golden Ash and the Sea-Oak, the Baobab and the Kypress pine. And then there was the darkling Skelow, flourishing in a little plot inside a magic wall. Its leaves varied from deep purple to midgreen, its trunk was black and grey, with smooth black patches of dark that seemed to absorb the light. I felt—I could not help myself but feel—oddly drawn to it.

One spring night, between the dawn and the day, I came into the tree garden, leaped lightly over the magic wall—no bar to one such as me—and, with a prayer to the Skelow, I plucked free two of its dark leaves. I was unharmed of course—came back over the little fence and the moat and went straight to the Carach. I knelt down in the place where other suppliants had knelt and said:

"Blessed Carach, do you see what I am holding?"

And the Carach tree replied in its dark, purring voice:

"You are brandhul, Dannell Thorn."

"Do you know why, good Carach?"

"You have it from your father the King," replied the Carach. "Use this strange gift wisely."

Then three gold green leaves fell down upon me; I gathered them up and stowed them in my collector's satchel, separate from the leaves of the Skelow. The Carach spoke no more.

It was about this time that Raben Curren returned from his voyage to distant lands with a splendid cargo of rare herbs and spice plants. He settled in the Pendark lands, for their warmth; he came back to Thornlee, and he married my mother. I get along pretty well with my stepfather and have often spent time on their farm at Pencurren, but I was schooled to take over Thornlee. My mother has borne two more children, Rowan and

Rosemary, and I love my half-brother and half-sister. In time, my Uncle Elias made over the herb farm to me and went with my aunt to live down the valley. He died four years ago, and my Aunt Phylla went to live with my mother at Pencurren and help with the children. At Thornlee, for some time, I have had only my true servants, Han Lockyer and his wife, Jean.

A matter had arisen that caused some pain to my mother. I had been marked out for some time to play Shennazar at summer pageants in Oakhill. I was not the only one chosen—there were many men of the right type, with the right hair and features, but she thought I was cheapening my heritage. But I must say this *heritage* has not meant the same to me as it has to my poor mother. For so long, it was more like an ancient tale, it was not my own experience—I wondered if I might one day travel in the Chameln lands, and I have often wondered if it would be possible to tell the truth to some true friend of the Zor family. But these thoughts seemed to me only a foolish dream.

But my mother was right. I should not have taken my father's role. My play as Shennazar exposed me, brought me to the attention of those who would otherwise have left me alone. Two years past, I was approached by the artist Chion Am Varr, from the Shennazar workshop in Oakhill. He praised my looks and my performance at the Pageants and expressed a wish to paint my portrait. It was clear that he was sounding me out for something more, and he spoke of the courts of the Chameln. There dwelt the two queens, one old and wise, the other beautiful but coldhearted and a little mad. The marriage of Queen Tanit had just been arranged with Count Greddach. I had no idea where this was leading, but I agreed to meet one he called his patron, the commissioner of the portrait.

I keep in a room apart, a secret room, all my books and scrolls on the history of Hylor—the Chameln lands, of course, and the Daindru, the two rulers, also Lien and its links to old Eildon, which has ever been my home. The man who came to see me was a certain Lord Evert—his father and grandfather had all served the Dukes of Greddach. Some of these noblemen have a strange reputation, especially the one who turned his great park at Boskage, in the south, into a kind of menagerie, then his heir, the current duke, who made it a museum. Yet many of the branches of this ancient line have proved fine and respectable—for instance, the parents of young Count Liam, Count and Countess of Greddach, who served the house of Pendark and were known for helping the tin miners and pit workers. Count Draven Greddaer, Liam's father, even served Eildon as an envoy into other lands and, before his death, was known and respected at the Conference Hall in Lindriss, where envoys from all lands meet and talk.

This Lord Evert who approached me is about fifty years old, handsome, easy, and not proud. He was very persuasive—asking first about my family, and praising my appearances in the Pageant and the splendid reputation of Thornlee, the herb garden. I suspected that he knew of my mother and her second family. I gave back the story that my mother and I had arranged some years earlier. Her family came from the Pendark lands, and her grandsire, a farmer, had spoken of Pendark blood, a very distant but lawful connection. I admitted that I would have liked to travel into the Chameln lands some day and see the true memorials of Shennazar, the King I was supposed to resemble.

Then he came out with it. There was a tale that Prince Carel Am Zor, the Lost Prince, had been completely innocent of any treachery. There was evidence that he escaped death at the hands of the barbarians, the Skivari, passed through their lands behind the mountain barrier, and came at last to the River Bal. His true companions had brought the wounded prince downriver to the Western sea and so into Eildon.

There he had lived quietly for a number of years but now he was dead. His grave was to be seen in the north. Yet, continued Lord Evert, in these times of uneasiness with the Kingdom of Lien, it was of supreme importance for a watcher to be placed in the court of the Zor. Count Liam would naturally send his own intelligences to his family, but he was no spy. What if a suitable person, carefully introduced, took the place of the Lost Prince? Yes, indeed, there was an age difference between myself and the prince, but there were methods of aging by magic, by the application of certain salves and potions. I could grow a beard . . .

What was behind this curious offer? I could hardly say, though it seemed to me Lord Evert spoke with no approval of Count Liam's marriage, which the Count, being long-since orphaned, and having reached his majority some years past, had undertaken without the blessing of the immediate members of his remaining family, though this had not been widely spoken aloud, the marriage being a very honorable one, and reflecting well upon the power and prestige of the Greddach family. I awaited two things—a threat and an offer of payment—and they came promptly. Thornlee and its famous herb garden was in fact "under the cowl," held by the priestly colleges of the Druda—it might be reclaimed and the tenants evicted if anything displeased the landlords. Then, of course, if I proved apt for this task, I would receive rich rewards in land, gold, and goods—I had surely, said Evert, thought of marriage. In fact, I had not considered it very much—I had two dear mistresses, both actresses from the pageant, but the hidden circumstances of my birth held me back from a more permanent commitment. Despite all my reason told me of the futility of my mother's ideas, perhaps I have always had this dream of traveling to the Chameln lands.

I could see no way out of the offer that had been set before me; all I had to protect myself was the hidden secret of my birth, which must remain hidden, lest it offer some new idea for my *usefulness.* So, with a pretty show of reluctance mastered by greed—and a hidden, true eagerness to go into the Chameln lands—I agreed to the plan.

Chion Am Varr, who had already suggested I allow my beard to grow, arrived the very next day, with a smug look—as if he had known I would be open to suggestion. He painted the portrait in the large drying room for certain herbs, which is above this room, my study. He explained to me all the symbolism of the picture—from the oak tree to the letters printed on the saddle for Prince Carel's lost horse, Ayvid.

He has worked carefully to make me appear older both in the portrait and in the flesh. I had already a ruddy complexion from outdoor work—not for me, the sheltered life of the gentle born—and some of his salves have produced wrinkles. I refused any attempt to alter my appearance by magic because I knew it would not work on a brandhul, and I did not want them to uncover my secret. Lord Evert would have challenged my refusal, but Chion pointed out that the very folk who welcome a Lost Prince can accept a Lost Prince who wears his years lightly. Besides, there would be those in the Chameln who would have recognized any whiff of magical fakery.

It took the painter four moons to complete the portrait—when it was dry and aged a little in the dry air of the loft, it was given to Evert. I understand it was held for a time, then sent mysteriously to the new-wed queen, arriving the day after her wedding. I don't know how this has been done.

Lord Evert has come often and provided me with a tutor. A handsome kedran ensign, who gives the name of Quelin—she is a good tutor, and I believe I am being tested again. Should I or should I not try to make love to my teacher? Is there some curiosity about whether I love women—or men? I have compromised by showing her fond attention, even taking her in my arms once or twice, but then drawing back—out of shyness, it seems.

From the first, Lord Evert has been concerned with keeping his tame pretender safe from other spies, especially from Lien and from the Chameln lands, even the court of the Zor. He showed me half a dozen stalwart men who patrolled the grounds and shielded Thornlee against magic. Nevil, steward for the lands "under the cowl," is privy to the whole plan.

I am a quick study of lines and facts. I already know the history of poor Prince Carel very well; I have heard rumors that place him in the distant lands of the barbarian tribes, long dead in the border country or living in the Southland, in Eildon or in Mel'Nir. I believe I will make an excellent Lost Prince. May the Goddess and the family of the Zor forgive me for this masquerade that is about to begin. I have sent word to my mother at Pencurren—I am off on a visit to a Festival in the north in the lands of Eorl Kimber, then a voyage in a pleasure boat to some of the western isles. In truth—come fall, they will send me to Lien, and I will be in the Swangard for a final month of tutoring before being sent on into the Chameln.

I pray sometimes that I might be rescued from this pretense, but who could there be to overcome the magic of my guards, let alone those who have set them over me?

The document was signed: Dannell Thorn, known as Dan Royl

Hadrik had read last. There was a silence, then he said:

"Poor devil! Captain—do you believe his story?"

"Yes," said Gael. "He told me nothing of his parentage, but he asked for my help. He knew that as the *Wanderer,* I was the one to help him—but more than that, he sought to protect me in his own turn. This 'Wanderers Bane,' he speaks of in his tale, the dread Skelow tree—he must still possess the leaves. If it is truly a magic tree . . ." She shrugged, looked down at her hands. "I would be most unwise not to fear it."

"Yes," said Gwil, "that sacred tree. That is the strongest evidence that he is speaking the truth, that he truly is brandhul, and Sharn's true son."

"He has read widely in the history of all the lands of Hylor, particularly the royal houses of Lien and the Chameln lands," said Gael. "He trusted me to carry away this precious account that he has given of his life and his part in the conspiracy."

"Is it certain that no harm is meant to the rulers of the Chameln lands—only a spy to report to Eildon?" asked Mev Arun.

"What of the real Prince Carel—was he a traitor? Is he dead?" asked Hadrik.

Gael Maddoc could not remain silent before her true helpers.

"I have some thoughts on that!" she said in a low voice.

"You answered his prayer, Gael Maddoc," said Gwil. "You overcame the magic of Lord Evert's guards."

"With the help of my brave troop of adventurers!" she said. "I think, before we make any more plans, we should treat ourselves to a good supper!"

So Imala went down to order from the kitchens, and they feasted on quail and brook trout and fancy breads and pastries, washed down with fine vintages of Eildon.

"Thank the Goddess," said Mev Arun. "We can cast off these damnable skirts!"

"Tomorrow," said Amarah, "I must send word to Chion Am Varr at *Shennazar* workshop. I am sick and must cancel the sitting for my portrait—with a payment of course."

"We must leave Oakhill at once," said Gwil Cluny. "I am still not sure that we have escaped Evert's guards, his men of stone!"

"No!" said Gael. "Amarah must return again to Chion Am Varr for at least a final sitting. We must know the name of the man who set the painter upon Dannell Royl. I believe Dannell—but the plot is deeper laid than he has imagined. It is no matter of chance that he is being sent to Lien before he will be allowed to visit the Chameln." She pulled the amulet she had taken from Steward Nevil from her pocket, and showed it to the others. "This is a token of the Brown Brotherhood of Lien," she said. "The wheat ear symbol was designed by the prophet Matten's friend and spirit-brother Hiams, who founded the Brotherhood after Matten disappeared on his final pilgrimage." Her long nights with Tomas and his dusty scrolls made all plain to her. "There has been plotting between Lien and, at the very least, some scion of the house of Greddaer here in Eildon. Perhaps this Evert even believes the story he has spun to our poor Dannell Royl—but I do not doubt that our poor 'Lost Prince' will be hard used in the Swangard fortress. And who can say what those who have formed this plot will do if they discover Dannell is brandhul, and cannot be bound by spells or charms? And worse—what arguments might the Brown Brothers bring against Tanit's succession if it can be proved this bastard-born son is in truth King Sharn Am Zor's oldest child?"

The room went quiet around her as her good comrades absorbed this information. Gael tapped the cover of the journal, then gave them all a serious look.

"This record must be carried home, regardless of whatever else we accomplish here in Eildon. Gwil, it is time for our dispersal. We must ensure that this news comes home safely! I am trusting you to take Dannell's account and carry it home—you will travel more swiftly than we do, and, surely, if anyone notices our presence here, it will be you, a single man alone, who will draw the least attention."

The supper party ended, and since it was not late, Hadrik went down, paid for their sojourn so far at the inn, and ordered their covered carriage for their appearance at Chion Am Varr's early morning. In the quiet of her sleeping alcove, Gael thumbed her magic slip of wood and beheld Tomas. No, Gwil was coming home first, and it would be a few more days at least before she, too, turned her face homeward. Then—then he might pray for a good wind. Was all well in Coombe? Never better, Tomas assured her. They exchanged a quick greeting—love, love and longing until they met again.

In her dreams, she beheld a map on old soft vellum, the kind she might have seen in Tulach Hearth. There were darting silver arrows on the map that all seemed to go southeast from some point in Mel'Nir—was it Goldgrave, or farther north, even as far as Balbank? She awoke in the cool Eildon morning and recalled that they were in the middle of the Oakmoon, with Midsummer not far away. She recalled old Jared Wild of Wildrode's words, spoken with a certain weight of foreshadow, in the night she had removed his house's ancient curse: *Who knows what else will befall in the lands of Hylor before Midsummer?* And she wished of a sudden that she was safe home with Tomas, indeed among all her family, Bran the dog exuberant, overjoyed to see her.

What had Lien and Eildon planned together against the Land of the Two Queens? Were these countries working in tandem or at cross purposes, Eildon only desiring of a hidden ear in the Chameln court, while Lien's purpose went deeper and more deadly? She touched the gold band upon her arm, Luran's gift, feeling again for its coldness, amidst all the summer's heat.

Why indeed had the Shee authorized her journey here, plunging her ever deeper into the morass of the dark folk's politics?

II

It was five days since Gwil Cluny had sailed away home, bearing the Journal of Dannell Royl, the true son of Sharn Am Zor. Amarah's portrait was not finished—but they had their answer, they had broken their contract with the painter, and they were going home. They gave up their horses and set sail in a hired pleasure boat down the river Laun, all the way to fair Lindriss city. Hadrik had gone on just a few days ahead to secure them passage at the port.

Gael was set down first in the district called Old Hythe. She made a tryst with the others, left her saddlebags and lance, but kept her sword. Their boat with painted sails went off toward the markets. Gael had sent off a message in the early hours of morning before their docking, using a certain amulet. Now she climbed the mossy steps from the river and walked along the cobbled street to stand before a tall house of red stone. The sign on the lower story showed a bunched shock of golden grain and before it, a new-baked loaf—from the shop itself came a delicious scent of baking breads and pastries. On the upper floor, there was a second device and this one in metal, hammered flat upon the stone—crossed rapiers and the letters A.H.

As she gazed upward, a double window was opened, and a dark beauty leaned out, smiling:

"Gael, my dear comrade!" Yolanda Hestrem cried. "Welcome to Hythe!"

She went in through the bakeshop—busy with male and female apprentices and with customers. As she approached the stairs, a door was flung open, and there was a tall old woman, her hair now worn in a crown of well-coifed plaits about her head, rather than loose and straggling. Elnora Hestrem embraced her rescuer, and Yolanda came racketing down from the fencing rooms up above, where Alban Hestrem, the famed fencing master, was occupied putting his noble pupils through their paces.

The private rooms of the house were spacious and comfortable, decorated with rich hangings—even the ceilings—swirled with sea creatures and waves, the designs of the Merwin folk. The three women sat by an open window that showed the stableyard and behind it green fields and were brought Kaffee with cream and fresh pastries.

"Yes," agreed Mistress Elnora, "I not only left the sea, left my Merwin folk, but I insisted upon learning a useful art for the land. Alban, my dear swordsman, lived in a half-world, between nobles and soldiery—it is difficult for those who perform a service for the lords and ladies and their children. The bakehouse was a great gift."

"Because *you* were gifted, Mother," said Yolanda. "At baking and at handling the shop."

Gael asked gently if Mistress Elnora had fully recovered from her ordeal.

"I tire easily," said the old woman, "but I think I came out of things better than one other . . ."

"Have you not heard?" said Yolanda in a low voice that Gael recognized as her conspirator's tone. "Brother Sebald came home to Lien, and, soon after, he vanished from Balufir's court. Rumor has it his old bear-leader Justian, the Brother-Advocate, had him committed to Blackwater Keep, in punishment for the Athron debacle."

"By the Goddess," exclaimed Gael, feeling a strange thrill of excitement and of guilt for a task left undone. "I have come to Eildon on a mission, and I have not sought any further news of the Witchfinder's way since he crossed the Adz and returned to Balufir!"

"I had it as a thin whisper," said Yolanda. "There are great movings in Lien this summer. King Kelen has entered his final days—it is rumored he can no longer rise from his bed, or indeed answer to the world around him. Prince Matten will not reach his majority until the last day of the Winter Feast—that gives the Brown Brothers barely six short moons to once and for all secure their hold upon him. Small wonder that Justian should have no patience with a brother, even one so inspired as Sebald, who has brought ridicule upon the Brown Robe, just when they want it to be taken as the land's sole authority."

Gael shook her head, baffled by this unexpected turn. "We must be grateful for this removal. Surely this Justian has taken a wrong step. Sebald was a most valuable man to him." Yet she spoke with doubt, for something in this action did not make sense to her.

Elnora, marking Gael's puzzlement, nodded. "I agree. My Yolanda might rejoice, but I find the rumor most strange. To me, Justian was to Sebald as father to son—if any in Lien these days may be credited with warm family relations!"

"When I return to Lort, I will try to discover the truth," Gael promised. "And I know one who might tell us more. Remember the young adept who came into Athron with the Witchfinder's Progress? I do not know his name. He was not a Brother, could not be because of their stand against magic. And more, it seemed to me he did not serve them in his heart. Do you know of whom I speak?" she asked Yolanda's mother. "Now that I have visited this land and seen the folk in the streets, I would say he came out of Eildon."

"He can be found," said Elnora, smiling, gesturing for the girl who had come in to refill their cups to bring pen and paper. "I will write you his name, and all I remember of the others. Now—can you say anything about your travels in Old Eildon, our strange land?"

"Not until I have spoken with others," said Gael.

"See," said Yolanda. "Our *Wanderer* is a woman with a tight tongue."

She smiled at Gael from under her lashes. "I would not *pretend* to press you on this . . ."

"Go along with you, Yolanda!" laughed Gael. This was the very line the dark beauty had used when she courted Gael for Lord Auric, in those heady days following on the Silverlode rescue. "You love intrigue for its own sake!"

Mistress Elnora received her writing box and brought out a scrip of parchment, a pen and ink. She wrote out the list of all the names she had marked among those who had been her persecutors, her hand, if not her fingers, fine and strong. "This one," she said. She pointed to a name as she handed Gael the tidily written sheet. "This one was the young adept. And I think you were right—he was Eildon born, and perhaps even of the blood."

As Gael turned to look at the name, there was a noise in the yard below. Yolanda rose to investigate, and Mistress Elnora—Goddess be thanked!—was distracted as well, giving Gael a moment to cover her astonishment. The name Mistress Elnora had written was *Devon Bray*. The very same name Amarah had uncovered in Chion Am Varr's records: the man who had paid and commissioned the artist to complete the portrait of the 'Lost Prince.' Gael could hardly imagine all this connection might mean—though for certain it meant danger for Dannell Royl!

Yolanda came back from the window, laughing—it was some accident from the kitchen below that had caused the noise, nothing further.

They talked a little while longer, mostly of pleasantries. When Mistress Elnora became too fatigued, she went off to rest. Yolanda took Gael strolling in the sunny back garden; she was grave and serious now.

"My mother sees a good outcome to many things, but there is a strange dark strand across the magic web. From the Kingdom of Lien, of course . . ."

Gael nodded. "I fear for that poor young prince, for Prince Matten. Yet he may surprise us . . ."

Yolanda touched Gael's arm, below the gold band of Lord Luran. A shiver passed through her into the tall kedran's body. "The trouble that has been foreshadowed will arise in King's Bank, where there is a border with Mel'Nir!"

"What? Where have you heard this?" said Gael. "How do you know?"

"I cannot say," said Yolanda. "No more than you can tell me of your own business here in Eildon."

Gael had not considered that this matter of the Chameln and Lien might spill over into her own country. There had not been *that* kind of unrest in Mel'Nir since General Yorath's glory days. "I've heard nothing," she said, uneasy in her turn. "Thank you for this warning, Yolanda! Now—I fear it is past time I took a hire boat to the city markets."

From a corner of the garden in Old Hythe, they could look across the cobbled street to the river.

"Go well!" said Yolanda. "Until we meet again!"

Gael echoed her farewell with the same words.

BOOK IV

CHAPTER XVI

INHERITORS

Now the adventurers were homeward bound on the fishing boat *Moon Child.* The Master, Captain Caleb, was a man of Eildon, the trusted friend of Captain Treyn, who had brought them from Banlo Strand. He had a mate and a crew of four, and they netted for herring, which they quickly salted and put down in the forward hold.

The passengers made themselves useful. After so many days of mincing in cumbersome skirts and lacing, the kedran were eager to work with their hands. Ignoring the smell, Mev and Imala ventured into the hold and made themselves busy packing the casks of fish. Gael and Amarah, with noses more delicate, took over the galley from the elderly cook. They had victualled the boat for the journey as part payment, and their chicken stew, spicy Southland dumplings, and pan bread from Coombe were loudly praised by the fishermen. Hadrik, fit for idleness no more than the rest of them, took turns at the wheel and at helping the fishermen.

Still, Gael feared some kind of magical pursuit, a great storm sent after them. She wondered about a bird, flying impossibly high in the sky above the *Moon Child.* But the voyage continued unhindered, and in six days they came to Banlo Strand. They left their seafaring companions with the Treyn family at the Strandgard anchorage.

It was early morning, and they could not bear to trundle all the way back to the Long Burn in the cart provided. In a small cantreyn behind a dune, they stood close together, Gael, Hadrik, Mev Arun, Amarah, and Imala. Mev Arun made a joke, saying Gael was hurrying home to be with her big scribe, Tomas.

"And with my horse and dog!" protested Gael, blushing, which only made them laugh all the louder.

She sketched the magic circle with the blue fire from her lance and uttered the familiar words. Then, in a few pulse beats, shrouded in the magic mist, they were in the cantreyn beside the tall elm, not twenty yards from the hay barns of the Long Burn Farm.

As they drew apart and heaved up their saddlebags, men from the farm came out and hurried toward them. There was a loud familiar sound, between a bark and a howl of joy, and there was the great dog Bran bounding to greet Gael. She hugged him. Then Tomas appeared in the main doorway of the house and began to stride across the green.

She knew at once that something was wrong; there was bad news of some kind. She thought of death, sickness—was it in her family?

"Oh, what is it?" she cried, as he took her in his arms.

"I feared you might be too late," he said, holding her close. "We must go down to Ardven House. Emeris Murrin will rejoin her old comrades."

She took a little time to visit Ebony in his stall. Then Tomas drove a cart, and they let Bran come with them. The kedran cook at the Long Burn—for there was still a guard in place, despite the Cup having been removed to the Holywell—made them up a basket of good food and drink such as the others were enjoying. They drove past the standing stones, the Maidens, and on toward Coombe, the new, prosperous town, bright with summer. They talked freely, without sadness but also without gaiety. It was simply a blessing to be together at the end of another journey, their longest apart since they had spoken words of troth.

"There are strange feelings in Coombe," said Tomas. "Maybe the aftermath of all the wealth and good fortune. I've heard that there are voices raised against the so-called New Rulers."

"Meaning the fiscal, Culain?" she asked.

"And his helpers—including the *Wanderer* and the scribe at the Long Burn . . ."

"I've done my best for Coombe," said Gael sadly. "Where does this come from?"

"You've hardly seen the new Ardven mansion—and the present owners, come out of the north . . ."

As they came through a street of shops behind the reeve's house, they were loudly hailed. There stood an old man with a staff and a kedran on a tall brown horse: Druda Strawn and Jehane Vey.

"Praise the Goddess, you are here, Gael Maddoc!" said Druda Strawn. "I do not come to this vigil—I am a town officer, so Culain tells me."

At his side, Jehane dipped Gael a worried nod, confirming the Druda's words—but then her irrepressible spirit rose again. "I will ride with you!" cried Jehane. Gael saw that she wore the badges of a captain in the Sword Lilies. "I'll be your standard bearer! Kedran together will show honor to their old comrade."

"Take my lance then, dear comrade!" Gael called to Jehane. "It has a banner for Coombe!"

"Gael and Tomas," said the Druda, holding up his hand in blessing. "I am sending you both into a strange encounter with the heirs of Ardven. Bring me back a thorough report!"

There was a fine, improved road winding down to Ardven. Gael saw at last how Culain Raillie had had the mansion rebuilt, as part of the beautification of Coombe. Now the Cresset Burn flowed in a new channel, held back by flood walls, and there were gardens behind the tall house. It had all its tall chimneys again, glazed windows with good shutters, and some half-timbering on the upper floor, in the manner of Lien. Gael recalled the time not long past when she had sat with Old Murrin in the cold above the flood waters and heard marvelous tales of the old kedran's life in the wide world.

There were more people than she expected waiting in the new courtyard, keeping a vigil. When they entered, with Jehane leading the way, there was a reaction—a voice cried:

"A banner for Coombe!"

But another voice answered, "Maddocs all come up in the world!" and yet another, "Incomers from the Long Burn!" Then a voice she recognized cried out loudly, "Give a hail for the brave *Wanderer,* summoned to the bedside of her old comrade, and for our own Sword Lily, brave Jehane!"

The hail was given, a decorous form of a cheer for the sad occasion, and then there was a chant, so sweet and sad it could hardly be called squint-singing:

Here come kedran,
One brave and one fair,
To stand by an old companion.
Kedran and kern,
Those who yet may ride home:
Bring voice to all ears of this action!

Shim Rhodd and Bress Maddoc, large as life in their uniforms for the Westlings, with ensign sashes, came to greet their cart.

"Sister, Tomas, we'll see you to the door!" grinned Bress. "Greetings, Captain Vey!"

The watchers were not quite silent; they murmured, and sometimes a voice was raised, then hushed. A groom in the Ardven colors, grey and crimson, took Vey's horse to the stableyard, and another drove the cart. Bress took charge of Bran as Gael stepped up to the wide porch before the door, with Jehane at her side. There were windows and fretted stonework, full of watchers inside the house—but no one opened the doors.

Jehane rapped with the lance a second time, and there came the sound of drawn bolts. A big man in livery stood framed within the doorway. The spacious hall at the base of the fine staircase was filled with as many as twenty men, all strangers, some of them out of livery, finely dressed, others in guard uniform, like a fighting force. All stood back as the door was opened and stared at the two kedran.

"Greetings in sad time," said Gael to the big man. "May I speak to your master?"

"What's your errand, kedran?" he asked.

"We have come to sit vigil beside our old comrade, Captain Emeris Murrin."

Among the watchers a young boy said, "Captain? Captain? Old Aunt Captain?" and laughed aloud. Gael was shocked and angry; Tomas spoke up behind her.

"Is your master Oweyn Murrin of Balbank there, please?"

"Not sure," was the answer.

At the landing where the stairs divided, Gael saw a woman in a long, pale healer's cloak, holding towels. It was her mother; she beckoned them. Gael took the lance from Jehane and said loudly:

"We will go in!"

She rapped gently on the paving stones, and the tip of her lance held a blue spark; then at a whispered word or two, her shield encompassed Jehane. Gael looked at Tomas, who shook his head, unsmiling, and stepped back, indicating that he would not join them. The tall steward gave a great rumbling laugh, with some fear and unbelief in it. Gael, losing patience, jerked the tip of her lance and he fell backward on the polished wooden floor. She marched in with Jehane, and they stepped over his legs.

The new heirs and their servants cried out at this simple act of magic. As they reached the middle of the stairs, a loud voice called:

"You there! Captain Maddoc!"

She turned her head, and there surely was the new heir himself—Oweyn

Murrin, the nephew of old Emeris Murrin, son of her brother, who had remained in Balbank after it was purchased by Lien. It was said that the Melniros who chose to stay had been fairly treated by the authorities in King's Bank, the rulers of Lien. There was a name for them, Aldmen, or simply Alders. It had become a title: Aldman Murrin was tall and well built, a brown-haired man, tanned by the sun; he did indeed bear a strong family likeness to Emeris Murrin.

"This is my house!" he said loudly. "I will have no magic, no witchwork here! It is not my custom!"

Gael held his gaze.

"We will sit vigil by our old comrade Emeris Murrin," she said firmly. "This vigil at a deathbed is a custom here in Coombe. The folk outside are keeping vigil as well. But we—we must go up."

Jehane was already at the landing; they both continued up to Shivorn Maddoc and followed her. There were a few jeers from the Aldman and his followers. So they came at last into what was surely the last vestige of that upper room where Gael had spoken with Old Murrin years past. There was new plaster on the walls; a rough tapestry covered the old door to the alcove where the old woman had in past days stored her accoutrements of battle. The captain herself lay on a pallet bed, propped up on pillows, and the late summer light shone in through a new window.

Gael was nearly at the bedside when she saw that the large room was filled with all the women of the household. In the furthest corner, to her left, there were strangers, quietly sipping Kaffee or tea. One was finely dressed, the wife, perhaps, of Oweyn Murrin, and she had two female attendants. On the floor there sat two young girls, probably kitchen maids. Then there were two other women, unknown to Gael. From the woven patterns of their dress, she knew they came from Rift Kyrie. These two must be the child of Captain Murrin's sister and the housekeeper, Matilda. Of all the faces, only this last pair bore the mark of sorrow.

"What is this?" she said to her mother in a low voice. "Where are the men of the house?"

"It is a King's Bank custom," said Mother Maddoc. "Men and women do not sit together."

Gael joined Jehane, who was already in a chair beside the bed. She looked into the face of Emeris Murrin and felt nothing but a helpless love and admiration for a proud spirit.

"Dear comrades . . ."

It was a breathy whisper.

"Hush," said Gael. "We are here . . ."

"Content . . ." the halting voice continued. "Ylla—my dear Ylla waits in the golden fields—"

From below there came the sound of raised voices, shouting, and laughter. A heavy door slammed. Gael felt a surge of anger for the heir from King's Bank. Old Murrin said, her eyes fixed on Gael:

"A word for the *Wanderer* . . ."

Gael bent closer.

"Take the banners," came the halting voice. "There is a message . . ."

The old woman caught her breath, and Mother Maddoc came with a cup of water. After a few sips, Murrin's breathing changed. Her frail body arched up from the pillows; a strange sound grew in her throat. She turned toward the lighted window, showing the gardens, the Cresset Burn. Gael and Jehane held her up; then she was gone.

A heavy silence spread through the room; the cousin from Rift Kyrie began to weep softly and was comforted by the housekeeper. The women from Balbank set down their Kaffee cups. Shivorn Maddoc made a sign of blessing and removed the pillows. Then she drew up a pale sheet and covered the body of Emeris Murrin.

"Help me, girls," she said. "We'll move the pallet into this room for lying out."

The lying-out room was the cool alcove behind the tapestry. Here, also, lay Emeris Murrin's belongings, in an untidy jumble, as though her room had been all quickly cleared to make way for those sitting vigil. Gael's mother pulled the tapestry flap down, leaving them in partial dark, but also making them some privacy as she opened the old woman's clothing. On a sudden thought, Jehane asked:

"What has become of Oona, the grey cat?"

"Gone to the gold fields that await all good mousers," said Mother Maddoc. "She was sixteen years old. Lies under an ash tree down in the gardens."

"Mam," Gael asked. "Where are Murrin's treasures—I mean her wall banners, from old time? She charged me to keep them safe."

"Why they're here, in this press," said her mother. "These things will be stored, I think . . ."

Gael shook her head. "I'll take the banners out—under my cloak, maybe, or vanished some way."

They went swiftly to the dark cupboard and sorted through the cloths kept there. There were four banners—Gael had only remembered three—one in a cloth cover, to protect its gold and silver thread. The last, brown and silver, was the banner for Krail that Murrin had had from Yorath Duaring, at the first muster of the Westlings. Gael and Jehane folded them beneath their cloaks, tying the laces around their necks.

Shivorn Maddoc gave instructions:

"Go and pay your respects to the good folk from Rift Kyrie. Send Matilda to help me here. Then speak in private to Mistress Murrin, if you can."

In the bright room, the new Mistress Murrin and her women had all covered their heads with scarves. The Balbank women were arrayed by the narrow windows now, looking down into the gardens and pointing into the grounds of their new domain. The two kedran were greeted by a fresh-faced young woman, the niece, Rieva, from Rift Kyrie, and by the good Matilda. They whispered together while the women at the windows talked aloud and laughed.

"I'll go to help your mother, Captain," said Matilda.

"Oh Goddess," said young Rieva. "Balbank must be a strange place. Do you see those head scarves? I thought they wore them for mourning—but no, it is their law and custom. They must cover their heads because they are women—lest the men who see them are defiled."

"Say rather that *King's Bank* is a strange place," sighed Gael. "These are the customs of the Kingdom of Lien!"

She approached the women at the window and the new Lady of Ardven House, Mistress Murrin, turned to confront her. She was a handsome blond woman, about forty years old, and her manner was indeed very strange. She took a harsh, high tone with Gael from the first, but had little tricks of a prescribed modesty: covering her mouth when she spoke, plucking the scarf across her face and over her hair, even covering the tips of her fingers with her sleeves.

"Mistress Murrin," said Gael. "May I ask what funeral services are planned for my comrade, Captain Murrin?"

"We could bring her forth, kedran," came the reply. "If you wanted her. Ask that healing woman who attended her."

"The healer is Shivorn Maddoc of the Holywell, my mother," said Gael. "Our family have served Ardven House for generations. In the last years we have cared for Emeris Murrin, who is well-beloved in Coombe."

"What do you seek?" the blond woman asked coldly. "Some kind of reward or payment for your services?"

"By the Goddess, no!" said Gael, raising her voice. "I seek respect for a member of your family, your husband's kin, even if you *do* worship the

Lame God! Even if you have been enslaved by this life hatred that rules in the Kingdom of Lien! Remember, you are not in Lien now!"

"You defile my house!" snapped Mistress Murrin, dropping her hands from her face. "With your foul kedran dress and your bold speech and your vile magic! I am only a humble Altwyf of Balbank, but I know how you would fare in King's Bank!"

"You are not in King's Bank now," said Gael grimly, a little regretting her outburst. "But if you do not wish to bring your kin to burial with the honors she has earned, I will arrange that officers of Coombe will come and take Emeris Murrin for her funeral rites. Your husband will be informed."

She went down the stairs, leaving the Mistress of Ardven whispering angrily with her women. Rieva—the poor girl was this woman's cousin by marriage now—went with Matilda to assist Shivorn Maddoc; Jehane and Gael went quickly out of the house. The front doors were wide open and the hallway was empty except for one house servant, who pointed to the open door, to bid them get out. After they went, the doors were shut and bolted.

The word of Murrin's passing had been given, and those who kept vigil were drifting away. Gael could not tell who the hecklers were who had jeered at the name Maddoc, and at the *Wanderer.* There were Bress and Shim standing by the cart, which had been brought from the stable along with Captain Vey's horse. Now Bran the dog came down from the cart and ran to greet her.

"Where is Tomas?" she asked.

"In the house," said Bress. "He went to parley with Oweyn Murrin."

There was a long trestle table set up in the courtyard by the Coombe wives; it was usual for food and drink to be brought and also sent out of the house, but this had not been done today. She and Jehane went and helped themselves to barley water in a stone cooler and trout-fish pasties.

"Will Tomas get sense from these people?" asked Jehane.

"Of course," said Gael shortly. "For one thing he's a man, not a defiled creature in kedran dress, and for another, he was born in Lien—his father was a known scribe there."

They waited for about another quarter hour. Then the doors were opened, and Tomas appeared with Oweyn, as friendly as you please. The two men shook hands. Murrin's companions and his young son spoke farewell to Tomas. The party returned indoors, possibly to avoid the sight of Tomas driving off in the company of two kedran. Jehane unthreaded the banner for Coombe and gave it to Gael.

"It might rest with our old comrade," she said.

The windows of the great house flashed in the lowering sun as the cart trundled down the track toward Cresset Burn.

Tomas laid his hand on Gael's arm. His face was tired, drawn. "That was difficult," he said. "They were barely creatures of reason. I could hardly keep them to the point." Gael saw then the hard line he must have walked, trying to see Emeris Murrin honored, and she laid her hand over his, some of her hard feelings passing.

There was a short silence between them, and then Tomas asked her:

"Did you mark the man who stood behind Ardven's master, just as I came to you from the hall?"

Gael had barely seen the man—tall, strong, she guessed an officer—so only shook her head.

"That was Merrin Treyes," Tomas said. "Aldman Murrin arrived in Coombe well supported. Treyes is his captain." He gave Gael a steady look. "It is Treyes who makes the trouble for Cullain Raille."

"Why should he do such a thing? What could be his business in Coombe?" Gael twisted in her seat to look, but the front of the house was already out of sight.

"I can hardly guess," Tomas said. "Treyes is an Aldman, like the others, but the name is from a Lienish family. This said—his manners are more of old Lien than new. He has been courting young Bethne at Long Burn Farm. His manner, out of uniform, would seem to hold great charm for her."

Another turn in the road, and the stone circle, the Maidens, hove into view. Jehane dug in her heels and cantered her horse joyously out onto the verge.

Gael sighed, turned her hand into Tomas's, and for a moment closed her eyes. She hoped this Merrin Treyes would not be a frequent guest at the Long Burn while she and Tomas remained in residence.

Emeris Murrin was buried two days later. A throng of people came to see her laid to rest. Her grave was on the top of the hill behind Holywell House, the home of the Maddocs. There it was, the same hillside where Gael and her father had ploughed and coaxed a living out of the hard soil. It had shared in Coombe's blessing and was more fertile and pleasant in these days. Druda Strawn and Master Rhodd, the innkeeper, together with half a dozen sturdy helpers, had called for the wooden sarg at the gates of Ardven House, and it was carried in procession on one of the roads round the hill. Gael and her mother brought holy water from the sacred spring. Others were buried here on the western side of the hill. Maddocs of old time and the children of Shivorn Maddoc who had not lived. So the Druda offered prayers, and everyone sang a farewell chant. Captain Murrin was left to look down upon her family mansion. There were tables set up in the courtyard of the Maddocs's house for a good funeral feast, but Gael had no stomach for it. She was still distressed by the experience at Ardven with the new folk; she took the chance to slip away once the baked meats were served.

Down in the grotto, in her old secret hiding place, she had placed the banners of Emeris Murrin. She had not had a chance to carry them home to the Long Burn to search for the mysterious message her old comrade had spoken of on her deathbed; now she simply gathered them up in a willow basket and carried them back up to the wake. She bade farewell to all the guests as soon as it was possible and mounted up outside in the roadway, upon Ebony. Tomas had Valko, his good roan; Bran the dog accepted a last tidbit and came trotting along behind.

Tomas tried to cheer her, and this clear day, halfway through the Applemoon, the month of plenty, worked its own magic. The farmed hills about Coombe were unusually empty and quiet, with many of the folk up at Murrin's funeral.

"A puzzle," said Tomas, who enjoyed puzzles. "Whose path crossed that of the *Wanderer* and of Emeris Murrin, so that a message was left with her?"

They rode over the second bridge and looked at the standing stones, and Gael was struck by a sudden misgiving.

"I think Taran has sent me a clue—"

"Give it to me then, sweetheart!"

She only shook her head, kicked Ebony's side, quickening the pace to a canter on the approach to the farm.

The Long Burn had no guests—Mev Arun and the others had lingered on at the wake. They were welcomed in by the steward and the housekeeper, Bethne. In the large parlor, Gael spread out the banners on a table—there were no hidden signs in the banner for the Westlings or the banners from Eriu and Athron.

"No," said Tomas, "it must be this splendid thing woven for the fighting women of Palmur." They gently removed the cotton cover and spread out the banner—a kind of gonfalon with two peaked ends—upon the table. There was a small raised place near a tree with silver fruit, and on the underside Gael found a folded parchment. It was as she had thought, and she knew that it must have a sad meaning.

"It is from Lord Luran," she said.

The Eilif lord wrote in a fine antique straightletter:

Gael Maddoc, I am alone in Tulach. It is finished. But this need not be a time of mourning, for more of our folk have passed safely over the waters than we had reason to hope. My Mother, Ethain of Clonagh, sends her greetings. We have agreed to give you a certain stewardship as a return for all your work on our behalf, and particularly your last service to us in Eildon. We know now that you are indeed THE WANDERER, an envoy for the people of Hylor as well as for its rulers among the dark folk. I will send this letter by messenger to Captain Emeris Murrin of Ardven House, who will keep it safe for you until you are free to claim it. Then I must speak with you. Accept a blessing:

Luran of Clonagh

Gael passed the letter to Tomas. She leaned her elbows on the table and put her hands to her face, blinking away tears. Once again, she seemed to feel the soft wind that had touched her as she stood upon the hilltop overlooking the Palace Fortress of King Gol, the Eilif lords and ladies all about her.

"Dear heart," said Tomas. "Do not weep!"

"I will speak with him," she said. "This was news which must come!"

Gael sat alone, looking out on the fields in the room where Culain Raillie had once kept Taran's Kelch hidden in a chest. She thumbed the magic slip of cedarwood, and Luran looked out at her.

When they had exchanged greetings, he said:

"Ylmiane has departed," he said. "Sir Hugh has gone with my mother to the Pendark lands, where he will pass a little time with the Lyreth Lords, the Children of the Sea. The others—they, too, have passed beyond Eriu, and this without fading. For this, we must give you thanks. You carried the golden thread," he told her, and she knew he meant the bracelet she had worn for the Shee into Eildon. "That greatly soothed their journey."

"So soon?" Gael asked.

"If you had not indeed been the *Wanderer,* our time would not have been called," Luran admitted. "True, it came sooner than even we had expected, but that should have not been a surprise to anyone. But I bid you to be happy in your mind: for we were fading swiftly. If you had not come when you did, if the thread had not followed you across the waters, there would not have been many left to await the coming of a fresh hope."

Gael put her hand over the gold band upon her arm. For the first time, it felt warm from the heat of her own flesh. Some magic, some spell had departed from it as the last Lord of the Shee had spoken; beyond that, the gold seemed of itself suddenly heavy, a weight of loneliness upon her. Yet she managed to not speak aloud her sadness. The Shee had used her neatly: she had not understood, in this last venture, how closely the Shee's tasks had paralleled the course of those she had taken on in this dark world, seeking the answer of the "Lost Prince."

She had her part-answers of Eildon, of Lien, and of the "Lost Prince" himself—but by the same token, she had also finished her service to the light ones, and this unknowing. It was almost more than she could bear, for the passing of beauty can never be anything but painful.

They spoke for a time of Captain Murrin, and Luran sent a final greeting to Druda Strawn.

"What will you have me do, lord?" asked Gael.

"See to this place, Tulach Hearth," he answered briskly. "We have left you with the spells that will bring its gates and gardens out of the land of the Shee. Those at least will stand in the dark world for all to behold, a monument to what has passed from the high ground."

"Oh, that is fine, lord!"

"You must be poor Tulach's chatelaine," Luran told her. "People it as you will, to keep secure the last of its ancient treasures. A guard or two, perhaps a scribe to point out its wonders?" Luran's sweet smile was touched with sadness. "Though its Mistress continue to wander still, Tulach will surely outshine the attractions of Old Greddaer's estate in Eildon!"

"I hope I will never earn it such a comparison," said Gael seriously. "Fear not, my lord, I will keep Tulach private and safe. But where will you go now?"

"To Eildon," he said cheerfully. "I will seek an Eildon bride. I will leave in the last days of this Applemoon. Keep patient, then you may come after the first day of the new month. In the meantime, Tulach will wait in its shadowland until the *Wanderer* bids it appear."

A last blessing, and he was gone from them.

II

Gael sat bolt upright in bed next to Tomas, unsure what had woken her. The embers of the little fire within the grate had burnt to the faintest glow. It was three nights into the new moon, Maplemoon, the Month of Blood, though the fire colors of autumn had not yet clad the trees, the autumn storms had not yet come upon them.

They had talked much in these past days of Tulach, though neither had made any move to go there. It was too sad, knowing those fair folk were forever gone. Yes, Gael felt a certain curiosity to traverse the halls and chambers of that great manor, hidden from her eyes in all her visits there. Would Hurlas, the Widow Menn, the other mortals who had served the Shee, also be departed with their masters? Yet she deferred the moment while she could, wanting to remember Tulach as it had been, well peopled by the folk of light. Besides, there was harvest to bring in, and Rab Maddoc not so spry, and Bress soon to be called away for duty again in Krail, the golden city. Gael and Tomas had delayed by days, then a week, their departure, lingering with family and friends.

There came a sharp stab in her hand, as if of heat. Looking down, she saw that Annhad's precious ring had woken her. She touched its stone, and a great light blazed up, brighter than anything she had yet beheld from its depths. She cried out her surprise, full of foreboding, and Tomas came awake.

"What is it?"

She was at her chair, pulling on her boots, fumbling for her weapons. "Call the kedran. Call Hadrik. Have themselves make ready for a lift. There is trouble at the Holywell."

He did not hesitate, but ran down the hall to where the Long Burn's other guests were quartered. She heard him rousing all the kedran—Mev Arun was the first to rise, and the first at the door of Gael's bedchamber.

"What has happened?" The dark Chyrian girl fastened her sword belt at her waist, bent to tighten her greaves.

"I am not sure," Gael said. "But I fear an attempt upon the Star Kelch."

"Blood and Fire!" Mev swore. "The Goddess will not stand for this."

"No she will not," Gael said grimly, "and so we have been called."

"Is it Eildon?" Mev dogged her steps to the yard's door. "Come to steal back our treasure?"

Gael only shook her head. "No. Liam of Greddach is our friend. His

Uncle—nay his family entire—is not, but I believe they will do nothing while Liam remains consort to Tanit."

Overhead the new moon was hidden behind thick clouds, the light a strange quality of dull silver. Gael strode swiftly toward the cantreyn behind the tall elm, casting a brief longing look at the stable. But she thought of the narrow passage that reached the inner grotto of the sanctum and knew she would not risk bringing Ebony in upon that floor.

Golden-skinned Amarah, her friend Imala, and Hadrik soon joined them, Tomas and Bran at their heels. Tomas held the thick collar at Bran's neck, keeping the big dog back when he would have run to her. "I would come with you," he said, but she only shook her head, and it was what he had expected.

"Ride to Coombe," she charged him. "Find the Druda, rouse up the town. There has been anger in Coombe these last weeks, but this, no one will argue."

He took her hand. "The Aldmen must have come to Coombe seeking more than a landholding."

"I fear it must be so."

"Then you will see Merrin Treyes when you come to the Holywell," Tomas said. "Take care. There will be others alongside him."

"The Goddess has called us forth," Gael said. "We will hold them."

All she had summoned were now within the cantreyn. She gave Tomas a hasty kiss and unsheathed her kedran longsword. It felt uncomfortable to call the blue fire upon the tip of a sword rather than on a lance's point, but a lance would be no good to her in the Holywell's narrow passage. Sketching a prayer to the Goddess, she began the spell, and at first all went as she expected: the spreading circle of fire, the shrouding mist. Then came a horrid lurch, a disorientating waver. Mev Arun, or one of the others, cried aloud in terror. When the mist cleared, the sloped hill Gael Maddoc saw above her was not the tiny cantreyn below the Holywell where she had intended to bring them. A cold wind touched her neck, and at first she thought she had erred and brought them all to a place where they were under attack: dark figures stood around them, women, all of them, with grim faces and long, rising hair that flew about their shoulders.

Then Gael saw that in the shadows of these faces were stars, rushing black water, trees—whatever stood behind them. She thought at first these strange folk were wraiths, then, looking around, she realized where she and her comrades were standing: they were within what should have been the stone circle of the Maidens, near the Holywell, but instead of the Maiden stones, all that stood there were these grim-faced women, robed in darkness: the chill wind was rising from *them.* Below ran the dark water of the Cresset Burn, and beyond that, the white-paved road to the Holywell and her parents' croft.

"Why have you brought us here?" Gael cried. "We must away to the Well!"

One among the six was their leader—she made a gesture when the tall kedran would have broken away, freezing Gael in her tracks.

"We are the Ruith Nighean," the woman said. *"Taran's Maidens. You have been called here to receive arms."* She spoke a Chyrian so old, Gael could hardly comprehend the words. *"The Kelch has come again to its home. It went away of old time by* permission *of the Guardians."* Gael was not sure of the word; "permission" was as close as she could construe its meaning. *"Now, by the hand of the* Wanderer *and those who help her, it will not go away again.* Punishment *will fall on any who attempt to remove the Kelch without following the old-time ceremonies."* Again, Gael was unsure of every word's meaning, but the woman's tone brought a shiver down her spine.

The wind from the dark women rose higher still. Four of the Ruith Nighean turned to Gael's companions—Imala, Amarah, Mev Arun, and Hadrik—and armed them with fresh-cut switches, heavy with autumn dry leaves and thorns. Gael recognized the odor—these were Whitethorn, tree of magic and of sacrifice, which had grown so long by the mouth of the Holywell. At another time, these thin boughs might have seemed a frail weapon; tonight, granted from these wraithlike hands, no one doubted they would prove a fierce scourge.

When the time came for arming Mev Arun, there was a hesitation, and the woman who held the branches turned to the leader. The leader then held both her hands to Mev, as if in benediction, the expression on her gaunt face sober. *"You are of true Chyrian blood,"* she warned. *"If you take this weapon to your hand on the Goddess's bidding, you should know, you will never leave the Holywell. The Goddess will not take you unwilling or unwitting to this pledge."*

Mev looked a little scared, glanced nervously at Gael; still, she held out her hands for the sacred branches. "If Pfolben loses another kedran tonight," she cried bravely, "it will not be because I shied away from my last battle."

So Mev was armed, like the others, with the branches, and the leader turned to Gael. *"You will find your weapon in another place,"* she said, almost sadly. *"Tonight, for the Kelch, we can do no more but strengthen those spells you already hold."*

She parted her dark robes and brought forth a staff, not a war staff, but something like a shepherd's crook, elaborately carved and not strong looking. All the same, she struck it sharply across the edge of Gael's sword, and there came a spattering of sparks, blue and green, that died away, only leaving the blade faintly glowing.

"Go now, Gael Maddoc," said the woman. All six of the Ruith Nighean raised their hands in benediction, palms held outward above their heads, the wind streaming from them like a storm, their hair lifting like wild black streamers. *"Run to the Holywell, Tuannan, and put stop to the defilement that would be made there."*

So they ran, splashing across the low water of the Cresset Burn to reach the road, and then stumbling along the white road in the half-dark. Imala fell. In the pulsebeat as they helped her rise, Gael took the chance to look back. On the hill above them, all that remained were the six ancient stones, standing once more in their eternal circle.

They sprinted on up the hill to the Holywell. At first they feared for the noise they made, then up ahead, they heard great cries, as if of one in mortal peril. Gael thought her heart would burst. It was her mother's voice.

She feared then that the others—Bress, her father—were already dead, and a mist came down across her eyes, staining all the world with blood.

Mev Arun and the others—they had never seen Gael Maddoc like this. Planning the attack—there was no chance for that. All they could do was follow her. They ran together up the lower path, straight to the cave, Gael Maddoc well in the front. She was lit by that anger Melniros call the God-rage. For those first moments, nothing could stand in her way.

The scene at the mouth of the cave was already terrible: the cave mouth lit by shining blue fire, so intense it burned almost green. A crush of men in dark cloaks stood before this shining entrance, prevented by the magic fire from entering the passage. Yes, they had been already to the croft to rouse the Holywell's guardians: Rab Maddoc lay unconscious on the ground, blood seeping from a terrible blow to his head. Bress was on the ground as well, a knee in his back, blood on his face: they were questioning him. Shivorn—one man had shorn a great hank of her fallen hair, straggling loose about her shoulders; now he pressed it brutally in her mouth, whether to gag her, punish her for crying out, or to force Bress to speak the words that would allow them entrance, could not be determined.

Gael cleaved the first man from the back; a moment she would remember, out of all the haze of her God-rage, for the remainder of her days. Her sword, with the light of the Ruith Nighean upon it, went through him like an ax splitting a thin rod of wood.

Mev Arun and the others, for there was little else they could do, fell in upon the other Aldmen with their branches. There was a horrible crackling, a blossoming of white fire, wherever those scourges landed. Still, they were five against upward a score of men. Merrin Treyes was there; he called his men to order; the Aldmen caved inward for another moment, then found their swords, drew together, and raised their defense.

Then it seemed all would have gone ill for the Holywell's defenders, save that in this same moment Gael threw back the man who had held Mother Maddoc's arms, and when her hands touched her mother's flesh, the God-rage left her. She came to herself quicker than reason could have expected, saw and understood what must be done. Bress was down, fresh-wounded, Amarah also—had she held her temper, called the Stillstand from a distance, this would not have happened.

She raised again her sword, let it fall, called the spell. Then came, not crackling in the air, but thunder, and she understood in a sudden fear the strength of the gift the Ruith Nighean had laid upon her. The Stillstand spread in a blast of power that left only Gael standing, Gael and her mother, clutching her daughter's waist for support.

This was truly the Hour of Stone. Gael cried out—her mother loosed a second piercing cry. The knot of men at the circle's center—Master Oweyn Murrin was among them—their faces went unnatural pale, their hair. As Gael watched the spell unfold, she saw the flesh of these men swell, coarsen, lose the color of its blood. This was not the strange costume pantomime she had seen at Thornlee in Eildon: truly the stone was taking them, transforming them out of life.

All within the circle faced this danger. Mev, Amarah—none of them were shielded. Gael thrust her mother to safety, donned her own shield—with a prayer that it would be proof against the angry magic of the Ruith Nighean—and waded within the Stillstand's edge. A flush of dread chill coursed through her as she stepped within; she seized the first body that came to her hand, dragged it to safety beyond the edge of the spell, returned for another . . .

There was no one who could aid her in this desperate task. She worked in horror beneath the pale of the moon, entering and exiting the chill circle; there was nothing she could do to dispel magic so strong; she could only pull those within to safe ground; that was all she could accomplish. Shivorn moved among the bodies as her daughter dragged them free: "O Bress—Gael, you must try for Bress, for Mev Arun, for Hadrik . . ."

When Gael was too worn to continue, eleven bodies yet lay within the Stillstand's hold. It was too much for her. In stone, they had become too heavy to shift . . . and Rab Maddoc was among them. Her mother would not let her return within the spell: Gael's cheeks had grown patchy and grey as the magic touched her, began its work. Her shields had worn thin; the Stillstand's magic had seeped through. She fell down upon the grass and began to cry, bitter tears, if only the God-rage had not fallen on her, if only there had been a chance to order their attack . . . her father . . . but there was no time even to mourn, for here was Bress, bleeding upon the grass; here was Amarah, chilly grey and unable to breath.

"You must bring those who live the Cup!" Shivorn cried. "Bring them the blessing of the healing water!"

There was a little room to squeeze by the edge of the spell, to reach the mouth of the sacred cavern. The blue fire that had kept the Aldmen out did not repulse Gael. She stumbled up the passage, lit so unfamiliar and bright by the blue green flames.

The Cup was in its proper place, in the niche over the Mother's altar. She filled it from the font, from the blessed spring, and brought it out to her mother beneath the stars. Shivorn knew the ritual; she went from one body to the next, giving each a short sip.

Gael was there when the Cup was brought to Mev Arun. Mev had suffered a grievous cut the length of her arm, even down onto her hand. Gael could not tell if her friend would ever again have the strength to hold any tool, let alone a sword. But her eyes were quiet, did not show her pain, and her uninjured hand, raised to steady the sacred Kelch, did not waver. "Thank you, mother," said Mev Arun, swallowing deeply of the holy water, and Gael saw that the fate the Ruith Nighean had spoken was true, though nothing so unhappy as any of them had feared: Mev Arun would stay by the Holywell; she and Bress would have a child—perhaps even love, be married. Mev would become Shivorn Maddoc's daughter, would give her the first grandchild. A precious gift had been granted, even as the Maddocs had suffered great loss.

Gael squeezed closed her eyes, for a moment could not look upon the scene. She had only glimpsed her father's face: the thin kind features, his curling hair, now set forever in stone. She could not look again. Later, when the spell had faded, she would look again, and see that the Goddess had blessed those features in their final moment with an appearance of calm and peace, but she could never come to believe it; in this piece of her life, she would never live to feel anything other than regret.

Another of those they tended had received a different sort of gift. Merrin Treyes had been struck across the face with one of the whitethorn branches. Its imprint remained across his cheek, an almost pretty, seared pattern of leaves. When Shivorn brought him Taran's holy cup, he deeply drank. Gael saw he was a handsome man. His manners reminded her a little of Auric Barry, something in the *politesse* of the way he wiped his mouth and looked past Shivorn and into the *Wanderer*'s eyes. Gael knew she was looking on a man intimate with the inner circles of the Lienish court.

Like all those who had fallen within the Stillstand, he was still weak. Gael pushed him back against the turf, opened the clothes at his neck. Yes, here was the brass wheat ear, partner to the one she had taken from Steward Nevil at Thornlee gardens. She tore it free, and watched as fresh waves of nausea swept across the man's features.

"You have come from the Brown Brothers," she said, accusing.

His eyes went to her mother. Shivorn was already moving on to the next man, raising his head to the Cup. "If that is true," he said in a faint voice, "you are the one who called us here." His tone was almost mocking. Perhaps he still thought she would kill him, and wished to die unbowed.

"What do you mean?"

"It was the Tuannan who were in Athron, was it not? Did you think one such as Sebald would rest, before he found vengeance?"

"Sebald is in Blackwater Keep," replied Gael, a little confused. "Or so goes the rumor."

Merrin Treyes's gaze fixed upon the center of the Stillstand, which had not yet diminished, on the clustered figures of Oweyn Murrin and his bravos. "A convenient rumor," he said. "While Sebald discovered the home of the one who had deprived him of his quarry."

Then Gael truly understood, and fresh sorrow swept her. In naming the Tuannan, she had sought to protect her winter home in Lort, sought to divert attention from her involvement with the Shee. Coombe—little Coombe had always seemed so far out of the wide world of the *Wanderer*. Now—she was the one who had drawn this bane down upon them.

"What else has Sebald planned?" She did not believe the Brown Brother she had so briefly glimpsed in Athron, the priest with the warrior's face, would stop at anything so simple as this punishment. "What else is that terrible man plotting?"

Merrin Treyes closed his mouth, but Gael shook her head, would not accept his silence. "If you know, you must tell me. I have lost much this night, and committed acts such as I have never in my life desired. What does Sebald plan? Why would he risk a raid so deep into Mel'Nir? What can be his hidden purpose?"

"What has started will not be held back," the Aldman officer told her.

She looked at him deeply. "That is not for you to decide; besides, I hold it for an untruth. Now—you will tell me what you know, or I swear by the Goddess, I will drag you back within that stone circle and leave you there."

Merrin Treyes was a brave man, but he looked within the circle, at the figures that lay there, so hunched and still, and Gael could see he did not wish to join them.

"Certainly, I was given a trust when they elected me to come here," he said, speaking carefully, choosing his words. "How else could I effect that which they desired? But I am not so far into their secrets that I can in truth tell you their greater plans or purpose."

"How were you to carry the Cup home?" Gael asked. "Across the land, or through the water? Who would have aided you on this retreat?"

Merrin Treyes made a blessing sign and shook his head. "We were sent to destroy the Cup," he said, "not flee with it."

Gael almost choked, but she could not disbelieve him, and she understood at last the great anger of the Ruith Nighean. She looked worriedly to her mother, still busy among the fallen men, and wished the Kelch was already safely back inside the cave. "Now you have seen the Cup," she said to Treyes. "Can you tell me in truth you believe its destruction would be a blessing? To Hylor—to Lien—to anyone?"

Merrin Treyes lowered his eyes. "I am not a fit judge," he said, though she saw by his reaction that the Kelch's magic had indeed touched his heart. When he looked again at Gael, his eyes were steady. "This, however, I do know: Kelen, King of Lien, does not have another moon of life left to him. Until Prince Matten reaches his majority, there will be a regency government. But Matten's birthday is not far away, and the Brown Brothers do not trust him. It is whispered throughout the ranks that among the Brother-Advocates, there are hopes for a war, a war that will prolong the regency—for it is not fit that a new King be crowned while a Kingdom is embroiled in battle."

"Who will Lien attack?" Gael cried. "The Land of the Two Queens?"

"You might think so," Treyes said, almost grinning, though not happily. "But you would be wrong. No, here lies their madness: it is whispered among the fighting men, those who would be sent to face battle, that the good brothers are planning an attack on Mel'Nir. There have been plaints from King's Bank, you see; a matter of some estates that were divided when Mel'Nir ceded Lien those lands. There are those in Lien who make claim that, in the south, Lien's Kingdom has yet to find its proper border . . ."

CHAPTER XVII

IN THE BORDERLANDS

Gael stood on a large uneven plot of ground—some of it paved with ancient stone, some of it green and fresh. The sky was dark, tinged only on its eastern rim with the pale light of predawn. Here on the High Plateau, the chill of autumn was in the air.

She looked to Druda Strawn—her sole companion, save for Tomas and the dog Bran. He nodded—the time had come—Gale raised her lance, uttering the words of the spell, the last magic Luran and the Shee had passed to her.

This time there came no sound, no crackling in the upper air: only a gentle shimmering in the predawn sky, a darkening, a thickening of shapes. There came the tall familiar double aisle of elms, the rough walls, ancient and half-corroded, that marked the outer boundary of Tulach's gardens. Within, Gael saw the plantings of the Shee, all in silence, mysteriously making their place: pushing, or setting aside, the rougher grasses of the high ground.

At the end of the avenue between the tall elms, there stood Tulach's portal: two great wooden doors surrounded by a frame of ancient stone—the house itself, the yard, did not follow the gardens and the wall through to the land of the dark folk. Beyond, all that was to be seen was the ground of the High Plateau, stretching empty into the distance. As Gael uttered the final words that fixed the portal and gardens in this dark dimension, in the world of mortals, she felt a great weight lifting from her shoulders. This was all as Luran and the last of the Shee had desired.

"I never thought to see this place," breathed Tomas in a low, reverent voice, breaking at length the silence. A whisper of wind struck the avenue of elms, delicately moving their branches. Their tops were touched gold by the early morning light; all else yet remained in darkness.

There was a movement at Tulach's portal, half the great door opened: the old steward, Hurlas, the tiring woman, Widow Menn, others, half-Shee and dark alike, all those who had been called to people the house in the Eilif lords' last days. They were waiting for Gael Maddoc, had somehow known of her approach. Hurlas held a great ring of keys, ready to lay them in the new chatelaine's hands. Gael looked at Tomas. "I had not expected this honor," she said shyly. The path, the avenue between the elms, loomed before her.

"Tulach is a house of retreat," he replied. "After what has passed in Coombe . . . far safer that the *Wanderer* at least should make her home here, even if *Gael Maddoc* choose to dwell in other hearths."

There was inescapable wisdom in this. Gael turned to the Druda. "Will you lead the way?"

She could not read her old master's face, could not tell if he was happy or sad. He made the Mother's sign, nodded, and took the first step forward.

Tomas held the horses for them, and they all went down the quiet avenue together. Through the portal, they caught their first glimpse of the yard beyond, the massive walls of the inner keep, the rambling outbuildings. Dawn opened, and the sun caught them just as they passed in through the great doors. To Gael's astonishment, the light that was on the elms was there also in the yard of New Tulach, as if the same sun were in the sky in both places. Beneath this pale morning light, everything within Tulach's yard appeared pale and unnaturally clean, even scrubbed on its dark stony walls. Gael did not doubt that this was a last working of the Shee, before the hall, or at least its entrance portal, was tied to the dark folk's world.

Druda Strawn stood tall before the people of the house, raised his strong voice, and spoke a blessing:

"Let us all give thanks to the Shee, the Bright Folk, who graced our land of Mel'Nir in Hylor with their presence for so long! Let us walk in, with respect, remembering those lost ones who have sailed into the sunset, following a golden thread."

The vast hall was much brighter than Gael had ever seen it, with lights and fires upon two hearths and all the casements and unglazed openings in the fabric open to the sun. So they went slowly, in company with all the mass of Tulach's people, exclaiming sometimes in wonder, through all the grand staircases and the secret stairs, the galleries and the chambers and the workrooms, the rooms containing books and other treasures. Bran the dog kept close by them and was strange and sad. He understood that the Shee had gone—Gael would have said he missed Luran his former master a little; he often came to her and Tomas for reassurance.

After a time, she and Tomas wandered alone down to the rooms deep under the Great Hall. They admired the fine, clean storerooms full of grain, winter vegetables, parsnips, carrots, turnips, and so on. There was a wine cellar next door and great tuns of ale; there were exotic foods, earth-apples or potatoes from the Lands Below the World and sacks of rice from the wet fields in Rift Kyrie.

"In any other keep," said Tomas, "some of these rooms might have been prison cells, part of a dungeon."

"It is too much," said Gael, looking around at the vast riches, the plenty. "I have called Gwil Cluny—he has agreed to come, with members of his family, to help keep all this ordered."

"A fine plan," Tomas said. "Folk of the half-Shee will perhaps best understand the ways of keeping Tulach's heritage fresh."

Seeing all this food, hunger seized upon them. They made their way out of the cellars to a certain room, up the stairs from the Great Hall. It was one of the rooms she would claim for her own in New Tulach; it was Little Hearth. A small brazier had been lit for the beginning of autumn, and there was Bran, lying on the hearthrug, perfectly at home, waving his tail when Gael and Tomas came in. There was a tray of cold food, covered, upon the table where she had seen so many things appear by magic.

After a time, the door opened, and in came Druda Strawn; he had a look that Gael remembered—concentrated but not solemn. He carried a wide band of golden brocade, woven with Chyrian symbols.

"To crown the day," he said, "let us please the Goddess and the Gods of the Farfaring and the Shee who have moved on . . ."

There was some rearrangement. The Druda stood with his back to the hearth, with Tomas on his right and Gael on his left. Then he spoke to them, softly and privately; he bound their wrists loosely with the golden band, and so they were married. The two silver rings with which they had plighted their troth in the tower of the Swan lay on the tabletop, and, when the band was loosed, they exchanged the rings a second time, and so the ceremony was complete. Tomas strode round the table and kissed his bride. Gael was crying and laughing together, trying not to let herself wish that her mother was here, not to think on how her father might have felt . . . Bran, catching at least the happy part of their mood, bounced for joy, leapt up to lick her hands and face.

When they had got Bran settled, Tomas drew a package from the deep pocket within his scholar's robe. "Your family could not be with us today," he said seriously, "but look, see what they have sent along, in honor of our wedding!"

This was hard for Gael, for she knew that her parents had been long in planning for this moment, even if the Druda had not been able to carry along all the contents of the troth chest they had prepared for her. Now there was a bracelet for Gael and a set of ivory pens for Tomas, and with these fine things there was a sheet of parchment, in fact a broadsheet. The ballad was called *THE WANDERER—Battlemaid of Destiny*. The Druda glanced at it, smiling, and wondered if it might be sung to some air. Gael looked, too, and did not know whether to laugh or cry.

"Who writes such stuff?" she cried.

"Hush, wife," said Tomas, grinning. "There's great deal of knowledge in here."

So Tomas read out the first verses of the ballad:

O Wanderer riding through the world,
Tall Kedran, bold and free!
With Chyrian banner wide unfurled,
How great your destiny!

Rulers of Hylor know her well,
The Bright Shee know her worth,
But it is for the common folk
Our Wanderer roams the earth!

By Wildrode and by Wennsford Town,
By Silverlode she goes,
The Wanderer heals ancient wounds
Brings mercy to her foes . . .

Then Gael indeed began to cry, for all she could think of was the battlefield that yet lay outside the Holywell, the frozen figures of stone, her father among them, who once had been men. Yet this must be Bress's gift to her, Bress her brother who must think no more of battles, must take his father's place to guard the Cup . . . Tomas did his best to comfort her, while the Druda stood back, a certain sadness in his expression.

"There is one more chamber here you must visit," said Coombe's Guardian-priest, when Gael at length recovered herself. Then Gael saw upon her chatelaine's chain a certain key, ancient in its appearance, that she had not previously beheld—a last, softly jangling tap of magic.

"What is this room? Where is it?"

They descended to the Great Hall; Hurlas the Steward was waiting for them. He bowed his head, pointed out a faded tapestry. Gael saw then that the cloth was a mere magic shade; a word, and it had vanished, revealing a broad passageway beyond, deep cut into the earth, ancient. This time, Gael led the way, descending the wide, shallow steps. The walls were illuminated to either side with the bright light of magic, with beautiful swirling patterns. At the bottom of the steps was a beautifully carved door. The lock yielded to Gael's key . . .

This was the shrine of the Shee, the "tigh-Aoraidh," a place of worship. There was no altar, only a place for kneeling and a simple wooden table beneath a high window, cased with precious colored glass, leaded in images of blue summer flowers and green leaves. Gael caught her breath: waiting on the table was a black lance, a black so fine it truly did absorb the light, bound round with cracked golden tape, and beneath it a sheet of parchment:

This is the Krac'Duar, the sacred Hallow of Mel'Nir. It remains here that Gael Maddoc, the Wanderer, *a woman whose blood balances the old magic of the Chyrian people with the new strength of Mel'Nir, shall come to hold it.*

Ghanor, the Duaring King, lost this sacred Hallow for his people through the matter of the foul slaying of Mel'Nir's last true Champion, Simeon Red-Letter, called "the Fair, the Gracious," son of Ethain of Clonagh, and Effan Swordmaster, a dark man of the Great Eastern Rift.

This parchment was signed, in a firm straight hand:

Lady Ethain of Clonagh, ever-in-mourning

Gael settled her hand upon the weapon. The ring of Lady Annhad flared like a star, then died down. She read again the parchment: this Simeon Red-Letter would have been Lord Luran's half-brother. The sad story was not known to her—perhaps Ghanor himself had suppressed it, along with the name even of the Duaring Kings' great Lance, of Mel'Nir's own Hallow.

Grief overcame her. Her own loss, her father, was too fresh. Hot tears stung her cheeks, and she was filled with doubt and sorrow. One man's death—was that the source of all these decades of doubt and sorrow for her land, all its hardships? War-leaders contending for power, kings who did not have the power to rule them? Yet she could not know, would never know, for the Shee had gone, and this was all the explanation left behind them. Could she have served the Shee any better? How could *any* dark ones, any mortals, have gained their understanding, their love? And what was the meaning of this, the weapon in her hand, their repayment for her service?

"Goddess bless me," she said softly, knowing this at least for truth: "That this weapon come to my hand for peace, and not for the making of war."

II

Gwil Cluny rode in two days later, come late afternoon, on a fine warm day followed by storm clouds, the last of the summer weather. He was followed by a cart that bore his new bride, his pretty young cousin, Lyse, who had once served as tiring woman to Lady Malm, back in those heady days after Silverlode. He had come to serve at New Tulach, brought all his household with him, but also he bore great news:

"The Council has met in the Eastern Rift—Keddar has been chosen Lord of the Eastmark!"

Tomas looked at Gael, half amazed, as if to say "it has begun!" And truly, this was a matter of amazement. Mel'Nir, the land so long unbalanced between its marches, East, West, and South—and now, within just days of the Hallow's recovery, already this happy portent!

"This has been long in the planning," said Gael, taking Gwil's hands in greeting, for she did not want to lay too much of this good fortune to the simple matter of her hand upon the Krac'Duar. "I heard talk of it last winter. But it is great good news!"

"Keddar is a good man," said Gwil. "The documents and patents, even as I speak, are being sent to King Gol at the Palace Fortress."

"He'll do better than Huarik the Boar, or Corvin, his Wilding son!" Tomas smiled.

"Come," said Gael to Gwil. "You must see the great house, for all within is cleaned and new. By the Goddess's good graces, there will be a happy home here."

They turned to go inside. Yet, before the closing of the great door, she chanced to glance to the west. There she saw that great palaces of cloud had reared up over distant King's Bank, far away, and below the High Plateau's heights. She shivered. The trouble Merrin Treyes had foretold for King's Bank had not yet appeared; Yolanda Hestrem's warning back in Eildon had yet to come to pass. She hoped these ominous clouds were not a warning, and sent up a prayer.

The clouds outside continued to thicken as the day came to its closing, followed, just after dusk, by strange torrential rains, such as were seen more commonly in coastal towns like Coombe, not up on the high ground. Then, at night, there came a dark-clad rider, riding in terror along the great avenue of elms. Her horse was foundered, blowing its breath in agony as it sank down before Tulach's great door. The servants brought this rider to the Great Hall; Gael and Tomas descended, hastily pulling on their clothes.

It was the lovely woman-child Zarah Beck, the innkeeper's daughter from the Swan, half-dead with cold and exhaustion. At first, she could not talk. The Widow Menn brought her a warm posset, wine, then stronger liquor. The last loosened her tongue, and then tears began to fall.

"Danger has come from King's Bank," pretty Zarah at last brought out, hardly above a whisper, "and gods alone know how many precious souls are in danger, by Goldgrave!"

"Tell us, Zarah," Gael said, leaning in to better hear. "Who is now at Goldgrave? Is your good father there?"

"He was," Zarah replied, weeping, "but now he has gone closer to the border. Brother Robard the Carrahill Tutor is there, among the battle sites, with three young scholars."

"This is bad news," said Gael. She thought of Brother Robard, so lean and sharp, and many happy nights at the Swan, with Robard and Terza, passing a scholar's jokes, sharing good wine.

"O Captain Maddoc," cried Zarah, gathering her breath. "You have not heard the worst of all, the names of Brother Robard's callants: They are Till and Tomas Am Chiel, the sons of Princess Merilla Am Zor, in the Chameln lands. They are with their younger cousin, Prince Gerd Am Zor, the brother and the heir of Tanit Am Zor, the new-wed Queen!"

Gael took it in, and understood. This again must be Sebald's doing, the feared blow against Mel'Nir, combined with one against the Chameln, as chance brought that land's young heirs within range of a fast-acting strike. This action must be completed before Degan of Keddar had taken on the full mantle of Eastmark's charge, perhaps with the intention of sending the marches of Mel'Nir, East and West, spinning back out of balance. For the King's Bank lay between the Eastmark and the West, touched also by the smaller Dannermark, where King Gol held the titles. There would be much laying of blame, much arguing, which march of Mel'Nir must hold responsibility for allowing such a raid its success.

"See that Ebony is prepared," she called to Hurlas as she strode across the Great Hall and upstairs toward her chambers. "Prepare my weapons."

For Mel'Nir's honor, she would ride out with the Lance, she would bring succor to these Chameln Princes—*all four,* she thought. For if "Rolf Beck" had reached the young princes to give warning, the time must surely have come to share the good innkeep's secret with all the world.

"Will you ride with me tonight, Tomas?" she asked, as she fumbled within their room, making ready. He had come to stand, silent, by the door, his hand upon the good dog Bran's great head.

"I will come," he said softly, "if you would have me by you."

"I need your steady head," she told him. "We must make our way to the border, and I am not sure what we will find. I will not make war on these poor folk of Lien," she said, pulling on her riding gauntlets. "They are pawns in a cruel master's game. This raid—it is ill planned, but those poor soldiers are not the ones who made the decision to act. Tomas, my heart, it is time to teach this Brother Sebald a lesson—and it is not the lesson of punishing violence the Great Mother taught him when he sent his men to violate her Well."

No—she would not have him arm himself—only a sturdy staff, to keep a man at distance, should this prove necessary. Then they were outside in the blessed cantreyn where Gael had started so many journeys, only this time it was the Krac'Duar, the Black Lance, that she held up to call the magic.

"The Gods go with you!" cried Gwil Cluny, and it was a cry taken up by the entire house of Tulach as Gael and Tomas, mounted on their horses—Zarah Beck riding pillion, her arms clenched tightly about Tomas's waist—were taken by the spell.

They made landing in a rain-drenched wood amid a flash of powerful lightning and a resounding thunder peal—Gael was *not quite sure* that this was not caused by her spell. Rain poured down in a dark torrent through the frail roof of leaves overhead as the two horses from Tulach and their riders made their appearance, and the mist of their arrival was torn apart by the wet. Gael saw before her a dark line of soldiers, of fighting men spread among the trees; the miserable prisoners' cart, drawn by a pair of unhappy looking ponies, heads bent down beneath the downpour, lay directly before her, surrounded by guardsmen. She would not repeat the horrible melee of the Holywell: even before the mists of the spell had cleared, she raised again the Krac'Duar, calling the Stillstand. The Lance's power was both sweet and harsh, strong, yet with this casting, she felt herself completely in control; it was not like the terrible magic set upon her by the Ruith Nighean that night at the Holywell. With this weapon in her hand, it was but a small matter to shield Tomas and herself, the horses, Zarah; then all that was needful was to step within the circle, open the shutter at the back of the prison cart and count the men within, all uninterrupted as the guardsmen lay in postures frozen around them.

Five of the guards who had escaped the Stillstand's first effects—no six—threw themselves within the charmed circle in the short time it took to make that count, and were instantly trapped; those who remained outside saw the effect, hesitated. There was much calling and crying among the force: here a raid that had gone forward with such high success was of a sudden disrupted. The Lienish force had been hieing homeward in great good soldiers' humor despite the rain; self-congratulation was in the air; now all that was gone, set awry, and this by just one woman and her companions on a single second horse.

Gael Maddoc spoke up in a voice clear and proud, once again raising the Black Lance. "It has been given to me in good understanding that Lord Vane, the Governor of King's Bank, is a moderate man. Whoever sent you here today—accept that your mission has failed. Fall back upon the good governor's mercy, beg his pity, say you were sent unwilling into Mel'Nir—Lien's good neighbor—on an errand, successfully consummated, that could only have brought our two nations to a bloody and unneedful war. For you indeed have not succeeded here today because I will not allow it, and I am the *Wanderer,* the last gift of the Shee to all good Hylor's lands, and I will not see war and ravages visited upon our nations where the power lies in my hands to hold this back!"

There were cries around her of rage—these must be Aldmen, carefully chosen, who could only find outrage at being so spoken by a kedran. But Gael only brought down her lance—there was no cantreyn, no blessed round here, only magic, powerful and direct. The mist shrouded all, and they were gone: cart and horses together, and nothing was left, save for guardsmen still frozen within the Stillstand's hold.

The young men came up from their stupor, gasping; Zarah Beck, reunited with her father, embraced him, weeping, in the shadows at the back of the cart. They had come away from the raiding party to the cantreyn near by the Adderneck, where Gael had one time before landed, on her journey to the Royal Chameln wedding. She was not sure why she had chosen this place: the little corner where the lands of the Chameln, Mel'Nir, and Lien all came together at the Dannermere's edge.

It was not raining here: the night lay calm and peaceful around them, with a settled feel, as though perhaps an hour had passed since hard rainfall. They were uncomfortably close by the Lienish border, but the ride from here toward Lort was an easy one, along the Nesbath Road, and they needed only pass across the bridge at the confluence of the Ringist and the Bal to be securely on the road to safety.

Brother Robard was the quickest of those rescued to make his recovery—he was excited to see Tomas, asked many questions, one scholar to another, seeking to gain full comprehension of all points of the action that had just gone forward. Gael almost smiled to hear him posit the possible strategies, the likely source, of those soldiers who had ambushed him and his highborn pupils. Not for nothing was Robard renowned as an expert in military affairs.

"Unlucky venture for the man who planned this!" he said meditatively. "It must have been pressed forward in secret—how else? Now, without hostages—royal hostages—these raiders will have started a wave of trouble that will be a long time settling. Balbank—King's Bank—holds three distinct areas of command, and large forces split between them. The Governor's household men; the Brondland regiments; and, near at hand, the Border Regiments, often associated with the Brotherhood. In all the confusion—for our Melniros soldiers will certainly rally against them, we saw three villages burned, upon the retreat—these forces of Balbank will set upon each other like suspicious dogs, each blaming the other for provoking such an unwelcome fight! It will need a strong hand come down from Balufir, from the King's own court, to settle them. But with Kelen so lowly . . ."

"Your Highness," Gael turned to the young Gerd Am Zor, known in his own land as a Seer. She wondered what he was making of all this uproar, whether he might have had time to glance within "Rolf Beck's" mind, to see what had brought the good innkeeper of the Swan running to bring warning, to see why this man had proved so loyal to the Chameln at this crisis moment . . . By Gerd's expression, the glances and keen attention he was giving to Brother Robard's words, she guessed not. "There is little time for talk here," she told the prince. "We must go along the road—a few hours riding, and we will come to Nesbath town, where we will find you and your cousins good sanctuary. I am afraid you must make do with your current contrivance—" The closed prison cart was worse than inconvenient, but what could be done about that? "We must move swiftly, I would see you—all of you—safely home before this night ends."

She turned her horse within the small light of the cart's single lamp—Robard, for the first time, caught sight of the great black lance. Recognizing the weapon at once, he could not contain a cry of sheer joy, excitement:

"It has come again!" he cried. "It has come again!"

The young princes wanted an explanation—Gael looked at her own Tomas in dismay. She was tired—the long lift of the cart, as well as the horses, without the aid of a cantreyn at one end, had taken much from her. Besides, she was not certain that the recovery of the Krac'Duar was meant to be widely known. The sacred Hallows—it was not for nothing they were called "Secrets." They were not toys for political games; they were the gods' gifts to Hylor, not intended for any one person's aggrandizement. "Dear Brother Robard," she called, rushing to interrupt him before he spoke the Lance's name, its history. "It is just as you have said. Much *indeed* has been found this night." Here would be a diversion indeed: she called a bright blue light to the Lance's tip, illuminating in one quick moment all whom she had saved, princes, scribe, and innkeeper together.

Prince Gerd Am Zor, yes, he was a powerful Seer, she could almost see the touch of the Sight running through him—he was puzzled—she could see that reflected on his handsome face. Then he flinched as though he had been struck, turned, and met "Rolf Beck's" eye. "*You,*" he said, in a voice filled with shock. "You are Carel—my Uncle Carel Am Zor. I never thought to cast my eyes on *you.*"

"In you go," said Gael, chivying them briskly within the cart. "All this can be discussed later—talk amongst yourselves, if you must. For now, we must start moving."

Then she truly did grin, patting Ebony's neck and casting a teasing look at Tomas.

Chameln lands, it would seem, had recovered their Lost Prince.

Tomas grinned in his own turn, and climbed into the front seat of the cart. "That was unkindly done," he said, but she could tell he was amused.

"Perhaps you will talk to Brother Robard for me," she said. "Can he keep *my* secret? I am hoping that he will." Tomas's Valko was tied to the tail of the cart, and then she moved Ebony up by the cart's front. Tomas clucked to the ponies, and they began moving.

They could hear voices in the back of the cart, but they were not—so far—angry ones.

"Had you guessed?" Gael asked her husband.

"About our good innkeeper? I had. But there was so much talk that Prince Carel had betrayed his brother, betrayed the King . . . knowing 'Rolf Beck,' I could hardly think this could be true; then again, come this Thornmoon, it will be fifteen years since King Sharn Am Zor's death. A man can greatly change between the ages of twenty-five and forty—particularly one who regrets a betrayal, his own actions."

"If I did not wish us swiftly safe in Nesbath town, I would give much to be inside that cart!" said Gael. Yet they could not risk picking up the pace too precipitously, lest it prove too much for the ponies.

Ahead lay the great stone bridge across the river confluence. There were guard posts at either end, manned by Melniros. As they came within hail, Gael felt a pang of nerves, even as she gave the call. Would the guards stop them? Would they allow them passage, so late and strangely come through the night? The guards emerged from their little hut, bringing a light. Then it was with unspeakable relief that she saw their broad open faces, crowned with ruddy gold hair—here were true sons of Mel'Nir! Surely they would be allowed to pass on, unhindered.

"Whither bound?" the watch-leader called. "And what your names and business?" Gael let Tomas answer: he gave his name and Brother Robard's, did not name their "pupils," though he gave them number. This was an acceptable explanation to the bridge guards—news of the Balbank raid had yet to reach them; they had no reason to be suspicious. Gael gathered from a few words they let drop: on past nights the Scribes of Lort had treated them to stranger visitations than this!

The cart rumbled across the stone of the bridge—it was an impressive piece of engineering, all told, built to withstand the seasonal flooding of the mighty rivers. A center span was wood; it could be swung aside to allow tall vessels passage. Just beyond, Gael caught sight of a small cluster of hooded figures, standing as if waiting, against the side of the bridge. Surely the bridge-guards should have warned them of this presence . . .

"Tomas!" she cried out, a low warning.

He pulled up the ponies, startled, as the trio of figures—men, two tall and strong, the third thinner, short and frail—stepped into their path.

"Well met, Gael Maddoc, Tomas Giraud," said their leader, throwing back his hood. It was Auric Barry, together with his henchman, Captain Tully—accompanying them, most surprising of all, was Brother Less, his old bones shivering in the chill of the wet autumn night.

"How did you come here?" Gael said coolly, reaching to unstrap the Krac'Duar from its traveling bands.

"Stay your hand, *Wanderer,*" said Tully. "Allow my master first to speak."

"Speak then," said Gael. "For we are in a pressing hurry, and we have no time to talk."

"The road from here to Nesbath is clear," said Lord Auric. "I can swear this upon all Hylor's Gods: We have not come to slow that part of your mission. Rather, I have come to beg your mercy, your mercy upon Lien, and beg that you will lend yourself to an act of dangerous charity, but one that will prove a boon true to Lien and to all Hylor's lands, if it can be successfully carried forward."

Gael looked to Brother Less. "Do you give yourself to this?"

The old man nodded. "The young lord speaks truth. But truly, it will be a great danger to you to take up this task, for you must come with us into Lien, and alone, unaccompanied by any companion. Also, you should know, in Lien we do not have so many *cantreyns,* to bring you safely home again."

Tomas and Gael exchanged a look. Gael thought of how she had itched to find her destiny, how impatient she had been with Lord Luran of the Shee when he had not set her tasks of any great peril. "You need to tell me a little more," she said to Brother Less. "Tell me more, or I will not come."

"We know you are the *Wanderer,*" said Brother Less. "Come with us, I pray, and we will tell you the story of how Lien lost its *Hallow*, and yet might come to be healed."

Gael looked again at Tomas. She did not want to leave him—she did not want to carry the Krac'Duar into Lien, where it could be lost with her, lost again to Mel'Nir, if she undertook this "dangerous task" and failed. Less saw where her glance had fallen, then saw in his own turn the Black Lance. Like Robard, he immediately recognized this weapon, and his eyes widened. He cast a sideways glance to Lord Auric but did not further speak, either in encouragement or in additional caution.

In his silent understanding of her quandary, Gael made her decision. "I must go," she said to Tomas. "This is not a choice." She gestured to the prison cart. "Take them fast as you can to safety."

"My beloved wife," he answered. "Take all good care. For you must know you are taking my heart with you, and I will be wanting it back." She saw, this time, that he was not so willing that she should ride out, that in this venture, his acceptance of her calling was a strain for him. Yet, still they both understood that she must go.

She drew Ebony to his side, and they violently, sweetly kissed, until the foul ponies startled and broke their embrace apart.

"Blasted animals!" said Gael. Before she further lost her composure, she turned away. "I am ready," she told Lord Auric.

"Brother Less will give you the picture."

Gael saw it in her mind: the perfect cantreyn field. The clipped grass, rolled flat, was dappled with white flowers underneath the dull silver light of the new moon. "I see it," she said.

Casting only one final glance to Tomas, sitting proud upon his seat in the new beginning drizzle of the rain, she lowered the lance and took them there.

CHAPTER XVIII

THE HAUNTING OF THE GROVE

Light flooded in through pretty mullioned windows. Gael, rising from her comfortable bed to look out—two straw mattresses and a down feather one atop—saw she had come to still another magic place. She was looking across bright yellow autumn fields to a rushing, mist-covered river—she knew from her arrival last night, this was the Ringist—and across the water, the sky was sullen, full of rain. Here, the weather was a matter of craft: it was autumn, yet summer lingered, and pale morning sunshine glinted upon the grass.

This was Erinhall. It had been the famous Markgrafin Guenna of Lien's private retreat, the place she had made from herself, hidden from the world, in her stand against the Archmage Rosmer, the man who had stolen the heart and mind of her only son, had set him upon the path to Kingship. Once this had been a hunting lodge, standing within the Great Border Forest of the Chameln, overlooking the river boundary. It had passed to a Lienish lord in payment of a debt . . . and then Guenna had claimed it.

Gael understood a little more than she had the night before: Guenna, from her deathbed, had passed this hidden place to Garvis Merl, Lord of Grays. This Garvis—Tomas had spoken of him once, but never explained all the details. He was brother to Zaramund, Kelen's first wife, whom Rosmer had ordered murdered, that Kelen be freed to marry the young and then biddable Fideth. Rosmer had intended the death of all of the Grays, for they were Lien's most powerful lords—but he had missed when he struck at Garvis, the youngest of old Lord Merl's sons. Gone into hiding,

Lord Garvis had at first lived the life of a desperate man, an outlaw; now, for more than fifteen years, he had been master of this safe place of retreat, riding out, along with his Green Riders, when opportunity came, on secret ventures to fight against those who had usurped his rights. Rosmer had been the first enemy of Garvis of Grays; now Garvis fought the Brown Brotherhood in Rosmer's place. Brother Less, Lord Auric of Chantry—these were the public face for Lien's reform. Meantime, Erinhall had become the secret heart of Lien's resistance to the Followers of the Lame God at Balufir court.

Gael pulled on her outer clothes—some servant had taken them away and brushed and cleaned them in the night—and went out to find her hosts. Erinhall's main hall was pleasant, painted in friendly colors; there were flowers and autumn leaves arranged in the long fireplace. A woman sat waiting in a chair that had been moved to catch the sun; otherwise, the room was empty. Catching sight of her visitor, she stood and gave her welcome.

"We are grateful you have come, Gael Maddoc. You bring us fresh hope."

This was Mayrose, the wife of Garvis Merl of Grays, and elder sister to Fideth, Lien's Queen. She was a plain, angular woman, a little past middle age, with a face coppery and lined from days of riding in the sun and wind, and brassy greying hair, half-hidden beneath a sort of coif. But her eyes were full of light, and this was not the light of magic: it was the light of love, of life, and Gael could see that Lady Mayrose had given everything, since the day Zaramund of Lien had been murdered, along other family members of the Grays, and Fideth of Wirth had risen to replace her; Mayrose had given *everything* to try to right this wrong, to bring light and hope to Lien's people. She was not at all as Gael pictured a fine lady of Lien; instead of silks and tight velvet lacing, she wore a plain—if finely made—leather tunic over a loose rustic skirt. Now she was not speaking at all to charm Gael, or impress her. This was not the "common touch" Gael had seen so many fine lords display, it was a simplicity of manners almost poignant for its humility. The life of a reforming outlaw could not be an easy one; there was little that Mayrose took for granted.

"I do not know why you have called me," Gael answered, trying to keep her words short. "But one such as Brother Less holds my admiration and respect. If he would venture out on such a night to beg my aid, I knew I had to answer."

"It was an effort for him." Lady Mayrose said, candid but not unfriendly. "But I think it soothed his heart to accompany those who brought our pleas to you. Besides . . . he is ever the questing scholar, and cannot resist a chance to see history made."

Laughter on the lawn outside interrupted them. Gael glanced out the window. In the garden were four beautiful children, wearing white. The tallest, a brown-haired boy, was carrying the youngest, golden-haired, on his shoulders; two other sisters were laughing, making a playful battle over a basket of fresh-cut flowers. At first Gael thought these children must belong to the Lady of Grays. Then she looked again—something was wrong; the flowers overflowing the basket were bluebells, white myrtle, snowstars . . . the fair blossoms of spring. What she saw was out of season . . .

"They will always be here," Lady Mayrose said gently, coming to stand behind her. "And see—who comes behind them."

There was a woman of middle height, with flowing black brown hair, threaded through with strings of pearls. Her gown glittered as if green light was trapped within its folds; her face bore an ageless beauty, neither old nor young. Then Gael knew without being told: these were a vision of Guenna of Lien and her children: Kelen, Hedris, Aravel, and little Elvédegran.

"They are less than wraiths," said Lady Mayrose. "Bright memories of a happy time."

"Why have you brought me here?" Gael asked.

The Lady of Grays smiled. "My good men—see how bravely they have left us, to talk women's matters over between ourselves—for these are a woman's matters of which we must speak. Pray you, Gael Maddoc, be seated. I have a story for you."

Gael found a chair, positioned it where she could still see the children, the woman their lady mother. So much history lay before her: those two young girls, with their bluebells—they would marry the Daindru Kings, Firn and Zor, enjoy at least for a time happy married life—until the spider-vizier Rosmer crept forward again to claim them. Little Elvédegran, the youngest, would die before her seventeenth year, giving Yorath Duaring life. The boy—his fate would prove the worst of all, for in his weakness, the lovely life of Lien, its poetry, music, and magic, would fall under a shadow.

"She was a loving mother," said Gael, watching the Markgrafin smooth her daughters' hair.

"And later she would become a powerful sorceress," said Lady Mayrose. "We have been here more than fifteen years, from the time of Guenna's passing. In that time, little has faded of the magic she left behind her."

"Her existence here was well ordered."

"Yes, though she lived always with deep regrets." Lady Mayrose again and took her sun-filled seat. There was a tall wooden box, almost large enough for a linen-press, by this chair's side. Leaning over her chair arm, she ran her fingers over this chest's darkly polished lid. "She had loved Zaramund; she never could accept what had been done so Fideth could take her place. Yet by her life's end, when King Kelen's son—his heir—was almost five years old, she began to recognize, belatedly, she had another grandchild. She had failed Kelen—then she died, bitterly certain that she had also failed young Matten, and Lien as well, for her lovely swans—they had flown to other nests, and none would be coming home again."

"I have heard tale that the young prince has stood stubborn against the Brown Brothers," said Gael.

"That is true," said Lady Mayrose, "but because of an old decision Guenna made, he lacks an essential protection."

She made a movement with her hands, then she was holding a folded piece of white stuff. The ring on Gael's hand leapt to life—so simple as this, there was the Hallow of Lien, the missing Fleece.

"What is this story you would tell me?" Gael asked, as the lady unfolded the ancient skin for her visitor to examine. This Fleece, like the Cup, the Lance, had on first glance a worn appearance. There was faded, indecipherable script branded into the leather around its outer edge, and the wool had long since rubbed bare in the places where it had been folded. Yet the time-softened skin retained still a tremendous power, a warmth, a soothing . . . She remembered where she had seen just such a blanket before: it had been the most treasured possession of Lady Malm, brought from Eildon to serve her when she came as midwife to Princess Elwina of Mel'Nir.

"This is intended for a swaddling cloth?" she asked, tentative.

Lady Mayrose nodded. "This Hallowed Fleece has served to swaddle every Markgraf and Markgrafin of Lien from time of old. It was brought out of Eildon by those who founded the Mark of Lien, so distant in the past now. It holds a great healing magic, from the Goddess. A babe swaddled in this ancient cover will earn a great destiny: a ruler's destiny, a ruler-consort's destiny—not, of course, the same thing as a happy life. The women who first vested it with this power, even this piece's name—all this is lost to us.

"But Guenna left to us at least this sad history in her archive: when she was brought to bed with her firstborn, Kelen, the birth was hard, and the young Markgrafin fell into a deathly fever. The child himself—he was born so healthy and fair, he was given in haste to the milchwomen, while within the birthing chamber, a great struggle was made to preserve Guenna's life. Edgar of Pendark—he loved his beautiful young wife. When it became clear that she was dying, he insisted that the healers use the Fleece to bring succor to his lady—the babe would do well enough without such cover. Even so, Guenna lay in a fever dream for weeks . . . and Kelen was never brought to the Fleece.

"Hedris, Aravel, Elvédegran after them—Guenna's daughters were all wrapped within this precious Hallow, they all received its blessing—but never Kelen. Back in those sweet days, when all the children were young, it was not obvious this was a grievous error. It was only much later, when Edgar himself was long dead, and Kelen fell so easily prey to Rosmer's blandishments, did the great error became apparent, for it has always been Kelen's *counselors* who have ruled Lien, never Kelen. When the full extent of Rosmer's power became plain, and the last of her daughters was gone from Lien, the Markgrafin fled—and she took the Fleece with her when she retreated to Erinhall: it was a woman's piece; she would not leave it to Rosmer or to Kelen."

"And so Matten also has missed his chance for the Fleece's Blessing," said Gael, filled with a deep sadness. She had seen the return of the Chyrian Cup, the Lance of Mel'Nir; already she saw how prosperity returned to these hard-pressed lands as these sacred Hallows again found their place. But the Fleece . . . she rubbed the worn softness of its wool gently between her hands. Surely Lien must wait another generation before the Fleece could be restored, before the shadow of the Brotherhood's rule could be swept back.

But Lady Mayrose was shaking her head. "Not so. There *is* a spell that might yet bring Matten to the Fleece's Blessing. Guenna left many writings. She researched deeply the Fleece's history, and knew it had not always passed smoothly from one ruler of Lien to the next. There is a spell, not practiced now for upward of a hundred years. It is called the *Haunting of the Grove.* Once there were many who might have performed this spell, but over time much knowledge has been dispersed. Now this magic can only be performed by one born to a certain destiny. Only by one such as yourself, Gael Maddoc, who balances great forces of magic and power within, and this is why we have called you here: to ask you if you will attempt to perform this *Haunting.*"

Gael could tell by the lady's tone that the spell must be a fearful thing, and dangerous. But it was what she was here to do—this was why she had left Tomas, left the young princes of the Chameln, alone on the dark Nesbath road. She nodded her head. Yes, she would do it.

The lady allowed herself only the smallest of smiles. Gael could not be sure Mayrose was gladdened by her answer. She must have given some sign; it was only moments before Lord Auric came to the door, accompanied by two young girls—yes, *these* deep-tanned hooligans were Lady Mayrose's children, and not those pale beautiful creatures out in the garden. They were Zarah Beck's age, perhaps a year or so younger. Not twins, but born so close together, they had not even a year apart in their ages.

The elder—heir to all the fortunes of the Grays, to all those wide lands and power, should the Lord of Grays ever return from an outlaw's exile to retrieve them—was trothed to Auric Barry. Gael hemmed, for with this news, much was made plain to her—although she was much impressed by Lord Auric's gentle manners with this child, and clearly the girl herself adored him in her turn. Neither sister could be called beautiful—they had inherited their mother's plain face, her brassy dark hair, but Gael could see in them the life, the intense spirit, that brought so much animation, so much *vitality,* to their mother. She wondered if this had been a family trait, shared by Mayrose's sister Fideth, the trait that had drawn Kelen of Lien to her.

"You have chosen to play a dangerous game," she breathed to Lord Auric, when they passed one another in a lull of privacy.

"This is no game," he answered. From his air of suppressed excitement, she could see he was not entirely speaking the truth, though perhaps he did not choose to know himself so well that he was aware of this. "It does not matter if it takes years—certainly it will be years before Lady Ellain and I can marry. Brother Less thinks it will be years beyond that for balance in Lien to be truly restored. But his Followers of Truth—the reformed Brotherhood—it must prevail in the end."

Gael could only tell him that she hoped this would indeed come to be truth.

II

The *Haunting of the Grove* was an ancient hunting spell of Eildon, so old that half the words were spoken in the Chyrian tongue—Eildon's original settlers. A party was prepared: it would include Gael, old Garvis of Grays himself, Lord Auric's Captain Tully, and also a strong, tall old man known only as Hunter, as subtle a master of woodcraft and tracking as ever Gael had known, though when she complimented him, he only hemmed and said, with an ironical gleam, that he was in truth a city man, and proud of it. Garvis Merl of Grays was a handsome, aging man, with all the courtly manners Gael expected of Lien's gentlefolk, though he was touched by a bitterness that only lightened when he looked upon Mayrose, she who had shared all the years of exile from Lien's courtly circles, or upon his lively daughters. And these daughters . . . to Gael's dismay, Lady Guendolin of Grays, Garvis's younger daughter, was to accompany them on the *Haunting*. Gael would have spoken against this, and strongly, but to work the spell, there must be a virgin in the train, and she must be a fast rider.

After some practice in the meadows and woods close to hidden Erinhall, Gael saw that the choice of Lady Guendolin was not so foolish as it had first seemed. Lady Guendolin was a small girl: short, wiry, intense. There was no foolishness in her . . . save perhaps for those moments when she cast her eyes Lord Auric's way, and Gael—along with everyone else—could see how truly she adored her sister's handsome betrothed, his fine gentle manners. Such a contrast to the rough girls of Mayrose, their plain straight figures and training!

Lord Auric did not practice with them; he was to join them after the spell had begun. After two days, he made his way to Balufir Court. He was to join a hunting party—the prince's hunting party, for Matten, Heir of Lien, though hemmed in on all sides by the Brown Brotherhood, was still allowed some of the princely prerogatives, hunting for pleasure among them. In four days' time, those training to make the *Haunting* would ride out to Fountainfields, one of Lien's famous hunting forests, where the Prince and his court would take their pleasure, hunting the fat red roebucks that were bred there for just this purpose. Gael sent a message to Tomas—she would not risk using her slip of cedarwood, for Lady Mayrose warned her there were ways within Lien of detecting such magics; the witchfinders of Lien never tired of tracking such threads. But at last they were ready, and the fivesome rode out.

They rode cross-country, for they wished to avoid scrutiny. Gael gained in flashes a sense of a well-ordered, thickly-populated land, with elegant houses of the gentlefolk nestled among the trees, and wide estates. Still, for one who had been raised in Mel'Nir, it seemed a small, heavily-burdened place. They passed an astonishing number of punishment places, tucked back away on quiet lanes and within lonely fields. In one place, they passed a pair of blackened stakes, and she knew that women accused of using magic—nothing more than this!—had been burned there.

At Fountainfields, they reached the forest enclave's long boundary wall, made of mellow, golden red brick. They rode along beside this wall for more than a mile, through unkempt brush—Gael could hardly imagine the labor that had been lavished upon this barrier, and all to keep a parcel of deer from running wild—the wall was surely too low to deter a determined poacher. Finally they reached an old, neglected-looking door, and Garvis of Grays had the key. Inside was a broken-down row of coops for pheasants and other game birds, disused and fallen into ruin, along with a pair of wicker pens, overgrown with grass and empty, where the red roe deer were fattened in season and brought to fawn. Passing these pens, they went on through the woods, immaculately cleared and maintained; Gael saw why old Garvis had scoffed at her reluctance to bring Ebony, her fears that in this magical chase he would fall and harm himself on "uneven ground." Even the low-hanging branches were trimmed, to prevent fast riders from coming to injury; all around, the ground had been smoothed and shaped; she could not tell what was nature and what was artifice.

Lord Garvis was intimately familiar with this forest; of course, he had hunted there through all his youth, probably right up until the terrible spring when Rosmer had conspired to have his family, his lovely sister, murdered. He led them through a maze of planted glens and then up to a little table of sheltered high ground, under an enormous spreading oak. If all went well, Lord Auric would bring the prince's party along the open vale beneath: they would call the spell, ride down and overtake them, cull young Matten away from his people, and then give him chase, hunting the young prince through to the completion of the spell, the grove ceremony.

While they were waiting, Guendolin napped with her head in her father's lap. Garvis of Grays stroked her rough hair—Gael saw in him a terrible fear that his daughter would somehow fall sacrifice to this *Haunting*. He dearly wished to send her home, but he could not quite bring himself to do it. This showed the extent of the terrible hope he lay on the *Haunting*'s success, made Gael afraid in her turn. She would have brooded on this further, but Hunter spoke up—perhaps he recognized the turn of her thoughts—diverted her with some questions about the Chameln. He had lived some years in Achamar and was curious to learn about this recent wedding of Tanit and the Eildon count. And Aidris, the Witch-Queen? Did she still have her wits about her? Morning passed away to afternoon. It was almost twilight when they heard the first horn, still far away, but coming swiftly to them.

They leapt up and drew together on the crown of the hill. Gael had the Fleece in her hands: she held it to the center of their circle, and they all caught hold of its folds. They had to go carefully, for this was not a call to the Dark Huntress, but to the Mother, for her Blessing. Gael and Lady Guendolin spoke aloud the intonation, then they all went hastily and mounted up. Gael uncouched the Lance from its traveling straps. She could not keep it in the bands if they were going to gallop. All four of the adult riders cast anxious looks at Guendolin, they could not help themselves, but the girl's eyes were only for the head of the vale, where the first of the princely hunt's riders would make their appearance.

A movement came—no horse, but a magnificent stag, delicate legged, its sides heaving. Foam streamed from its lips, its eyes rolled in terror. The poor animal was lagging—its end was near. Three lanky deerhounds followed, then a bunched pack of heavier hounds, then the grand cavalcade of the courtly Lienish hunters, tightly bunched together. Lord Garvis moved his horse forward, the signal that he had seen Lord Auric and Prince Matten among this crowd; at this cue, Gael raised, brought down her lance—pale blue fire spread, encircled them. She felt a tearing, somehow familiar, yet distinct, then there were streaks of light all around them, and it was as though they had entered the current of a swift-moving stream, and it was pulling them forward. As Ebony began to move, as she pressed him down the hill, she sensed she was only half riding in this dark plain, down this dark hill. There was a strange flowing lightness all around her; the trees, the stones of the hill, and, then, even the riders of the prince's hunt seemed to stream and fade away.

Ebony was thundering downward through this pale blue shadowland; ahead, she saw white faces turned to them, as if seen through water. The movement of their attack had finally caught the hunting party's attention. At the point of a little group, she saw a slender young man on a beautiful white and grey horse. He wore a brown tabard of rough cloth over a silken shirt in blue and white; he pulled round his horse's head without realizing what he was doing as he turned toward the distraction. Now the animal almost stumbled, skewing sideways through the other riders. Gael turned Ebony's head to track this man's tail—this was surely Matten of Lien, the man they must ride down for the grove-ceremony.

His eyes, even at this distance, seemed to meet hers, and in that moment quarry and hunters took a bond. Gael and her party, riding the stream of pale blue light, were moving faster than mortal steeds could ride, and as they came up toward him, Prince Matten's horse, too, fell into the stream, gained a preternatural quickness, slipped away, rode involuntarily out and away from his companions. Gael had a flashing glance at the royal hunting party as she rode through them and beyond—she saw Lord Auric, who would be left behind after all because he was not in the spell, then at his side she glimpsed two familiar faces, one golden-haired and sun-touched, one dark-haired and pale—just a flash, then they were gone—but her startlement was so great she would almost have pulled Ebony up, save that for the spell, there was no stopping him.

Dannell Royl; Devon Bray the Adept. What were they doing here? Had the poor pretender out of Eildon been forced upon this hunt, that he might glean some last courtly polish before being sent out among the Chameln? Even within the swift flow of the *Haunting,* Gael felt a stab of dread for this poor lost pawn. What was happening in Mel'Nir? Was the news already spread abroad that the Chameln's Lost Prince was at last found, would be brought home? Gwil Cluny had brought the Pretender's Journal safely to Nightwood and the house of Vanna Am Taarn. Surely Tomas would make the story known to Gerd Am Zor and his family; surely measures would be taken to protect this poor forsaken bastard of the Zor, trapped within Lien's web.

Streams of blue mist dragged past her. She was moving faster than the mist itself, closing in on the young prince—he kept glancing back to her over his shoulder; perhaps he did not know this was the worst thing he could do if he truly desired to outrun her. Garvis of Grays, Hunter, Tully—she could not hear their horses, would not look back herself to see where they had gone. The only one who had kept pace was young Guendolin, bent light as a feather over her short horse's neck—Stryder was a Chameln grey, and fleet of foot—urging him forward with her voice.

They chased the prince on and on—if all this was enclosed in the Fountainfields wall; Gael could hardly conceal her amazement at the distance. She could see the prince's steed was tiring—if all had gone as planned, Lord Auric would have delayed Matten in taking his remount; this horse should have been tired even before they'd come charging down the hill.

As their pace began to slow, the mist broke into swirling currents, trammelling them back toward the dark world. They were in a part of the park that was populated with ancient trees. The prince turned his horse sharply—he knew where he was. Perhaps he was trying for guile rather than sheer unthinking flight, but it was too late—his pretty mare was done. She stumbled, Prince Matten gave an angry cry, half-jumped, half-fell, to the turf. He had to go back to his horse for his sword, then he pulled it free of the saddle strap and slapped her away.

Gael, reining in Ebony, remained mounted, scanning the territory. They had come to rest in a verdant glade—not that any part of Fountainfields was not green and well-tended!—but autumn here seemed held a little in abeyance. A premonition came to her: this glade might prove witness to more than the expected effects of the *Haunting*. She prayed she would retain control, not lose possession to some unexpected great coil of power,

power that might rake the young prince ungently, as well as all those around him. Behind the prince, there was a little pool, almost perfectly round; it was overgrown with moss and flowering plants, withered a little from the fall's first cold nights. An age-patinaed dipper tied to a rough length of twine stood nearby, perched on a rooted staff by the water's edge.

"Do you know who I am?" she asked the prince.

"You have been described to me." His voice was steady, though his face was white with fear. "You are the kedran *Wanderer* from the Chyrian Coast."

"If you know I am the *Wanderer,*" she said, "you must also know it is nothing for me to call the Stillstand, the Grand Bewitchment. You are frightened, I am sure, but you are also a prince, and I will offer you a choice. I have come here today for a single purpose, and it is not to harm you. Shall I cast the Stillstand, or will you give me your word of honor, and accept what I am here to do?"

"You dare not call the spell," said Prince Matten. "There are witch-finders all around—even now they will be closing in. Call your spell, and they will surely find us."

"Is that your choice?" Gael raised the Black Lance.

"No," the prince said, shivering. Someone must have told him of the Stillstand, the awful helplessness; he could not bear the thought. "I will submit. This I swear on the Goddess, the Great Mother, and all who serve her."

"Don't trust him!" cried Guendolin, coming down from her horse, half-frantic. "To one such as him, the Mother is only the foul Marsh-Hag! What would it cost his honor, for him to cross such a pledge? Make him swear to something else, to something he believes in!"

Gael stared at the young prince, deeply met his eyes. In his face, she could see a shadow of the manly handsomeness that molded the striking features of Dannell Royl, the sensitive brow of Gerd Am Zor, even a curve of cheek she had seen in the young giant of the east, Chawn Yorath-son. Here was an uncomfortable choice. She slipped down from Ebony, came toward him, the Lance still in her hand. "Let us drink on your words," she said, catching up the dipper by the pool.

"I will take your Blessing," said Matten, bowing. Gael felt a heady rush of surprise, understanding all at once what he was asking from her: this was a ceremony she knew from her life at the Holywell, a Blessing called from the Goddess to sanctify a pledge. She had not expected this; perhaps no one bred outside of Coombe would have known what to do . . .

The scene by the Aldwell of Lady Race was like something from an ancient picture: the beautiful boy, hooded by the shining white fleece, held the young virgin's hands, pressed his brow gently to her breast, and called aloud the blessings to the Goddess. Then the tall, fire-haired kedran gently drew him away. She splashed a last dipperful of Blessed Water from the Aldwell about his face and shoulders, then she directed the virgin to take the Fleece and mount up upon her pony. Then last, the tall kedran herself sprang to her tall black horse, ready to make the final blessing. The steed stamped, in fiery temper, but the *Wanderer* took him firm in hand, turned to the Prince of Lien, and lowered her Lance to touch his shoulders.

"Today the Mother has made you a King, a truer King, than any created by force and guile. Return to Balufir, and rule peacefully." These ancient Chyrian words contained great force, though no one here but the *Wanderer* herself could comprehend their meaning.

It was all like a scene in a sacred book: then came a cry of rage, almost of agony, and swift arrows. The first struck the *Wanderer* in the back; it tore across a shoulderblade and did not lodge; the second, hastily aimed, took the child Guendolin in the arm, piercing the muscle through, for she wore no armor. But something was wrong—though the tall kedran was the least wounded of the pair, it was the *Wanderer* who cried out and slumped forward on the saddle, the great black lance dropping from her hand.

"Devon! Devon!" Prince Matten cried, as two horses crashed into view from between the trees. "What have you done?"

The young adept went straightway pale; he had heard the horror in his prince's voice. He had hunted all through the woods for his beloved liege, forcing the big man on the other horse along with him; now he dropped the hasty noose he had slung about this man's neck, jumped down from his own saddle, shaken, seemingly not believing he had found his master whole, unblemished—and in such a rage! "My lord," he said, almost weeping. "I hardly thought to find you well."

"How can I be *well*?" said the prince, tearing away. "What have you done?" He stared at the bow in Devon Bray's hands. "That is my bow," he said, amazed, though he knew Devon Bray had carried this weapon for him, strapped to his saddle. "It is *my* arrows you have used . . ."

The big, handsome man, still up on his foaming horse, was shaking his head. Matten saw it was the Eildon Pretender, and once more he did not understand. "What have you done?" he asked again.

"It was the Skelow," said Dannell Royl. "The *Wanderer's Bane*. It was on the arrow's tip."

Devon went deathly pale. "She was going to kill you," he whispered. "I used the brandhul man to come to you, to cut a path through the spell and follow. Then, when I saw the lowering lance . . . Sebald—" he said, his voice sinking to a whisper. "Sebald told me—"

They would have spoken further words, harshly, but there came more crashing through the woods. "Father!" called Guendolin. She was almost dropping from the shock of her pain.

The Lord of Grays galloped into the clearing, pulled up his horse, took stock. Not for nothing had he led the Green Riders, the hidden outlaws, for fifteen years. He read every face within the glade, decided what needed to be done.

"You there!" He told the prince and his adept companion. "We have done all we can for you! Away with you!"

He shouldered them aside and pulled his daughter onto his own saddle. And then—then, Garvis of Grays did not hesitate. Pulling the Fleece from between his child's chilled fingers, he rode to wrap it tightly around the *Wanderer*'s shoulders. Tully he sent to recover the Lance, and Hunter to the great horse Ebony's other side, to hold the *Wanderer* up in her saddle. All settled, he turned them to make way from the glade, to ride the green roads to safety.

But before they could depart, Dannell Royl pushed his horse in front of Garvis of Grays' steed, boldly spoke. "You must take me with you," he said. "For I am brandhul, and a master of herbs, and something of a healer. I alone in all the world can keep the *Wanderer* with us."

Garvis glanced to his daughter, pale with pain, and then back to this man, unknown to him. "You can come," he said. "But only if you can keep with us through the woods. We will not wait for you."

Then they were gone, and all that remained within the quiet of the glade were the young prince, his companion, and the Aldwell's serene waters.

CHAPTER XIX

THORNMOON

In their friendly tower rooms, Gael and Tomas relaxed over a good supper and joked about being an old married pair. Dark days of shadow had passed from them. Gael would always bear the Skelow's mark, a jagged scar across the back of her shoulders. A young girl had lost her arm that Gael Maddoc might live: Garvis of Grays, Lady Mayrose, the Keepers of the Fleece of Lien: all had been put to a terrible choice. Even then, without special healing knowledge held by Dannell Royl, the sacrifice of their youngest child's arm might not have been sufficient to save her.

There had been many, many days of sorrow and pain; now that sorrow was spent, Gael was returned home. She had lost much flesh, her clothes hung loosely from her tall frame, but she was in Tomas's arms again—she had rejoined him.

It was already Thornmoon, the Moon of Sacrifice, the last of autumn—Gael had lost more than a month to the poison of the Skelow, the black tree. Tomas filled her cup with golden wine, kissed her on the mouth. A rumor had come and gone that the Swan would be closing. Rolf Beck—for the Prince Carel Am Zor still answered to that name—would winter in the Chameln lands, but the scribe's refuge he had created in the Swan was also his life, and he intended to keep it going.

Across the room, hung on the wall, were dress clothes for Gael, brought over from Tulach. An invitation had come: tomorrow, Gael would give it answer. For her action on the border, the rescue of the Chameln's princes, King Gol had commanded her appearance at the Palace Fortress.

Tomas and Gael lay together in the welcoming bed, speculating about this invitation.

"The public statement concerning the princes—that will surely not be all of it," Tomas said. "It has long been the word that Gol will abdicate—pass the kingship on to Rieth, his sister Fadola's son. But this line is not direct—now that the Krac'Duar is recovered, perhaps our goodly king has heard word of this and wishes you to sanctify his choice."

"What do we hear of Rieth's young wife and her little son?" she asked, troubled in her mind that the Black Lance might be commanded to such a purpose, as though it were merely a formal stamp of approval, nothing greater in it. Yet how could she say *no* to her own king if he asked her such a thing? "It proved a hard task to bring Lady Malm to her duty as a royal midwife. But I found you, my dear, as a reward."

"The little prince, Kirris, is already walking—a true Duaring, as they say. Just nine months old, and already hardy and strong on his feet. His grandfather is dead—old Baudril Sholt. He gave up his name for his wife Fadola's child—Rieth has always been called Duaring, for the succession. Some day I would like to hear Lord Yorath's account of the Bloody Banquet of Silverlode—his meeting with Fadola and Sholt. Did he really believe they were innocent of old Ghanor's murderous plot?"

"Someone—was it Mistress Vanna?—said that he deliberately allowed those two poor things to go to the Southland, to put them out of the reach of the old despot."

Tomas nodded. "If so, it was a kindly act. Now—the little boy's mother—Elwina of Eildon—they say she is capricious and spoiled. Didn't you meet Kirris Paldo, Elwina's brother, in the Burnt Lands?"

"Yes," she said, "and he was a decent fellow."

"I've heard—you'll call it gossip—that the young royals and their friends are arrogant and clannish. They are impatient with the old king and his circle—eager for him to be out of their way."

"Oh Goddess," she sighed. "Gossip is worse than secrets. Now, has word come from the Chameln lands about our friend, the pretender? He was gone from Erinhall so many weeks before I left there."

"Queen Tanit was gracious—she welcomed her lost brother. But there has been no public announcement as yet—Dannell Royl, though bastard born, is indeed King Sharn's oldest child. There will be much work, documenting the legitimacy of Tanit's own succession, before any public announcement can be made."

Gael Maddoc came to the Palace Fortress in her finest clothes—although as New Tulach's Chatelaine, she had chosen simple colors: brown and green, with a small yellow crest of a rising sun, and today all felt ill fitted, for the weight she had lost to her great sickness made all hang loose upon her. She raised no banner—the Krac'Duar was slung in its carrying straps; she did not flaunt it. In the bright light of day, its strange quality of absorbing light was less notable, and the broken gold tape wreathed round hardly marked it as a weapon of power—like the Star Kelch and the Fleece of Lien, it only showed its greatness when its power was called forth.

The ancient pile of the Duarings' palace was a fortress still—the lower floors and terraces thronged with the warriors of Mel'Nir in all stages of their military career, their training. There were boys from the King's Longhouse, in their grey and gold, alongside pensioned officers, white bearded, who had fought in the armies of King Ghanor. Mihal Carra, Brother Robard's lord those months when he served as tutor at Carrahall, was one of Gol's equerries, and it was this Carra, familiar to Gael from the tail end of her ride with the Malms, who had been sent to greet her. He met her at the gates, where she was looking back wistfully at that hilltop road where the Shee had honored her. He greeted her warmly, and they turned their horses toward the first ramp.

As they rode through the soldiery, she was suddenly recognized by a company of the Palace Guard, handsome fellows—she had no idea where they might have seen her.

"By the Gods, it is our own Far-Faring Maid!" boomed an ensign. "Cheer for the *Wanderer,* lads!"

And cheer they did, with the quick, ritual shouts of "Long Life! True Blades!"

She laughed aloud and doffed her hat to wave at them. A voice came out of the ranks: "Trust Captain Carra to find himself such a fine duty!"

"—to a scarecrow!" cried another, which drew friendly laughter and another salute. Gael was not offended; she recognized in the jape a warrior's recognition for a proven comrade in arms.

When their horses were stabled about the third round of the mighty hill, they at last reached corridors that could properly be called a palace. Gael was led through the fine rooms of state and presented, as a guest, to guards and waiting women. In an anteroom to the present throne room, the young Lord Carra paused to show a famous artifact that stood behind a dark red arras.

The great throne, Azure, was built for giants: a huge construction of metal and dark wood, still with its upholstery of deer skin, its claw grips upon the heavy black metal arms. It told of the awful might, the lust for power that had ruled Ghanor Duaring, the so-called Great King. It suggested to Gael what it might have been like to have and to serve such a father.

"Legends," she said to her companion. "I have heard that the small creature, Drey, who crept out from the King's robe to kill with Sting, his dagger, lived for many years after Ghanor's death."

"Yes," said Carra, unsmiling. "He may have been a deformed Kelshin—at any rate a midget. No one would put an end to him, for fear of some magic. He lived like a small, raging, twisted animal in a padded room, high up in the eastern tower. At the last, he took a fever, and Hagnild put an end to his sufferings."

Yet now, after so much misery and bloodshed, here was the good king, Gol Duaring, in his eighty-fourth year, sitting in the sunshine with his third wife, fair Nimoné, in a pleasant room at the top of the Palace Fortress. The royal pair greeted Gael Maddoc with ease and gentleness—praised subtly the rescue of the Chameln princes, the discovery of Carel Am Zor—yes, they had heard of this matter—remarked upon that other rescue—the Malms brought out of Silverlode. They were familiar with the work of Tomas Giraud, described him as a leading scribe and archivist for Mel'Nir.

Then came a pause, and when the king spoke again, it was of deeper matters, closer to his private heart.

"I will pass on the crown," said King Gol in his smooth deep voice. "My dear Queen and I would make a final progress along this southern shore of the Dannermere into the lands of the new Lord of the Eastmark, Degan Keddar. After that—I am ready to retire from this hard seat." He patted the cushion of the soft settle on which he sitting at the moment, then smiled at his little joke. "Degan of Keddar. Very sound man, eh Carra?"

"Indeed, Sire!" said the young equerry.

"The new Lord of the Eastmark has found something for us," smiled Nimoné. "The beautiful horse farm at Cloudhill, where Strett of Andine trained so many *famous riders*."

"You must mean your stepson Knaar of Val'Nur, my Queen," said Gael, catching the Queen's eye. Nimoné, who had indeed been married to the great Valko Firehammer in the last years of that lord's life, blithely smiled, her true thoughts masked by a bland expression.

"Yes—yes!" blustered King Gol. "You two bold gals are hinting at my true-born son, Yorath Duaring! Do not speak so slyly—today, it is his birthday, you must know, and a sad twenty years, almost to the day, since I have last seen him."

Gael was surprised—she had not expected the king to speak of such manners so openly—and this before three pages, Mihal Carra, and herself.

But it seemed even a king must wax on, melancholy, on what would have been his son's fifty-first birthday. "I cannot tell you how I miss him—but in truth, it is all my own fault; I never earned such a son. But I've heard rumor you've seen him, Captain Maddoc, in some scrying glass . . .?" His ill-shuttered eagerness could only prompt Gael's pity.

"Indeed, Sire," she said. "He is a great wonder to behold, together with his son, Chawn Yorathson . . ."

"Tell me my grandson is born straight, without any of the crookedness that has plagued our ancient line!"

"Yes, Sire," said Gael, with a good will, for speaking truth could not be a hardship. "Straight and tall together. A fine figure—a true man of Mel'Nir!"

The King closed his eyes for a moment, picturing this vision with manifest pleasure. Then he spoke of his sister, Princess Fadola, mother of Mel'Nir's heir-apparent, Prince Rieth—her husband, the old vizier Baudril Sholt, had passed on, but she still lived very quietly in her own apartments.

Listening to him intently, Gael felt she understood what he was saying. The old king knew his son, the great Yorath, had made his choice: he would not come again to Mel'Nir; he would never rule it. "Good King Gol," as all called him, had no choice but to look elsewhere for the passing of his kingly trust. He was tired, he wished to retire—yet he did not seem wholly settled in his mind that Fadola's son must be his heir.

"Captain," asked the old king, "are you an adept in magic?"

"No, Sire," replied Gael. "I may have some aptitude from my Chyrian blood, and I have a large store of magic from the Shee and from others, but I am not a true adept."

"The great Hagnild is gone," said King Gol, "and he was thought of mainly as a healer—but would it be valuable for a ruler to have a resident magician, a true adept at court? I ask this for my nephew and heir, for Prince Rieth."

"I can only say yes," replied Gael. "For one so Blessed by magic must hold even the notice of the Gods, I think. But finding a reliable adept, man or woman, is a difficult task, one for which I am not myself well suited."

"In past times, Mel'Nir's Kings were supported by great champions," the old king said abruptly, his manner becoming a little sharp. "Do you think, Gael Maddoc, those days will come again?"

Gael looked down, did not know how to answer. The Krac'Duar felt slippery in her hands. Was this why she had been called here? To claim this old title, this ancient trust? "I heard story that Mel'Nir's last champion died a treacherous death," she said seriously. "It seems to me the times have passed when Hylor's Kings believed in sharing power and honor so close to their thrones."

King Gol blinked. He had never considered the matter in this light. "Perhaps that is true," he allowed. "Then perhaps I must ask you only to accept of me a smaller honor, that you avoid drawing 'jealous' attention. A pledge of land . . ."

His gesture brought a young page smartly forward, and there was the deed to the ground of Tulach on the High Plateau and the empty hills around, half the way to Aird. "There can be no title to accompany this gift," he sighed. "For there are those who would be displeased by that. But I thought this at least might bring you some precious privacy, some relief from intrusion . . ."

By tradition, there were no lords of the High Plateau, from respect to the Eilif Lords of the Shee, no parceling of the land there. Gael felt her heart sadden that she would be the first to be given ground there, yet she could not say no to such an offer.

So the old King and his Queen were well pleased—they all took a sup of exquisite wine from the vineyards of the Chyrian lands, below Coombe. Then Gael took her leave and wandered with the equerry Carra to another part of the palace. He brought her to a gallery, and from there she looked down upon a terrace, where the young royals were gathered.

There was Prince Rieth Duaring, Fadola's son, a tall, handsome young man, whose red gold hair, from the Emyan picture of him as a lad, had darkened to a rich brown. He sat in an upright garden seat and laughed aloud. Some kind of contest was in progress between two of the courtiers—they had armed themselves with light bows and were taking turns shooting at brightly painted targets set about the lawn.

Princess Elwina, on a gilded garden bench, was a striking blond beauty, surrounded by ladies in whispering silk dresses. A nursemaid stood by, and now the Princess gave back her infant son, the little prince,

Kirris. Gael saw that what Tomas had spoken of this child was all true: he was not yet ten months old, but already strong on his legs. As his mother set him on the grass, he ran off across the lawn and had to be chased by his nurse. There were ten or twelve young folk of the court taking their ease near the Prince and Princess, or waiting to take their turn at the archery targets, or simply walking hand in hand. Gael did not like the negligent ease with which these courtiers employed their arrows with the child so near, so ill attended.

"I will leave you to approach them," said Mihal Carra.

"You're cruel," said Gael Maddoc. "Why do you do this?"

"I am not part of their court. I serve the Old King." The young lord evenly met her gaze, and Gael saw suddenly that she must do this. Gol might have been put off by her talk of past champions betrayed—but truly, it seemed, he must know something of what she had brought to him in her carrying straps.

"I hope I am expected, at least," she grumbled.

She pulled her brown green finery to rights, couched the Krac'Duar at the trail, and strode off down the steps, carrying her hat. No one seemed to watch her approaching; she came from the east, toward the Prince's bench. Then she was roughly grasped and pinioned by two giant warriors in the livery of the Duarings. Gael remained very still and said nothing.

"Armed," said the ensign on her right. "Making for his Highness the Prince!"

Still Gael did not speak.

"Declare yourself!" said the captain on her left.

Gael looked at Prince Rieth—he was looking at the guards and their prisoner, and so indeed were all the court—even the archers at the butts seemed to have paused. What would the next move be with an unexpected, armed intruder? She smiled at the captain and made as if to free her poor arm from his mighty grasp.

"Highness," he called. "Prisoner won't speak!"

"Oh, bring it here," said Rieth impatiently.

The captain nodded to the ensign—already the spectacle of two huge men restraining one kedran seemed rather forced. "*A scarecrow!*" she heard in an undertone as they walked her forward. This time the word was not spoken with affection. The junior officer led her to stand before the prince, who nodded so that her arm was released. Rieth's eyes were blue; if she had not known Blayn of Pfolben, Lord Auric of Chantry—Tomas Giraud of Lort!—she would have thought him a handsome man.

Now she had learned to judge such things differently. He was only a handful of years older than herself. She recognized in his face an unpleasant teasing look that told her she had, in fact, been expected.

"Do you have a name, kedran?" he asked in a clear, amused voice. There was a hint of laughter from Princess Elwina and her ladies.

"I am Gael Maddoc, Highness," she said. "I was sent to meet you by King Gol."

"We expected a creature of legend," said Rieth. "One who deals in magic, who flings open Tulach Hall and consults with dark folk and light, in every land under the sun!"

"The old King will quit his throne," said Gael evenly. "I suppose he sent me here to look upon the man he expects to follow him onto that hard seat."

Rieth was suddenly angry. "I will have nothing from *you,* Captain! Take your leave, or I will have you taken off by my guards!"

"Oh, the guards!" she said, smiling. Back so early as her journey to Queen Tanit's wedding, she had learned how to use just the mere whiff of the Stillstand. She remembered, with nostalgic sadness, how it had knocked the fierce Durgashen warriors on their backs, the men who had attacked the young Fareo juggler, threatened an innocent boy. Now she did not even need to point her weapon—only to close her eyes, to concentrate. The guard captain and his ensign who were guarding her fell quite gently to the ground and lay on the greensward in ungainly attitudes. There were hoots of laughter from the court. Gael bowed low to Prince Rieth and wandered across the lawn, heading back to the western staircase to the gallery. But then, needing in her heart to salvage some small piece of dignity from all this foolish play, she paused and made a bow to the princess.

"My service to you, Highness," she said, "and to your noble son!"

Elwina tossed her pretty head. "You must be that uncouth Chyrian wench, the one who made poor Lady Malm such a poor companion on the high ground."

The jibe hit home. Gael had intended to mention her meeting with the cheerful Prince Kirris, Elwina's brother, in the Burnt Lands. Now she swung away, stung—and there was the young prince, baby Kirris, right in under her feet.

Trying to protect him, to prevent injury to the child, she fell clumsily down on one knee, fumbling to keep hold of her weapon. Raucous laughter met her ears from every side—yet not a single voice raised for the safety of the child next in line but one to the old King's throne. Perhaps they thought the Lance was too long, the point too far away, to do the child injury.

Gael knew otherwise—the weight of the Krac'Duar in her hand alone would be enough to give the child a grievous hurt—perhaps she was the only one who thought of that! From the kneel, taking a deep breath to steady herself, she stared at this precious royal child, his level, trusting gaze. She could not help a stab of guilt, thinking on young Guendolin of Grays, and all that had fallen on that child so that Gael could be saved. At least *this* innocent she had not harmed.

The child—the baby, with his fringe of red gold fuzz, his slate blue eyes—it was not possible to tell if they would stay that color, or darken when he became a little older—darted toward her. His nurse, appalled, would have seized him back, dragged him away, but already the little prince was too fast for her. He buried himself against Gael's tunic, not at all afraid, for a child such as this must be very accustomed to towering "giant warriors." He had come to her because he wished to touch the Krac'Duar—its cracked band of golden tape had attracted his interest.

"Fie, it's dirty. Your Highness, come away." The nurse cast her dagger glance on Gael as the child squirmed from the tall kedran's arms and laid both hands upon the shaft of the Lance, bracing himself, chortling with childish pleasure as his pink fingers broke free a small cracked square of the shining stuff—

Gael did not know what to do. She felt strong magic shifting within the shaft of the great weapon—certainly there had been a passing—she looked down at the child, clutching the tiny square of broken tape in his little hands, turning again to Gael, to protect it from his nurse—

How had no one else sensed it? How had no one else felt the almost sick-making, strong spasm of power, only Gael?

She looked round at Prince Rieth, the obnoxious Princess Elwina—now all she could do was feel sorrow for them. Yes, they were full of arrogance and pretension—but none of that would ever be rewarded.

This had not been Gael's doing: it had been fate.

"Tush, on your way," she whispered warmly to little Kirris, laying her hand on his small skull, stroking briefly the soft bright hair. No one was close enough to hear; the child himself would not comprehend: "One day, you will make a good king for Mel'Nir; yes you will, perhaps even a great king, *but not today,* my bonnie boy." She pushed him back toward his nurse.

Now she simply gave another bow and hurried away to the staircase. She did not neglect to take her spell off the unfortunate guardsmen.

On the gallery again, she stood in shadow, gazing out over the Dannermere. She had entered the shadowy room through the louvered doors, following the way that she had been led by Mihal Carra. He came toward her with a rueful smile.

"That looked very bad," he said. "But you seem to have carried it off."

She wondered if he had seen deeper than the unfriendly interplay—but she would not ask him. "It was an unpleasant meeting," she said stiffly. She had no wish to attempt to explain the rest of it.

"Before I take you back to the gate," he said, "the King and Queen asked me to think of something that might please you."

Ah, but at least Gol and Nimoné had been well-satisfied to see her today, and yes, in truth, she had performed a good service for the old king—and perhaps for Mel'Nir too. She set the Krac'Duar back in its traveling bands, hoped it would be called no more to this unhappy court.

She followed the young equerry across a pleasant room where older men and women were taking a meal, and then they went down a winding stair to a lower level. The room was busy, full of paper, with journeymen and apprentices; the head scribe sat at a raised table, before a fortress of books. Three copyists wrote the work out fair. The man who met them at the door murmured: "It is the *Dathsa*. We are completing a whole binder!" The head scribe, at the top of the room, looked up from his work now, and it was Tomas Giraud.

He smiled and called for a pause. The bustle stopped, and the team of helpers relaxed and drifted away. Tomas came down from his high table, greeted Mihal Carra, and embraced Gael. He held up his hand, and they listened: a mysterious rhythmic sound came from behind a heavy door.

"Oh, I know what it must be!" said Gael. "It is a machine called a press, for making printed books, Lien Books!"

"So it is!" said Mihal Carra. "But do you use paper?"

"No, we use parchment or even the reed paper, papyrus," said Tomas. "But we move with the times, and the results can be very fine."

The controller who had let them in now came with two servants, a boy and girl, who carried wine and salads, with cold game birds. As the repast was set out for them in an alcove, Tomas drew Gael aside, and his face was grave, yet full of the curiosity she knew so well.

"Something has happened," he said. "I see it in your face—"

She shook her head. "Tomas," she said, "what I have performed here today will one day appear in your own book, the *Book of Sooth,* the *Dathsa*. But please, my heart—it is not timely that it should make its appearance there today."

Tomas glanced at the Krac'Duar, and his gaze grew solemn. "I will wait," he said. "The great book can wait. But come, my love—you must eat. Your strength is not so fully recovered that you can miss a meal."

Gael, completely drained, was happy to put herself into his charge throughout the meal, and then for a further time afterward.

CHAPTER XX

TULACH AGAIN

The chamber of the Shee's tigh-Aoraidh felt chilly after the warmth of her supper, shared with a tired Tomas, who had just ridden out to Tulach two days before, in Little Hearth. She had brought a candle down, to light her way once inside the chamber—it was after dark, and she had closed the door to the perpetual illumination of magic on the wide staircase that descended to this hallowed place.

She had removed the golden hallow-coins from their string, laid them upon the table, in a certain order: the Cup, the Fleece, the Lance. Below these, a second row: the Crown, the Lamp, the Stone. The Hallows she had yet to meet.

Since her meeting with the king—and with Prince Rieth, Princess Elwina, little Kirris—she had been deeply unsettled. Immediately after that unpleasant day, she had swiftly brought the Lance again to Tulach—overland, not through the magic cantreyn fields, for a lingering effect of the Skelow wound was great pain when she called the mist of the traveling spell down around her. It had been a hard journey, in bad weather, a journey that had set her down for a few uneasy days in bed, feverish, tended by a worried Widow Menn and pretty Lyse Cluny.

But the effort had been worth the pain: the Krac'Duar was not a weapon properly carried about in the dark world, flaunted like an ordinary weapon. She was reminded of the stories Mother Maddoc had told throughout her childhood: how the Star Kelch had traveled through the hands of one Chyrian hero, then another, until old King Baradd thought so little of its sacred nature that he used it to serve out the mead to his drunken soldiers. Lively, loving stories, all told, but some essential power had faded with every changing of hands, every uncaring usage.

Then had come the Melniros through the mountain passes from the Svari and the cursed Dettaren, and the Chyrians could do nothing but fall back before them, all the way to the shores of the Western Sea. There were great Chyrian ramparts, earthworks, as far east as the Daneskan deserts, but the Chyrian peoples were gone from those places. They had kept their hold only on the ancient heart of the land, its long, jagged coast, and that only by capitulating to their conquerors.

Gael fingered again the hallow-coins, moving them on the table. The Hallows, she had come to believe, granted power in inverse proportion to their active use. The Cup—so carelessly bruited about in the world, so haphazardly employed—had been greatly diminished. Now, restored at last to its secret home of old, the Druda sent word that the sacred Kelch was regaining strength, soothing to the hearts of Coombe.

The great healing powers of the Fleece of Lien . . . it seemed to Gael they had left that land's rulers with an irresistible urge to use its power to overcome every sickness, every ill . . . a misuse, she believed, that had stirred a bitter power within the magic. Now the Fleece was dangerous. It healed, yet it drew disaster close by it. She did not think it was chance that left both herself and young Guendolin of Grays wounded, left Garvis of Grays with the terrible choice which one he would see healed, in those moments so hard upon the heels of the grove ceremony.

She threaded the top row of hallow-coins back on their thong. The Lance-coin went on last, and then she set the half-threaded thong down, went to rest her hand on the real weapon, the great Krac'Duar, lying across the wall below the high, night-darkened window, in the brackets Gwil Cluny had devised for its keeping.

At least Mel'Nir's Hallow had not been overused, not turned bitter, or been squandered—or if it had, the long tenure it had lain, unused, with the Shee had mellowed it, readied it again for its proper use. The Lance had lain in the secret shrine of the Shee for more than seventy-five years, from before the time Ghanor had taken Mel'Nir's crown. Yes, it had been hungry for use from the moment she had taken it into her hand, and how much it had accomplished in the little time she had held it! But this hunger was not to be taken for granted—she thought of the Shee, and their swift departure from Tulach's Halls. Magic could pass quickly from a land, and by rules far from her capacity for comprehension. It was best to remember that a life could be well lived outside its purlieus, best to not become *too* dependent.

She smiled, touched the Lance a final time, came back to the table to retrieve her coins. Pretty thoughts, for one who had retreated within Tulach's gates . . . and yet she was not so bad as the Priest-Kings of Eildon! From what Druda Strawn had told her, the Priest-Kings had lived in retreat from the world for hundreds of years now—the Hallow Crown with them in their seclusion. She wondered if the power that had been gathered there could account for the strange, magical quality that suffused that entire country—and perhaps also for its almost tragical waywardness.

She did not guess she would ever see Eildon's hidden crown—so closely kept, so carefully guarded. She picked up its coin, threaded it back again on the thong, moved on to the next, Cayl's Lamp. Poor occupied Cayl! She doubted it would ever find its independence. But if Cayl's Lamp was held in the same Larkdel Sanctuary in Lien that housed the Prophet Matten's two hundred and fifty year old supposed-life stone . . . a stone with a light that had never gone out, "evidence," it was said, of the Prophet's undying nature . . . Well, she had her guesses about the force that might truly keeping that stone alight, whatever faith the Brown Brotherhood might place in Matten's immortality!

But she had already done her part in Lien—and more. She did not think the call would be coming to bring her to Larkdel any time in the near future. That coin also went back on the thong—then she held up the last Hallow token in that row.

The Stone of the Chameln—yes, *that* she was eager to see, and Tomas with her. She would stand before it and admire the foresight of a people who had vested the best of their magical strength in a stone, laid it as the foundation for their double thrones, the Daindru—still running in an unbroken line for almost twelve hundred years!

Already, she and Tomas had spoken of a winter visit to Achamar, to visit this sacred Hallow—and perhaps some other friends, along with it. The Chameln lands were milder than the bleak plain of the High Plateau; "Rolf Beck" had sent word that they would be welcome there.

For a little time—why not take a "grand tour" and enjoy some pleasure in traveling and the company of good friends? When she considered all that had happened in this long year, since her first journey across the High Plateau with Lord and Lady Malm—why shouldn't she take a rest?

Surely hers was not a destiny that could be pursued. She must be patient, and wait for it to find her.

There was light snow on the ground the day she and Tomas rode out for Lort. Bran was with them, loping along, skidding, dashing his nose playfully into the little drifts and then running, ears flown back, to catch them again. Gael scolded him and told him to keep close—the ride to Goldgrave, where they would spent the night, was not a short one. "I wonder if we will ever come to winter here," she said, looking back at the dark walls of Tulach's gardens, the skeleton double row of bare elms, the distant gate where Lyse and Gwil were still waving their good-byes.

"The Shee would not grudge you the comfort of the lowlands," said Tomas, speaking seriously. "Anything to make you stronger—I think you were not sleeping long last night."

She had not told him of her visit to the tigh-Aoraidh, the Lance—he had been asleep already when she had returned to their room. Sometimes, being the wife of a scholar was a liability: since she had gone to the Palace Fortress, the Chronicles of the Krac'Duar had been opened, the edict that had banned its name quietly revoked.

Gael knew this must be King Gol's doing: it was, if not subtly done, then at least done in a manner so as to cause the least disruption, the least resentfulness. Gael knew at last the story of Simeon Red-Letter, the mortal son of Ethain of Clonagh, the man who had dared to love the woman Prince Ghanor Duaring had chosen to be mistress, dared to carry her away—Gael and many others, too. Though it seemed folk were enjoying the stories, there was no talk of raising a new champion for Mel'Nir: this was spoken of as something legendary, something of the far past. The Lance—it was spoken of as a perilous weapon, a weapon that could draw forth the soul, all mortal love.

Gael Maddoc, who had held the Krac'Duar in the strongest moments of its magic, knew intimately its powers, recognized this story to be a parable for the desire for power, not for the magic of the Lance itself, but she had not entirely been able to convince Tomas of this moral lesson. He was happy when they rode out from Tulach—and left the Lance safely behind them in its holding brackets.

"Ah, but I am strong enough!" she told him. This was not completely true—the Skelow wound still troubled her, more even than she wanted to admit; but it was true enough for her to delight now in pushing Ebony forward playfully, making the horse dash out away from him, her doting husband, forcing him to chase her. Valko at least caught her teasing mood, and they rode on together, making good speed and in good temper. Bran had to stop playing in order to keep up.

The ride was hard and cold, yet pleasant. At day's end, they came in to the Heroes of Goldgrave, that good inn where Gael had once stayed in the train of the Malms, and they stood inside to take their rooms. But the hosteller, alas, was in no good mood; there was some confusion, the big public room was full, their rooms not kept, particularly, they did not want the dog.

"An unexpected party," the hosteller explained, looking down his narrow nose.

"We have paid already for places," Tomas said mildly.

"Unexpected parties on the road!"

Gael and Tomas looked at each other, trying to be amused. She was wearing the plain clothes of a kedran captain; Tomas was warmly dressed in his scribe's tabard and cloak. They did not wish to reveal themselves, but also after a long day's riding, they did not wish their day ended in a drafty room up under some cold ceiling. "Who has come here?" Gael asked.

It was a great party, a family reunion—all of great ladies. The hosteller, Shim Doon, a little unbent, for this was an awkward time of year to provide great ladies—three of them!—with all the comforts that were expected—and one come all the way from the Southland, and unhappy with what she called the cold. The cold! Was this cold? Master Doon did not see it that way! But one among the ladies, she was renowned as a Seer, and thus—no choice in it! All three must venture forth! What could their husbands—they were great lords indeed—what could they be thinking?

Gael did not need to ask, she knew. This could only be the Strett sisters: Annhad, Perrine, and Pearl. "Take in our names," said Gael. "They will see us." She put her hand over the green stone of Lady Annhad's ring: it had served her well since that bright morning in Pfolben when Elim, Lady Annhad's servant, had watched her put it on her hand. Tomas met her eye. He saw her worry and put his hand reassuringly around her waist.

Master Doon was surprised when Gael and Tomas were brought swiftly to the "great ladies'" chambers; Gael was surprised when they were ushered into a big room with a blazing fire, and all three sisters were there to greet her. In four years—five!—Lady Pearl had changed little in her appearance. She still shone with the light of magic; the touch of age was yet in abeyance. Lady Annhad was also well.

Perrine, the new-made Lady of the Eastmark, looked older than both her sisters, and very tired, as though her new responsibilities lay heavy on her shoulders. Gael would learn, a little after this conversation, that she had only just received the sad news that her first grandchild had been born with the cord around its neck. It was not thriving, but neither had it died. Perrine was polite enough, but she made her welcomes and retreated. Her sisters' company was all she wanted, this cold evening of new winter.

"Gael Maddoc," said Lady Pearl, after all had made their welcome, and Tomas was properly introduced. "You are looking tired."

"There were troubles back in the Maplemoon."

Lady Pearl nodded, with knowing eyes. "We had news of this at Cannford," she admitted.

Annhad called Master Doon to bring refreshment—he came himself with the tray, whispering to Gael in an aside that room had been made ready for them, Bran had been taken there already. Soon after, Tomas bid his adieus and went out to see that everything was well prepared for them.

"He is worried about you," Lady Pearl smiled. "Surely a virtue in a husband." She had never married, thus this light jest.

Gael, having paid her respects, sought now to make her escape, leave these long-separated sisters their privacy, but Annhad bid her bide a moment. She wanted to see her old ring—Gael held it out to her.

"That was mischievously done!" The Lady Pearl tapped her sister's hand. "Taking the *Wanderer*'s protection, putting this bauble in its place!"

Gael could not quite see what had provoked this. "It has been very useful to me," she said hesitantly, "and I think . . . I think I have come safely through all you foretold for me."

"Yes," said Lady Pearl, looking at her deeply. "I think that you have. Is that why our paths have crossed here tonight? Do you imagine your destiny fulfilled, and wish another forward-peering glance from my crystal ball?"

Gael thought of the lovely afternoon at Cannford Old House, how she and Jehane had come so lightly down the avenue, and gone away from there . . . burdened. She thought of the things she might like to see: a child . . . not soon, but not too late, also, that her mother would not see it. Baby Kirris crowned king? No, he was yet too little. She wanted that to wait. The other things she wanted to see . . . she had a feeling as though her Skelow wound had twisted, and she was touched by the memory of her father's corpse upon the ground. Where there was adventure, there would also be pain. "When last we met," she said, "you indeed gave me a great gift. You foretold some pictures from my life . . . a man, a royal boy, an old woman before a mirror. These set me on my destiny when I was a raw young girl, and could scarcely see that there could be any such strange road before me."

"I remember that man held a pen," said Lady Pearl, smiling. "It can be no mystery that you have found him!"

"The other pictures came to pass also, as I'm sure you know. But in truth," Gael said, "I do not accept that my destiny, my questing, is played out. But I am no *green girl* now. I can wait for my fortune to find me out in its own way."

Lady Annhad gently closed Gael's hand around the precious ring. "You must keep this," she told her. "For you are right. There is much in your destiny yet to play out, of that I am sure."

Gael said her good-byes soon after—Annhad and Pearl were casting discreet looks of concern toward their sister; it was time for her to go. She came up a cramped, winding stair, found Tomas already in bed—no, Bran had to go back on the floor, the bed was small, and truly the boards were not so cold there—and waiting.

"Did Annhad reclaim her ring?" he asked, sleepily moving to take her in his arms.

"No," she said, snuggling in beside him, grateful, that at least for this night, they had found this warm berth. "For I am the *Wanderer* still, and Hylor yet has secrets it will open for me!"

APPENDIX A

CHRONOLOGY OF THE EVENTS IN THE CHRONICLES OF HYLOR

I.

A Princess of the Chameln
Yorath the Wolf
The Summer's King

284 Farfaring—In Mel'Nir, the death of Ankar Duaring, the Wizard King. Ghanor Duaring, the "Great King" begins his reign.

300 Farfaring—birth of Raff Raiz; in the Chameln Lands, birth of Princess Aidris Am Firn.

301 Farfaring—Beginning of the "Long Peace" in Mel'Nir.

304 Farfaring—In Mel'Nir, Prince Yorath born, son of Gol, Ghanor's only son. Because he is marked by a twisted shoulder and a vestigial tail, his grandfather, King Ghanor, orders his death. Yorath's mother, Elvédegran of Lien, preserves his life by sacrificing her own to magic, committing her infant son to the care of Hagnild Raiz the Healer, a noted magician at the Melniro court. In the Chameln, Prince Sharn Am Zor is born.

310 Farfaring—Princess Merilla Am Zor born.

311 Farfaring—murder of Racha Am Firn, King of the Firn, and Hedris his Queen, by agents from Lien.

314 Farfaring—Prince Carel Am Zor born.

316 Farfaring—Death of King Esher Am Zor, following a suspicious hunting accident. Annexation of the Chameln Lands by Mel'Nir's forces, as ordered by King Ghanor.

319 Farfaring—Visit by Hagnild the Healer's family to Nightwood (Jalmar,

with his son Raff Raiz). Markgräfin Zaramond of Lien is 30. Ghanor campaigns in the north and Huarik of Barkdon, Lord of the Eastmark, revolts. End of the 18-year "Long Peace" in Mel'Nir.

321 Farfaring—Yorath, at 17, starts to have dreams of Guenna of Lien.

323 Farfaring—The massacre of the Melniro army by the Chameln (led by Queen Aidris Am Firn) at Adderneck Pass. Yorath is a young soldier serving in Strett of Cloudhill's household.

324 Farfaring—In Mel'Nir, King Ghanor's treacherous massacre at Silverlode, which turns half his country against him. Princess Fadola of Mel'Nir is pregnant. Yorath, after distinguishing himself at Silverlode, enters the service of Valko Firehammer, the Melniro Lord of the Westmark.

326 Farfaring—In the Chameln, the official coronation of the Daindru rulers, King Sharn Am Zor and Queen Aidris Am Firn.

327 Farfaring—battles between King Ghanor and Valko of Val'Nur at Aird and Goldgrave on the High Plateau.

328 Farfaring [1172 since the laying of the stones in the south wall of Achamar; third year since the humbling of the Melniros and their expulsion from the Chameln; civil war in Mel'Nir in its second season; year 2221 in Lien, which shares its dating with Eildon; Year 37 in Athron since the Carach Tree returned]—Kelen of Lien and his wife Zaramund have given up hopes of an heir. King Sharn is 23, Prince Carel and Princess Merilla return from Lien to the Chameln.

329 Farfaring—In Mel'Nir, Valko victory at Donhill; in Eildon, birth of Dan Royl, King Sharn's bastard son.

330 Farfaring [1174 Chameln]—King Sharn arrives in Eildon for an unsuccessful courtship.

331 Farfaring—Yorath sent west into the Chyrian lands. Prince Rieth of Mel'Nir, Princess Fadola's son, is 4 years old. The rebellious Southland takes Lowestell and lays siege to Hackestell. Yorath sets up base in Coombe to repulse the Southlanders, and raises "the army of the west" (Chyrians). Yorath called Ruada (prince of the blood) on freeing Krail—first hint that the truth of his birth is coming into public knowledge. In the Chameln, Princess Tanit Am Zor, daughter to King Sharn, is born at some time during this year.

332 Farfaring—Yorath "kills an old man" after the second battle of Balbank. Caco Bray's amulet is read (revealing proof of Yorath's birth); death of Valko Firehammer. Knaar rises in his father's place as Lord of the Westmark.

333 Farfaring—Gael Maddoc is born, toward the end of winter. At the year's end, Knaar of Val'Nur prepares for a treaty with Prince Gol of

Mel'Nir—and Yorath voluntarily jumps off the cliff at Selkray after Knaar tries to have him killed, effectively abdicating his claim to Mel'Nir's throne. In the Chameln, Princess Merilla's twins Till and Tomas are 4; Sasko, son of Queen Aidris and heir of the Firn is 8; Prince Gerd Am Zor, Sharn's second child, is born this year. Queen Aidris is pregnant with her daughter Maren, Tanit is 2½. In Lien, Fideth of Wirth (who is not yet 17) is pregnant with Matten by Kelen of Lien (who is nearly 50).

334 Farfaring—death of King Ghanor at the year's start—Ghanor is the "old man" mortally wounded by Yorath after the second battle of Balbank, and his death this year fulfills the prophecy that he will die at the hand of a marked grandchild. Prince Gol, Ghanor's son, Yorath's father, succeeds to Mel'Nir's throne. Prince Rieth, the heir apparent of Gol, is seven. In Lien, at the Swangard fortress, Queen Aravel (Sharn's beknighted mother) is healed of her madness by Yorath's mercy. While hidden at Guenna of Lien's retreat in Erinhall, Yorath learns that Fideth is pregnant, and that the Markgräfin Zaramund has been killed by Rosmer—on Swan Greeting, end of Birchmoon and the beginning of Summer, Zaramund and her family have been assassinated by Rosmer, Lien's treacherous archmage vizier. Guenna lays a curse on the roses of Lien, not in the Chyrian tongue, but in the Old Tongue of the North—the people of Lien believe it to be the curse of the Goddess, and many turn to the Lame God for his protection. Kelen and Fideth marry soon after Zaramund's death, and Prince Matten of Lien is born this year.

335 Farfaring—Yorath leaves the land of Mel'Nir. He travels east to the Chameln and meets with King Sharn Am Zor—who is the same age as Yorath, almost to the day, as well as Queen Aidris Am Firn.

336 Farfaring—In the Chameln, King Sharn Am Zor rides west and pushes back the rebellious Skivari tribes.

339 Farfaring [1183 Chameln]—Balbank, rich lands of Mel'Nir, are ceded to Lien for cash. In Lien Garvis of Grays leads the Green Riders against the tax collectors of Lien, accompanied by Mayrose Wirth. In the Chameln, Aidris visits Sharn and hears "The Rose Lament" (written by the poet Robillon Hazard for her grandmother Guenna 20 years past). The death of Guenna of Lien (of apparent old age) swiftly follows. Back in Lien, Garvis of Grays and his wife Mayrose are brought to Guenna's secret retreat, the magically hidden Erinhall. Aidris Am Firn's old scourge, Hunter of Lien goes to join Garvis of Grays.

340 Farfaring [1184 Chameln]—Lien annexes the peaceful land of Cayl. In autumn, Kelen is crowned King, and all his vizier Rosmer's plotting

seems to have met success. But Rosmer has pushed too far, timing for this moment also King Sharn Am Zor's murder. Though Sharn does die, falling victim to Rosmer's plotting, he performs the "Harkmoor" curse with his last breath, and takes Rosmer to the grave with him.

II.
The Wanderer

349 Farfaring—Summer, Gael Maddoc is 17 and trains with the Summer Riders for the Westlings.

350 Farfaring—Gael is 18 in the Willowmoon, meets Blayn Pfolben, and joins his service.

354 Farfaring—On her arrival in Aghiras as part of Blayn's escort, Gael has reached the rank of Acting-Captain. Maplemoon and Maurik of Pfolben's birth celebrations, Gael arrives home, age 22.

355 Farfaring—Prince Kirris Rieth Elwin Duaring is born, early in the year. Spring, Gael begins her service to the Shee.

Turn of the moons in Hylor:

Tannenmoon—"Old Man's Month"
Crocusmoon—"Last Snows"
Willowmoon—"Month of Planting"
Birchmoon—"Young Girls' Moon"
Elmmoon—"Young Men's Moon" (in Athron: Lindenmoon)
Oakmoon—"The Midsummer Month"
Applemoon—"Month of Plenty" (in Athron: Carachmoon)
Maplemoon—"Moon of Blood"
Hazelmoon—"Harvest Month" (in the Chameln, the "Month of Plenty")
Aldermoon—"Moon of Death"
Thornmoon—"Month of Sacrifice"
Huntress Moon—an extra moon wedged into the late autumn calendar
Ashmoon—"Month of Changes," includes the 5 day Winter Feast

APPENDIX B

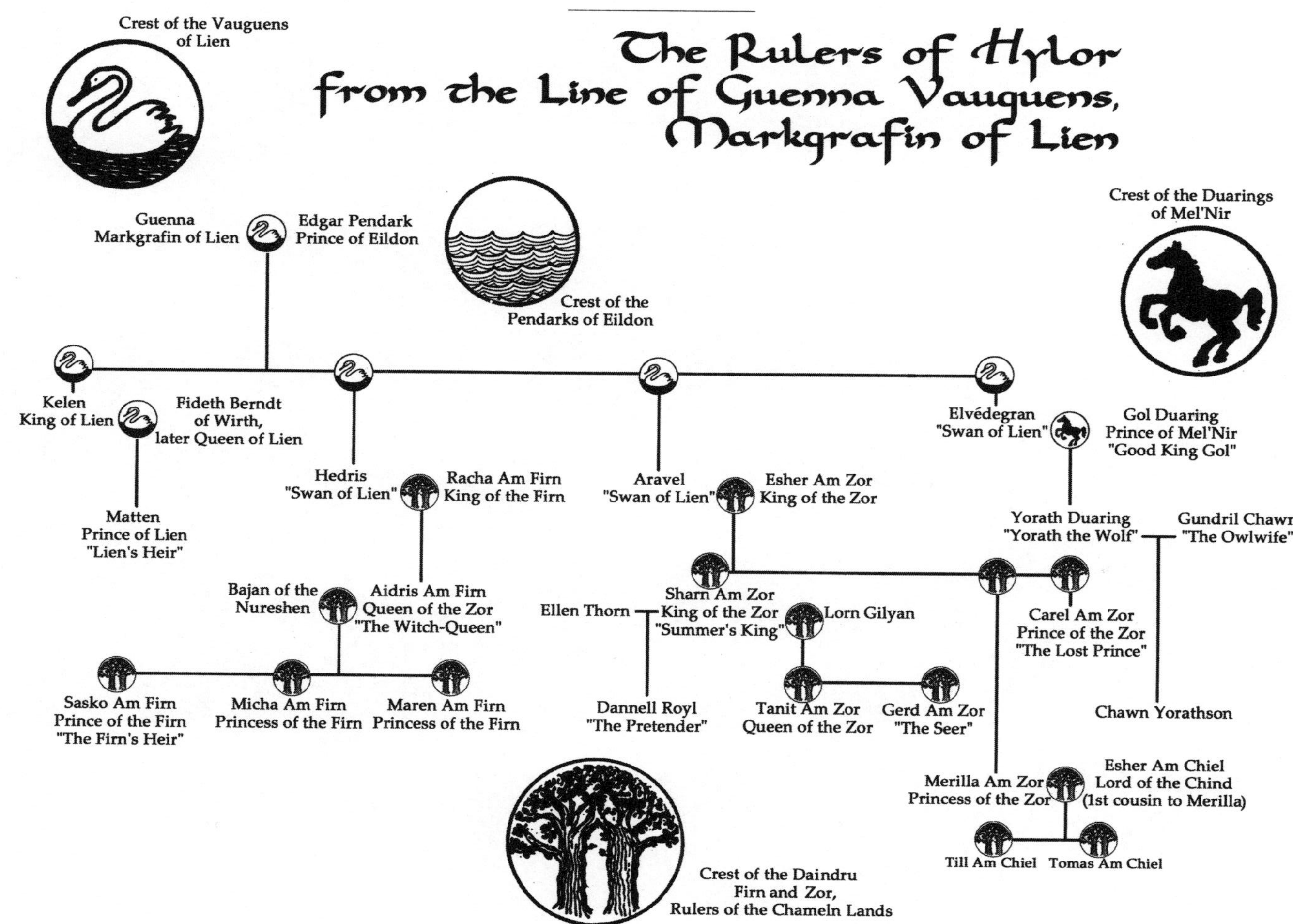
The Rulers of Hylor
from the Line of Guenna Vauguens,
Markgrafin of Lien
Crest of the Vauguens of Lien
Crest of the Pendarks of Eildon
Crest of the Duarings of Mel'Nir
Guenna
Markgrafin of Lien
Edgar Pendark
Prince of Eildon
Kelen
King of Lien
Fideth Berndt
of Wirth,
later Queen of Lien
Matten
Prince of Lien
"Lien's Heir"
Hedris
"Swan of Lien"
Racha Am Firn
King of the Firn
Bajan of the
Nureshen
Aidris Am Firn
Queen of the Zor
"The Witch-Queen"
Sasko Am Firn
Prince of the Firn
"The Firn's Heir"
Micha Am Firn
Princess of the Firn
Maren Am Firn
Princess of the Firn
Aravel
"Swan of Lien"
Esher Am Zor
King of the Zor
Ellen Thorn
Sharn Am Zor
King of the Zor
"Summer's King"
Lorn Gilyan
Dannell Royl
"The Pretender"
Tanit Am Zor
Queen of the Zor
Gerd Am Zor
"The Seer"
Elvédegran
"Swan of Lien"
Gol Duaring
Prince of Mel'Nir
"Good King Gol"
Yorath Duaring
"Yorath the Wolf"
Gundril Chawn
"The Owlwife"
Carel Am Zor
Prince of the Zor
"The Lost Prince"
Chawn Yorathson
Merilla Am Zor
Princess of the Zor
Esher Am Chiel
Lord of the Chind
(1st cousin to Merilla)
Till Am Chiel
Tomas Am Chiel
Crest of the Daindru
Firn and Zor,
Rulers of the Chameln Lands

APPENDIX C

The Rulers of Hylor
the Duaring Kings

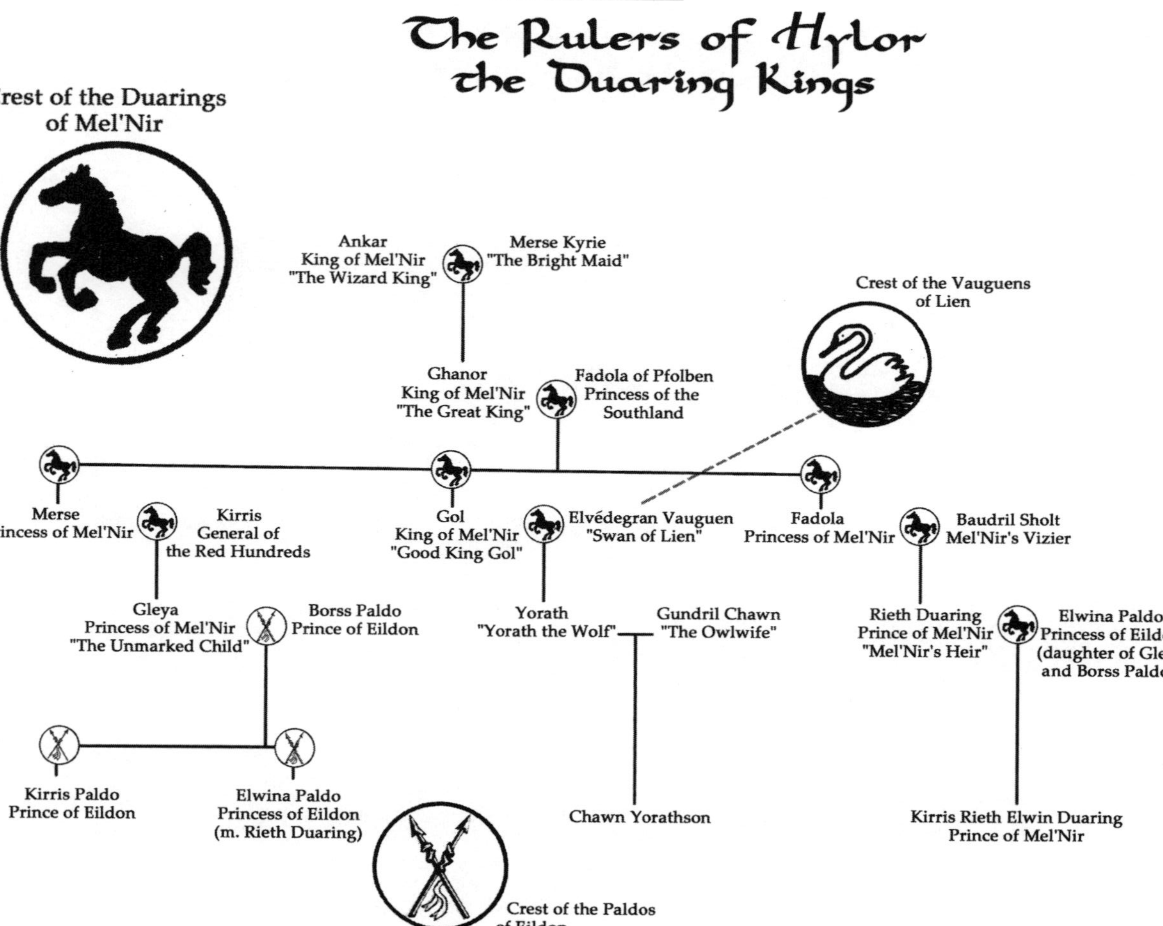

ACKNOWLEDGMENTS

It is not possible to make a complete list of those who have contributed to this work. Cherry's agent, Jim Frenkel, her editor, David G. Hartwell—without their efforts, this book would certainly never have been published. All Cherry's friends, her readers, her inspirations—I cannot speak to these, I do not know the names of all those who helped her in the last months of her life as she struggled to bring the manuscript of *The Wanderer* to something like completion.

I first read the Rulers of Hylor trilogy when I was in college. I couldn't know then that these books would be among those that would have the greatest impact on my writing life. Why Cherry's books appealed to my imagination so strongly remains to this day an incompletely solved mystery: when I read *Yorath,* at least, I was of an age where I was very keenly disappointed when Cherry's hero, the great general, decided to turn his back on his birthright. At 19, it was clear to me that a man who was born to be king must *certainly* take up the throne when the moment came on him. There was no nobility that I could see in his abdication—besides, how disgusting that he had taken as his lover an older woman he had first met when he was but twelve years old!

Almost twenty years later, I can still remember the strong feeling of my post-adolescent disgust.

I was at Oxford when I first started writing fantasy; I had not thought of Cherry's books for years, but for some reason I found myself searching for her in the Bodleian library's card catalogue—the attractions of my dissertation had temporarily palled. In the Bodleian I discovered Cherry's most recent book, *Cruel Designs*—a chilly Viennese arts and crafts murder mystery, as I remember it—most striking to me because of the heroine, Katya Reimann. Not long after that, I completed the first draft of my first book.

When I heard of Cherry's orphan novel, this last chronicle of Hylor, I was filled by the same churning determination that fueled me through that first draft of my first book. I had some sharp discussions with James Frenkel and David Hartwell, trying to keep on a leash the ludicrous hunger I felt that *I* should be the one to work on, and complete, this book. Some more rational discussions with my own agent, Shawna McCarthy, brought things into a calmer perspective, and then—the actual wrestling with the unfinished book.

I want to thank everyone who offered me their perspectives on Cherry's writing—not least John M. Ford, who gave me permission to redraw and expand the beautiful map he had made for *Princess of the Chameln*. I want to thank my family, for putting up with me.

More practical (but no less fervent!) thanks go to the unflappable Moshe Feder, David's editorial assistant, and to Gerri Lynch, Amanda Haldy, Amanda Vail, Sarah Galbraith, and Chloe Kiritz, for the child-wrangling services that have made my writing possible during this past year.

And lastly I want to thank Cherry, for a wonderful creation that has lived with me for many years now, and all the great mystery that allowed me to be a part of the completion of this book.